Born and educated in London, Andrew qualified as a civil engineer and has worked and travelled throughout the world, gaining a wealth of experience. His journey has been the source of inspiration from which he creates his historic novels. Married to Lynne, he now lives in Queensland, Australia.

For Lynne

Andrew Mudie

THE MAGWITCH FORTUNES

AUSTIN MACAULEY PUBLISHERS™

LONDON * CAMBRIDGE * NEW YORK * SHARJAH

Copyright © Andrew Mudie (2021)

All rights reserved. No part of this publication may be reproduced, distributed, or transmitted in any form or by any means, including photocopying, recording, or other electronic or mechanical methods, without the prior written permission of the publisher, except in the case of brief quotations embodied in critical reviews and certain other noncommercial uses permitted by copyright law. For permission requests, write to the publisher.

Any person who commits any unauthorised act in relation to this publication may be liable to criminal prosecution and civil claims for damages.

This is a work of fiction. Names, characters, businesses, places, events, locales, and incidents are either the products of the author's imagination or used in a fictitious manner. Any resemblance to actual persons, living or dead, or actual events is purely coincidental.

Ordering Information
Quantity sales: Special discounts are available on quantity purchases by corporations, associations, and others. For details, contact the publisher at the address below.

Publisher's Cataloging-in-Publication data
Mudie, Andrew
The Magwitch Fortunes

ISBN 9781645362357 (Paperback)
ISBN 9781645362364 (Hardback)
ISBN 9781645368571 (ePub e-book)

Library of Congress Control Number: 2020909730

www.austinmacauley.com/us

First Published (2021)
Austin Macauley Publishers LLC
40 Wall Street, 33rd Floor, Suite 3302
New York, NY 10005
USA

mail-usa@austinmacauley.com
+1 (646) 5125767

My special thanks must go to those who have helped with advice and research to consolidate the historical information contained between these pages.

Of particular note, I must thank all Dickensians, historians, archivists, curators, and officers of the Metropolitan Police, all of whom gave off their valuable time, sifting through evidence in the pursuit of answers to my strange and probing questions.

Without exception, everyone associated with this work has shared in the reality that a mere 175 years ago, New South Wales was a very different place and, between these pages, all contributors have helped to provide an insight into those convict and free-settler lives, many of whom became a legend in their own right.

Author's Note

The reader may feel that this novel is the work of two authors. This is, in fact, the case as, where appropriate, certain text from Charles Dickens's brilliant novel, *Great Expectations*, has been lifted verbatim from the master's own words to give authenticity to the former years of the major Dickensian characters' lives. The rest of the work has been a creation from the mind of the author.

A Foh Fum Legend

A novel based on historical events in the convict transportation era between London and New South Wales in the 1800s by William Andrew Mudie.

Fact

Convict transportation to America ceased after American Independence in 1775, and commenced to Australia with the First Fleet in 1788. A total of approximately 80,000 souls were transported to the Land of Promise.

- Terms for transportation were for seven years, 14 years, or the term of a man's natural life. Freedom was the process of a *Ticket-of-Leave, Conditional-Pardon,* or *Full-Pardon,* courtesy of the Governor of N.S.W.
- At the height of convict transportation, over 1200 female convicts were incarcerated in the Female Factory at Parramatta.
- Botanist, Sir Joseph Banks, had *Jute* (hemp) shipped out on the First Fleet in 1788, with the intention of developing the Australian Penal Colony as a major producer of hemp products.
- The East India Company provided significant logistical support to the Australian Penal Colony from its offices in Calcutta, West Bengal.
- The Bank of New South Wales opened for business in 1817, and today, is known as the Westpac Banking Corporation.
- The Australian Gold Rush commenced in 1853, four years after the Californian Gold Rush.
- The clipper, *Dunbar*, sank off South Heads, Sydney, in 1857, with the loss of 121 lives, most of whom were business tycoons and returning settlers. Fifty-eight were crew. There was only one survivor. To this day, the disaster remains the worst maritime tragedy in Port Jackson's (Sydney harbour) history.
- The racehorse, Moses, won the Epsom Derby in 1822.
- The racehorse, Archer, won the first Melbourne Cup in 1861.

Foreword

It was Christmas Eve when that terrifying convict appeared in the church graveyard on the edge of those unforgiving Kentish marshes:

"Hold your noise!" cried a terrible voice, as a man started up from among the graves at the side of the church porch.
"Keep still, you little devil, or I'll cut your throat!"
A fearful man, all in coarse grey, with a great iron on his leg. A man with no hat, and with broken shoes, and with an old rag tied round his head. A man who had been soaked in water, and smothered in mud, and lamed by stones, and cut by flints, and stung by nettles, and torn by briars; who limped, and shivered, and glared and growled; and whose teeth chattered in his head as he seized me by the chin.

That man was Abel Magwitch, the convict in Charles Dickens's brilliant novel, *Great Expectations*.

So how did Magwitch make his money? Charles Dickens intimates through sheep farming, however, to have generated enough wealth to be able to fund Pip by his ninth year in New South Wales seems unlikely, given the amount of land and stock Magwitch would have required and that he could have only become a landowner in New South Wales if he were emancipated. Some say it was because of the gold rush. That too cannot be the case, since gold was only discovered in quantity in 1853, some seven years after Magwitch returns to England.

The Magwitch Fortunes unveils the early years with events that led up to Miss Havisham being abandoned, events more sinister than the simple breakdown of a loving relationship.

Then there is the hidden fact that Magwitch turns out to be Estella's father, and gypsy, Molly (Jaggers's housekeeper), turns out to be Estella's mother, saved from the hangman's noose by Jaggers who arranges Estella's adoption by Miss Havisham.

Estella learns the evils of Miss Havisham's teachings through two failed relationships of her own, yet love has been shadowing her since she opened the gates to Pip at Satis House. Surely there is the future possibility that Pip and Estella can come together.

But Magwitch does, indeed, make his fortune; how else would he have funded his Gentleman, Philip Pirrip, known as Pip? And would you really allow the Crown to confiscate your inheritance?

There are prison hulks and transportation to Australia, and floggings and murder trials and hangings as we witness life with the convicts in New South Wales, some of whom deliberately committed crimes in the miseries of industrialised Great Britain just to get a free ticket to be transported to the Land of Promise.

The Magwitch Fortunes provides a window as seen through the eyes of Abel Magwitch during his formative years before he meets Pip in the graveyard and, more particularly, the 15 years or so, he spends in exile in New South Wales where he is exposed to the harsh years of convict life, and, later, how he capitalises on opportunities before his return to England.

And finally, we see how the lawyer, Jaggers, sets the stage for Pip and Estella to pursue their inheritance in New South Wales.

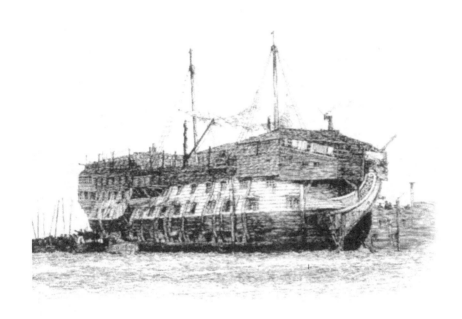

The Prison Hulk

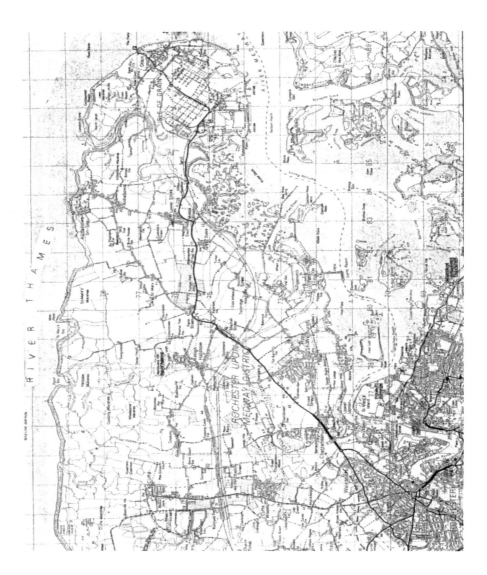

Rochester upon Medway

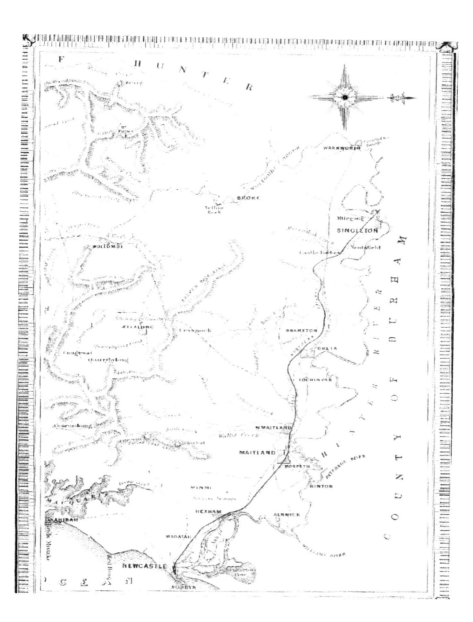

Castle Forbes
James Mudie – Free Settler, 1822
Farm where Magwitch worked

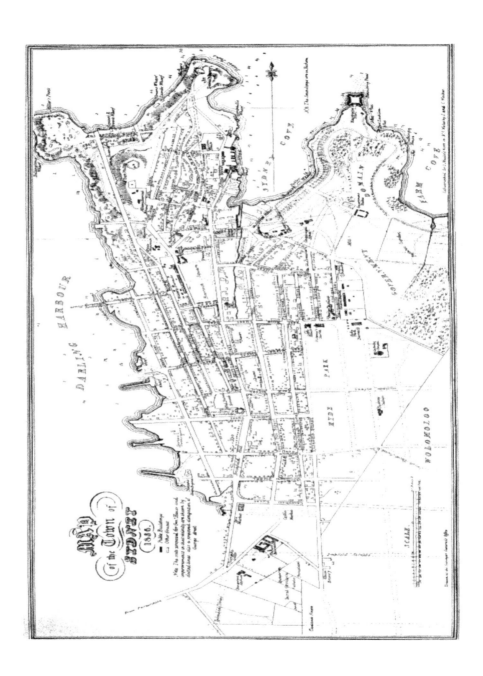

Prologue

"Square away," ordered Captain Green, confident that he was entering the mouth of Port Jackson.

"Aye aye, Captain," shouted the two seamen hauling the ship's wheel in an anticlockwise direction, one seaman instantly knocked off his feet by another mountainous breaking wave.

"Keep the luff," shouted Green through his megaphone as the clipper headed broadside into the wind. He felt weary as he looked up into the close-reefed fore and main topsails. He ordered the foresail to be clued up, adrenaline alone keeping him awake, having had no rest for the past two days.

"Breakers ahead!" screamed able-seaman Johnson.

"Hard to starboard," shouted Green; he looked desperately up at the sail-less rigging. The wind having forced him to strip most of the canvas, and with no small sail hoisted, the clipper failed to respond. In the ink-black heinous night, they drifted towards the rugged cliffs. Trapped broadside to the wind and parallel to the mountainous waves, *Dunbar's* hull became a sail.

Part 1
England – 1820

Chapter 1

The funeral pageantry played out under the wintry afternoon sun as it attempted to shine through the partially overcast sky. Steaming muscles rippled under the leather tack and polished-brass harnesses of the six, plumed, black mares that hauled the loaded hearse along Rochester High Street. Two upright gentlemen crisply dressed in black tunics over white ruffled shirts, sported top hats. They drove the well-groomed horses at a careful walking pace. Behind the drivers rested the mahogany casket adorned with wildflowers and roses gathered from around the town. Behind followed the mourners some 20 yards distant. Slowly, the church bell sounded its deep monotonous toll as the procession made its way sedately up the cobbled High Street and turned gently onto the private road to the church.

"When's the will reading?" Arthur's face was sullen. Belligerent.

Miss Havisham threw an angry look at her half-brother.

"I heard next week," she snapped.

"Do you know where?" Arthur pursued, barely able to keep his greedy motives concealed from his half-sister.

"The Town Hall," she frowned, her annoyance at Arthur's rudeness beginning to show.

"When?" His weak face feigned a sombre expression. A façade to other mourners in the funeral procession.

"Good God, Arthur, not now!"

Escorted by her half-brother, Miss Havisham, the deceased's only beloved daughter, led the funeral procession. They walked quietly and in silence, in the chill autumnal breeze under the grey sky, the only sounds being the steel tyres of the hearse as the artillery wheels meshed with the cobblestones beneath and the gentle plop of the horse's hooves. Behind them shuffled the townsfolk, a vast number, their faces saddened by the sudden loss of their valued brewer.

Having outlived his beautiful wife, Brewer Havisham had married his pretty young cook, who, after six months, promptly provided him with a son, Arthur. Her kindness and ample feeding, rinsed down by copious quantities of his own beer, had eventually conspired to prematurely consign the brewer's greatly swollen, yet generous person, to the next world.

The pallbearers sweated profusely as they slid the casket gently from the carriage and carried it on their shoulders over to the side of the open grave. Reverently, they lowered the town's brewer into his final resting place, stood back, and breathed a respectful sigh of relief.

"Ashes to ashes, dust to dust," said the minister, throwing a handful of soil onto the top of the coffin in the grave. Direct family followed his lead, individually stepping up to the side of the grave and tossing a single bloom onto the lid of the casket. Slowly, the mourners dispersed and made their way back to the inn.

A fresh wood fire had been lit for the wake in the main lounge at the Blue Boar Inn. Free beer was served to those who had attended the funeral. Slowly, conversation warmed and, as the beer took hold, the hubbub escalated from red-cheeked well-wishers as they gave their sympathies to the principals, Miss Havisham and Arthur Havisham. All that is, save and except for Anthony Hitchcock, who sat by the open log fire. With his trouser leg rolled up, Hitchcock, nicknamed Hath, scratched the rapidly healing scar on the back of his calf muscle.

Miss Havisham stood to the side of the horsehair sofa in the bay window whilst Arthur collected the drinks. Fascinated, she studied Hitchcock and his apparent disinterest in the activities of the private gathering. He was scruffy. Weather-beaten. A thin turkey-like neck emphasised his Adam's apple that rose and fell as he swallowed ale. In between gulps, Hitchcock stared into the fire. She shivered. His alien presence gave her a feeling of detachment from the room and the desire to get back to Satis House and privacy.

"May I introduce you to my colleague, Mr. Compeyson?" said Arthur, disturbing her detachment.

Young and handsome, he presented a swarthy complexion under well-groomed black hair. Compeyson stepped forward and bowed his head slightly as he offered his hand.

"Miss Havisham," announced Compeyson in his eloquent, public, boarding school voice. He bent forward to kiss the back of the extended, black-gloved hand. "My pleasure to make your acquaintance, ma'am. Please accept my deepest of sympathies at your bereavement."

"Thank you, Mr. Compeyson, but if you will excuse me, I feel the need to return home to Satis House to be with my own person for a while." With a detectable flush of interest, Miss Havisham politely excused herself and walked steadily out to the waiting hackney carriage.

Read by the justices, the will reading took place in the Town Hall the following week. It was a simple will, granting a small lifetime annuity to the second wife and the same for Arthur Havisham. But the bulk of the Estate went directly to his daughter, Miss Havisham. More importantly, by way of special bequest, she was to receive the brewing business adjacent to Satis House, and indeed, Satis House itself.

"I need a drink," cursed Arthur, as he resigned himself to his paltry share of the Estate. Scowling at the assembled guests, he pushed his chair back and stalked aggressively from the beneficiaries meeting in the Town Hall, marched across the cobbled road and into the private bar of the Blue Boar Inn. He ordered a treble whisky and a pint of ale.

"I get a poxy lifetime annuity, and she gets everything else, including the brewery and Satis House." He took another swig of ale, emptying the pewter tankard. Slamming the mug back down on the bar, he ordered a refill. Tossing a coin across the bar, he grabbed the refilled mug, sloshing the surplus onto the polished wood of the bar. "Jesus wept," he blasphemed aloud, his thin frame and watery eyes showing signs of inebriation. Eating nothing, he drank continuously for the rest of the afternoon, serving only to deepen his emotions and bitterness. By the time it grew dark, Arthur had decided he should consult with his old school friend, Compeyson. He dragged himself to the booking office across the road and reserved his box on the next morning's stagecoach to Chiswick.

It was approaching lunch the next day as the coach arrived in London. Half an hour later, Arthur hurriedly related yesterday's experience at the Town Hall.

"How about the City Barge?" interjected Compeyson, secretly pleased at Arthur's jealousy and bitterness. In mutual agreement, they hailed a Hackney coach and set off for the riverside pub. There had been plenty of rain over the past few days, and the moon was growing. High tide pushed the Thames westwards and now lapped at the backdoor of the tavern. In silence, they entered from the tradesman's door and ordered two pints, then settled in the rear corner of the scruffy bar.

"My good fellow, quite frankly, all you really want is that moneymaking brewery. Just the cash alone will make you a rich man. Who would want a mansion in Rochester anyway? All you need to do is to employ a bookkeeper to do the counting and just check the books whilst living a life of plenty up here in London. Not so?"

"Quite so," replied Arthur. "But how in hell's name do we get our hands on it, now that the will has directed the business to my damn half-sister?" Arthur grabbed the empty beer tankards, squeezed himself out from behind their corner table, and went for replenishments at the bar.

"Ask the barmaid for some paper and a quill," shouted Compeyson to Arthur's back, just as he reached the bar. A few minutes later, Arthur returned to the table. Setting the full, still-frothy tankards down on the table, he handed over the quill and paper. Compeyson pulled the paper towards him, opened the portable inkpot, and began to write. Minutes later, the missive was completed and Compeyson sat back, proud of his work.

"Take this to your sister," said Compeyson with a sly grin. "Maybe I can strike up a certain acquaintance with the little lady. Just hope it's not too soon after the funeral. Don't want to disturb her any more than she may already be." Arthur threw a quizzical look across the table at Compeyson.

"But she's only just met you?" he bleated. "And what about your wife, Sally, what will she say?"

"You can forget that harlot," said Compeyson aggressively. "She won't know anything unless you are stupid enough to tell her. Nobody down in Kent knows of her existence. But as to Miss Havisham, well, she's a different kettle of fish. Didn't you see her face when we met at the wake? Definite interest there or I'm not my father's son," said Compeyson, chuckling. "Now, if she accepts my approach, I plan to be on the following Saturday morning's coach, so let's take it from there. You stay behind the scenes and keep out of the way. We never had this meeting. Now, did we?" Arthur resisted the temptation to speak. With another sly wink, Compeyson quaffed the last dregs of his pint.

Returning to Rochester on the late-night stagecoach, Arthur decided to spend the night at the halfway staging post, Guy-Earl of Warwick, at Welling Kent, his decision prompted by the lack of whisky in his ample pewter hip flask. He failed to notice the escalation in his consumption of alcohol, let alone his loss of appetite.

He woke early. It was one of those magnificent September days, early morning birdsong, dew-laden lawns, and brilliant autumnal foliage clinging to the trees. Arthur climbed aboard the morning coach and settled into the tapestry bench seat. He reached for his hip flask. "Hair of the dog," he muttered to himself, his trembling hand raised the flask to his lips.

The coach jerked forward to the sound of the driver's whip cracking in the air, instantly hooves dug into the rough-metalled road. With the back of his other bony hand, Arthur quickly wiped the trickle of whisky spilt on his chin. He looked out of the open window space, ignoring the other travellers seated opposite. Alighting at the staging post in Rochester, Arthur scurried to Satis House, his hand regularly checking Compeyson's letter buried deep in the breast pocket of his tweed jacket. He arrived at the front gates just as the church bell struck 11 a.m. Surreptitiously, he let himself in through the massive wrought-iron gates of Satis House and walked through the courtyard towards the front door. He stopped halfway, reached for his pewter hip flask, and took a swift gulp. Consumed with envy, he glanced across at the steaming brewery. The delicious smell of brewer's yeast filled his nostrils, giving greater purpose to his mission.

"Bitch," he cursed jealously under his breath. Quickly, he took another wet gulp from the flask, and instantly coughed, nearly choking on the fiery liquid. Stuffing the flask back in his pocket, he proceeded along the stone pathway to the front door. He pulled the bell handle and waited. The late brewer's butler appeared and ushered Arthur upstairs. Dismissing the butler, he knocked on the heavy mahogany door. Arthur was not expected.

"Enter." He turned the heavy brass doorknob, opening the door into the great lounge.

"Good morning," he said briskly. Seated comfortably in the large tapestry-covered armchair by the fireside, Miss Havisham expressed surprise at the arrival of her half-brother. Reaching inside his left, breast, jacket pocket, Arthur withdrew Compeyson's letter.

"As I have business to attend to in Rochester, I offered to act as courier," volunteered Arthur, walking into the room.

"Oh, how nice of you to visit. Would you like some tea, Arthur?" He shuddered at the thought of sweet tea and cake.

"Thank you, no. Actually, I cannot stay, but I have a personal letter from Mr. Compeyson," replied Arthur, presenting the letter. A slight flush glowed in her cheeks as she opened the envelope and read the contents. Smiling innocently, she carefully refolded the letter, thanked Arthur for the delivery, and bid him relay her message of acceptance. Arthur acknowledged the request, and excusing himself, hurriedly retreated. Outside the gates, Arthur took another couple of swigs from his flask whilst coveting the brewery.

"I've done my bit," he muttered to himself as he trudged back to the Blue Boar Inn. "It's over to Compeyson now." In the bar, he ordered his first pint and sniggered aloud. The mental image of his half-sister sleeping with Compeyson began to take form.

Chapter 2

Christmas Eve, and it was going to be a white Christmas, or at least it looked like it, as fat snowflakes fell. The great lounge at Satis House glowed from the reflection of the main central fire. High ceilings surrounded by scrolled and floral cornice work added dimension to the lounge. Flickering flames from the fire reflected from the twin, central chandeliers. The burgundy, velvet, window drapes added warmth as they hung, swept away at the sides, then fell to the floor, revealing the snow and ice-frosted double-hung windows.

They sat arm-in-arm on the settee, their feet resting together on the soft, down-filled leather footrest. Silently, they gazed into the constantly changing flames of the fire licking around the glowing coals. Miss Havisham sighed and snuggled deeper into Compeyson's arms. "I never thought I could feel this way," she said, sighing again. "I wonder what next year will bring. You have made me feel so strong and wholesome. I don't want it to end." She fidgeted again and turned her head from the fire to look up into Compeyson's dark-brown eyes. He smiled tenderly back.

"And why should it, my love?" replied Compeyson in a low whisper. "We have the rest of our lives together and nothing can come between us. We share the same interests." There were a few seconds' silence. Compeyson lent forward and poked the fire, then settled back. "I can help you with your business, if you would like?"

"I would like that very much, and I have been thinking along those lines about the brewery. It needs a man to control it. They say that the workers don't respond to me very well, but I think that's because I am not familiar with management."

"Ah." Compeyson grabbed the moment. "I would be honoured to represent you. Indeed, I have management experience and training. Darling, say no more, you can leave that side of things for me to worry about." Miss Havisham reached up and slid her arm around Compeyson's neck, raised her head, and kissed him lightly on the cheek.

"I thought so, my darling, we shall talk more of this in the New Year."

Both January and February were bitterly cold, with north winds and gales creating massive snow drifts across Kent. Compeyson had taken well to his new position, and Miss Havisham found herself boasting of her newfound manager to her lawyer, Mr. Jaggers, and her other relations and friends. They had all remained non-committal, preferring to keep their negative opinions and advice to themselves, and, most certainly, never to be spoken within earshot of Miss Havisham. As if an independent spectator, Arthur sat in the wings of the elaborate charade, but, quietly, he served to encourage the relationship.

"He's a really nice fellow, don't you think?" He chose his words carefully. She loved his input, and by the middle of February, had offered Arthur a position at the brewery as Sales Manager. He had been delighted to accept, especially as he had an interest in consuming the brewery products at every alehouse they supplied in Kent.

Towards the end of February, the great thaw came and little fat snowdrops burst through the melting snow along the roadsides, and in the gardens, and in the fields. Next, up popped the first green shoots of wild daffodils that suddenly burst forth in profusion. The watery sun strengthened and shone each day, and by the end of the month, most of the snow had gone. Miss Havisham noted that this year was a leap year, and as the full moon approached, she made her fateful decision. It was the night of the 28th of February.

By the next day, her mind was made up. Compeyson arrived to escort Miss Havisham on her regular weekly tour of the brewery. As they entered the building, the brewery clock chimed 10 a.m. Having toured the vats and production lines and large stocks of barrels, their last port of call was the sales and dispatch office where Arthur proudly claimed that the recent sales achievements were due to his brilliant work, although the weather was probably more the cause rather than his charlatan input. Arthur went on to boast about his future sales forecasts, bringing great comfort to Miss Havisham and a smirk to Compeyson's assumptive expression. They left the sales office and the tour was satisfactorily completed just past noon.

"I'm so happy," said Miss Havisham, as she took Compeyson's hand and gave it a special squeeze.

"Darling, I would like you to join me for lunch."

"It would bring me infinite pleasure, my dear," responded Compeyson with his sickly half-smile.

Luncheon was served in the great dining room, and Miss Havisham indicated that Compeyson should seat himself at the head of the table, with herself to his left. The first course consisted of steamed mussels in a rich garlic-and-cream sauce, and was followed by a brace of roasted pheasant, glazed vegetables, and gravy. Gin and quinine tonic had been the prelude, followed by white and then red Burgundy wine. The heat from the blazing fire brought enormous comfort to the large room as the happy couple shared each other's company, and talked about their prospects for the future. Luncheon ended with port and Stilton on freshly baked, warm, crisp bread. "Shall we take coffee and brandy in the withdrawing room?" suggested Miss Havisham, already rising from the table to change venue.

Compeyson gulped down the remainder of his port wine and followed a few paces behind. Miss Havisham indicated that Compeyson should seat himself in the comfortable winged armchair. He promptly did and, stretching his legs out towards the fireplace, drew the little side table to within comfortable reach in readiness for the brandy. With her delicate legs folded underneath the flowing material of her frock, Miss Havisham comforted herself next to him on the fireside rug. She rested her arm over the tapestry-covered arm of his chair. They talked continuously about the brewery and how well Arthur was doing. The door opened and the butler arrived to serve the coffee and brandy.

"Satis House," sighed Miss Havisham. "Did you know that Satis is Latin for enough or plenty? And that's how I feel this day," she said, smiling, her eyes looking up at Compeyson's handsome face. He casually returned the smile.

"A little toast?" he said, raising his glass of brandy. "To us and the future." The hint of a wry smile appeared on his face.

"To us and the future." Momentarily, the crystal glasses touched. They smiled at each other and drank the toast. Delicately, she placed her glass on the side table. Her hands reach gently for Compeyson's free hand. "Darling, did you know today is the 29th of February?" Her cheeks flushed, evidencing her underlying emotions.

"Of course, my dear." His mind was racing.

"This is a leap year, and today is the day when a gentleman cannot say no to a lady." Her pale cheeks flushed deeper at the thought of what she would say next.

"Go on," said Compeyson, with a feigned look of surprise spreading across his brow.

"Darling, will you marry me?" It was out before Miss Havisham had any further chance to reconsider, but no matter, she had to do it. Almost in shame at what had been said, she quickly looked back at the fire, frightened at the reaction her words may have. With thespian skill, Compeyson slid from the chair to his knees, and reached over to hold her in his arms.

"My darling, how could I ever reject one as beautiful as you? I fell in love the very first day we met and, as we grew close, I had not the nerve to propose to you as I am not a man of means able to match your status."

"Not important, darling," her words came in a whisper. The prickles behind her eyes blurred her vision as she accepted the embrace and kiss.

"Does that mean that you accept?" she whispered gently in his ear.

"Wild horses would not keep me from you, my darling. Of course, yes. And yes, and yes. Maybe some champagne?" Compeyson's mind kept racing.

"Better than I could have ever done myself," he chuckled, as, hours later, he descended the backstairs and exited Satis House. He walked across the manicured grounds and commenced his last round that day of the brewery. "Not long now," he mused, fondling the brewery cheque book whose only authorised signature was that of Miss Havisham. Turning the heavy lock in the wrought-iron gates, he laughed out loud and, exceptionally proud of his work, left the Estate for his dingy little apartment in Rochester High Street.

"So, what happens now?" asked Arthur, swallowing his third large whisky in the Three Jolly Bargemen, the haunt they had selected for discussing their traitorous little conspiracy.

"Patience, Arthur, patience. There will be wedding plans and lots of paper to sign. One of which will be the arrangements for the brewing business," said Compeyson, as he winked at the voluptuous barmaid in the process of clearing away empty beer tankards and replacing the overly full ashtrays.

"Christ, Compeyson, what in the hell will Sally say if she hears? It's against the bleeding law. I think, even to be betrothed to another is criminal. It's bigamy. Go to Newgate for that," warned Arthur. "It terrifies me and makes me sick to my stomach to even think of it. God alone knows what will happen if she finds out."

"Not so fast, you stupid idiot. Who said I'm going through with the wedding? And anyway, what the hell will you care? You and I will be rich men. The key is to get her signature on a business agreement, and the bank account. Then it's all over, and we will own a brewery." Compeyson's confidence shone around the room as he strode over to the bar for replacement drinks. Arthur sat alone at the corner table, whimpering. Compeyson returned with the beers.

"You don't really need me now. Do you?" whined Arthur.

"Of course, I do. You are part of it. That lovesick female feels you are the family, which, I suppose, you are. She trusts you implicitly and will be happy to feel that you're getting a share of the action in return for managing the sales. After she has signed the papers, we'll put her into retirement. With two-thirds of the business, we control, and she'll get voted out." Compeyson greedily gulped at the froth on the top of his tankard. It had been an exciting day.

"And another thing, you can take up residence in that quaint little cottage behind Satis House. No rent to pay, of course. I'm sure Miss Havisham won't mind. All part of our cosy little family."

Compeyson's voice trailed into sarcasm. Grinning again, he sat back in his chair and lit up a fat cigar. Arthur's apprehension showed in his miserable expression. Drenched in beads of perspiration, he mopped his sallow face using his soiled handkerchief.

The date was set and preparations had been in full swing for over a month. The church had been booked and invitations sent. The reception was to be held in Satis House. On the eve of the wedding, Compeyson appeared at the gates.

The long evenings had arrived and it was still light. He walked to the front door of Satis House and let himself in with his own key. He found Miss Havisham seated at the top of the dining table which now groaned under silver cutlery and porcelain crockery in readiness to receive great trays of food waiting in the pantry. The enormous five-tiered wedding cake already occupied pride of place in the centre of the grand, oak, dining table over which had been spread a thin veil of white lace. "My darling, tomorrow is our special day," she said, entranced by this handsomely suited gentleman, complete with suspended fob chain. She indicated to Compeyson that he should seat himself next to her at the banquet table.

"Indeed, it is, my dear, and I cannot wait for tomorrow. Last night, I dreamt that I was waiting for you at the altar and then we walked back down the aisle and out into the sunshine. We were arm-in-arm together for all to see, and in the eyes of God." Her heart fluttered and she flushed at his response.

"And we shall have two children. A little girl for you and a little boy for me. Maybe they'll be twins. It's almost as if I can see them playing together in this room, and out there in the courtyard, and in the sunshine," she said, her gentle hand waved towards the westerly windows, the leaded panes glittering through the refraction of a brilliant red summer sunset. "Oh, sorry, my darling, I must be dreaming. What is it that you have there?" Her attention drawn to the leather pouch beneath his left arm.

"Just a few papers to dispose of before tomorrow, darling," replied Compeyson, nonchalantly placing the treacherous documents before her, and offering her the quill pen. He reached for the black inkpot whilst still talking about the arrangements for the flowers at the church. Unwittingly, she received the quill pen, and dipped it in the inkpot.

"Where do I sign, darling?"

"Here. Here. And, oh, here," replied Compeyson, appearing unconcerned. It was all over in less than two minutes. He carefully blotted the signatures and repacked the papers in his leather pouch. "I must rush, darling. Last minute arrangements for tomorrow are pressing. Until tomorrow, then."

Compeyson had gone as quickly as he had arrived. He went straight to the Three Jolly Bargemen where Arthur sat in the corner, drinking himself under the table, his nerves reaching breaking point. Compeyson crashed in through the bar door and shouted, "Barman, two large whiskies if you please." He ordered loudly and then rushed over to Arthur, giving him a playful punch on the shoulder.

"Deal's done, partner. Three perfect signatures. One for me. One for you. And one for the bank. Now that's what I call real business." Compeyson raised his whisky and toasted himself, then rapidly swallowed the contents. "Barman, two more large whiskies." Abruptly, his expression turned to a frown. He grabbed a seat and sat down next to Arthur.

"One last letter," said Compeyson with a sly wink. "And, barman, get me writing materials." Arthur looked shocked. "Drink up, man; lots more where that came from. And it's cost us nothing." Compeyson oozed with confidence. "Now, get those writing materials and the next lot of drinks. And I want red ink!"

"What last letter?" slurred Arthur, struggling to stand, concern etched across his sallow face. Compeyson frowned.

"Don't go soft on me just yet," he sneered, as he dipped the pen in the red ink. The letter was short and to the point. It contained harsh words. Words designed to inflict pain, such that there could be no misunderstanding. No hope of reconciliation. "If you strike a blow to the heart, make sure it stops," said Compeyson. "If it doesn't, that heart is coming back for you." He gave a sly grin, knowing his evil future would be left intact. The grotesque letter arrived at Satis House at 20 minutes to nine on the morning of the wedding. It found its mark.

Horrified as he read Compeyson's evil words, the lawyer leant back in the tapestry-covered chair in the great lounge. Composing himself before speaking, he dabbed the droplets of perspiration from his strained face with his enormous silk handkerchief. He braced himself to begin the offensive, paused for thought and, to the best of his ability, gently interrogated Miss Havisham.

Still in her early 20s, Miss Havisham had broken down and, through tears and shame, had admitted her lack of caution. She admitted that she had no knowledge of the papers she had signed. Silently, Jaggers contained his infuriation. Her only comment was that she thought the papers were to do with the brewery business.

"There is but one option open," Jaggers chose his words carefully and deliberately. "You still retain the property and all your rights as landlord. My advice is that you serve notice on Compeyson and Arthur to vacate the building and that you permanently lock the brewery premises until we are in a position to challenge this evil fraud through the courts."

"Do that, Mr. Jaggers. Do that now." Her face ashen and deeply lined with the strain of the past few days, Miss Havisham gave her instructions.

"Lock them out, but disturb nothing, save that everything is left as it was and shall be forever more. Now close my curtains, and leave me, Mr. Jaggers. I wish to be alone."

Chapter 3

The children gasped in horror as the dishevelled man bashed his wife with the rolling pin. Over and over again, he struck her on the back of the head and shoulders. She weakened and collapsed, falling prostrate to the floor, striking her head on the wooden platform as she fell forwards.

Seated cross-legged on that May afternoon, the terrified children watched, hardly daring to look at what the nasty man was doing to Mummy. Mummy lay silent and still. Her long, wiry, reddish-blonde hair hung over the front of the platform.

The horrid man kept shouting at her. He hit her again on the back. Every time the rolling pin struck, she struggled to turn her head to shriek back at him. She tried to lift her arm to protect herself, but that didn't stop the brutal husband from thumping the rolling pin on his ragged-looking wife, as she lay, defenceless, face down on the floor. A deep, gruff voice came from outside the room.

"Stop that. Stop that. You're under arrest," challenged the furious policeman. "Come along with me." He was smartly dressed in a dark blue, domed helmet and uniform, with silvery buttons down the front. Without waiting, he raised his truncheon and attacked, repeatedly smashing the horrid man on the head, until he too, fell to the floor and lay next to his battered wife. The policeman strutted backwards and forwards, proud of what he had just done. The children applauded their hero. Without any warning, a huge crocodile appeared at the other side of the room. The children gasped as it slithered behind the policeman.

"Behind you," they shouted, as it slithered to the other side, but the policeman looked the opposite way.

"The other way," shouted the children. The policeman turned round too late, failing to see the crocodile as it quickly slithered to his other side. With horror written across their innocent faces, the children cupped their small hands over their mouths. Again, they shouted through little fingers, "Behind you," frustration floated on their little voices.

The crocodile opened its enormous jaws to reveal rows of vicious xanthodontous teeth. Slithering towards the policeman, the crocodile began snapping at the policeman's legs. A big yellow tooth caught the policeman's trouser. The children gasped as he tugged to free his leg. He raised his truncheon and started battering the crocodile. Miraculously, the husband and wife regained consciousness and stood up. They saw the policeman who, by this time, was being dragged away by the crocodile. Both the husband and wife came to the aid of the policeman and beat the crocodile to death. The children cheered and laughed as the husband put his arms around his wife and gave her a big bear hug. Then they all walked happily from the room, pulling the dead crocodile behind them.

The red and white curtains jerked closed and quickly opened again to reveal the puppeteer hiding behind the canvas. He stood up with the gloved puppets, and all the children cheered again, as Punch and Judy waved and bowed to the children and their parents enjoying the medieval puppet show on Epsom Downs.

The atmosphere around the gypsy fortuneteller was different. There were no children, and there were no spectators. Passersby seemed to give the mysterious tent a wide berth. Just within the opening, the gypsy sat at a small, square, trestle table on which was laid a dark purple velvet cloth and, quietly, she turned the hand-painted Tarot cards, commenting at the pictures. She was young and beautiful, and possessed fine features. Raven-black and lustrous hair peeped from under a red and white spotted headscarf. Around the fringes of her headscarf had been sewn strange coins.

Coins not of the British realm, but of some foreign and mysterious land. They glittered in the reflection of the sun that bounced from the rapidly drying pool of muddy water at the side of her temporary stall. In her ears were rings with long drops of gold, and around her neck hung a string of tarnished pearls. Each long, slim finger supported a ring fashioned in either silver or gold filigree, adorned with blue or green or red jewels.

Sitting opposite the gypsy, was the querent, a mature woman in her late 50s, grey-haired, and in obvious distress. The woman reached into her grubby handbag, rummaged around, and retrieved two, silver, three-penny pieces. Carefully, she placed them side-by-side across the fortuneteller's palm. The delicate hand closed on the coins and spirited them to a safe haven. Having dropped the exit curtain to within three feet of the ground to increase privacy, the gypsy moved the crystal ball to the centre of the purple velvet cloth and, next to the crystal ball, carefully placed the deceased's gold watch. Resting her elbows on the table, either side of the crystal ball, with her fingertips touching her high cheekbones, the gypsy instructed the woman sitting opposite. The woman shut her watery eyes in obedience and listened.

Epsom Downs played host to many thousands during the week before the Great Race, not least of which, were the gypsies. Considered vagrants, they were not welcome to join in the festivities at Epsom village where local families would celebrate the traditional spring festival by crowning their May Queen and dancing around the maypole.

The gypsy-dingle nestled at the edge of the bluebell-carpeted woods on the north side of the Downs. Mostly oak trees and beech trees and chestnut trees, their new, lush green leaves shone in the spring sunlight. The wagons at the edge of the woods belonged to the Ingram family.

Drawn up in a semicircle, there were two Bow-Top wagons, a Burton, and two old Readings. Well-maintained and brightly coloured, they added to the excitement of the build up to Derby Day, the classic race for three-year-olds over one and a half miles. The final wagon, hidden in the trees, was an open lot in which the Ingrams stacked the barrels of ale, mead, and homemade wine.

They boasted knowing six generations of Ingrams and, each night, sitting around the fire under the starlit skies in the county of Surrey, they would tell tales of their forefathers' treks across the Byzantine Empire and Europe, and before that, the Holy Land and Babylon. Few knew that their origins had developed farther east, as far back as the antiquity of India herself, where the great river, Ganges, washed Hindu customs, and the belief in reincarnation. Through the millennia, spiritualism had developed deep within each Romany, the reason why, today, every Romany possessed the mystic powers of fortunetelling.

Released from Kingston gaol following his incarceration for vagrancy, Magwitch had decided to head in the direction of Epsom Downs. Door knocking seemed the only way to prevent starvation, although, when the sun went down, a little bit of vegetable scrumping seemed to be fair game. On his third day after release, Magwitch managed to secure temporary work in a market garden in Worcester Park.

The pay had been unusually good, and he had taken the opportunity to purchase some better, second-hand clothing. He looked in the reflection of a shop window and dusted off his tweed jacket and fawn trousers. "Dapper! That's wot I is. A dapper gent," he chuckled to himself; his right hand slipping into the neat material of his trouser pocket, his first two fingers and thumb feeling the various coins. He identified the serrations on the edges of the two individual shillings, and the sixpence, and then the 12-sided three-penny bit, the smooth-edged of three individual pennies and two ha'pennies. "A total of three shillings and one penny," he whispered to himself. "I'm a rich man," he chuckled again.

The work at the market garden had come to an abrupt end, but no matter, like all freelance hucksters at this time of year, he made his way to Epsom to try his luck at the races. His black boots grew white as the chalky mud started to dry. And his face and neck began to redden under the hot afternoon sun. He shielded his eyes to watch the pale, young, gypsy girl disappear into her mysterious tent and, behind her, carefully closed the silky privacy curtain.

"Allo, ducks." Magwitch swung round to see an old woman. She clutched a few sprigs of heather. Her one stained fang protruded from the front of her wrinkled mouth, thrusting her top lip forwards. Magwitch stared back at the mystic's tent. "Good luck charm, kind sir," offered the old woman, the fang prohibiting her lips from forming the words. "Brings ya love from a beautiful woman, ducks." Startled at the intrusion, Magwitch stopped observing the strange tent and, to appease the old woman's insistence, dug deep into his trouser pocket for a single ha'penny.

"Two sprigs for a ha'penny," he bartered.

"Oh, guv, a dapper lad like yoursel', guv? What's a ha'penny to the likes of yous?"

"Rabbit's foot; I'll pay more," he said. "But not for heather." A twinkle formed in the old woman's eyes as she dug deep into the ragged folds of the multilayers of her dark cotton fabric. White clay mud clung to the hem. Her sudden laugh reduced to a cackle, dredging up a wet cough. She swung her scraggy head to the side and spat into the soft chalky-clay mud.

"You're a believer, ducks, and that be true if I never breeves ano'ver word. Best see the girlie fortuneteller if yous a believer, 'cause wot she tells you comes true if yous a believer, gord strike me dead." The old woman straightened up as she produced the dried rabbit's foot. "Tupence ha'penny, and not a farving less," she challenged.

"Tupence the lot."

"Saucy bugger, an' may luv and luck be yourn for the rest of the year, but see 'er in the tent." The old woman pointed to the mysterious tent and slipped away into the growing crowd. Magwitch turned towards the tent.

"My name is Molly," said the gypsy gently, indicating to Magwitch that he should seat himself opposite. "Now shuffle the cards and place them back on the table." Magwitch busied himself shuffling the cards.

"Buy a special book for writing?" suggested Molly, pointing out the little black book with a gold surround and clasp lying partially buried under silk scarves at the back of the tent.

"And how much, luv?"

"Seven pence, luv," replied Molly, handing him the little book and clicking open the pretty gold clasp. "See, nice pages to make notes. Keep it like your own history for dealin's on yourn travels."

Hardly able to read or write, Magwitch put on a pretentious face and dug out the coins and carefully laid them on the table. He selected an additional coin and handed it to Molly. She smiled as he started shuffling the cards again. His thick, calloused fingers clumsily squeezed the deck, accidently forcing a card to jump out. He glanced at it, recognising the skull. Molly grabbed it, and quickly turned it over as if it were sacrosanct.

"My apologies, ma'am." Magwitch finished shuffling and placed the deck back on the purple velvet cover.

"Now cut them with your left hand and pass them to me with the hand you use least." Stunned by the beautiful face before him, Magwitch did exactly as bid.

"First, I need to know your name. All of it."

"Abel. Abel Magwitch, and I's a little over 30," he said, raising his right hand to scratch an irritation on the side of his slightly hooked nose.

"Before I begin, Abel, I must explain that I use *mi douvals zee,* the energy of *Zee,* but truth will only come to those who truly believe," Molly's voice was clear yet charming in its innocence. Magwitch nodded in acceptance, allowing his eyes to look deeply into Molly's shamanistic, ebony eyes. He lifted his left lapel and smelt the fresh heather, then secretly returned his left hand to the furry paw in his pocket. He sat forward, eager to hear the cards speak. Having carefully lowered the silk curtain to complete their privacy, Molly spread the cards face down in a fan. The card that had jumped out already placed face down, the way it had fallen, at the side of the fan.

"Abel, we will begin with the gypsy spread. Pick three cards please. They show your past, present, and future. Then hand them to me, one by one." He selected carefully. Handed the first, then selected the second; it seemed to stick to another card next to it.

"I'll have that one too," said Molly, reaching forward and grabbing both cards as they slid from the fan. And strangely, Magwitch's third selection also stuck to its neighbour.

"And that one as well." Molly snatched the card. "The cards must have lots to tell you," she remarked, closing the fan and removing the pack from the table. She adjusted all six cards, face down in front of Magwitch, both in the order and orientation in which they had been chosen. "I shall start with the card that jumped out." Molly turned the card to reveal a bleached human skull with a fresh red rose growing from the eye socket. "It appears the right way up in the spread, which shows you are reaching the end of one stage in your life and will soon begin a new one in a different direction. Death of the old ways, and the birth of a new and blossoming period." Her index finger pointed at the card.

"About time," mused Magwitch, a hint of a thrill ran beneath his skin. Molly's hand reached for the first selected card. "Your past," she said, turning the card.

"The wheel of fortune – Reversed." Molly took a sharp intake of breath.

"I didn't expect this. You've had a bad time, many losses and troubles and setbacks. But it's going to change." She pointed to the death card with the little finger on her left hand, and then turned the second card.

"Empress. The right way up. This is a generous card." Molly smiled and looked across at Abel. "The Greek God of fertility. Your new life is about to begin, probably going to get married and have a family." Magwitch grinned and winked at Molly.

"Little baby girl just like you?" Molly smiled politely and then turned her attention to the card that accidentally came out with the second choice.

"The Tower reversed." Molly took another intake of breath, sharper than the first. "That's better than if it were the right way up," said Molly, attempting to smooth the interpretation. "But remember where this card lies in the spread. This is for your present, either just past or maybe, say, the next few years. But its meaning is still serious. It signals change. Could be seen as big change. Maybe emotional shock or even disaster. You can expect big changes and upheaval. Remember, if you have a dream or imagine seeing the ghost of Romany rye at sundown, he'll be dressed in black with a chimney-pot hat. The most common sight will be of him stalking the river angrily. If that happens to you, then you will know that this reading is true. You would understand if you were of gypsy blood," said Molly, moving on quickly and turning the third card, the card for the future.

"The Chariot, it's the right way up," announced Molly, smiling again.

"This card is brim full of action. Shows you have faith in yourself and what you can do. But there will be hard work where you are heading, and yes, you are definitely going to travel. It's a bright card. There's lots of sunshine. Seems a long way off in the future." Molly returned the card to its place in the spread and then turned the final card.

"The World. Right way up again, see, the sun is at the top!" exclaimed Molly.

"It's a tremendous ending to your long and torturous road. The world will be yours for the taking, Abel. Everything comes to he who waits, and you're going to receive the rewards you so richly deserve." The temperature had risen inside the young psychic's tent. Molly sat back and looked across the intimate little table at her querent. Not sure why, but she felt that sitting opposite her was a special man. Magwitch wiped the perspiration from his brow. "Would you like me to gaze into the crystal ball?" invited Molly.

"I think I needs to know everything," replied Magwitch, sweat from his left hand having saturated the furry paw in his pocket; he took another refreshing sniff of the heather.

"Cover my palm with silver," instructed Molly, conscious of the anguish spreading across Magwitch's face. Magwitch pulled out all his coins and placed them on the purple velvet. "That one'll do nicely," she said, holding out her palm. Magwitch placed the corroded three-penny piece in the palm of her hand. Her slender fingers closed and spirited it away.

Molly's elbows rested either side of the crystal ball; her fingertips pressed gently against her high cheekbones. Her ebony eyes focused as she stared down into the picture forming below.

"Abel, you come from good Jewish stock?" her words came as a question. Before he could answer, she continued, "You are a gambling man. Not good with money." Magwitch nodded again.

"I see a Hebrew word here. Maybe a name, but I can't make it out. There's long grass, maybe weeds? And water. Yes, water. The marshes maybe. A wicker basket floating in murky waters like bull rushes, a long time ago. There are horses, lots of horses. Yes, it's to do with the horses." Molly suddenly stopped, wiped the perspiration from her brow, and quickly took a drink of water from her old clay bottle hidden behind her. She concentrated again.

"No, it's gone, but I see something else." Molly reached across the purple velvet and gently clasped Magwitch's right hand.

"Now I see a beautiful little wedding, there's a campfire and a gypsy band. A little girl is running around. She's calling out to her mummy." Molly shivered, but it was blazing hot inside the little tent.

"She's looking at me!" exclaimed Molly, shivering again. Quickly, she jerked her hand from Magwitch and replaced her fingertips back on her cheeks.

"It's gone dark. Very dark." Perspiration burst from her forehead and dripped onto the purple velvet. Magwitch sat bolt upright, mesmerised, frightened at the picture forming in his mind. She reached for the water again and took another sip, her eyes not leaving the crystal.

"The sea, it's blue, and the sun is shining. It's very bright." She paused and lowered her head. "But there's a big sailing ship, and men standing around in rags," she frowned. "They're shackled in irons, shuffling around on the deck. It's gone again, but it's very, very bright. Yes, here's something…"

"What is it?"

"I'm not sure. Maybe it's clothes, and tents, and sacks, and hammocks, and rope." Molly gave another involuntary shiver, her left elbow slipped and her head dropped towards the crystal ball, waking her from the trance. Magwitch made his first pathetic entry in his little black book.

Chapter 4

As dusk approached on the Thursday, the eve of the Epsom Derby, the crowds slowly dispersed, leaving the once fresh grass dry and trampled under foot. Magwitch entered the booth where he had had a snack lunch earlier in the day and approached the polished wooden bar, behind which, stood his old publican friend.

"Evening, Magwitch, what's your poison?"

"Usual pint, guv," said Magwitch, feasting his eyes around the room, taking in the assembled patrons. One loud, well-dressed man seated at a large side-table close to the bar, along with a few of his associates, caught his attention.

"I think this is the man that might suit you," suggested the publican, catching the suited man's attention.

The publican discreetly leant across the bar and whispered to Magwitch. "See that obvious gent; he's been looking for a partner like you. Name's Compeyson, a wheeler dealer, but be careful what you get into." The publican turned away and completed pouring Magwitch's ale.

Magwitch flashed a glance in Compeyson's direction.

"To judge from appearances, you're out of luck," Compeyson spoke publically. His friends chuckled at the words.

"Yes, master, and I ain't been in it much, neiver," replied Magwitch, turning his back and securing his pint of ale.

"Luck changes," replied Compeyson, looking fraudulently at his fob. "Perhaps yours is going to change."

"I hope it may be so. There's plenty of room," replied Magwitch, before taking another long swig of ale, and sitting himself down on the nearest barstool.

"What can you do?" quizzed Compeyson, swivelling around to continue the conversation.

"Eat and drink, if you'll find the materials," replied Magwitch, with a cantankerous grin spreading across his sunburnt face. He studied the slightly younger man.

"A good'en, I believe. Ripe for the plucking," said Compeyson, nudging Anthony Hitchcock, alias Hath, sitting to his left. Reaching into his jacket pocket, Compeyson withdrew two florin coins and looked seriously at Magwitch. "Tell you what. See this four bob? They say you'll meet me here same time tomorrow night." Magwitch's eyes moved from Hath's weather-beaten, fisherman's face and dropped to the two coins Compeyson had placed in front of him on the table. "One now. The other, tomorrow night." Compeyson pushed one of the silvery coins towards Magwitch and slipped the other back into his left fob pocket.

Chapter 5

The Epsom Derby was scheduled for three o'clock in the afternoon. Magwitch scratched around for information on the horses. He looked at the racing page of the local paper. There was something familiar. Hardly able to read, he studied the pictures. There it was, the Bible, Old Testament, and a baby in a basket. *What had Gypsy Molly said? A Hebrew word?* "It's got to be Moses in the bull rushes," muttered Magwitch.

"Sssssh," he whispered to himself, as he approached the bookmakers. The sign read Moses, 40-to-one, Jockey, Thomas Goodison, trained by William Butler, and owned by the Duke of York. "Definitely not the favourite at those odds." Magwitch grinned to himself as he bet the whole florin to win. "Easy come, easy go," he muttered, walking to a vantage spot to watch the race. He sat on the post and rail fence, screening his eyes from the afternoon sun. Waiting for the race, he sketched the horse and copied the word, Moses, in his book.

"And they're off," blared the man through his handheld megaphone, but it meant nothing to Magwitch until he heard his Moses mentioned. Halfway around, Moses was running seventh. That was the only time its name was mentioned as far as he could tell, until the end. Magwitch couldn't believe it. Four pounds plus his bet back. He went straight to Gypsy Molly's tent and gave her a ten-shilling tip.

"How kind of you, Abel." Molly found it hard to contain her surprise.

"A pleasure to 'elp a nice lady who 'as 'elped me," replied Magwitch. "Reckon me luck's changed all right, luv, and reckon I must come back and treat yous some more. May I ask Miss Molly if she would like to walk out with a lucky man?" Under her colourful headscarf and raven-black hair, Molly's face flushed.

"How kind of you to remember me, sir."

Chapter 6

Shaking uncontrollably, Arthur's hands could hardly hold the cutlery.

"Have a gentle glass of French wine," invited Sally, attempting to relax her husband's business partner.

"Give him a bucket of gin," growled Compeyson, not caring in the slightest for Arthur's alcohol abuse and resultant sickness. Sally, a slim, frail woman, and Compeyson, lived in a house in Brentford on the edge of Hounslow Heath. Arthur lived alone on the top floor. The bad business in Rochester and his half-sister had provided significant capital and income to Compeyson. But Arthur had buried his shame by submerging himself in the demon drink. Alcohol had become his constant companion, particularly as it was supplied free from the brewery business.

Magwitch watched from his seat at the bottom of the dining table as Sally tended to her latest wound inflicted by Compeyson. She was covered in bruises through his habitual beatings. Invited the previous night at the pub when he had collected his second florin, it was Magwitch's first visit to Compeyson's matrimonial home, so he sat politely and observed. The thought of securing a proper job had become uppermost in his mind.

"So what do you think of my family?" jested Compeyson, ignoring Sally and pointing at Arthur. "He's trying to drink the whole brewery." Compeyson's laugh turned to a sneer. "What with gambling and drinking, he's all but wiped out the brewery money. Stupid, pathetic fool." Magwitch nodded and took a breath to reply, but was cut short, as Sally emerged from the kitchen, carrying a hotpot of steaming stew. "Just look at him, will you? He's dying of the horrors as I speak. Reckons he betrayed his cow of a half-sister down in Rochester. His brain is gone, affected by his excessive and prolonged use of alcohol. He sweats and trembles and is loaded with anxiety and hallucinations. Got the delirium tremens if you ask me. Says he gets the same nightmare, over and over again."

Magwitch looked from Compeyson to Arthur, and then to Sally, struggling to ladle the stew from the pot.

"Let me help yous," volunteered Magwitch, offering a tablemat to set the pot on.

"Leave her to it," said Compeyson angrily. "That's her job." Compeyson took a swipe at her free arm, but missed. He felt nothing for any of them. His only interest lay in making money by means fair or foul. Mostly foul.

"So wot's my job?" asked Magwitch, deliberately changing what little conversation there was.

"Ah," said Compeyson. "So you're interested in being a partner?"

"I's never says no to workin' for to keep a roof o'er me 'ead," replied Magwitch, nodding his head to Sally as she served the stew.

"It's simple. I case the joint. You do the heist, and we quickly shift the swag through the fence, Hath, in Chatham docks. His real name is Anthony Hitchcock, but he goes by the name, Hath."

"Wot! Yous set me to go a thievin'?"

"Free board, and lodgings, and a bit of money in your pocket besides. Pretty good job if you ask me," said Compeyson condescendingly.

"I ain't askin'."

"Yes, you are. And I've just offered you a proper one, if you're game." For a few seconds, Magwitch sat in silence, spooning the soupy stew into his hungry mouth.

"I's game all right," sighed Magwitch. "When's the first job?"

"Patience, man. Don't rush me," replied Compeyson. "When the time's right, I'll let you know."

Chapter 7

Molly Ingram had made an impact.

"Who is she? Where does she live? I need her in my life," Magwitch talked to himself over and over again. Besotted, he walked over the Downs the next day.

The festivities at Epsom were winding down, yet the gypsy encampment at the side of the woods was still there. Little fires pumped sweet-smelling wood smoke upward through the high branches of the trees. A great fat oak and another tall beech tree provided the two corners to the camp.

"Wimbledon and Henley Regatta will be next. I've got to find her." Clutching his rabbit's paw, he whispered the words. "A thievin' job with Compeyson; for what that's worth. I'm already over 30, and it must be time to make a family. Molly said that's what the cards spoke of." He walked across the top of the Downs and then downward over the coarse grass towards the Ingram encampment. He ran over in his mind what he was going to ask Molly when he found her. He knew what he wanted. "And if I do ask, maybe she'll say yes. Especially if she reckons, I'm a lucky man."

It was approaching midsummer's day, the summer solstice, and the longest day of the year. It certainly would have been a very special night for the Druids at Stonehenge.

"Most unlikely couple," the gypsies whispered. "The beautiful Gypsy Molly, raven-black hair on top of white, petal-smooth skin, and not yet 21." They believed she could have done better for herself. "And him, that huckster, Abel Magwitch, more than ten years her senior. No past, and probably no future. Hooked nose, thinning fair hair of no descript colour, taller than the average man, yet thick-set and strangely masculine." The criticism went on and grew, but Magwitch didn't care; he was thick-skinned. "Can't speak the Queen's English," they muttered amongst themselves. But then, who could, amongst those peddling their wares on Epsom Downs?

"He's a Gorgio," said Sylvester, the gypsy chief, angry that an Ingram should wish to marry outside the Romany race.

Chapter 8

"I pity you," sneered Compeyson, listening to Magwitch pour his heart out about falling in love with some gypsy at the races.

Magwitch had refused to live in the big house in Brentford, only visiting when requested to do so for business reasons, usually to get his instructions from Compeyson.

"But yous haven't saw the lady yet," he argued, as they sat quietly together in the parlour of the Brentford home. It was yet another of his many visits to receive the next set of business instructions, accompanied by the usual insult from Compeyson. Since the bad business in Rochester, Arthur had become a total paranoid alcoholic. Sally and Magwitch watched helplessly as he threw himself into yet another alcoholic fit. The fits were becoming more frequent. Sally ushered Arthur back up to his bedroom and called down the stairs for Magwitch to come up and help. Magwitch excused himself from Compeyson and climbed the stairs. He entered the bedroom to witness Arthur sitting bolt upright, staring into the corner and pointing.

"She's there, I tell you, and she's coming to get me," he shouted, grabbing at his pillow to protect himself. His face went white as if he had seen a ghost. He waved his hands in front of his head as if defending himself, arched his back, and fell back onto his pillow. His sallow complexion drained. Sally lowered her ear to listen for breathing. Arthur was dead.

"Good riddance if you ask me," said Compeyson. "Now he's out of the way, Magwitch, we can get down to some proper business. Now, you and I must swear our allegiances to each other. On the Lord's book, if you like?"

"I have a special book," said Magwitch, producing his little black book with the gold clasp that he had purchased from Molly.

"Lord strike us dead on the spot if we ever split in any way," said Compeyson, nodding to Magwitch. "Now, kiss it." Magwitch bent forward, closed his eyes, and reverently kissed his little black book. Respectfully, he offered it back across the table. Compeyson lowered his head as he received the book in his right hand, pursed his lips, and kissed the gold clasp. His eyes looked away. Secretly, he crossed his fingers.

Chapter 9

Molly carefully cut the two-inch diameter shaft for her besom from the great oak at the side of their camp on Epsom Downs. Her coarse crosscut, pruning saw, specially sharpened to avoid tearing the bark, ensured a perfectly clean cut. Carefully, she severed the slim branch from the great trunk. She clutched the shaft to her small bosom, the few remaining oak leaves, succulent in their newness, sprouted from the bottom of the shaft. "Power, confidence, and fertility," she almost sung the words to herself.

Walking over to the single, wild apple tree, she neatly cut three slim saplings from the base of the trunk. "Prosperity and romance," she chuckled. "That's him." Molly knew he was destined for greatness one day. Next came three sprigs of ash for compassion, trustworthiness, and fairness. And finally, she selected the willow for flexibility and resilience. She sat down quietly in the forest clearing, and using a fresh piece of vine, carefully bound the twigs onto the oak shaft. The vine represented joy, lust, and prosperity, completing the symbolic qualities of her broomstick.

The wedding ceremony would commence at dusk and last for nearly two hours. But the summer solstice meant that it would still be light until late. The cauldrons bubbled and the candles flickered. The windless evening was humid, yet the insects had all but disappeared. Even the moths seemed preoccupied.

Magwitch slipped into the back of Molly's Bow-Top wagon just as the gypsy band started to play. There were four of them, the fiddler, the wind instrument not unlike a clarinet, a baby cello, and a sort of drummer. After the first instrumental, the drummer stopped drumming, lit his briar pipe, and exhaled pipe smoke as he mouthed a song with a hoarse voice. They either stood or sat around the fire, watching the cauldron boiling. The spits were ready for the hedgehogs just before the end of the blood-mingling ceremony.

Dressed in traditional costume, the happy couple emerged from their wagon to be witnessed by the Ingram family and a few friends. Ursula, Molly's twin sister, picked up the symbolic broomstick, and proceeded to sweep the ground in front of the couple as they entered the circle. Magwitch and Molly stood hand in hand as Ursula swept around the outside of the circle, sweeping away all the bad omens from the ritual centre. Sylvester stepped forwards to receive Magwitch and Molly. Ursula bowed to the Elder and gently lay the broomstick down in front of the wedding couple. Next, Ursula lit all the candles around the circle. And finally, the cord was produced and handed to Sylvester, who, in turn, handed it to the first of his two young female assistants. The two assistants, girls, barely out of puberty, stood together, one holding a bunch of ceremonial twigs obtained from seven different kinds of trees, and the other girl held the silk cord. Sylvester began to mumble incantations into the still air, reached out, and snapped the individual twigs, throwing each broken sprig into the air with each chant. His incantations included the forbidding of acts of adultery, and spiritual affairs, and to be faithful to each other until death.

"Molly, you must fetch the bread, and the salt, and the water," instructed Sylvester. Molly turned and walked gracefully to her wagon for the prepared basket containing a loaf of bread, a small bag of coarse sea salt, and a small bucket of fresh stream water.

"Now drink together," instructed Sylvester, as he poured the fresh and pure water into one cup, and bid them drink from the same vessel. Sylvester reached for the ornate silver dagger. He instructed Magwitch and Molly to extend their arms. Magwitch held out his right hand, and Molly held out her left hand. Sylvester took Molly's wrist and squeezing, formed a ridge of skin into which he drove the dagger, piercing the soft flesh until blood began to trickle. He did likewise with Magwitch's wrist, and then put both wounds together so that the blood would mingle. With ceremony, he bound the silk cord around the joined wrists in a figure of eight, the sign of infinity, representing eternity for the couple.

Finally, he tied three love-knots into the loose end of the cord, one for constancy, the next for fertility, and the third for a long life. He then entered into prayer, culminating in the ritual untying of the silk cord. Smiling to the couple, Sylvester gently squeezed Molly's cut wrist again, his other hand reached into the basket for the bread, and tearing off a chunk, dipped it into the excess blood dripping from Molly's wrist and handed the bloodstained bread to Magwitch. He then squeezed Magwitch's wrist, broke off another chunk of bread, and dipped it in the surplus blood dripping from his wrist, and handed the blood-soaked bread to Molly. Magwitch and Molly looked deep into each other's eyes whilst they ate their betrothed's bloodstained bread.

When every bit of bloodied bread had been eaten, and rinsed down with elderberry wine, Sylvester broke the remaining bread and spread the crumbs over the couple's heads. Silently, both Molly and Magwitch reached down into the bag of salt, retrieved a handful, and threw some over their left shoulders. Sylvester presented the silk cord previously tied around their wrists, the marriage cord that must be kept for at least two years, and unless requested otherwise, retained by the gypsy Elder, for life.

"With this bloodied cord," announced Sylvester to gathered witnesses and friends. "Should there be any reason that this couple should separate, then it can only be so by the presentation of the sacred cord to me, together with the declaration of a justifiable reason. If this it to become the case, it can only be me, or my successor, who may perform the solemn annulment of the union through the ritual burning of the sacred cord." Sylvester's face and voice delivered the severity of the last Romany law. He turned from the gathering and prepared to make the final presentations at the close of the ceremony.

"We come to the end of the ceremony and to drive away evil spirits, I solemnly present the besom and kharvie-saster." Sylvester pointed to the broomstick now resting on a stool in front of the campfire, then to the campfire on which bubbled a cast-iron kettle. Hand-in-hand, and amid roars of laughter, and cheers, and applause, Magwitch and Molly skipped towards the broom, and jumped over it, turned and walked back from the fire, and, together, they ran and jumped over the boiling kharvie-saster. Successfully over, they turned, and laughing breathlessly, waved goodbye to all the guests and ran off into the night. Away from prying eyes, they mounted their spirited horses, and rode off at a gallop to their honeymoon wagon, already parked on the edge of Hounslow Heath.

Chapter 10

"So soon, Molly, gord knows we only got married a few months ago. How do you know?" questioned Magwitch, stunned at the news.

"A woman knows," replied Molly with a gypsy's twinkle in her eye.

"Then the cards must have been right." Magwitch leapt up and danced around the campfire, shouting, "I'm to be a father. I'm going to be a father."

"They certainly were," chuckled Molly. "And it was the Empress, Greek goddess of fertility, one of the most important cards." Molly slipped her hand in through the buttons of her frock and stroked the taught skin on her stomach. Standing a mere one quarter of an inch over five feet, thin framed, particularly her chest and arms, Molly looked almost too young to be heading for motherhood. Her hair, combed back into a single plait and rolled into a bun at the back of her head, gave sharpness to her facial features. High cheekbones with scalloped cheeks emphasised her dark, ebony eyes above her button nose. She exhibited a gentle demeanour, but beneath that, lurked an intense passion, only few would ever experience. Magwitch was the first male she had truly fallen in love with, but having witnessed his degenerate business dealings with that ponce Compeyson, she was beginning to doubt her wisdom in becoming his wife.

"When do we choose names?" shouted Magwitch, grovelling on his knees in the mud beneath the wagon whilst fixing the linchpin of the nearside front wheel.

"Now, if you like. Boy's and girl's names, but I know it's going to be a girl," said Molly. The wagon gave a jolt as Magwitch wrenched at the rusted linchpin.

"Need to make a new one," said Magwitch, as he tapped the broken linchpin from its housing. "What, you think I'm going to make an old baby?" replied Molly angrily.

"No, silly, a new linchpin," grumbled Magwitch, sweat running from his brow as he loaded the fire with more wood. The fire crackled as the flames took hold. Fanning the growing flame beneath the dry wood, Magwitch placed a few lumps of jet-black coal on top. Half an hour later, he loaded more coal and sat at the fireside, working the bellows to increase the heat. The fire roared at the increase of oxygen and, the mild steel rod, from which the linchpin would be forged, glowed red in the coals. He withdrew it and started beating it on the heavy steel anvil. Driving the hardened steel punch through the flattened end, he created a hole for the clevis pin. It only took seconds and, hammering out the rough edges, he proudly quenched the new linchpin. The steam hissed and droplets of condensing steam belched up into the cool autumnal air.

"Have a name like steel," shouted Magwitch up at the wagon. Molly came to the door.

"Not a good name for a girl, really," she said with a furrowed brow. "I would like it to be like a French name," said Molly, looking down at Magwitch covered in charcoal, and ash, and grease, as he slid the new pin into position.

"La," suggested Molly. "That's for girls. La steel. Make a name out of that." Magwitch frowned, his writing abilities restricted to signing his name and a few more four-letter-words being the sum total of his literary capability.

"I'll ask them in the other wagon. Them Woods people yonder. Them'll know names I reckon."

Chapter 11

Madonna Woods was fully literate and ten years older than Molly. She was head and shoulders over her, and heavily set. Her head supported coarse brown hair, with a fine down at the fringes, and her voluptuous facial features and body left Molly feeling somewhat inadequate. Magwitch almost dribbled at the sight of her.

"Enormous heaving bosom under that loose-fitting blouse and bet there's big thick dark nipples too," surmised Magwitch. He took every opportunity to watch her washing in the stream.

It was a typically cold and foggy November night for Guy Fawkes' night, and on Hounslow Heath, the locals had built a huge bonfire that had been lit half an hour previously. The gypsy gathering around the fire had swollen with the arrival of other family members. The mead and mulled wine flowed, helping the Woods family warm in their acceptance of Molly and Magwitch. For Magwitch, this arrangement was perfect. He could walk to work or, rather conveniently, attend his numerous meetings with his partner, Compeyson, in the big house in Brentford. So far, they had been successful, but now planned for bigger fish. Compeyson worked on his social connections in the West End.

"Yes, that'll be good," said Magwitch, patting the ground next to him, inviting Madonna to sit. He had just moved back from the heat of the massive bonfire, now consuming the hastily prepared mock-up dummy of Guy Fawkes, long ago forgotten that he had been a treasonous catholic who had failed in his attempt to blow up King James as he spoke in the Houses of Parliament in 1605. The annual celebration had become a ritual re-enactment.

Every year, carefree children, went around singing, *A Penny For The Guy,* usually getting a farthing, sometimes a ha'penny, and knocking on the doors of the expensive London residences at the time when the owners were having their evening whisky, always gaining greater generosity for their efforts.

This year, the Woods had collected one pound, 13 shillings, and seven pence ha'penny. That was almost enough money to buy all the materials to build an urgently needed open-top wagon, the wagon to be used to collect all the rag-and-bone cast-outs from the wealthy homes around Hounslow Heath.

Magwitch patted the ground. Gypsy Madonna came and sat beside him, his rugged features in the firelight becoming strangely attractive to her. Secretly, Madonna felt for his right hand, they connected and she squeezed. He turned his head and winked.

"So by next April, you want me to work out a pretty little girl's name from La Steel," she jested.

"Gord, I'd be an 'appy man like," said Magwitch, the stirring in his loins forcing him to adjust his dress. She couldn't help but notice and squeezed his hand again. Madonna leaned closer and whispered in his ear.

"Well, I've already played with the letters. Hope you will like it." She slid her hand into the top of her blouse and produced a piece of folded parchment wedged in her abundant cleavage. Seven letters had been written in black ink, three of which had been slightly smudged through folding the paper when the ink was still wet. "I have found this name, what do you think?" Magwitch looked at the letters and stuttered to decipher their meaning.

Madonna chuckled, and whispered the name written on the parchment into his left ear, "Estella." Magwitch repeated it.

"Estella. Gord, that's bootiful. I can almost see 'er now." From the other side of the growing fire, Molly looked on, her physical condition making it difficult for her to find comfort sitting in the open. She moved her hand to her stomach, responding to the occasional kick from within her growing belly. The mead was going down well, too well. Fortified with rather more wine than usual, courtesy of a successful amount of elderberry and dandelion wines produced last year, and which had been mixed with rich gypsy honey from the beehives. It was delicious.

The Woods' family Elder stood and shielded his face from the heat of the ceremonial bonfire. Flames licked up the suited chest of the Guy Fawkes effigy. *"Bang!"* The noise and explosion shot across the heath as the gunpowder in the effigy's sacking chest exploded. Then another two smaller bangs. One after the other, as each eye socket blew out. This time, the flash had a green tint mixed with orange. Madonna and her father stood up, waved their hands for attention, and chanted:

"Remember, Remember, the fifth of November,
The Gunpowder, Treason, and Plot.
I see no reason why Gunpowder Treason,
Should ever be forgot.
Guy Fawkes; Guy, 'twas his intent
To blow up King and Parliament.
Three score barrels were laid below

To prove old England's overthrow,
By God's mercy, he was catched,
With a dark lantern and burning match.
Holla boys, holla boys, let the bells ring;
Holla boys, holla boys,
God save the King."

More mead was poured during the applause. Then came the spit-roasted hedgehogs. Seventeen in all, providing dinner for the Woods and their guests. Magwitch laid back.

The gypsy doctrine, *marimè*, had instilled in Molly that pregnancy, and childbirth, made her unclean, and, therefore, she could not allow Magwitch near her. Jealously, she watched him as he lay on his back, allowing his eyes to follow Madonna during her performance. The aroma of roasting hedgehogs and potatoes filled the damp November air. Magwitch had little appetite as he fantasised over Gypsy Madonna. He failed to notice that Molly was becoming conscious of his thoughts.

Chapter 12

Compeyson's personal invitation to attend cocktails at Porchester Terrace, Bayswater, arrived on Tuesday. The date set for the party was next week, Thursday, 6 p.m. to 8.30 p.m. He studied the card:

Sir Rupert and Lady Marlborough are delighted to invite Mr. Compeyson on the special occasion of the engagement of their daughter, Teresa, to Malcolm Trentham, son of the esteemed London Banker.

"They can afford it," muttered Compeyson, as he ascended the marble steps to the London residence. He knocked the polished, brass knocker on the heavily panelled front door and stood patiently, noting the access to the servants' quarters beneath the stairs below. The window was ajar and the catches looked rusted. "Access point number one," he mused, making a mental note as the front door opened.

Handing over his gilt-edged invitation card, heavy overcoat, top hat, scarf, gloves, and cane, Compeyson ordered. "Large pink gin," he said in his snooty accent, his nose in the air.

"Certainly, sir," replied the young waitress, indicating that he should enter and join the other guests. Circulating, Compeyson introduced himself to his host and hostess, boasting about his new investments in the Scottish jute industry, a subject he had overheard at the last cocktail party he had attended in Marylebone on the previous Tuesday. The previous cocktail party still foremost in his mind; he had witnessed an almost secret meeting at the height of the party. He had noted the two gentlemen standing together, away from the main action of the party. One burly type, who had a strange habit of biting the side of his index finger. By all accounts, a lawyer specialising in criminal law. His miserable clients, wretches to be tried for murder and either hanged at Newgate, or transported to New South Wales. The other gentleman, the host, was engaged as a merchant with significant interests in Calcutta. Compeyson had pricked up his ears at the mention of a plant called marijuana and jute.

Jute. The strange word had floated in the air. Compeyson had sidled over specifically to eavesdrop, overhearing about its commercial application.

"Tremendous opportunity, it is capable of making rope, and cloth, and sacks, and tents, and hessian, and webbing; the applications are endless." The host had continued and the list the merchant had talked about got better and better. "And they believe a Scottish weaving company is experimenting with mass production in Dundee, using whale oil of all things." The lawyer had made notes about the investment opportunities.

"Rich, very rich," Compeyson had muttered to himself, following his little survey of valuables during the two-and-a-half-hour cocktail party. His mind returned to his current situation. "The burglary in Marylebone should now be in full swing," he chuckled to himself, as he slipped from the ballroom at Porchester Terrace, excusing himself from the trumped-up cocktail party pleasantries and stealthily climbing the carpeted stairs to the private suite above. The door at the top of the stairs brushed the deep pile carpet as it opened. He surveyed the room's comprising parlour, study and two bedrooms.

"Ah, windows and no proper catches." He walked over and tried the handle. "Small diamond panes, simple and easy to remove from their lead surrounds," he muttered, easily opening the window and sticking his head out. "Ah, perfect, cast-iron drainpipes. Access point number two." Compeyson made another mental note, and then quickly assessed the ornaments. Solid silver and gold, all recently polished. He walked into the double bedroom and over to the chest of drawers. Gently, he clutched the large central wooden knob and slid open the right-hand drawer.

"Obviously the lady's side; I've hit the jackpot." Compeyson chuckled, a half grin appearing on his handsome face. A beautiful diamond tiara sat invitingly on its burgundy velvet in pride of place. The fat, mahogany drawer was dedicated to jewellery. His eyes feasted on the contents: a string of pearls, bracelets, and earrings. It went on, too much to count. Compeyson placed his hand back on the huge knob, but pushing too quickly, the drawer squeaked, twisted, and stuck fast. He felt sick with excitement.

Suddenly, the dog that had been locked in the private study behind the parlour barked. Compeyson jumped out of his skin. Panic set in. He bashed the drawer with his fist. The dog barked more aggressively and clawed at the door to get out. The drawer moved, twisted to the other side and stuck again. Compeyson bashed the other side of the drawer with his fist. It slid back. He swung round to see the butler filling the doorway to the bedroom, ready to enter the room.

"Oh, err, sorry, I was looking for the privy," explained Compeyson, wondering how long he had been watching. "The one downstairs always seems to be busy with the ladies. My need was getting urgent," continued Compeyson, pointing to the study door. "Sounds as if that dog wants to savage me."

"Of course, I'm so sorry, sir," apologised the butler. "If you would kindly follow me, sir, I will show you into the master's private suite." Compeyson breathed a sigh of relief.

Chapter 13

Thirteen minutes had elapsed since Magwitch had entered the Marylebone property. Nearly finished, his sack was full of candlesticks, and cutlery, and ornaments. "Gord, stuff wot glisters maybe not gold," he told himself attempting to be selective. Madam's jewellery proved a waste of time. Costume, and most of it fake. Magwitch's teeth had proved that. "Bet the old dowager don't know she's got cheated," grinned Magwitch, as he climbed down the drainpipe with the swag in a hessian sack slung over his shoulder. But the safe had held something else. Papers to do with a property along Chowringhee Road, Calcutta, West Bengal. Magwitch looked at the strange document; the colourful government seal in the bottom, right-hand corner signifying that the papers were something of value. Quickly, he tucked the parchment into his inside jacket pocket for later.

Chapter 14

Ursula pressed down on Molly's shoulders. "Push, luv, push. One last push. Harder, push." Molly took another breath, deeper this time, determined to produce. She screwed up her face and pushed, the exertion ending in a low scream. Her petite frame stretched to capacity. The head arrived. She breathed again, the excruciating pain all consuming. She took one final breath and a last push. Estella arrived. A beautiful, new, baby girl had been *born on the straw at Hounslow Heath*. Her physical features just like her mother, Molly, yet with a fair complexion and long limbs, possibly taken from her father, Abel Magwitch. Maybe she had a quieter and deeper personality and an analytical temperament. Time would tell. The delivery amazed both the Ingrams and the Woods. Two hours from feeling the first contractions, Estella had been born. Half past ten, in the morning on the second of April, 1823.

"I has a bootiful baby girl," sighed Magwitch. He gazed into the campfire burning peacefully outside their Bow-Top wagon. He looked across Hounslow Heath, his feelings complete. What more could a man want. He swilled another few gulps of mead and prodded the fire again. It was spring, and rich wild daffodils burst from the heath. New leaves adorned the once dead-like trees, and the hedgerows fattened. Life was good and the cards had foretold what was to come. Magwitch tossed some more wood on the campfire as he thought, *Broken Tower comes next. What in hell's name does that mean? And the ghost of Romany rye dressed in black with a chimney-pot hat and fiercely stalking along the river.* Magwitch chuckled to himself.

Chapter 15

The roof of the barn on the Powder Mill Lane's side of Hounslow Heath was high and at its apex; thick, steel plates bolted the rafters in place. Great, thick, 12-inch, square, horizontal, timber cross-members braced the walls and provided the bearers for a storage stage high above the barn floor. The high stage, boarded with one-inch-thick flooring, held bales of lucerne, the winter animal feed.

At the side of the barn, a split-pole ladder provided access to the storage area and, at the end of the barn, located in the triangular section of the gable-end wall servicing the top stage, was a little door, three-feet wide, four-feet high, through which an iron joist protruded. An overhead pulley system ran on the bottom flange providing lifting equipment to winch up the bales of hay. There were no windows. What little light there was grew from openings in the vertical planking, but when open, light would stream in through the massive quadruple doors at the front of the barn. It was dry, bone dry, and dusty if disturbed. The boarding creaked when walked on. But it was cosy, and strangely warm, even in winter.

The heavy barn door creaked in refusal, then the rusted hinge grated and groaned, as it gave under the man's pressure. The door had dropped on its rusted hinges and scraped the surface of the soft mud formed at the entrance. There was evidence of an earlier opening. A smaller footprint recently having buried itself in the adjacent muddy grass indicated the passage of another. The man closed the door quietly behind him and walked through the scattered hay on the floor and over to the split-pole access ladder.

"Is that you?" said the female voice from above. Magwitch's heart pounded as he placed his booted foot on the bottom rung and climbed the ladder.

"How long has yous been 'ere, luv?"

"I think longer than an hour. It was broad daylight when I arrived," replied Gypsy Madonna. Leaning back, she quickly removed her underwear and adjusted her frock. Magwitch's head appeared at the top of the ladder.

Swinging himself from the ladder, he scurried through the hay to the back of the platform and, to let more light in, opened the small access door in the rear.

"It'll be dark soon," commented Magwitch, studying the tombstones poking their heads up through the long grass in the Hounslow cemetery 50 yards away. He shivered, his fascination for graveyards forming vivid images in his mind about the activities of the body snatchers and experimentation by the medical men. His mind flashed back to his last meeting in Brentford. Compeyson's new plan: 'Cut them down at Newgate before the life was throttled out of them. Broken neck or not, didn't matter. Buy them from the undertakers, or steal them from the graves. The ones with deformities fetched a bigger price.' Dr. Emmett paid cash and asked no questions.

"Come over here," invited Madonna. "I'm getting cold." Magwitch scurried back, and snuggled in. She gently pushed him backwards and undid his thick leather belt. Magwitch helped. Caressing and kissing his white skin, she took charge. He lay silently, propped up on his left elbow, breathing in the sweet-smelling lucerne.

It was nearly dark, but sufficient light penetrated through the little door. Magwitch raised his head to look at the detail, but soon lay back in the hay again, leaving Madonna to do all the work. The dust from the hay rose into the air. Magwitch sneezed. "Do that again," whispered Madonna in Magwitch's ear.

"Can't," said Magwitch. "It's your turn to cough." They giggled, reaching the perfect moment together. Gypsy Madonna slumped forward, rolling to the side. For minutes, they lay, panting. "Don't tell Molly."

"Do you think I'm mad, or something?" whispered Madonna. "Anyway, she hasn't worked it out for the past two years. Even if she does, she's much smaller than me, so doubt she could do me any harm. Find a four-leaved clover."

"Wot for?"

"Gypsy's magic cure for deception," explained Madonna.

"Gord, don't be clever 'cause she's got the mystics. Yous aunty, Madonna, and says no more on it," grunted Magwitch, dragging his clothes back on. "She mustn't think nuthing. And oh! Molly's to give Estella a summer party. Never does it in April, 'cause it's always too cold. It's just 'er excuse fur to show 'er off. She'll make raspberry pie an' custard. Reckon yous an' me can come up 'ere again. Same time. Wot d' yous say?"

"Am I invited to the party?" asked Madonna, struggling to pull her underwear over the heel of her shoe.

"O'corse yous are. I'll make proper sure."

"I'd like that," said Madonna.

"But I'll 'ave to go arter the pudding 'cause I's got business in Regent's Park first," said Magwitch, scratching the itching roots of his pubic hairs. Madonna frowned. "So I'll come over later in the afternoon, about two-and-a-half hours after helping Molly clear up after Estella's party."

Chapter 16

Boasting an abundance of heather and red berry fruit, wild brambles grew in profusion everywhere all around the edges of the vast, open wasteland. With Estella in the middle, each parent held one hand, and, together, the family strolled through the meadow grasses over to the copse on the far western side of the heath. Still early morning, the dew drenched their shoes, but they didn't notice.

The air was perfumed with wild jasmine and honeysuckle, and the warm sun soon penetrated their bodies. Magwitch sat down on a thick, fallen tree trunk and retrieving his Negro-Head plug from his pocket, proceeded to shave small slices of tobacco. He carefully loaded his briar pipe. Lighting a piece of straw from his flint, he offered the flame to the pipe bowl and puffed, discarded the burning straw, and sat back to watch his family gather wild raspberries and blackberries.

"My little angel, here, you hold the basket and I'll pick the raspberries," said Molly, handing her the basket. Estella took the basket in both hands, her arms almost fully extended. Molly lent into the tangled mass of thorns. Aggressively, the brambles caught the hem of her frock. "Ouch!" she exclaimed, quickly pulling her hands from the thicket, the soft skin on the backs of her hands becoming lacerated by barbed thorns. She reached down to rescue her frock viciously hooked onto the trailing bramble. Blood from a deep laceration across a vein in the back of her right hand spurted onto the bramble leaves. "Oh look, blackberries as well, my favourite. Makes for a much better flavour in the pie," commented Molly, attempting to make light of her wound.

"Mummy, can I make the pastry?" pleaded Estella, not noticing Molly wrapping her handkerchief around her damaged hand. "I can stand on the chair, Mummy," continued Estella, remembering that the table was too high for her to reach.

"O'corse, that's if Mummy says so," called Magwitch from his vantage point on the fallen trunk.

"We'll see," said Molly playfully. "But we've got to fill the basket first. We need enough for everybody."

Chapter 17

Murder, and the promise of *Blood Money*, attracted the gang of Bow Street Runners and gypsies. Swarming around the barn, they sifted through the hay and inspected the ground around the door. They studied the grass, and the mud, and the footprints.

"Why did you come up here this afternoon?" challenged the cold-eyed Runner.

"I had just fed that woman on my blackberry pie and custard, and she made a poor excuse to leave my Estella's party," said Molly, her ebony eyes flashed. Her suspicions alerted further. "She'd gone before I knew it. Invited me to visit her in her wagon, but I didn't go. Well, not immediately. When I did, she wasn't there."

"What did you do next, Molly?"

"I came up here, looking for them," said Molly angrily.

"Them? What do you mean, them?" The investigation became more invasive. Molly flushed.

"Jesus, I'll kill 'im."

"So where is your husband now, Molly?" the cold-eyed Runner changed tack. Each question becoming more intrusive.

"Abel, oh, he left the party much earlier." Suddenly Molly screamed, her mind connecting him with the affair. "I'll kill 'im 'an all." She screamed. The Runners heard her words.

"Jealousy's as good a motive as any," mused the Runner. It was enough to make the arrest. "Now, lady, that's enough of that." The Runner clamped the cuffs on Molly's wrists.

"I'll kill 'im. I'll kill 'im. And he can forget his bloody little daughter too," Molly cursed, and mumbled alien Romany gypsy words. "Made like 'im, cold as steel. I'll teach 'im to have affairs. Kill 'im; kill 'em all," Molly ranted, and raved, and wriggled to escape her captors, but her petite frame was no match for the gang of Bow Street Runners as they dragged her off to Newgate, kicking and screaming.

Molly had settled somewhat by the time they slammed the iron door shut. She threw one last curse through the small, iron-barred window, deep in the bowels of Newgate prison.

It was the gypsy's curse.

Chapter 18

"Gor blimy," gasped Magwitch, as he wrenched open the front door at the Brentford house. He stood, trying to collect himself in the doorway, but almost immediately started bleating on over the tragedy at the barn.

After retrieving the swag lifted from the property overlooking Regents Park two days earlier from a disused house in Archery Close, just off Hyde Park, Magwitch had returned to the barn for his date with Madonna. When he got there, she had already been found dead. He had hidden in a thicket and watched the Runners as they dragged Molly away.

"Murdered in the barn, yous understand. I 'eard the gypsies say she'd been strangled," Magwitch blurted out everything he had seen, his voice flustered and beads of perspiration formed on his wrinkled brow.

"So what?" said Compeyson disinterestedly. "Where's the swag?"

"Nobody knows who done it, but the gypsies reckon Molly. Runners charged 'er with murder. I reckon she done it an' all," said Magwitch. "And I see'd her, just for a second, a'cursin' and a'spittin'. They dragged 'er off, shouting I'll never see my Estella again. Says she's killed her an' all. I reckon that's wot she done. She's mad angry. Already killed my little Estella and buried the body just to spite me."

"Christ, Magwitch. Forget it. Now, where's the swag?" challenged Compeyson, getting angry.

"They ain't found no little girl's body yet." Magwitch's eyes misted over and watered. "If the Runners ain't took her, she'd 'ave come for to kill me an' all." Magwitch sniffed and wiped his hooked nose on the back of his sleeve. Turning and bending down, he reached for the sack he had left by the front door.

"Give me that," demanded Compeyson impatiently, grabbing the sack of stolen trinkets. "Do you see this?" he snapped. "Grow up, man. What do you want to be bothered for? Sounds to me as if it's the answer you've been waiting for. You just got rid of both of them in one hit." Compeyson broke into callous laughter.

"But I daren't go home," moaned Magwitch.

"Then stay here, you stupid fool. You can use Arthur's old room."
"But what about Sally?" Compeyson looked back in disgust at Magwitch. "Who cares about what she thinks."

Chapter 19

Gypsy Madonna's Ledge-type wagon was parked neatly at the end of Pulborough Way on the northwest side of the Hounslow High Street leading into London. It lay empty, with the exception of her personal things.

Struck down, murdered when she was only 32. Her murder had shaken the Woods family to the very core of their existence. The Ingram family denied everything, but would not be invited to the funeral. Molly, an Ingram, locked up in Newgate, approached committal proceedings prior to going to trial.

"She can rot in hell."

The Woods's Elder would do everything in his power to see her hanged.

Jaggers thought differently.

Chapter 20

Dedicated to Gypsy Madonna, the private funeral attended by family and friends had but one hidden observer. He secreted himself in the shrubs and brambles at the edge of the heath. His interest was the body contained in the simple coffin. He watched the burial proceed in Hounslow cemetery. The weather had been dry during the day, and the sky promised a dry night. The moon would be out and nobody would know. Except Dr. Emmett, but then that didn't matter; he never asked questions and always paid in folding money.

"She would understand," Magwitch said to himself. "Her beautiful body donated for the benefit of the human race and the cause of medical science. The coroner had said it was strangulation, but what would be the effect on the brain in such cases? Dr. Emmett would find out."

The grieving family walked past the open grave one by one, each tossing a wildflower, or lavender, or heather, or rose, onto the coffin lid. They spoke in Romany. The silent observer was oblivious to the words. The mourners dispatched the undertaker's carriage and proceeded to walk northward across the heath as the evening approached. They walked to Pulborough Way, taking a little under an hour. Madonna's Ledge-type wagon stood elegantly at the end of the lane. The Woods's Elder bowed his head in ceremony before ascending the four stairs to the brightly coloured door. It was open, and he entered. With his right hand, he signalled for female assistance, whilst the men proceeded to light the campfire. The large flint stone would serve as the anvil. All the crockery within the wagon was the first to be smashed on the stone. Next came the vases and any breakable item. Bed linen and clothing was left hanging, as was Madonna's food and personal items. The Elder descended the stairs to the campfire and with a pair of tongs, selected the hottest log and threw it in through the open wagon door. Within seconds, the wagon burst into flames. Three quarters of an hour later, the remains of the Ledge-type sat as a smouldering ruin; only the mild steel tyres to the wheels, and axle shafts, and metal brackets, and nails, and bolts, sat glowing in the ashes, now a distant reminder of Gypsy Madonna's passing.

Chapter 21

His London Harley Street address was close to the Cavendish Square end of the road. Actually, Dr. Emmett's research laboratory was located beneath road level. Many would term it a cellar. Previously, he had been a highly successful barber in premises on the Old Kent Road. His experience in attending to amputations and, other bloody intrusions into the human body, had become invaluable. But now, the red and white, rotating, 'Blood and Bandages' sign, advertising his barber's business, was long gone. Discretion and secrecy had become of paramount importance, given the skepticism towards surgery.

The two men struggled to carry the shrouded body down the narrow stone stairs. At five-feet six-inches tall, and still clothed, she was heavily boned and strong, weighing over 12 stone. Ten shillings or more each was a king's ransom for a couple of hours' work. When the mourners had dispersed, grab the body from the casket and close the lid. Catch your breath for a while, then backfill the grave. He had brought bodies to Dr. Emmett before, but this was different. A healthy, young female murdered by strangulation. A fresh corpse.

Pocketing the large, white, five-pound note that Dr. Emmett had given him, Magwitch hailed a hansom cab and rode in style back to his top room in the big house in Brentford.

Chapter 22

The coal fire burned gently in the grate of the large room at Satis House whilst Jaggers and Miss Havisham took tea together. The grandfather clock sat frustratingly silent, its brass-inlaid face reported 20 minutes to nine.

"Ma'am, it seems that it is a new material. Well, having said that, maybe not, the newness comes from the fact that they have managed to mass produce the product in Dundee and, I believe as an investment, it will serve your interests profitably."

"Mr. Jaggers, it certainly sounds interesting," agreed Miss Havisham. "And, indeed, be instructed to place a small investment. The amount, I shall leave to your good offices to decide. Now, whom did you say? Mr. Cox of the Camperdown Jute Works or some such name?"

"Quite so, ma'am, quite so." Miss Havisham's eyes misted and her cheeks flushed. She gave a fraudulent cough and shuffled in her high-backed chair.

"Em, Mr. Jaggers, I must also bring to your attention that since the demise of the brewery and, of course, the failure of my marital arrangements at the hands of that now-deceased half-brother of mine and his unscrupulous friend, I have other personal needs." Jaggers sat forward in his tapestry-covered armchair, selected the brass poker, and poked the large piece of unburnt coal, stimulating the coal tar to ignite. The flames shot up the chimney in an attempt to escape the stifling nature of the heavy conversation within the barren room.

"No, not men," snapped Miss Havisham, avoiding the obvious assumption her lawyer may make. "Mr. Jaggers, you are aware that I live a solitary life, but, as yet, I feel I have the need for a companion." Jaggers continued to attend the fire. "And it occurs to me that I should seek the company of a foster child, a little girl whom I can cherish and raise as if my own." Jaggers replaced the poker and sat back in his armchair, raised his big hand, and aggressively bit the side of his forefinger.

"Am I to understand, ma'am, that a young lady, say, about the age of three, would serve your purposes? And if I have understood you correctly, ma'am, you wish to become the legal guardian of such a child." Miss Havisham nodded as Jaggers continued.

"And, ma'am, assuming I am in a position to request the courts make such an award, would a child with a fair complexion suit such a role in Satis House?" Miss Havisham gave a half smile and nodded her head in acceptance.

"Then, ma'am, I may have such a child, but you understand there are others who will need to sanction such an adoption before the courts would make an award possible. I shall send word within the month and revisit you early next month to attend to the finer points." Jaggers stood to leave, pulled his spotted handkerchief from his inside pocket, barely touching the side of his large nose. He bowed respectfully, and turned towards the heavy door.

Chapter 23

"Molly, Molly, Molly." With a wave of his right hand, Jaggers silencing yet another tirade from his client. "If you want my help, you must do exactly as I say. Is that clearly understood?" Jaggers stood for a moment as Molly quietened before sitting down at the table provided in the squalid little cell at Newgate prison.

"Yes, sir," replied Molly, bitterly.

"Before we come to the matter of your committal and what I'm sure will become a trial by jury, I have certain matters before me, the answers to which require urgent attention. Do you agree?"

"Yes, sir," she answered, a little less grumpily.

"When and where were you born?"

"Maybe, I think, 21 years ago, sir? Maybe less, and they say I was *born on the straw* on Epsom Downs," replied Gypsy Molly, beginning to relax. Jaggers made a simple note in his leather-bound pocketbook.

"Is it true that you have a little, three-year-old girl by the name of Estella?" Gypsy Molly flinched, her fists clenched, forcing, and her ebony eyes flashed. She jumped up and paced the floor of the cell, then suddenly swung round and faced Jaggers.

"Make no mistake, guv, nothing is to happen to 'er or there'll be the gypsy's curse on them who wrongs 'er." Molly hit the wooden table with the open palm of her hand.

"I quite understand," began Jaggers, amazed at how small her palm and fingers were. Without touching, he studied her pale white wrists and the scratch marks on the backs of her hands. It gave him an idea, embryonic, but an idea, nevertheless.

"You must not conceal the child from me as she may become important to the trial. And if not for the trial, then for the child's sake," said Jaggers. Molly's face flushed in sudden rage, and was about to speak. Jaggers raised his large hand, barricading her vicious words before they could be emitted.

"Molly, Molly, Molly. I often see children tried at the criminal bar, where they are held up, accused of the crimes they scarcely know they commit. I see them every day, lost to their mothers who are taken by the rules of society. I see these children whipped and transported and neglected and cast out, qualified in all ways for the hangman, and growing up to be hanged. Just about all the children I see in my daily business life, I look upon as so much spawn to develop into the fish that will come to me to be prosecuted, defended, forsworn, made orphans, or bedevilled somehow. Even the work of Quaker, Elizabeth Fry, I fear, is under threat. Her school for the children of convicted women, children born in goal and with no hope, is full, and lacks the support of the authorities' charity. Once wealthy, her husband now faces bankruptcy as a result of her huge and generous endeavours to help those pitiless and disenfranchised children. Estella is but one pretty little girl out of all of them whom I can save. No father to speak of, possibly dead, hopefully so, lest he returns to disturb our trial with convicting evidence, that only he can speak of. Molly give the child unto my hands, and I will do my best for her. If you are saved, your child is saved too. If you are lost, your child is still saved." Jaggers reached for his large, spotted handkerchief, dabbed at his troubled brow, and paused whilst Molly tried to assimilate his ominous words, and make her decision.

"Will I see her again?" asked Molly, almost in a whisper, her eyes near to tears.

"There are some questions a man in my profession is unable to answer, but you have my word that you will know that she is well cared for."

"Where will you send her?"

"I cannot answer that, for you must say goodbye, and wish her everything of the best in her life. But, Molly, be assured that Estella will want for nothing, and blossom into the new world that awaits her."

Chapter 24

"All rise," bellowed the duty sergeant.

The public gallery of the Old Bailey was empty. No witnesses attended, only the cold-eyed Runner, and counsel for the prosecution. From the cell below, Molly was goaded with a stick from behind as she climbed the stairs. She stood in chains alone in the prisoner's dock. The judge entered from the door behind the bench and nodded to the sergeant.

"Court is in session. Justice Gates presiding. Be seated." The Old Bailey sat to consider the committal of Gypsy Molly. Peering over the top of his wire-framed spectacles, the judge nodded towards counsel for the prosecution.

"May it please, your Lordship. We have examined the evidence before this honorable court and submit that the prisoner at the bar is guilty of the murder of Gypsy Madonna and, accordingly, should face trial and suffer the full penalty of the law."

"Counsel for the defence, do you have anything to say in the defence of the accused?"

"Yes, your Lordship. If it please, your Lordship, we submit that the accused could not possibly have committed the crime as stated by the Crown, and during the trial, we will bring further evidence exonerating the accused at the bar of all implications in this crime." The judge reached for his gavel.

"The trial of the Crown versus Gypsy Molly will be set at some future date and at a time convenient to His Majesty's Court of Sessions. As to the grant of bail, it is the decision of this court that the accused be retained at her lawyer's pleasure for which, security of 100 pounds shall be lodged with the bailiff prior to the removal of the accused from these premises. That will be all."

The gavel crashed down onto its damaged oak block. Mesmerised at the speed of the proceedings, Molly jumped out of her skin, looked up, and scowled at the judge. Still clamped in chains, far too big for the size of her, Molly was led back down the stairs to her squalid little cell where she rejoined the other women awaiting trial. All with differing crimes, some theft, some arson, some assault, but Molly was the only murderess. Gentle and petite, yet she frightened the other women with her threats of the gypsy curse. They left her alone and she watched them through ebony eyes as she sat, looking sullen and forlorn from the corner of the large communal cell. Some had already given up hope, but Molly had been awakened by the presence, for the first time in her life, that someone was interested in her welfare. Jaggers. The proposition to become Jaggers's housemaid seemed infinitely more appealing than the end of a rope, or life in the cell, or transportation to that infamous penal colony of New South Wales. "Mister Jaggers, I'm frightened for what is to become," said Molly, as the Hackney carriage made its way along Fleet Street and into the Strand heading for Jaggers's residence in Gerrard Street, Soho.

"Molly, we've just begun," replied Jaggers. "The justice has entrusted you to me, and that's the way it shall remain. But we have yet to deal with the preparation, more especially, we need time to assemble our evidence and, indeed, prepare for the trial itself."

"Yes, guv, er, sir," replied Molly, having no idea what Jaggers was talking about with bail, and committals, and trials, and still worried that Jaggers had another purpose for her. She looked silently at his powerful hands, and up at his overly large head and nose, surprised at the effect the cold of the evening had on his skin as it closed the black stubble holes in his chin and the porosity of the flesh on his bulbous nose. They entered the Gerrard Street residence; Soho nightlife had yet to begin.

Chapter 25

Dr. Emmett's laboratory consisted of three rooms and a converted washroom. The room farthest from the front door had previously been used as the kitchen for the maid's quarters. It was the smallest of the three rooms and, at one end, sat a massive cast-iron furnace. It was always glowing. He used it for incineration. At the back of the furnace was a large copper boiler for heating copious volumes of hot water for both the heating and washing. Most of it got used in washing down the floor, particularly in the vicinity of the heavy oak workbench.

The front of the furnace had four doors, two very large doors at the top, large enough to insert two turkeys in one and a whole sheep in the other at the same time. The smaller doors beneath were for ash removal. Behind the doors, thick, cast-iron grids sat glowing red, supporting clinkered coal that sucked air in through the spiral fan opening in the centre of the bottom doors. Combusted air forced its way up twin cast-iron chimneys through the back wall between buildings and buried in the masonry to the roof, five stories above, discharging into the rapidly-building, Sulphurous smogs of London. Brass handles hung like huge golden raindrops, their purpose to lift their heavy cast-iron doors over the protruding vee notch to secure the door. Both top doors were provided with thick glass windows, one-inch wide and three-inches tall, through which the doctor could determine the successful incineration of the discarded body parts.

Emmett's recent use of mercury to explore the human pulmonary blood vessel system had caused problems. The injected mercury had refused to allow the contaminated body to incinerate properly, forcing him to remove portions of lungs and thorax in small leather satchels, disposing of them in the garbage drops in Soho. The skull had taken the usual two hours to break down, but the brain also stubbornly refused to incinerate due to mercury contamination. There was no trouble in disposing of the abdomen. Bones from the pelvic girdle, legs, feet, and arms performed in a similar fashion to the skull.

The original pantry, built to the side of the smaller room, had been cleverly converted. Its new purpose being to delay decomposition of body parts awaiting examination. Emmett had constructed six, specially built-in marble racks, cantilevered from the wall on powerful cast-iron brackets. The bottom two racks, located on opposite sides of the pantry, were for the latest arrival of complete bodies. One rack was empty, whilst on the other, lay a heavily built female, with bruises to her throat and a yellow-black bruise above her right temple. Two bronze pennies, her only clothing, had been strategically placed to hold her eyelids closed. The middle and upper racks were reserved for disseminated body parts. On the left, Emmett lovingly retained the parts already in the process of experimentation, and on the right, he placed those parts yet to be employed.

He had carefully covered the lifeless bodies and dismembered parts in damp muslin, the moisture maintained by allowing the muslin to drop into slim water troughs running parallel to the racks at each level, continuously topped up by the incessant drip, drip, drip of three, brass taps, one above the other, at the end of the pantry. The overflow channelled to a central floor waste.

To limit the ever-aggressive flies, particularly in the stifling summer months and reduce their determination to contribute to the putrefaction process of the corpses by vomiting on their decaying meal, muslin was fixed over the air vents in the wooden door and open window which led to the pavement above. At pavement level, the hint of human decay was instantly welcomed by the stench of horse and other detritus, around which, bluebottle flies busily buzzed.

The second room contained a central worktable built in stout oak. The surface at one end of the workbench was scalloped from repeated blows from the heavy meat cleaver, shredding bone and material for incineration in the next room. Above the table hung three, whale-oil lights, casting circular shadows down over the subject beneath. Around the wall had been installed benches under which were cupboards. On the top of the side benches stood chemistry equipment, beakers, and bottles, and burners, and jars, with a range of coloured liquids, and crystals, and pickled body parts. In one, large, green-glassed bottle was the shadow of a heart complete with arteries and veins still attached, the tin lid which had rusted, making its removal difficult. At the other end of the room, located on a shelf, sat other prominent bottles, one contained a fetus submerged in a light brown liquid. Next were similar bottles containing a liver and a pair of linked human kidneys.

The final side of the room, the side with two double-hung windows that always remained closed and locked and were always covered by dark velvet curtains, was one deeper shelf. It was deeper and stronger than the others, and supported a range of 12-inch diameter glass-stoppered jars, each containing a human sample. The first sample was a hand, then a foot from which sprang the main Achilles tendon still joined to the calf muscle as it floated to the surface of the liquid. On the floor sat a large thick bottle of industrial alcohol. Farther along and in line, in front of the cupboards, stood bottles of acids marked in red. Cautionary names in large print appeared on each container, hydrochloric, sulphuric, ammonium nitrate, and phosphoric. The little mahogany corner cupboard, always locked, contained Emmett's private stock of whisky, never less than two bottles of his favorite single-malt. His principle being that when working, its medicinal properties helped his concentration, and obliterated the stench and shock discoveries within the decaying human anatomy.

The third room, through which the front door exited, led to the stairs that ascended to the street above. The parlour, as Emmett would refer, was for receiving distinguished guests. Surgeons mostly, all of whom had come from the barber's profession, and all of whom had come to rely on Emmett's research and physical study of human anatomy.

In one recent case requiring the removal of an intestinal lump causing a blockage of the faecal passage in the lower tract, Emmett had run a parallel operation on a male abdomen whilst the operation had been in progress at St. Bartholomew's Hospital. At the same time, they had even experimented with the removal of the little blind end of the smaller intestine and performed an appendectomy on the live patient. Emmett had opened up the abdomen of the latest man hanged at Newgate. The hanging had been a morning hanging. Emmett had waited especially for a morning hanging, in full knowledge that the prisoner would have been fed bacon and eggs one hour before the hangman tied the noose and slid the bolt on the trap. Once the police had left, the body was cut down and spirited over to Harley Street by hackney carriage. The eminent surgeon at St. Bartholomew's Hospital had waited and watched as Emmett worked, opening the body until the intestinal tract was reached.

"Ah, ah, masticated eggs and bacon," observed Emmett, scalpel in his left hand, prodding the contents of the bloody tube before him. The surgeon and he had discussed the offending components, establishing protocol for the extraction in the living patient, and how to sew the body back up. The surgeon had returned directly to the hospital and undertaken the operation, using alcohol as both disinfectant and anesthetic. The operation had taken a little under two hours and the patient had recovered perfectly within days. The surgeon wrote a revolutionary paper on the subject of the intestinal tract. The paper was an instant success, providing details of the operation and developed future protocol for other surgical techniques. Privately, Emmett stayed anonymous, receiving 100 pounds. The body had cost him seven pounds, ten shillings, and six pence, including the cutting down, and delivery, and settlement with the undertakers. No questions being asked as the gravediggers submitted records that they had dispatched the body in a lead-lined coffin to Gravesend on the Thames Estuary.

Emmett's parlour was ornate in its decoration; it was small, measuring a little over 500-square feet containing luxurious furniture, particularly a large sofa that he would occasionally use to sleep on if engaged in a particularly long research project. An always fully stocked drinks' cupboard, his leather-inlaid writing desk, and a glowing coal fire.

The walls were adorned with beautifully bound medical books, regimented on mahogany shelves from floor to ceiling. To the side of the front door was his small washroom that had been cleverly converted to a galley kitchen such that the apartment in Harley Street was fully self-contained, designed to suit a bachelor whose undivided attention was in the pursuit of discovery of the human anatomy in every respect. Emmett did his own housework and cleaning. Only those within the industry, as he called it, were allowed access. He did not boast his qualifications, nor did he erect his brass, medical practitioner's plate in the street above. At the behest of the exclusive body of London surgeons, there could be no leak to the authorities.

Chapter 26

Privately hired for the return trip to Rochester, the Hackney carriage pulled into the Three Jolly Bargemen. They had been travelling for two hours and shortly after noon, they felt the pangs of hunger and in need of lunch. The sun had shone all morning, and the countryside buzzed with bees fussing around the wildflowers along the hedgerows. Jaggers lent forward and opened the carriage door and stepped down onto the gravel path. He turned to assist little Estella by holding open the door.

Although only three years of age, she abruptly rejected his offer of assistance, the display of independence brought a wry smile to Jaggers's face. He watched, ready to catch her whilst she jumped from the bottom step of the carriage onto the ground below, her fair-haired ringlets bouncing as her feet hit the ground. Jaggers smiled at the pluckiness of the child. Lunch was brief and swift, and, within the hour, Jaggers and Estella set out on the final leg of their journey. Their destination, Satis House.

Entering the outskirts of Rochester, the carriage passed the old castle. Jaggers noted the windows had gone as if plucked out by carrion crows and, passing the Blue Boar Inn, they proceeded along Rochester High Street. Satis House was more than a house, but rather a mansion made of brick. It was old and dismal and had a great many iron bars to it. Some of the windows had been walled up. Of those that remained, all the lower were rust barred. There was a courtyard in front, and that was also barred. To the left was the brewery, but no brewing was going on. The clock on the wall had stopped at 20 minutes to nine.

"Good day, Miss Havisham," announced Jaggers. Little Estella stood next to him, the top of her fair hair level with his jacket pocket. Estella was tall and slim for her age, her fresh female face remaining expressionless at the sight of the strange woman, clad in her wedding dress.

"Ah, Mister Jaggers, so this must be Estella. What a beautiful little girl," observed Miss Havisham, stooping and taking Estella's hand. Estella said nothing. Stepmother and adopted daughter turned and walk back into the house.

"Now, ma'am, there is a small matter of the papers," said Jaggers, reaching into his inside jacket pocket. Miss Havisham looked back over her shoulder.

"Come in. Oh, come in," she tutted, then looked down at Estella. "I will teach you the ways of the world, my child." Estella looked up, a quizzical expression appearing across her flushed little face. "And I will teach you how to handle all the selfish and greedy men." Estella's expression began to glow.

"I'd like that, Missy Havam."

With the papers signed, Jaggers excused himself and disappeared down the dark staircase from the lounge; the drapes still closed from the last time he had visited. He climbed back into the waiting Hackney carriage and made his way to the Blue Boar Inn. It was getting dark outside as he settled himself into the armchair in the corner of the bar. He noticed the two Bow Street Runners enter the inn from the rear.

"Being followed," he mused to himself, as he sipped at his ample port. Taking another bite, he munched thoughtfully on the crusty bread, cheese, and pickles whilst considering his next move. He turned to beckon the two men to join him. But they had gone. Jaggers finished his snack, quaffed the remains of the port, acknowledged the publican, and departed. They had waited outside, and as Jaggers emerged from the inn, the Runners hastily turned away and one busied himself in the shadows, urinated against the wall. It was too dark to make out their faces. He quickly mounted his carriage and waited. Before turning around, they laughed at a secret joke then sang out.

Jaggers recognised the army song from The Bold Fusilier.

A bold fusilier was marching down through Rochester
Bound for the wars in the old country,
And he sang as he marched through the cobbled streets of Rochester
Who'll be a soldier for Marlborough with me?
Who'll be a soldier?
Who'll be a soldier?
Who'll be a soldier for Marlborough with me?
And he sang as he marched through the cobbled streets of Rochester,
Who'll be a soldier for Marlborough with me?

Jaggers sat stony-faced, listening to the taunting words chanted with a hidden meaning. He didn't rise to the bait and held his carriage waiting until they had finished. They emerged from the shadows and disappeared back inside the inn before he instructed his driver to head back to London and Soho.

Years later, Jaggers was to hear the song sung to different lyrics and with a new name, Waltzing Matilda.

Chapter 27

In her new position as housemaid, Molly had begun to understand Jaggers and his peculiar tastes. She quickly learned that he was an intensely private man, disposing of her earlier fears that her role would take on a different mantle behind the closed doors of his Gerrard Street mansion. Yet, strangely, she had begun to find his mannerisms growing in their attraction. Of particular fascination were his exclusive and varied dinner guests.

Molly was never allowed to dine with the master since that first night. To relieve boredom in the kitchen, she would seat herself on the three-legged wooden stool behind the kitchen door and pin her ear to the keyhole. The table had been laid for two, and his guest this night was his assistant, Wemmick. The Bow Street Runner had dropped in for a drink before the trial. Her adrenaline pumped at Jaggers's uncomplimentary comments.

"I believe nothing less than a shrew. She's a wild gypsy with a temper that I intended to control." Jaggers chewed away at his calloused forefinger, swung his arm and pointed aggressively in the direction of the kitchen door. Molly was furious.

"How dare he?" she whispered, her face flushing. "Speaks of me to others as if I'm the enemy 'stead of his client. Forcin' me to work for 'im so as to pay 'im back for the fees done for me. He's in ca'oots with the Runners. And that faded white-wigged justice and those who seek to demolish me and have me swing from the gallows at Newgate. For what? Killing that evil trollop, Madonna. A woman twice my size and more than ten years older. Ba! And damn the woman to hell." Molly cursed quietly to herself and thought back over past weeks.

After the arrest, Jaggers had tried to steer the interrogation and keep Molly quiet before she incriminated herself, but the Runner had been devoid of charity and in the cold, impersonal, and dank interview room, buried deep in that miserable stone building next to Newgate prison, he had challenged Molly. "Where's your husband, luv?" He had insisted on an answer, over and over again.

"Jaggers, gord bless 'im," she had muttered, feeling his hold on her thin wrist attempting to keep her quiet. "But I won't keep it in." She had refused to listen to him. "How in gord's name should I know? Run away if you ask me, and in fear of the hangman's noose, I'll be bound." Molly had eventually exploded. She hadn't seen Magwitch since they had all sat together in the wagon at Estella's party, eating raspberry and blackberry pie and lumpy custard. And then, later, after that prying interview, they had all walked back to Jaggers's office in Little Britain. She remembered his brass plate on the wall outside, and on entering his office, she found herself horrified by those dreadful plaster casts of dead heads fixed to that dirty wall, and his great desk, strewn with papers, and the hiss from the tired black leather of his coffin-like chair when his great backside settled itself down. The sword and pistol, bits of past trials scattered all over his desk as paperweights and ornaments.

The dirty, smog-covered skylight above his desk served little to lighten the heavy, lawyering atmosphere in the room. And add those piercing-cold eyes of the man who didn't believe anything anyone said. The memories flooded back into her agitated mind.

"Typical Runner, distrusts everybody, including himself, and will fabricate evidence to get me convicted so that he gets paid," cursed Molly. The eavesdropping on the conversation haunted her thoughts, troubling her mind further.

She stuck her little finger in her right ear and waggled her slim wrist to clear the wax. Wiping the nail clean on her apron, she leant forward again and, steadying herself by clasping the brass doorknob above her head, put her right eye back against the keyhole. She tilted her head to the side and focused. A fresh glimpse of the three conspiratorial faces around the fireplace confirmed what she already knew. "I'm in very grave trouble."

After the cold-eyed Bow Street Runner had left, dinner was served. It was late. Jaggers and Wemmick talked long into the night, reviewing their evidence. In the morning, Crown prosecution would deliver its damning evidence, all corroborated by witnesses. It seemed that Molly's trial would be based on speculation and pure circumstantial evidence. The only physical evidence would be dredged up by that person, whom no one ever saw, but whom they all talk about, the coroner.

Jaggers's last comment had shaken Wemmick. Before speaking further, he carefully prepared his last piece of Stilton and, with the beautifully engraved, silver cheese knife, bedded it down into his crusty bread. It was gone in one mouthful. After a quick gulp of port, he looked questioningly at Wemmick.

"Put the case, Wemmick, that the victim was attacked for another motive. A motive to do with her relationship with another woman." Remaining silent,

Wemmick frowned and took another sip of port. "And given that she was as big and as powerful as a man, put the case that she is a man, yet with breasts and a vagina. Yet, deep within, lurk the feelings and emotions of a man. Put the case that the jealousy our cold-eyed Runner refers to, is not as he is trying to make out, being that of a woman, but that of a man. And, indeed, consider the case that she tried to rape my client, who, in turn, was forced to defend herself against an unnatural crime. An unnatural crime of which the statute books of England and of His Majesty's government have, as yet failed to reflect." Shocked, Molly gasped at the keyhole, silencing herself with cupped hands; she lowered her head to conceal her shame.

"Molly! Coffee and cognac," shouted Jaggers, swivelling his large head towards the kitchen door as the grandfather clock sounded midnight.

Chapter 28

Drawn by matching palominos, the Hackney coach drew little attention as it passed the newspaper offices in Fleet Street. Molly sat next to Jaggers, her arm discretely linked in his. They faced Wemmick whose back was to the horses. The gentlemen wore dark suits under trim top hats. Molly had dressed in her straight-laced, black frock. On her head, she wore a red and white silk headscarf, below, which peeped raven-black hair, accentuating her fresh and innocent face. Driven by a single driver, the sedate coach proceeded down to Ludgate Circus and commenced the gentle climb up Ludgate Hill. The trial was on the role, scheduled for eleven o'clock that morning. Molly had awoken late, unable to sleep until the small hours the night before. Jaggers's words rang in her ears. *An unnatural crime.* She daren't ask what that meant for fear he would chastise her for listening at keyholes.

"Sessions House number two," announced Jaggers, just as the imposing dome of St. Paul's came into view. The driver pulled the left rein, turning the coach up Old Bailey.

"They should call it the Central Criminal Court," suggested Wemmick attempting to make conversation, the first court already full and overflowing with petty crimes. They stopped outside. Wemmick alighted first, holding the door for Molly, followed by Jaggers. They mounted the grey stone steps. Wemmick brought up the rear. It was ten minutes to 11. Molly felt sick and frightened and wanted to hold Jaggers's hand, but he would have none of it. Stepping in front of Molly, he removed his top hat and with a flourish, indicated that Molly should go first.

By five to 11, they joined senior counsel and took their places in the front of the court. The jury dock was vacant and would shortly be filled with 12 men, then sworn by that notorious hanging judge from Yorkshire.

"All rise," shouted the duty sergeant. The judge entered and once seated; the 12 jurors entered; their faces remained solemn as they were sworn by the justice.

"Counsel for the defence, how do you plead?"

"May it please, my Lord, the prisoner before the court, namely one Gypsy Molly, stands accused of murder in the first degree. Yet, my learned colleague and I," the robed Silk turned to acknowledge Jaggers, "can find no trace of animosity within her character to create such a motive. Further, it appears to us that, she, and she alone, given her small stature, could not have carried out such a heinous crime. The evidence will show that the victim was some ten years her senior and stood seven or eight inches over the accused. During the trial, we shall bring detailed evidence before this honourable court that will irrefutably prove that this waif, a young and delicate lady, not only had no motive, but that she had not the physical power to deliver such wounds as the coroner found upon the deceased. And further, we shall prove, beyond a reasonable doubt, that Gypsy Molly is a loving, and wholesome young woman. We shall prove that the evil and precarious nature of the pernicious insinuations delivered by the prosecution have no basis, and we, therefore, submit that counsel's application to commit the accused for trial be dismissed.

"We further submit that the biased and circumstantial evidence presented by the prosecution exhibits no threat to our defence, and that we shall challenge, and dispose of, each and every item. Furthermore, we would submit, my Lord, that we are confident that in the fullness of time, this honorable court will dispose of the criminal charge, and that this jury, comprising 12 true and just men," the Silk turned and paused, focusing on each member of the jury, "cannot fail but to unanimously return a verdict of Not Guilty." Defence counsel bowed to the bench, retreated, and whilst slowly locating his large posterior on his oak seat, winked confidently at Molly and nodded to Jaggers, satisfied at his first delivery.

"Counsels will approach," announced Justice Gates gruffly. The judge leaned forward to speak with both counsels as they arrived in front of the bar. "This seems to be developing into a longer trial than the Crown presented during our pretrial meetings. We will have one last meeting in my chambers." The judge frowned at counsel for the prosecution, an older man in his 50s, extremely thin and reeking of tobacco smoke, his tatty wig appearing too large over a thin, grey, featureless face, reducing the years left to him by a decade. Subconsciously, the experienced, hanging judge knew the man hadn't done his homework and, that in a long trial, it would be Jaggers and his counsel who would be winning all the way. Both counsels returned to their respective positions in the courtroom.

"Counsels for both defence and prosecution will join me in my chambers, where I shall consider an application for dismissal. That will be all."

"The court will rise," announced the sergeant.

The judge struck his gavel smartly on the wooden anvil, rose, and head bowed, moved to his private exit.

The judge exited the court through the rear door into the sanctity of his heavily timbered, private chambers at the rear, followed by prosecution and defence counsels and Jaggers. It started as a murmur and escalated as the spectators in the public gallery muttered and complained at the word dismissal. Fists began to wave in the direction of the prisoner and fingers pointed threateningly at the jurors waiting innocently for the justice to return. The sergeant moved forwards to intervene as the door behind the bench opened and the two counsels and Jaggers reemerged from chambers, followed shortly after by the judge.

"All rise," bellowed the sergeant, instantly bringing the gallery and jurors to their feet. "Silence in court," bellowed the sergeant, quelling the noise and reducing the pandemonium to hushed whispering in the public gallery. First to return to his seat was the thin, grey, prosecution counsel. Defense counsel and Jaggers remained standing until Justice Gates had settled in his high-backed leather chair. The judge nodded to the sergeant.

"Court is in session. Be seated," announced the sergeant. The noisy shuffling slowly abated as the judge reached for his gavel. The gavel tapped once, creating a pregnant silence.

"The trial of the Crown versus Gypsy Molly will be set at some future date and at a time convenient to His Majesty's Court of Sessions in the Old Bailey. That will be all." The gavel crashed down onto its oak block.

Confused and becoming increasingly concerned at the speed of the proceedings, Molly hunched her shoulders, buried her face in her hands, and began to weep.

Chapter 29

The Bow Street Runners were the thief takers. Clad in distinctive scarlet waistcoats under blue greatcoats and nicknamed, *Robin Redbreasts*, they were dispatched by the local Watch to secure physical evidence and extract statements and confessions, by fair means or foul, for the prosecution of suspected criminals. No more than 12 Runners at any one time, mostly ex-military men. Mistrials, falsified evidence, and corruption ballooned as London expanded. Either way, they got paid. Bought off by the felons, or paid for legitimately by the authorities, the Runners always got their *Blood Money*. The judiciary and interpretation of criminal law in England focused on punishment, but it was all about to change.

"The certainty of detection is a far greater deterrent from crime than the severity of punishment," said the Home Secretary, Sir Robert Peel, as he presented his new Metropolis Police Improvement Bill to parliament. At Peel's instigation, the debate was revolutionary. Against the usual objection that it was a restriction of civil liberty, the Bill passed in 1829, heralding the end of the corrupt Runners.

Backing on to Great Scotland Yard, just off Horse Guards' Parade and Whitehall, Scotland Yard was established at: Four, Whitehall Place. Colonel Charles Rowen, a retired soldier, and Richard Mayne, an experienced lawyer, were assigned to head the new force. Both justices of the peace, they immediately acquired the nickname, *Blue Devils and Raw Lobsters.* As respect for the force grew, they became known as *Peelers and Bobbies* and, following the enthronement of William IV, their slang name became known as *The Old Bill.* And nearly two centuries later, would still be known as such.

Chapter 30

Anthony Hitchcock had got 14 years for highway robbery and for fencing stolen goods in Chatham docks. His penalty, handed down in the Old Bailey, was transportation to New South Wales to serve out his 14 years and, if he gave no trouble, would receive a conditional pardon, but never allowed to return to England. The replacement fence had heard what had happened to him and realised that he too was being watched. Chatham dockyard was a good place to dispose of the swag. Plenty of cash-rich sailors coming and going both from the Royal Navy and merchant ships. Magwitch was trusted, but the fact remained that the penalty for receiving stolen goods was the same as carrying out the burglary in the first place.

Unperturbed, Magwitch and Compeyson continued the house burglaries. Compeyson did the research and Magwitch would carry out the felony. If he didn't, Compeyson would threaten him with eviction. They did three or four, maybe five jobs a year. It made a good living, particularly for Compeyson. Magwitch just got the crumbs from the giant's table. They had been robbing for nearly five years. The time lapse between cocktail party or, personal visit to case the joint, being set at a minimum of two months before Magwitch would carry out the robbery. In the City Barge pub on the north bank of the Thames at Kew Bridge, Compeyson took another swig of ale.

"Forget the silver trinkets and other nonsense, just take money and jewellery," insisted Compeyson, briefing Magwitch before the next burglary. "Silver trinkets are too easy to trace. Cash is better and the jewellery gets changed so the Peelers can't recognise it."

"Wot's the place?" grunted Magwitch reluctantly. He sat quietly opposite, not drinking, but smoking his pipe. Still in his mouth, he grasped the stained clay bowl of the pipe and pressed the newly lit expanding tobacco back down into the bowl. Quickly removing his burning thumb, he hurriedly dusted the hot ash that had dropped on his waistcoat.

"River Terrace. It's that large, sandstone house overlooking the Thames," said Compeyson with a wry smile. "They have their own landing stage, so you can get away by the river," he continued. "And there's something else in there besides." His wry smile fell from his mouth as he lent forward and golloped another swig of ale. "There's a huge iron door leading off the study. I didn't try to open it. Looks like a walk-in safe and, judging by the layout of the house, the size behind the door is big enough for a small room about ten-feet wide and 12-feet deep. I couldn't see any windows neither," Compeyson went into detail. "Now, don't fail me, Magwitch. You still owe for the rent, and, by my calculations, you owe me nearly four month's rent." Magwitch was trapped in a vicious cycle of crime in order to keep a roof over his head.

"Gord, I's been blackmailed, yous keeps me in the poor house and under yourn thumb whilst I's sent to the danger and yous just sit here, out of 'arm's way, pretendin' yourn well-to-do distant 'an out o' sight and not with danger doing the easy part," grumbled Magwitch, getting angry. "Yous keep treating me like yourn black slave! This is my last job and then I'm gorn."

"Well, you had better come back with plenty of money," scoffed Compeyson. "Or it will be the worse for you. Fail me and I'll call the bailiff and dispatch you to debtor's prison for unpaid rent."

"He's got craft and he's got learnin' that overmatches me 500 times and more," grumbled Magwitch, promising himself that this was the last job.

One hour after the tide turned and began filling the Thames, Magwitch started rowing from Putney wharf on the south bank. As dusk approached, he rowed with the tide across the river and into the shadows, drifting in close under the north bank. It was fully dark by the time he reached the private landing stage at Riverside Terrace. "Three-and-half hours of tide," he mused, estimating that there was sufficient time to complete the work, re-board, and row further upriver to meet with Compeyson at the City Barge. "Me alibi'll be solid."

Magwitch carefully moored, securing the stolen boat to the post such that the rope would allow for the rising tide. On his leather belt, he carried a large ring from which hung a range of skeleton keys. Over his shoulder, he slung the hessian sack. To protect himself from the cold night, he wore a dark greatcoat, flat hat, and woollen gloves from which his fingers protruded through the cut-away knitting. He crept stealthily up the timber deck, its incline slowly decreasing as it floated on the incoming tide.

He walked quickly to the east side of the building and jemmied the small window open. Within minutes, he was inside the deserted house. He groped in the blackness, frightening himself by knocking over a pot holding cooking utensils on the draining board in the kitchen. Through the faint light reflected from the moonlight on the surface of the Thames, he made his way to the bedrooms. Five minutes later, he had grabbed the jewellery from the drawer in the tallboy identified by Compeyson and made his way back down the oak staircase to the study. Breathing heavily with his heart pounding in his mouth, he heard little. Veiled in darkness, he surveyed the outline of the huge iron door. "The bugger's right," whispered Magwitch, his breath vaporizing in the cold air.

Reaching for the heavy ring of skeleton keys on his belt, he knelt down and tried his first key. It refused. He selected the second key. It too refused. In frustration, he shook the bunch and made a random selection. His fingers felt its shank. It was smooth, suggesting it was new or well-used. It entered the aperture perfectly. Gently, he held the elliptical end and turned in a clockwise direction. The end meshed with the mechanism. He applied greater pressure and, with his ear pressed to the steel door, listened carefully as the key found its purchase.

The lock turned with a dull clunk. The door opened easily. "Used often," he muttered to himself in surprise. He peered in, smelling the must and stale tobacco hanging in the air. He waited, hoping his eyes would grow accustomed to the ink-blackness within. They didn't and, feeling as if he had suddenly gone blind, he reached up and touched the side of his eye sockets to check his eyes were still there. Clutching the hessian sack in his left hand, he moved stealthily into the small room and hurriedly groped around for an oil light or candle. Nearly knocking the glass mantle over in haste, he dropped the sack, just catching the lamp before it fell. He clutched the metal base. It felt warm against his cold fingers. He raised the mantle and lit the wick, keeping the light as low as possible to escape detection. Quickly, his eyes scanned around the tiny room. In the centre sat a burgundy, leather-inlaid, oak writing desk around which stood four wooden chairs. The main armchair was fashioned in matching oak with soft-textured, crinkled, burgundy leather. Half open on the top of the desk was the plan of the basement of a building in London. He couldn't read the address of the property, Threadneedle Street, but instead, recognised the logo in the bottom right-hand corner of the famous Bank of England.

"Gor lummy," he whispered, his heart thumping. He opened the central drawer of the desk to witness a flat-rolled manuscript tied in a central, green, silk ribbon. He slid the ribbon to the end and unrolled the document. The word 'Calcutta' was embossed in the bottom right-hand corner. The manuscript appeared to be details of some large building. It meant nothing to Magwitch. Quickly, he rerolled the parchment and slid the green ribbon back on. Curiosity made him slip it into his inside coat pocket for later.

In the centre of the desk sat a crystal inkwell full of red ink. The supporting quill pen, its feathery plume pointing diagonally away from its mount, was accompanied by some sheets of parchment awaiting action from a writer's hand. A chunky crystal ashtray supported three, half-smoked, Montecristo cigars resting symmetrically in the notches, ash still hanging from their ends where they had recently expired. Magwitch selected the longest, stuck it in his mouth and bending forwards, relit it from the top of the oil lamp. He failed to notice that the stub end was still warm. Four pewter goblets, still containing whisky, sat next to a solitary bottle of The Macallan single malt.

"Temptation o' the Devil." He discarded the plan of the bank and settled himself in the leather-clad armchair. He swallowed the contents of the first goblet and lent back to savour his cigar. "How the other 'alf liv." He grunted in the gloom, reached forward and grabbed the second goblet. Just before quaffing the contents, his eyes arrested on a polished mahogany box in the centre of the desk, previously buried under the building plan. Quickly, he lent forward and opened the wooden lid, exposing a rich, green, velvet lining. There were imprints of two flintlock pistols. The weapons were missing. Disinterested, Magwitch swallowed the contents of the second goblet and put his head back to savour the taste. At the back of the room, he noted the single shelf on which rested little bundles of special paper held together with silk ribbons, each neatly tied in a bow. Magwitch looked at the shelf through a haze of cigar smoke. He rose from the desk and took a couple of careful paces forward. He looked down with disbelief at the bundles. "Fat one-pound notes." He gasped as he looked at the next two bundles. White bundles. "Even fatter sweltering five-pound notes!"

He suddenly felt sick; his heart rate pounding in his mouth again, both with excitement and fear. "Yous 'it the jackpot this time, my boy," he said to himself whilst stuffing the bundles into his sack. "Pay off Compeyson and yous can lead a proper life at last. But hold on a minute. No honour amongst thieves, now is there?" he muttered to himself.

Then, he heard the voices. He heard the front door slam shut. They were arguing above. Hurriedly, he slipped the remaining bundles into the sack, doused the light, and foolishly grabbed the bottle of whisky, slipping it into his sack. He groped for the third goblet and, losing valuable seconds, swallowed the whisky before exiting. He pushed the door closed behind him and crept back the way he had come, away from the voices. They were in the room above, and they were close. He climbed out through the small window and tiptoed down the landing stage. Ducking down, he slid into the rowboat. Quickly untying the rope from the bollard, he pushed off. Hugging the wharf and rather than splash the oars, he handled the boat along by the vertical planking. He heard the angry voices make the discovery above.

"Christ. We've been bloody-well robbed!" The shout went up. Then, he heard the sound of heavy, leather, hobnail boots clomping out onto the landing stage. Magwitch estimated there were two, maybe three or four of them, but it was dark and he kept hidden in the shadows of the wharf.

Over his shoulder, he saw the flash as the first pistol fired, the lead ball thudded into a thick iron bolt protruding from the wharf timbers above his head and ricocheted down into the murky waters of the Thames. Magwitch quickly pushed off. The second shot creased the shoulder pad of his greatcoat. In panic, he spat his glowing cigar over the side and rowed back into the shadows. Quietly, he paddled and rowed his way towards the City Barge. 20 minutes later, he climbed out and cast the boat adrift on the incoming tide. It drifted upstream, moving out into the centre of the river. He watched as it disappeared in the night. *Perfeck decoy,* he thought, as he entered the City Barge from the riverside. He kept the swag in the sack hidden under his heavy military greatcoat.

Inside the pub, Magwitch nervously relayed the experience. "And I reckons I's robbed murderin' bank robbers," said Magwitch, fear written across his flushed face. Compeyson couldn't stop laughing. Suddenly, he made a grab at the greatcoat.

"Give me the swag." Momentarily, Magwitch held on, but quickly gave in. Compeyson buried his interest in the contents. But Magwitch wasn't so happy. He felt the fear. Robbing the rich was one thing, but robbing from big, armed bank robbers was totally different. And, by all accounts, there were at least two, maybe as many as four of them. And they had guns.

"They'll come for us," said Magwitch with a pained expression written across his face.

"Wrong," said Compeyson confidently. "Where's your little black book?" Magwitch dug into his jacket pocket. Compeyson reached across the table and rested his fingertips on the binder, the gold surround well-tarnished with use and age. Unblinking, he looked directly at Magwitch. "We both swear that we know nothing about each other." Compeyson dropped his hand into the sack and rummaged around. "Here, this is your share, and consider the rent paid." Placing the bottle of whisky on the table, he handed over the few pieces of jewellery, a bundle of one-pound notes, and a couple of the five-pound notes carefully slid from under the silk ribbon.

"I swears." Beads of perspiration formed on Magwitch's troubled brow while slipping the book back into his jacket pocket. Then, quickly, he stuffed the jewellery into his inside poacher's pocket, the wad of one-pound notes into his higher inside pocket, and the handful of five-pound notes into the opposite inside pocket.

"So do I," said Compeyson, emptying the sack and greedily stuffing the numerous wads of cash into various pockets. "If anyone gets caught, remember, separate defences and no communication. We don't know each other." His words and actions mostly lost on Magwitch. Veiled concern growing in his mind as to what sinister new plan Compeyson was cooking up.

Chapter 31

The crooked Bookmaker at Epsom races had given the Peelers the tip off. Fifty pounds to win, paid with ten, great, white, five-pound notes, was too much, even for the likes of Compeyson and his flowery friends. The Bookmaker had smelt a rat. The odds at 30 to one indicated an imprudent gambler, unless he didn't care if he lost. Unperturbed, the Bookmaker had taken the bet. But the filly had won, prompting the Bookmaker to deny the bet and, to cover his actions, squealed to Scotland Yard. Realising that the ten five-pound notes taken at the races were part of the recent heist from the Bank of England, the Peelers took up the gauntlet. They considered bank robbery, especially the prime Bank of England, to be treasonable, and more evil than murder, exposing the King and the exchequer to financial ruin. They considered it their duty to crush this evil at source.

 London Bobbies swarmed, generating leads and connections. The trail led to the big house in Brentford. When the Peelers arrived, Sally was home alone, in bed, nursing her latest battering from Compeyson. Days earlier, Magwitch had flown as soon as he had received his share of the loot in the City Barge. The Peelers interrogated Sally, rapidly realising that she knew nothing other than they had a lodger who went by the name of Magwitch. The Peelers checked the record to find he had form. The Peelers hid in the scullery as Compeyson arrived back, the noise of his carriage giving due warning. He walked right into their waiting arms. No money or jewellery was found at the house, but by his association, he was charged as an accessory. Facing the magistrate the following morning, his legal counsel pleaded successfully and he was released on bail, pending trial to be set down at a time convenient to His Majesty. Meanwhile, the hunt was on for one seasoned criminal, Abel Magwitch.

 Scotland Yard had received an anonymous complaint about the jewellery lifted from Riverside Terrace. The description of the pieces came with a detailed jeweler's sketch. Days later, the trail led to Chatham dockyard and implicated the Fence. Earlier, Magwitch had offloaded the swag and had gone into hiding. But the Fence was still in possession of the few pieces linking both him and Magwitch to the crime. To save his own skin, the Fence quickly turned King's evidence and identified Magwitch in a lineup at Scotland Yard, unaware that there was another man behind it, Compeyson. At committal, given his prior criminal record which, in reality, had been created by vagrancy offences, bail was refused and, in chains, he was dragged off to the nearest lockup.

Chapter 32

When the tide was high, the lower floor level of St. Bridget's Well prison at Bridewell leaked river water from the Thames and, in his misery, he lay awake, listening to lapping water and feet crunching over the heavy-barred grating in the pavement above. They would be the feet of drunks on their way home, having spent hours drinking at the Prospect of Whitby. From his temporary cell, he could just glimpse the King Henry Stairs pier and watch the comings and goings during the buildup to the trial. Getting wind of the manhunt before his arrest in Chatham, Magwitch had hurriedly hidden his money behind a stack of timber in the dockyard. Then, strangely, during his committal hearing, he had received an offer of legal representation from a certain criminal lawyer named Jaggers.

Unable to retrieve his stolen money, Magwitch set about scraping up enough cash to cover a reasonable deposit on his legal costs through the sale of his clothes and the few belongings he had amassed during his years with Compeyson. The case seemed a foregone conclusion and Jaggers didn't hold out much hope, but he felt sympathy for Magwitch. The final shock, which hurt on the day of the trial, was to witness Compeyson's testimony in the same court.

During the trial, prosecution delivered damning evidence. Magwitch noted that it was always him who came forward. It was always him who was sworn at. It was always him who had received the payment from the Fence. It was always him who had done the breaking-ins, and, therefore, it had to have been him who had done the robberies. It was, therefore, him who had profited individually from the felony. Compeyson's defence lawyer summed up.

"My Lord and gentlemen of the jury. Here, you have before you, side by side, two persons, as your eyes can separate wide. The first one, younger, well-brought up, who will be spoken to as such. And the second one, the elder and ill-brought up, who will be spoken to as such. The first one, the younger, seldom if ever seen in these here sessions and only suspected. The other, the elder, always seen in the sessions and always will; his guilt being brought home. Can you doubt if there is but one in it? Which is the one? And, if there are two in it, which is much the worst one?" Compeyson's lawyer then turned to matters of character.

"And when it comes to character, was it not his schoolfellows that were in this position and in that. And was it not him as had been known by witnesses in such clubs and societies and, therefore, not to his advantage to steal from? And was it not Magwitch who had been tried before and has a record of being up hill and down dale in Bridewell and lockups? May it please, your Lordship, I call upon my client, Mr. Compeyson, to speak of his understanding of this unfortunate accused, and truly guilty partner in crime." The lawyer sat quietly back down, indicating to Compeyson to address the court. In separate chains and handcuffs, both Magwitch and Compeyson stood together in the prisoner's dock.

"Gentlemen, this man at my side is a most precious rascal," began Compeyson. "Out of the goodness of my heart, I gave him room and shelter. Somehow, he must have listened at keyholes to my friends of position when they visited. How else would he know whom to rob?" Compeyson continued to defame Magwitch, laying total blame at his doorstep, and that he had unwittingly and innocently become embroiled in this sordid affair for which he humbly apologised to his Lordship, asking that his character be taken into consideration. Following a brief recess in his chambers, the judge returned and extracted a guilty verdict from the jury.

"Once out of this court, I'll smash that face o' yourn!" Having listened to Compeyson carrying on with his pack of testimonial lies and then the crushing blow of the final verdict, Magwitch could have killed.

"See what kind of man he is, your Lordship?" whined Compeyson in his public school accent, his face flushed and in fear. Perspiration began to form on his brow.

"Sergeant, you will place two turnkeys between the accused to control the peace and provide protection," ordered the judge, hammering his gavel repeatedly for silence in the courtroom. "It would appear that you, Mr. Compeyson, have allowed yourself to become involved with bad company for which you have my sympathies. Accordingly, I sentence you to only seven years, with parole after the first year for good behaviour. As for Mr. Magwitch, had it not been for your counsel, this court would have seen fit to hand down the penalty of life. However, from the evidence before this bench, it appears to me that you are a repeat offender with a violent passion and likely to become worse. I, therefore, sentence you to 14 years without parole." During sentencing, Compeyson worked himself into an emotional state, but he theatrically checked it, took two or three short breaths and, swallowing often, and, at the end, he stretched out his hand to Magwitch in a reassuring manner.

"I ain't going to be low, dear boy." Compeyson had so heated himself that he took out his handkerchief and wiped his face, and head, and neck, and hands, before the judge could continue.

"He tells lies. Made me do it for to pay my rent," shouted Magwitch, waving his fist at Compeyson.

"Silence in court," ordered the judge, beating his gavel for attention.

"You will each be dispatched forthwith to a prison ship on the Medway for immediate execution of sentence." The judge slammed his gavel down in finality, furious at the unfettered outbursts.

The prison ship appeared out of the Romney marsh mist like a wicked Noah's Ark. Old rotting ships left over from Napoleonic wars lay beached at low tide in the ooze and mud of the Medway estuary. Rotten, rat-infested hulks that were once proudly afloat on the high seas now lay waste, soaked in the stench of crime and corruption, imprisoning the depths of humanity unlikely to see the light of day for years to come. Wrists and ankles manacled together, the convicts carried the chained iron ball as they were goaded from behind to walk up the gangplank and into the hulk. Magwitch was immediately dispatched to the black hole for solitary confinement, two decks below, whilst Compeyson joined other short-term inmates. Slung from vertical poles hung rows of hessian hammocks, most of which were already occupied with just enough space between each for a man to squeeze through. The warden indicated the vacant hammock nearest the corridor.

"So they says you're the good man?" said the warden sarcastically. Compeyson swung round, his face covered with expectation. "You're lucky, sunshine, 'cause you've been assigned to light duties and helpin' us warders administer this little lot of felons, includin' your mate in the black 'ole."

The black hole had no such luxury. Soiled hessian sacking lay strewn on the floor and a rotten barrel sat innocuously in the corner, on top of which sat a dented metal plate and mug. Water and bread would be given twice a day by the warders. The only light afforded in the cell was through a slimy porthole. Advanced corrosion had rusted the bolts from its surround, allowing the wintry weather to pour in.

They hadn't removed his handcuffs, and his ankles remained shackled together, restricting walking. Shackled to his left leg manacle was a short length of chain on the end of which was an iron ball. He struggled to the slimy porthole. It was dark outside and, from that distant savage lair, icy wind blew. In the faint light of the quarter moon, his heart lifted, as his eyes focused on the wetlands of the Romney marshes. A dark flat wilderness, intersected with dykes, and mounds, and gates, with scattered cattle feeding. It was nearly Christmas. He tried to recall his favourite Christmas carol.

"Away in a manger, no crib for a bed," He spoke the words aloud, turning back to survey his new surroundings. Magwitch sat down on the hessian sacking and began to think. Strangely, he slept. Day moved into night and back to day, but as the time passed, he hatched his escape plan. Awoken by the arrival of the warden's new assistant with his usual ration of bread and water, recognition precipitated Magwitch to curse and fly at the bars at his erstwhile partner, now enemy, even after weeks of separation.

"Now now, my old friend, that's not very nice, now, is it?" Compeyson goaded, chuckling at Magwitch's misfortune. "You only have another 13 years and 11 months left," he said, tossing the dried bread through the barred door onto the filthy floor. He smirked, teasing Magwitch with the water jug. "Now, say please to teacher." Magwitch growled obscenities as he pushed his dented mug through the bars. Compeyson made to pour the water into the mug, deliberately missing, allowing the water to splash onto the soiled wooden floor. "Oh, deary deary me, what a shame. Now, don't waste it, you've got a tongue, better lick it up." Issuing more obscenities from his thick jaw, Magwitch thrust both arms through the bars, stretching for Compeyson's throat. His right fist connected with the side of Compeyson's face, jarring his head, and making him drop the pitcher of water. "Now now," scoffed Compeyson. "There's that vicious passion again, what the nice judge warned you about." Magwitch slunk back into the corner of the black hole as Compeyson rubbed the left side of his face and disappeared back up the stairs amidst roars of sarcastic laughter.

The altercation renewed Magwitch's energy and escape plan. He had studied the tide, and had noted that bird's feet sank into the deep, slimy, sucking mud at low tide as they probed for worms. He couldn't swim properly anyway, so planned his escape at low tide.

"Nearly Christmas, guards'll be drunk on Christmas Eve," he mused. "Good time to make the break." He carefully removed two planks from the back of the barrel. "Mud skis," he muttered, almost grinning to himself at the brilliance of his plan. He carefully removed strands of jute from the bundle of hessian bedding and laboriously wove them together into thick string with which he would strap the curved barrel planks onto his feet. Since his wrists were still manacled, one more plank would suffice to help him push across the mud. An extra belt, made of jute from the soiled hessian, would make a belt from which he could suspend the iron ball from his waist so it wouldn't drag on the ground. There was nothing he could do about his manacled ankles, but there was sufficient slack in the chain to walk. "Jesus walked on water, and I can walk on mud," said Magwitch. "And the first thing wot I'll do when I get out of 'ere is go to church and say a prayer and thank the good Lord for my deliverance."

Without being noticed, it took another two days to break the frame of the porthole away from its rotten timber surround. A rusted, square nail extracted from the rotten planking of the hulk served to dig the final pieces of timber away. Carefully, he removed the rusted circular frame of the porthole and placed it quietly on the floor of his cell. Next, he stuck his head through the aperture and threw his skis down. They landed with a slapping sound on the mud and ooze below. His near starvation diet assisted as he wriggled through. Climbing down the outside of the rotten hull of the prison ship, the iron ball tied up to his waist came between him and the ship's side. His frozen fingers struggled to keep their purchase on the side of the ship and slowly, halfway down, he began falling over ten feet to the soft mud beneath.

Covered in slimy mud, he struggled to his feet and fitted his skis. An icy crust had temporally formed on top of the mud, helping him skate across its surface with comparative ease. It was dark and a new moon to boot. His breath steamed in front of him as he forged two furrows through the icy mud. Freezing fog fell as he reached the wetlands. He removed the barrel skis, retied the iron ball and walked, taking the weight of the ball in his right hand, his feet shuffling either side of the clanking chain. Muffled by the freezing fog, the warning gun thudded in the distance. "Games afoot," he muttered, as he increased his progress towards the village church at Cooling, determined to find shelter and give thanks.

Chapter 33

Compeyson stood paralysed outside the black hole. The stench of faeces and urine was masked by the nearly subzero temperature in the solitary cell. He couldn't believe his eyes. They flashed around the walls and came to rest on the vacant porthole. Rage mounted within.

"Done a bunk!" he gasped, instantly jealous at the escape and wanting to go too. He abandoned his bread and water trolley, rushed back to the upper deck, and reported the empty black hole to the warden. "He's gone I tell you. He's gone!"

The warden immediately gave the instruction to sound the alarm and fire the cannon. Compeyson slipped quietly over the side in the confusion. The tide was rising, providing floatation to the small rowing boat. Compeyson got in, pushed off, and he too was gone. His disappearance would not be noticed for another few hours.

Chapter 34

The afternoon was raw. Freezing fog and mist and iced puddles hampered his progress as he had struggled his way across the marshland, the hulk disappearing in the mist. Torturous hours passed before he reached Cooling Church. It was a bleak and miserable place, and totally overgrown with nettles. Half frozen, Magwitch stumbled between the gravestones, falling over the little children's graves hidden under the overgrown grass. He picked himself up and headed for the Norman door of the church. The noise of a young lad crying stopped him in his tracks. In fear of being discovered, he ducked down behind the headstones.

"Hold your noise!" growled Magwitch in a terrible voice as he stood up from among the graves at the side of the church porch. He made a lunge, grabbing the boy. "Keep still, you little devil, or I'll cut yourn throat!" he said, his appearance made more frightening by his grey prison clothes, broken shoes, and old rag tied round his head. He was soaked in water and smothered in mud, lamed by stones, and cut by flints, and stung by nettles, and torn by briars. Magwitch limped, and shivered, and glared, and growled; his teeth chattered in his head as he seized the boy by the chin.

"Oh! Don't cut my throat, sir," pleaded the boy. "Pray don't do it, sir."

"Tell us your name!" said Magwitch. "Quick!"

"Pip, sir."

"Once more," said Magwitch, staring at the boy. "Give it mouth!"

"Pip. Pip, sir."

"Show us where you live," said Magwitch. "Point out the place." Pip pointed to where the village lay on the flat in-shore among the alder trees and pollards a mile or more from the church. Magwitch grabbed Pip by the ankles and shook him upside down and then put him back down.

"You young dog," said Magwitch, licking his lips. "What fat cheeks you've got. Darn me if I couldn't eat 'em."

"Oh, please, sir, don't do it," said Pip, near to tears and hanging on to the nearest gravestone for support.

"Now lookee here," said Magwitch, "Where's your mother?"

"There, sir!" said Pip. Magwitch made a sudden start as if she were close, then stopped and looked over his shoulder at Pip.

"There, sir," said Pip timidly, pointing to the grave behind him. "Also Georgina. That's my mother."

"Oh!" said Magwitch, coming back. "And is that your father along with your mother?"

"Yes, sir," said Pip, "him too, late of this parish."

"Ha!" muttered Magwitch, considering. "Who d'ye live with?"

"My sister, sir. Mrs. Joe Gargery, wife of Joe Gargery, the blacksmith, sir."

"Blacksmith, eh?" said Magwitch, looking down at his leg, his eyebrows in a deep frown, and then looking back at Pip, he took him by both arms and tilted him backwards.

"Now lookee here, d'you know wot a file is?"

"Yes, sir," replied Pip, as Magwitch tilted him back further.

"You get me a file," instructed Magwitch, tilting young Pip back even further. "And you get me wittles and you bring 'em both to me, or I'll have your heart and liver out."

"If you would kindly please to let me keep upright, sir, perhaps I shouldn't be sick, and perhaps I could attend more." Holding Pip on top of the gravestone with his arms extended, Magwitch gave Pip one final tilt and shake.

"You bring to me, tomorrow morning early, that file and them wittles. You bring the lot to me, at that old Battery over yonder, you know, the old, ruined battery at Cliffe Creek. You do it, and you never dare to say a word or dare to make a sign concerning your having seen such a person as me, or any person sumever, and you shall be let live. You fail, or you go from my words in any partickler, no matter how small it is, and your heart and liver shall be tore out, roasted, and ate. Now, I ain't alone, as you may think I am. There's a young man hid with me, and in comparison, with which young man, I am an angel. That young man hears the words I speak. That young man has a secret way pecooliar to himself, of getting at a boy, and at his heart, and at his liver. It is in vain for a boy to attempt to hide himself from that young man. A boy may lock his door, may be warm in bed, may tuck himself up, may draw the clothes over his head, may think himself comfortable and safe, but that young man will softly creep, and creep his way to him, and tear him open. I am a keeping that young man from harming of you at the present moment, with great difficulty. I find it very hard to hold that young man off of your inside. Now, what does you say?"

"I'll get the file, and wittles of broken bits of food, and whatever I can get, sir, honest, sir!" exclaimed Pip. "And I'll be at the old Cliffe Battery early in the morning, sir."

"Say Lord strike me dead if yous don't!"

"Lord strike me dead if I don't," replied Pip, eager to get away.

"Now," Magwitch pursued, "you remember what you've undertook, and you can remember that young man, and you get home."

"Goo-good night, sir," said Pip, his voice beginning to falter.

"Much of that," said Magwitch, glancing around into the cold dank mist. "I wish I was a frog. Or an eel." Magwitch hugged his shuddering body in both arms, attempting to hold himself together. He limped off towards the low church wall, his feet and ankles crippled in pain. He continued out onto the flat marsh, picking his way through the stones popping through the water as the tide was in. The marshes and river appeared as long black lines, and the sky was just a row of angry red lines and dense lines intermixed. Two, ugly, black things appeared in silhouette on the edge of the Medway. One, a beacon for the ships to navigate by, and the other, a gibbet with loose chains still hanging, recently employed to hang a pirate. Magwitch limped towards the gibbet and beyond to the old Battery. Munching cattle jumped from the mist, their heads nonchalantly lifted to gaze at the intruder. Magwitch limped on. Alone. He waited at the Battery all night, hugging himself in the vain hope of retrieving his senses. He limped to and fro until the light came.

"Ah, at last, there yous are. What's in the bottle, boy?" said Magwitch.

"Brandy," replied Pip, handing over the file and untying the bundle of wittles carefully tied up in his pocket-handkerchief, and lastly, he emptied his pockets. Magwitch laid the file on the damp grass. He snatched up the round, crusty, pork pie, and proceeding to gobble it, rammed each massive mouthful down his throat. He kept shivering and, switching from the half-eaten pork pie, he grabbed the brown bottle of brandy and poured it down his parched throat, his urgency forcing brandy to overflow his frozen lips and trickle down his chin. He never stopped shivering; his teeth rattled on the glass as he struggled to retain the neck of the brandy bottle in his mouth without biting it off.

"I think you have got the ague," said Pip.

"I'm much of your opinion, boy," said Magwitch between gulps.

"It's bad about here," said Pip. "You've been lying out on the marshes, and they're dreadful aguish; rheumatic too."

"I'll eat my breakfast afore they's the death of me," said Magwitch. "And I'd do that if I was going to be strung up to that there gallows as there is over there, directly arterwards. I'll beat the shivers so far, I'll bet yous." Magwitch continued gobbling the minced meat, and the other whittles, meat, bone, bread, and rind cheese, all at the same time. He stopped his jaws in mid chew to listen. Then, he heard a sound.

"You're not a deceiving imp? Yous brought no one with you?"

"No, sir. No!"

"Nor giv' no one the office?"

"No!" said Pip emphatically.

"Well," said Magwitch. "I believe you. You'd be but a fierce young hound indeed, if, at your time in life, you could help to hunt a wretched warmint, hunted as near death and dunghill as this poor wretched warmint is." Magwitch gave a distinct click from his throat as if he would chime like a clock and then smeared his rough, ragged sleeve over his eyes. Pitying his desolation, Pip watched Magwitch gradually settle down to finish the pork pie.

"I am glad you enjoy it."

"Did you speak?" said Magwitch.

"I said I was glad you enjoyed it."

"Thankee, my dear boy. I do."

"I am afraid you won't leave any for him," said Pip timidly, watching Magwitch devour the food like a savage dog, continuously looking over his shoulder. "'Cause there's no more to be got where that came from."

"Leave any for 'im? Who's 'im?" demanded Magwitch, stopping in mid-crunch.

"The young man that you spoke of. That was hid with you."

"Oh, ah," acknowledged Magwitch with a gruff laugh. "'Im? Yes, yes! He don't want no wittles."

"I thought he looked as if he did," replied Pip. Magwitch stopped eating, and scrutinised Pip in great surprise.

"Looked? When?"

"Just now."

"Where?"

"Yonder," said Pip, pointing. "Over there, where I found him nodding asleep and I thought it was you." Staring, Magwitch grabbed Pip by the collar.

"Dressed like you, you know, only with a hat," explained Pip, trembling in fear of having his throat cut.

"And, and, and with the same reason for wanting to borrow a file. Didn't you hear the cannon last night?"

"Then, there was firing?" quizzed Magwitch.

"I wonder you shouldn't have been sure of that," replied Pip. "For we heard it at home, and that's farther away, and we were shut in besides."

"Why, see now!" said Magwitch. "When a man's alone on these flats, with a light head and a light stomach, perishing cold and want, he hears nothin' all night, but guns firing, and voices calling. Hears? He sees the soldiers, with their red coats lighted up by the torches carried afore, closing in round him. Hears his number called, hears himself challenged, hears the rattle of the muskets, hears the orders given 'Make ready! Present! Cover him steady, men!' and is laid hands on; and there's nothin! Why, if I see one pursuing party last night, coming up in order, damn 'em, with their tramp tramp, I see a hundred. And as to firing! Why, I see the mist shake with the cannon, after it was broad day, but this man, did you notice anything in him?"

"He had a badly bruised face," replied Pip, not sure where the conversation was headed.

"Not here?" exclaimed Magwitch, striking his own cheek mercilessly with the flat of his hand.

"Yes, there."

"Where is he?" demanded Magwitch, cramming what little food was left into the breast of his grey jacket. "Show me the way he went. I'll pull him down, like a bloodhound. Curse this iron on my sore leg. Give us hold of the file, boy." Magwitch grabbed the file from Pip's hand and started filing at his leg iron, the heavy ball still tied up to his belt. With his head bent over his knee and scant regard for the old chafing, he filed away at his fetter, creating deeper and bloodier wounds. He felt nothing, but his determination to be free. Pip slipped away for his Christmas luncheon at home.

Chapter 35

Warmed by the brandy and food, Magwitch kept filing at his leg iron. Eventually, the file won. Relieved, he sat back on the rock, rubbing his chafed and bleeding ankle. It was late afternoon and the mist had lifted, driven off by the wind, but as the evening approached, bitter sleet came rattling down and the mist returned, muffling the sound of the occasional sheep's bell. Through the mist, Magwitch saw Compeyson sitting on a grassy bank. Stealthily, he crept up behind and threw his whole body mass at his back, grabbing him round the neck. Seconds later, they were locked in mortal combat, and with fists flying, rolled down the grassy bank, and slithered into the Medway ooze. Water was splashing, and mud was flying, and they swore oaths and punched at each other.

"Here are both men," panted the sergeant from the top of the bank, having heard the noise first. The sergeant struggled down to the bottom of the ditch. "Surrender, you two," he challenged. "Confound you for two wild beasts. Come asunder." The other soldiers cocked their pieces and levelled them at the two convicts fighting in the mud. A few more of the soldiers struggled down the bank to help the sergeant. Both bleeding and panting and execrating and struggling, Magwitch and Compeyson were recaptured.

"Mind," said Magwitch, wiping the blood from his face with his ragged sleeves, and shaking torn hair from his fingers. "I took him. I give him up to you. Mind that!"

"It's not much to be particular about," said the sergeant. "It'll do you small good, my man, being in the same plight yourself. Handcuffs there."

"I don't expect it do me good. I don't want it do me more good than it do now," said Magwitch with a greedy laugh. "I took him. He knows it. That's enough for me." Compeyson was furious and, in addition to the old bruise on the left side of his face inflicted in the hulk, he seemed to be bruised and torn all over and couldn't get his breath back. He leant on the shoulder of one of the soldiers to keep himself from falling whilst climbing up the bank.

"Take notice, guard, he tried to murder me," said Compeyson, eventually able to speak.

"Tried to murder 'im?" scoffed Magwitch. "Try and not do it? I took him and giv' 'im up, that's what I done. I not only prevented 'im getting off the marshes, but dragged 'im 'ere. Dragged 'im this far on his way back. He's a gentleman, if you please, this villain. Now, the hulks 'as got its gentleman again, through me. Murder 'im? Worth my while too. To murder 'im, when I could do worse and drag 'im back."

"He tried, he tried, tried to murder me. Bear witness." Compeyson gasped.

"Lookee here," Magwitch addressed the sergeant. "Single-handed, I got clear of yourn prison ship. I made a dash and I done it. I could ha' got clear of these death-cold flats likewise. Look at my leg. Yous won't find much iron on it. I'd be clean gorn if I hadn't made the discovery that he was here. Let 'im go free? Let 'im profit by the means as I found out? Let 'im make a tool of me afresh? Once more? No, no, no. If I had died at the bottom of that there ditch." Magwitch made an emphatic swing at the ditch with his manacled hands.

"I'd have held to 'im with that grip that you should have been safe to find 'im in my hold."

"He tried to murder me," repeated Compeyson. "I should have been a dead man if you had not come up."

"He lies," said Magwitch, a new fierceness coming in his voice. "He's a liar born, and he'll die a liar. Look at his face; ain't it written there? Let 'im turn those eyes on me. I defy 'im to do it." Compeyson looked up into the sky, a look of scorn spreading across his face.

"Do you see 'im?" pursued Magwitch. "Do you see wot a villain he is? Do you see those grovelling and wandering eyes? That's how he looked when we were tried together. He never looked at me."

"You are not much to look at," replied Compeyson with a half-taunting glance. "Didn't I tell you that he would murder me, if he could?" whined Compeyson, shaking with fear again.

"Enough of this parley," said the sergeant. "Light those torches." During the fight, it had grown dark, three or four torches were lit and distributed. Magwitch remained silent and turned to watch, suddenly noticing Pip standing on the top of the ditch between two gentlemen dressed in civvies. He threw a secret look in Pip's direction. Pip acknowledged by shaking his head, demonstrating his innocence. Magwitch quickly looked away.

"All right," said the sergeant. "Now, march." A few yards farther, the deafening sound of three cannons burst the silence, shattering eardrums. "You are expected on board," said the sergeant to Magwitch. "They know you are coming. Don't straggle, man. Close up."

The pathway back to the hulk ran mostly along the edge of the river, Medway. There was a divergence here and there where a dyke came with a miniature windmill used to control the sluice gate, restricting the tidal flow in and out of the drainage ditches. The party progressed slowly, Joe, Pip's stepfather through his marriage to Pip's eldest sister, walked hand-in-hand with Pip, and the clerk of the church, Mr. Wopsle. They had just finished Christmas lunch when the police had arrived, looking for the escaped convicts. Curious, the three had left the forge and tagged on at the end of the police. They had watched the recapture and from behind, observed both convicts, lame from the leg-irons, slowing the pace. The party took an hour to reach the sentry's hut, and after the traditional challenge, entered the hut where there was a smell of tobacco and whitewash, and a bright fire, and a lamp, and a stand of muskets, and a drum, and a low wooden bedstead, like an overgrown mangle without the machinery, capable of holding about a dozen soldiers all at once. Magwitch watched the three or four soldiers lying on the bedstead, they raised their heads, gave a sleepy stare, and lowered their heads again. The sergeant sat down and prepared his report.

"I wish to say something respecting this escape. It may prevent some person lying under suspicion along with me," announced Magwitch, the party now seated haphazardly inside the hut.

"You can say what you like," returned the sergeant, his arms folded, looking coolly back.

"But you have no call to say it here. You'll have opportunity enough to say about it, and hear about it, before it's done with, you know."

"I know, but this is another point, a separate matter. A man can't starve, at least I can't. I took some wittles up at the village yonder, where the church stands alone at the edge of them marshes."

"You mean stole," said the sergeant.

"And I'll tell you where from. The blacksmith's house, that's where from."

"Halloa," said the sergeant staring at Joe Gargery holding Pip's hand.

"Halloa, Pip," said Joe, staring down at Pip.

"It was some broken wittles. That's what it was, and a dram of liquor, and a pie."

"Have you happened to miss such an article as a pie, blacksmith?" asked the sergeant confidentially.

"My wife did, at the very moment when you came in. Don't you know, Pip?"

"So," said Magwitch, turning his eyes to the man in a moody manner, and without the least glance at Pip. "So you're the blacksmith, are you? Then I'm sorry to say, I've eat your pie."

"God knows you're welcome to it. So far as it was ever mine," said Joe. "We don't know what you have done, but we wouldn't have you starve to death for it, poor miserable fellow creature; would us, Pip?" Nothing further was said, as the ferryboat arrived and Magwitch and Compeyson were pushed aboard.

"Give way, you." The party rowed out across the Medway, back to the prison hulk, and disappeared up the gangplank, as the flaming torches were flung, hissing into the water and went out.

Chapter 36

Old Bailey was the name of the street in which the London assizes were located. Later, it would be termed the Central Criminal Court, but, today, was called the sessions in which Jaggers would defend Gypsy Molly.

Accused of the murder of Gypsy Madonna by the Bow Street Runners, the warrant for her arrest confirmed the motive as jealousy, and was heavily supported by substantial, albeit circumstantial, evidence extracted in the form of statements from the Woods family, the resident Romany gypsies of Hounslow Heath.

The Crown would place before the 12-man jury, evidence detailing the why and the how, for the Runners already knew the where and the when, but the conundrum for the jury would be the what and the who. The Crown claimed that the tramp, Gypsy Molly, had planned the brutal attack of her defenceless victim, and that she, and she alone, had lain in wait that particular day, bent on delivering her message with rancour.

Jaggers thought and planned the defence differently. During the preceding days, as they prepared for trial, Jaggers was never out of Scotland Yard. Day after day, for many days, he contended against the committal. He took time to know and understand Gypsy Molly. Whilst highly spirited, he had found her to be bright-eyed and intelligent. To his surprise, she had greatly contributed to the management of his home in Gerrard Street, Soho. She was efficient and clean, delivering her work with crisp discipline and precision.

She was courteous and never complained. Her tasks were always completed by the time Jaggers returned from his office in Little Britain, and, on the many occasions when he would return frustrated and ready to resign from representing the poor down-and-out criminals of London, many of whom had done little else than to steal a loaf of bread to feed their wretched bodies and little children, she would give him a justifiable and logical reason as to why he should continue. Some nights, he would take her into his confidence, almost as if he was practicing for the jury.

'Put the case,' was his favourite introduction of a hypothetical situation and, combined with his huge black and white, spotted handkerchief, he would play act in front of Molly to see what the effect would be. He had taken expert care of her appearance, having artfully dressed her from the time of her apprehension, ensuring that she looked much slighter then she really was, in particular; her sleeves skillfully made to emphasise that her arms had a delicate look. She still possessed one or two bruises about her. She looked nothing like a tramp, and he considered that the lacerations to the backs of her hands were evidence, his question being, were the scratches inflicted by fingernails, or were they caused by the brambles? One evening, a couple of days before the trial, they had talked together in front of the coal fire in the lounge. Jaggers had relaxed as Molly retired to prepare coffee.

"Mister Jaggers, what has become of my Estella?" she had asked innocently as she returned from the kitchen and slid the tray on the table next to Jaggers. Jaggers had reached forward and grabbed her by the wrist. She had struggled, instantly breaking his grip. Jaggers had made a mental note whilst raising an eyebrow at the hidden strength.

"Molly, Molly, Molly, I have told you before and I'll shall tell you again that your daughter has no place in your mind. Nobody can know the outcome of your trial, and you must trust me. Now, on that subject, I plan to take the judge and the foreman of the jury to Hounslow Heath to visit the scene of the crime. But, before that, we must go together so that you can show me what you were doing to get those scratches on your hands. You will be present and, in my charge, and you will behave and follow my instructions. Is that quite clear?"

He had been brutally direct, chewing away at his index finger, occasionally ceasing chewing and aggressively pointing it at her. They had talked well into the night. Jaggers studied Molly, noting that although slight of build, she possessed hidden strengths. Definitely enough to throttle a human neck. He studied the coroner's report. He noted with surprise that the victim had sustained substantial bruising above the left temple, whilst there was only minor comment in the report relating to the bruising on the neck. The coroner's conclusion was that death was probably caused by strangulation. The word *'probably'* had stuck in his fertile brain.

To grow the picture for the jury, Jaggers found himself in need of a medical opinion and had made his way to Saint Bartholomew's hospital where he had engaged the services of the new species of medical men, a surgeon.

"Emmett's your man," the surgeon had replied in the midst of washing up after attending to his patient. "Doubt that he will wish to see you in his rooms, but we can try."

"You would join me with a visit to Dr. Emmett's rooms?"

"A pleasure," said the surgeon, hanging up his overall. The men exited the hospital and took the short ride to the Harley Street address.

"Put the case that the coroner overlooked a bruise above the temple simply because he had been told by the Bow Street Runners, who had reached a clumsy assumption, that Gypsy Madonna had been strangled. However, it seems to me that there may, indeed, be another possibility for the cause of death." Jaggers went into the evidence of the case he was working on without naming names.

"Strange," said Emmett. "A body was brought in around that time with exactly those wounds." Emmett jumped up and retrieved a buff file containing his autopsy.

"I removed the brain," he commented, but before continuing, walked over to the curtain and checked that it was fully closed, then returning, sat back down in his chair. "Do you want to see it?"

"See what?" quizzed Jaggers, disturbed that the man had retained the brain all these days.

"Don't look so surprised. I pickled it, and also pickled the lungs, and heart, and liver, and kidneys. Excellent specimen. It had an unusual death. Female too. I believe she would have been in her mid-30s. And she was pregnant," said Emmett, recalling the case. "Most of the bodies I get in here are hanged villains who smoke and drink and eat badly. By the time they get to the hangman, their bodies are broken and wretched. This one was perfect."

"Can I see your notes?" asked Jaggers.

"I'll do better than that," said Emmett, standing up. "Follow me and I'll show you the pickled specimens. You can judge for yourself as to the cause of death." The three men walked from the reception parlour through into the backrooms. Jaggers's eyes focused on the large jars containing body parts all pickled in a brownish fluid.

"Well, you have been busy," said Jaggers, removing his large handkerchief in a flourish. "But, certainly, your work will help my defence strategy—"

"Already does help mine," interjected the surgeon, enjoying the theatre.

"Thank you, gentlemen," Emmett acknowledged the interest from the surgeon and Jaggers. "Now, look at this." Emmett directed all eyes to the large jar standing on top of the waist high cupboard in front of them. "This is the brain in question. Note the discoloring just here. Evidence of hemorrhage in the area above the temple, and I would take an educated guess that death could have been caused by a fall, or, a blow to the head, and not asphyxiation. It's all in my report especially that the lungs appeared to have been functioning normally until death. Not for public consumption though," said Emmett, looking concerned at Jaggers's interest in the body parts.

"And why not?" replied Jaggers.

"I don't exist. Well, not to the authorities. My research is secret and the results of my work are for selected colleagues, especially for those who are intent on moving the boundaries of medical science forward." Emmett had provided infinite possibilities to Jaggers and, in turn, Jaggers could now relay his strategy to Molly's defence counsel.

Chapter 37

"Not guilty," replied Molly to the judge's question.

"Not guilty," she wailed again; anguish contorting her face. Her frail body and pale complexion accentuated by her attire provided grist to Jaggers's defence. The 12-man jury sat patiently as the emaciated Silk, counsel for the prosecution, led his evidence, intermittently interrupted by his uncontrollable smoker's cough. The men of the jury nodded at each point delivered, casting shocked glances across at Molly; her head barely showing above the brass rail of the dock. At the end of the second day, Crown prosecution had convinced the jurors and exhausted all their evidence.

"My Lord, gentlemen of the jury," began Jaggers's counsel in a powerful and distinguished voice. He rose from his seat at the front of the court and bowed respectfully to the bench and jurors. Clad in a pinstripe suit and a red rose in his left lapel, his wig and gown added an air of confidence to his words. He walked steadily towards the jurors, looking slowly from one to the other; his powerful stage presence bringing swift attention to his delivery.

"For the past two days, you have graciously and patiently listened to my learned colleague's forceful arguments and evidence, and I can see in your innocent and just expressions that you may be forming the opinion that this young lady, who appears before you in the dock, one Gypsy Molly, cannot be anything else but guilty." He paused for effect, watching the jurors fidget uncomfortably at the last statement and then continued to drive home the message.

"And, consequently, you will have subconsciously arrived at your individual verdict that the accused should suffer the supreme penalty of the law of England and Wales, and should be taken to the place from whence she came and there, hanged by the neck until she is dead." Frowning, most of the members nodded their heads in agreement as a small buzz of approval ran around the public gallery, mostly filled with members of the Woods family and the press.

Molly's counsel turned away from the jury and walked back to his desk, poured a glass of water. Jaggers slid across a single piece of parchment. The barrister studied the writing and returned to his previous position.

"You have heard from the prosecution that Gypsy Molly and her husband led tramping lives, but who is qualified to make such a ruling? Is not the life of the gypsy an ancient culture? A culture formed thousands of years ago, and, therefore, whose rituals are sacrosanct? To be married over a broomstick, indeed, a ritual wedding born of nature. Prosecution lays blame on the husband, their reasoning being that he too was a tramping man, but he is not on trial here." Defence counsel then proceeded to the dock and held up Gypsy Molly's left hand. "In evidence, my learned colleague points to these wounds, more particularly referred to as scratches. He uses words as conclusive proof of the struggle, scratches inflicted by fingernails. We say that these are not the marks of fingernails, but of brambles and, that during these proceedings, we will show you the brambles." The public gallery groaned at the statement. "Thank you, Molly," said Defence counsel, letting go of her hand and returning to his desk. He took a short sip of water whilst considering his next statement.

"Gentlemen of the jury, you have erroneously been led to believe that they are the marks of fingernails. My learned colleague has also suggested that the accused destroyed her own child. In this belief, you must accept all the consequences of the hypothesis. For anything we know, she may have destroyed her child and, the child, in clinging to her mother, may have scratched the backs of the accused's hands. What then? You are not trying the accused for the murder of her child. Why don't you?" The jury fidgeted as the impact of defence counsel's words hit home.

"As to this case, it is clear that the cause of the wounds has more than one possible explanation and, if you will have scratches, consider carefully how you accounted for them, assuming for the sake of argument, that you have not invented the cause for them?" Turning, counsel topped up his water glass and took another drink before continuing.

"Gentlemen of the jury, I invite you to rest your eyes on the accused." The heads of 12 male jurors projected 24 eyes that swivelled in their sockets to observe Gypsy Molly. She flushed and fidgeted at the attention the mention of her had drawn. Her head and shoulders hardly above the brass rail of the dock, and her small hands clutching a rail too big for her small fingers to encircle.

"In your strongest imagination, can you witness the struggle and why, especially when the victim appears to us all as a woman over ten years her senior, and, indeed, physically larger, and taller, and stronger, and heavier in every respect. And how do we know who attacked who, and for what reason?"

"Objection," challenged the prosecution near to choking on his rotten, nicotine-saturated lungs. "My Lord, where is all this leading?"

"Sustained," said the judge, tapping his gavel for order. "Counsel for the defence will please keep to the facts and refrain from embellishment. There is no need for embroidery in my court."

"My Lord, I am innocently pointing out the physical improbability that the accused even had the strength, height, or, indeed, the arms and hands with which to strangle the victim," responded counsel for the defence, returning for another sip of water before continuing. He swung round and verbally hit the jury.

"But what we do know is that there was a violent struggle. We do know that they were both bruised, and both scratched, and both torn. What else do we know?" He paused, inviting the jurors to reconsider. Returning to his desk, he picked up the buff file and walked back to face the jurors.

"Interestingly, we have the coroner's report, exhibit three." He waved the folder above his head as evidence to the court. Stepping towards the jurors, he opened the folder and read aloud, reiterating the sentence in the summation.

"Death was probably caused by strangulation. The word *'probably'* must cast further doubt in your minds. That word indicates that even the coroner could not be sure as to the cause of death, and it further raises the possibility that there may, indeed, have been another cause of death. Gentlemen of the jury, put the case, that the victim had invited the accused to come to the barn on that tragic day in order to pursue personal gratification. Abhorrent to you as it must have been abhorrent to the accused, who found herself alone, forced to defend herself against an unnatural womanly act. Put the case, that she sought to defend herself against the victim's advances made to appease her personal gratification. Put the case, that the bruise sustained above the victim's temple was the result of an accidental fall and that the cause of death was not as a result of strangulation as insinuated by my learned colleague, but the result of an accidental fall through misadventure."

"Objection," shouted the prosecution, "This is preposterous speculation."

"Sustained," the judge intervened, becoming further frustrated.

"Both counsels will approach." The two barristers approached the bar.

"Where is all this leading?"

"My Lord, I am merely establishing that there are other possibilities in this case, and it is my considered, professional opinion, indeed, I vehemently believe, that for the benefit of this trial, the time has come for the court to witness the evidence at the scene of the crime." Jaggers sat quietly, pleased at the direction the case was now moving in.

"Any objection?" said the judge.

"No objection, my Lord," replied counsel for the prosecution, his grey face lined with concern.

"Given the lateness of the day, court is adjourned. There will also be a recess tomorrow whilst I am on advisement of further evidence." The gavel crashed on the thick, oak anvil.

The visit to Hounslow Heath, where Molly had collected raspberries and blackberries on the morning of Estella's birthday party, completed Jaggers's picture. He pointed out to the jury, Foreman, that the brambles at the edge of the heath were not as high as Molly's face, and that they only reached her hands.

He demonstrated that her hands could have come into contact with the vicious thorns on the wild plant during the time she had gathered the fruit. He even identified the path she had taken through the brambles, and fortune had shone on his defence when he identified a piece of her torn frock still impaled on a thorn with a few drops of Molly's blood. On the final day of the trial, having retired to consider their verdict, the jury collapsed. Emerging from their deliberations less than two hours later, they solemnly filed back into court.

"Gentlemen of the jury, have you considered your verdict?"

"We have, your Lordship." The jury, Foreman, had risen to his feet before speaking and simultaneously handed a small slip of paper to the sergeant for transmission to the bench. Frowning beneath his wig, the judge silently read the missive and looked back at the sullen faces of the jury.

"And how do you find?"

"We find the accused, Gypsy Molly, not guilty." Pandemonium broke out with an enormous uproar in the public gallery.

"Silence in court," demanded the judge, repeatedly hammering his gavel on the well-used, oak anvil.

Underneath the bulbous nose, the hint of a smile slowly spread across Jaggers's face.

Chapter 38

He was a secret-looking man. His head was all on one side, and one of his eyes was half-shut as if he were taking aim at something with an invisible gun. He always maintained a pipe in his mouth and, every now and again, would remove it and blow smoke into the air. He wore a flapping, broad-brimmed, traveller's hat and under it, a handkerchief tied over his head in the manner of a cap, concealing his hair. His last work detail, before his release from prison, had been on the Romney marshes. "Mudbank, mist, swamp, and work. Work, swamp, mist, and mudbank," he muttered, as he received his release papers from the guards in the dockyard.

The stagecoach, loaded with Magwitch and the rest of the consignment of convicts for New South Wales, appeared out of the mist; the hooves of the twin teams being muffled in the thick, dank, and cold atmosphere. The coach drew to a halt on the side of the docks. Heavily chained en route to the convict transportation ship; for a few moments, Magwitch found himself alone and near to where he had hidden the remains of his swag. Unnoticed by the guard, he slipped from the coach and ducked between the stacks of timber at the back of the wharf, squeezing in behind.

"Gord, thank'e it's still 'ere." Magwitch breathed a sigh of relief as his hand came to rest on the small bundle of one-pound notes. He panicked at the sound of a pair of boots crunching on the road, but he kept hidden, looking about him as the man with the half-shut eye came into view.

"Psst." The man stopped. Magwitch beckoned him over. "I 'as a job for yous if you're game?" said Magwitch, holding some of the one-pound notes out for the other man to see. The man squeezed in and they sat together behind the pile of timber. Magwitch went into detail. "This boy, see, goes by the name, Pip, see, he giv' me help, and wittles, and I want you to find him and give him two, one-pound notes and a bright shilling," said Magwitch breathlessly. He watched the man's surprised expression as he cocked his good eye.

"''Ere, 'ere's the swelterers," continued Magwitch, shoving a bundle of notes into the man's hand. "And there's some for yous an' all."

"Where do I find this boy?"

"Try the Three Jolly Bargemen, his father, no, not his father really, Joe Gargery, goes there sometimes and takes this Pip with him, see."

"Where the hell's the Three Jolly Bargemen," challenged the man, peering cautiously through his half-shut eye.

"Near Rochester. Reckon, 'bout four mile out a'town." The man nodded, a frown spreading across his secret face. "What the blue blazes is he to this Joe? Nevvy then?"

"No, not nevvy; it's complicated, you'll find out."

"What do he look like?"

"Aha, this Joe is the blacksmith near the old church down by the village. I first see'd the boy by the graves on Christmas Eve," explained Magwitch.

"How will he know the money's from you?"

"Butt'n yourn lip on the money! Only the boy must get it for wot 'e done. Just buy 'em drink. I ow's 'em that too," Magwitch spoke with his hand over his mouth in fear of what he was saying. "Aha, an' another thing. Go to the old Battery, I 'id the blacksmith's file in the rock wall at the entrance. Pip'll recognise it and 'e'll remember wot 'e did. But don't let the blacksmith see it 'cause I don't want the blacksmith to know I stole 'is file 'cause I didn't say I did it when they took me. Now, swear on the book." Magwitch retrieved his treasured little black book from the inside of his tatty jacket.

"So what happened after you got captured?"

"They caught me next day. It were Christmas Day. Caught me fighting 'im wot did the trouble in the first place. They giv's me a lifer in Australia. Sailing on tonight's tide. Now, swear. Quick! 'cause 'ere comes the guard."

Part 2
New South Wales, 1830

Chapter 39

Castle Forbes had become one of the most successfully farmed land grants in the Hunters river district, if not the whole of New South Wales. Situated between Singleton and Maitland, approximately 150 miles north of Sydney, the initial grant, awarded by Governor Sir Thomas Brisbane, in 1822, had more than doubled in size to over four thousand acres, and now produced arable crops, cattle, and sheep. Eight years ago, when, as Free Settlers, James Mudie and his four daughters first set foot on the land, it was a wild place with impenetrable cedar and brush, choked with tangled vines and thickets. Massive trees towered above the plains; giant red cedar and figs and gums dominated the landscape.

The alluvial soils on the flood plains supported luxuriant temperate rainforests, and the vegetation on the fringes of the rivers was barely touched. Indeed, during their first eight years, James Mudie, referred to as the Major, and his four daughters, Emily, Maria, Isabella, and stepdaughter, Anne Scargill, had prospered. Originally from Dundee, Forfarshire, in Scotland, they had all established new lives in the Land of Promise. Emily had married John Larnach, who had accepted a Castle Forbes partnership as a wedding gift. Maria, Isabella, and Anne had also married well, and had been fortunate to establish their own farms in the area. Formally a Royal Naval officer in His Majesty's navy, James had also purchased land in Morpeth, the deep steamship port close to Maitland on which he proposed to construct a commercial wharf.

Mudie's family homestead appeared as an unassuming cottage, although it had six bedrooms and servants' quarters at the rear. Across the other side of Munnimbah Creek, now named Mudies Creek where it passed through the farm, were the convict's quarters, represented by a series of huts, and a main barn where Mudie would have food served, conduct the mandatory weekly convict muster, and read Sunday prayers.

With a labour force approaching 90, burgeoning to 120 at harvest time, hundreds upon hundreds of convicts had served their time at Castle Forbes. Mostly, they were reliable and of good behavior, but some ten to 15 per cent required regular discipline. Given the distance and access to and from Sydney, federal policing of the area was scant, leaving farmers exposed to providing their own methods of law enforcement and control. Punishment for the slightest misdemeanor at Castle Forbes was instantly and brutally meted out by Larnach, who, over the years, had become vindictive, relying on the lash to maintain order. Mutiny and rebellion against Mudie and Larnach lay just beneath the surface.

From his vantage point at Mount Manning, 60 miles south of Castle Forbes, Mudie watched the government iron-gangs slaving away on the construction of the new Great North Road. Building the section from Mount Manning to Wiseman's Ferry had been underway for a few years, and, resulting from the ongoing theft of grain during shipments from Castle Forbes via ship to Sydney, Mudie had decided to explore the possibility of transporting his grain to market overland by bullockies.

January was hot and dry, and the hinterland seemed to be having more than its fair share of forest fires. The eucalypts in particular, like tinder, messily dropping their branches. Sticky bark and leaves lay heaped for years in the forests. Lightning strike or, more likely, a careless convict scraping out glowing tobacco from his clay pipe, causing ignition. Mudie watched as the fire took hold.

"Frost turn the bullockies, and move them to more open ground," instructed Mudie.

"Certainly, Major," replied George Frost, mounting his spirited horse.

"Worried about the fire, Major?"

"I am. If the wind changes later, we could be in trouble in the night."

"Reckon you're right, sir."

"We camp here for the night," instructed Mudie, looking skyward at the billowing cumulous clouds.

"Rain. Hopefully rain tonight," Mudie commented to Frost as they set camp.

Government iron-gangs, the job maintained for the worst offenders. Cruel and inhumane, the iron manacles viciously chaffing at bony ankles, impeding production. Mudie continued his observation. He studied the construction of their temporary camp. The main tent consisted of three, forked uprights forming triangles and reaching eight-feet clear of the ground, a ridgepole 30-feet long between them, covered with bullock hides that stretched from the ground on one side, up over the ridgepole, and down the other side, making the width within the tent base some 16 feet.

The storm broke during the night, extinguishing the fire, but the volumes of water falling in the night brought another difficulty. Instantly, the surface of the track turned to mud under the artillery wheels of the bullock carts. Mudie decided to hold up for another day before continuing onto Sydney and the selection from Sydney Barracks of his next batch of convicts to be assigned to Castle Forbes.

Chapter 40

"Turnips, guv. Turnips and parsnips n' tatties and the likes, down in Essex," volunteered the last convict to be interviewed.

"Anything else about your farming experiences and your earlier troubles?" invited Mudie.

"Well, guv, I looked after the sheep. Shepherding I reckon they calls it, and a bit of laboring and a bit of wagoning and a bit of haymaking. Most anything to put food in my stomach. 'Appy to work at anything, guv."

"And who taught you to read and sign your name?"

"Strange one that was, guv. See, I was a deserting soldier sleeping in a traveller's rest, and he's lying there, this giant, see, under all these tatters. And it was wot this giant did for a livin'. Cost a penny for to learn me to sign me name. A penny a lesson like and he learn me to write," explained the convict, his ill-fitting, slop clothing masking his 44 years.

"What was your crime to be transported for life?" Mudie pursued his line of questioning in an attempt to judge his capability before allocating a position.

"In and out o' goal for petty things I was, like vagrancy, guv. And then got locked up on one o' them old Napoleon prison ships. You knows, guv, they calls them the hulks 'cause they're rotten. Anyways, I escaped them hulks, guv. O'course, they caught me 'cause of this other fellow that made all the troubles in the first place. They caught me on Christmas day, guv. The big gun made the alarm on them marshes, see."

"That will be the warning gun for escaped convicts," mused Mudie, allowing the convict to explain himself.

"And where was the tide when you made a bolt for it?"

"Low tide, guv, Christmas Eve. It was very deep mud on them marshes, wot sucked at yourn feet."

"Didn't you sink in the mud?"

"Nah, guv. I made shoes from old, barrel planks like. Aye, that's wot I did. Them planks slid me across the icy mud. Soldiers couldn't follow 'til the tide came in, guv." Magwitch's eyes twinkled at the thought of outwitting the soldiers. Mudie smiled inwardly at the man's cheek.

"Go on."

"Hid in a churchyard, and this boy, see, he 'elped me wi' wittles. I'll always remember that boy 'cause he saved my life."

"You'll do," said Mudie, comfortable that Magwitch was only guilty of petty crime, and his last statement demonstrating loyalty. Satisfied, he turned to leave.

"Do wot, guv?" said Magwitch, his knuckles whitening as he clutched the bars of the prison.

"Sheep farming at Castle Forbes," replied Mudie, making a note in his book; his weathered face giving nothing away.

The heavy, wrought-iron gate squeaked in opposition to being opened, as Mudie exited the high-security area. The clank echoed through the cold, stone building as the great, wrought-iron gate closed behind him and gravel crunched underfoot as he made his way to the assignment office at Sydney Barracks.

"Spare the rod and spoil the child," muttered the sergeant in charge.

"Aye, I understand entirely," agreed Mudie, sitting opposite the man responsible for assigning the convicts.

"Though I must say that after eight years and hundreds of convicts having passed through my hands at Castle Forbes, there are less than ten per cent with whom I have difficulty."

"Use the lash on them, Major?"

"Have to. John Larnach has them all weeded out," replied Mudie, watching the burly figure opposite affix his signature to the entry of ten new names registered in the barrack log allocated to Castle Forbes.

"Rumors flying around that Mr. Larnach has become vindictive since that incident with one of your daughters, James?" Mudie winced at the criticism, unhappy that knowledge of his domestic affairs had come to the attention of the authorities in Sydney.

"Anyway, why did you choose this little lot of felons?" continued the sergeant.

"15-minute interview is all I need. I can tell most times which ones will be any good. I look for experience in a useful trade, farming, smithy, sawyer, and mechanic. Any comments on that list of names?" inquired Mudie, changing the subject.

"Mostly harmless. This one seems a bit simple though. He did a bit of farming, I believe, in Essex, but that was a long time ago. Resigned to his fate I think, but he can read a little and sign his name. Don't know if he can write, and I haven't had to flog him yet," said the ex-army sergeant, indicating the last name on the list. Mudie leant forward and read the name upside down.

"Aye, I've just interviewed him; interesting story. Interesting name too."

"It is. He said to me he wanted to change his name from Magwitch to Provis after all the gaolers he has known."

"I think he means Provost," volunteered Mudie. "From Essex you say, because I already have a few from there. One in particular is a big problem. Anthony Hitchcock. They call him Hath and it seems as if he has sympathy from the other convicts. Worse is that he's become the ringleader of all the troubles. Always being flogged. Won't work, and keeps on putting the others up to mischief." Mudie went into detail about various incidents and the relationship Hath had with other convicts.

Chapter 41

Leaving the overseer to load the bullock cart with provisions and return via the inland road through Wiseman's Ferry, Mudie, with the assistance of one uniformed police officer, had opted to return by sea and take the steamship ferry from Sydney Cove to Morpeth. The sailing took a little over three days, including loading, but was a lot quicker than the inland route.

"The barn at the back will do just nicely," replied Mudie, as he checked in with his ten new convicts at Molly Morgan's Inn in Maitland. The party had left Sydney barracks a little under a week ago and, tomorrow, would finish the final leg of the journey back to Castle Forbes.

"And two separate rooms for yourself and the nice officer," suggested Molly Morgan, always respectful of the law. Wearing an unusually rich gypsy outfit, Molly Morgan ushered the two gentlemen to their respective rooms and slipped out back to inspect the latest arrival of convicts. Magwitch had seated himself in the far corner of the barn and was watching the door as she entered. He was instantly struck by Molly Morgan's appearance. His mind flashed back to that fateful day on Epsom Downs and the enormity of the events that had taken place since then. He studied her facial features and what little he could make of her frame beneath her bulky clothing. He compared her to his Gypsy Molly back home.

"Six inches taller and a couple of decades older, but nevertheless, she makes the same impression," he mused, as she strolled around, making her acquaintance of those who were interested.

"Does yous tell fortunes?" quizzed Magwitch as she passed. Molly Morgan stopped dead in her tracks.

"And who is it that might be asking?" she remarked, aware that they were all just starting their transportation sentences; hers, still vivid in her memory. A minimum of seven, or maybe 14 years each. In Magwitch's case, life.

"Abel Magwitch, but yous can call me Provis," replied Magwitch, sitting up straight.

"That's an odd name," said Molly Morgan.

"Special name," said Magwitch. "Chose it on the ship." Molly Morgan nodded.

"Cross my palm with silver if you want to know your fortune, luvy." Magwitch reached into his tatty, slop clothing and fished for a penny. Molly Morgan's eyes flashed whilst reaching for the small set of well-used Tarot cards hidden deep in her apron. "Funny-looking bit of silver," she said sarcastically. "But then, I suppose beggars can't be choosers." Still muttering, she took the coin and handed the deck of cards to Magwitch. "Shuffle; cut the cards, and place the deck back on the windowsill." Magwitch obliged.

"Wot's your name, ma'am?" asked Magwitch, still shuffling.

"Molly Morgan."

"Gord bless me soul," replied Magwitch, shocked at the similarity.

"I knew another Molly in England. A gypsy like yous. Went by the name of Molly Ingram," volunteered Magwitch. Still blinking with surprise, he placed the cards on the hardwood window ledge.

"Well, did you now, luv?" said Molly Morgan sarcastically. "Now, spread the cards out along the sill, choose one, and hand it to me face down."

"Only one? Gypsy Molly let me do three cards."

"That's all you gets for a penny, luv." Magwitch's thick, calloused fingers clumsily pushed the sticky cards along the windowsill, one card stuck ominously to the side of his thick thumb. He panicked and quickly withdrew his hand, dragging the card with it clumsily, allowing it to fall to the rough planking on the floor of the barn. He looked down. Lying face down, the card hid his future.

"There now, the cards have made the decision for you," commented Molly Morgan with a cynical half smile. Molly Morgan bent down and turned the card to reveal the Hermit, a wise, old man holding a lamp emerging from a sinister-looking cave. "It's time to withdraw far from all the people you have been associated with and consider yourself for once." Molly Morgan was deadly serious. Magwitch shuddered at the interpretation. Again, his mind flashed back to Gypsy Molly on Epsom Downs.

"Not a new beginning? Something different from what you have been doing for the past years," concluded Molly Morgan.

"So it could be a new beginning?"

"It says you should keep yourself to yourself," she replied, grabbing the deck of Tarot cards and walking away towards the door.

"That'll be up to the boss." Molly Morgan swung round.

"No, Provis, it will be up to you if you want to follow your destiny." Molly Morgan reached the door and was gone.

Chapter 42

Held in both hands, Mudie's eyes focused on the paper bearing General Sir Ralph Darling's signature.

"Power at last," said Mudie aloud in his home office at Castle Forbes.

"Now, I can legally deliver control and punishment and bring these wretched felons into line. We all need protection in Hunters river district." Mudie re-read the missive from the Colonial Secretary's office. "I have always agreed with Darling's stringent philosophies, and I'm the man to deliver it in the Hunter district." Mudie reached for the quill and wrote his acceptance of the appointment of Justice of the Peace and Magistrate in Maitland. Having signed his reply, he replaced the quill, blotted the ink, and tucked the letter into its official envelope. He sat back in his chair and considered his next move, his thoughts interrupted by a heavy knock on the door. Without waiting for a response, John Larnach walked straight in.

"Ah, John, pleased you have come."

"Well, you won't be too pleased with what I have to say," said Larnach, having just returned from his disciplinary meeting with his overseers down at the convicts' quarters.

"Let me tell you my news first then." Proudly, Mudie briefed him on his new appointment.

"Great news," agreed Larnach, "but I'm afraid I have to dampen your spirits by reporting on the latest situation with the convicts. Since the arrival of that last scruffy lot of felons, we have a headcount of 93, with additional brought in for the harvest of another 30, most of whom have been hired from government road gangs."

"So, what's wrong with that, John?"

"The rumor came from Ben Cribb."

"What rumor?" Mudie's jovial temperament changed to one of concern.

"Ben overheard one of Hath's gang whispering about a mutiny. This time, I'm sure they're plotting something."

"Aye, laddie," sighed Mudie, sick to death of the negative reports from Larnach and the problems with trying to keep control so far from Sydney. For over a decade, the number of convicts who had completed their time, or receiving Tickets-of-Leave for good behaviour, or in many instances finishing their time receiving Conditional-Pardons, were reaching near epidemic proportions. These time-served, emancipated convicts were beginning to challenge the entire system of governance in the penal colony.

"I thought that General Darling had been right when he introduced, *Trial-by-Jury*, but I'm not so sure now. It's stupid to believe that criminals, even though they have been pardoned, could act as fair jurors. Shouldn't be allowed, men with a criminal record, adjudicating for a convict friend. And now, we have convicts gloating about getting away with what should be a second conviction and further transportation.

"Men under custody are swamping the rule of law and jeopardising the farms and businesses developed by the free settlers who have invested their capital and time under the direction of both Governors Brisbane and Darling. A few extra police have been provided, but still nothing to that which is required in this huge, open expanse," Mudie continued, working himself into a frustrated tirade and not giving Larnach a chance to make his recommendation. He had noted that whilst the majority of convicts would toe-the-line, there was always that ten to 15 per cent of no hopers. Numerous gangs of criminal bushrangers formed by bitter absentees who absconded the minute they saw a chance to run away, free to roam the outlying districts, causing highway robbery, murder, rape, arson, and looting.

"Good job they brought in the Bush Rangers Act," responded Larnach, enjoying the fact that summary judgment for offenders convicted through the Supreme Court was now enshrined in law delivering the death penalty within 24 hours.

"Is it imminent?" asked Mudie, thankful that he had introduced his dogs, the Newfoundlanders, to raise the alarm at the approach of gangs. The dogs provided an early warning system, making it possible to provide protection to the family. But, away from the farmhouses, his four-thousand-acre farm was becoming increasingly impossible to police without help from Sydney.

"I'm not sure. The worst is that Hath. You know him, late 30s and treacherous. Feels nothing for others. I've had him flogged more times than I can remember, along with his hardened mates, and I've tried solitary and worked them in irons, but he keeps at it. He hates you and me and the other overseers. Hates anyone who represents authority. James Reilly's the same, skinny, Irish type, who acts as if he's Hath's righthand man."

"Aye, John." Mudie stood from behind his desk and paced up and down. "I'm well-aware of them, but keep on. Nothing we can do but to give punishment. We can't send them back once they are assigned unless they are convicted of another serious crime, then we could send them to Norfolk Island for good."

"Then they would know how kind I've been," said Larnach, laughing, enjoying the thought of the punishment meted out over there. Hard labour in heavy irons, and sodomy, and bread and water, and daily floggings, and hanging for attempted gaol-breaks. "I'm a saint in comparison," sneered Larnach sarcastically, relishing his power and new position as partner of Castle Forbes.

Chapter 43

Within a week of his arrival at Castle Forbes, Magwitch was dispatched to the high pasture to care for the new flock of Merino sheep. Larnach had threatened him with 50 lashes for any sheep found missing or dead. His simple brief was to shepherd, to keep out of trouble, and fend for himself beyond his rations which would be issued fortnightly. His biggest problem was drinking water. The relief would arrive on horseback with provisions and then check the number of sheep.

For once in his life, Magwitch had time to relax and think. Carefully removing his clay pipe from his jacket pocket and, having slipped through the lining, he reached deeper into the folds for the plug of tobacco and penknife, sat back, and leisurely shaved a few slices of rich, dark tobacco and loaded the bowl. His thumb rested to the side of the face of Queen Victoria cast into the front of the clay bowl; the pipe-maker's snub to Her Majesty who detested the habit of smoking. Magwitch sucked peacefully, drawing the flame through the tobacco. He thought back to his early days as a labouring farmhand in Essex and then to his earlier troubles. He chuckled at the little bit of money he had made through that body-snatching episode for Dr. Emmett. His mood darkened as he recalled the mistake he had made sleeping with Gypsy Madonna in the barn and, worse, the reaction when Gypsy Molly had discovered. He groaned aloud as he recounted her murderous threat to kill his little Estella.

"Gord, she'd said for to kill 'er child?" Magwitch groaned at his stupidity. He sucked at his pipe, pondering whether or not it had happened. "And if she'd dunit, why was no little girl's body for to see? Wot of a police enquiry?" Unbearable thoughts grew in his mind.

"How stupid for to do work for that swine, Compeyson. Low like a snake. He's the cause of the troubles. Why me? For wot? Just for to work and for to keeps the roof o'er me 'ead. Then I lose a bootiful lady wife who loves me?" Magwitch scratched at his rough jaw and, frowning as he thought, he thought some more. From nowhere, a family of kookaburras landed in the tree above and started their chorus. Magwitch looked up, mesmerised at the wonders of this new country.

"Well, 'ere I am for all that, alone in the hills, looking after sheeps. Maybe that's wot Molly Morgan's card meant. And wot of little Pip? He'd be about eight, maybe nine years now. He's the one who saved me, and he's the only one left who'll share in my future. They say this is the 'Land of Promise' for the likes o' me. Well, if I makes any money, I'll make him my gentleman. There'll be no dust on his boots, and he'll have the finest in London money can buy. And maybe, one day, 'e'll come to see me here. No, not like this, 'cause he mustn't see me like this. Anyways, 'e'll never find me up here, miles from nowhere."

Chapter 44

The stout walls of the first court in Maitland were 20-feet wide by 43-feet long, built of 14-inch thick brickwork and whitewashed. The courtroom itself took up two-thirds of the floor space from the four-foot six-inch wide entrance to the raised platform, at the back of which, the two-inch thick hardwood paneled wall was curved. At the rear of the platform, two, polished, mahogany doors hung on brass butt hinges, providing access to the magistrate's chamber on the left and the jury room on the right. Only the magistrate's room had a rear exit.

All ceilings had been constructed in lathe and plaster and whitewashed. Although late afternoon, autumnal sunlight streamed in through the four, cedar, casement windows along each side of the building, Magistrate James Mudie still maintained a gentle glow from his oil lamp. He perused the papers before him in readiness to brief the alternate magistrate due in shortly. He turned the pages of the list of Castle Forbes's felons to be tried in the morning. Written in his own hand, he ran his eye down the list. Quietly, he uttered each felon's name and their crime.

"James Reilly and John Perry were both charged with drunkenness. David Jones was charged with insubordination and swearing at the overseer. James Ryan had been absent without permission and caught cohabiting with a woman without permission. Maybe I can understand that, but as for John Poole, Singleton's worst, caught in the act of an unnatural crime. Sickening." Mudie sighed at the thought, and then he came to the next name.

"Anthony Hitchcock, alias Hath, the ringleader, and without doubt, the worst of the bunch, caught with other convicts at a secret meeting up at the Castle Forbes's windmill after work. They had been in possession of illegal alcohol, apparently the proceeds of the sale of Castle Forbes's grain." Mudie closed the file as he heard his colleague enter the courtroom.

Chapter 45

Christmas Eve saw the relief arrive and instruct Magwitch to return to Castle Forbes. In the stifling heat, Magwitch mounted the spare horse and made his way down the rocky hillside. The horse's hooves skidded on the loose stones as he descended into the valley. He looked up, shading his eyes from the merciless midday sun. "Now I know wot they meant in England by blue blazes. But I remembers another Christmas Eve when I 'ad them blue freezes, gord, that savage cold on them marshes." Magwitch leant down and rubbed his scarred ankle where he had filed away the leg iron. "Seems a lifetime ago," he muttered to himself.

He removed his tatty straw hat and wiped the dam of perspiration trapped beneath the cotton band with his torn sleeve, his balding head offering no resistance. He reined in his mount and surveyed the expanse before him. Thousands of acres of wheat, barley, oats, and vegetables, ready for harvest. To his left, he could see numerous Friesian cattle grazing leisurely, prompting him to wonder what his next role would be. He had heard the scary rumours about Larnach and that Mudie was too preoccupied with his new magisterial position in Maitland to take notice of the complaints.

Magwitch vowed to keep on the right side. He spotted the homestead and distinguished the outline of the huts housing the convicts. With a higher roof, the big barn, where he should report before nightfall, was more prominent and located at the rear of the compound. It was dusk when he arrived, just in time for the muster. He breathed a sigh of relief to find he was on the roll. He heard his name called by the overseer just as he dismounted.

"Here," Magwitch shouted, as a last-minute thought. George Frost looked up at him, nodded in acceptance, and applied a mark next to the name. Magwitch stood to the back of the other convicts, too many to count. They shuffled in the dust. Some fidgeted around, disinterested once their name had been called out. His eyes wandered from face to face, his presence hardly noticed. He screwed his dust-laden eyes towards the punishment triangle where a man hung limp from the leather thongs.

"Wot did he do?" he whispered to the convict nearest.

"Dunno. He was like that when I got here."

"Is he livin'?" asked Magwitch.

"Dunno. What's it to you?"

"Gord 'elp 'im."

"Hey, you. Shut up. Watch and listen," shouted Larnach. Magwitch quickly dropped his eyes to the ground. The muster complete, Larnach stepped over to the triangle, pulled his knife, and cut the thongs tying the man on the legs of the punishment triangle. The convict groaned as he hit the dry ground. Another convict stepped forward and chucked a pail of water over the limp body. The body jerked in shock. Two more convicts stepped forwards and picked the man up, one holding his arms, the other, the legs. They dragged him into the barn.

Slowly, the group of convicts dissipated. Magwitch quietly made his way into the barn. Visibility was poor inside, but he identified a spare hammock and proceeded to place his few possessions underneath. He slipped back outside and down to Mudies Creek for a wash before turning in. He peered through the long grass on the bank of the creek and thought he recognised one of the men. He froze, too late to crouch down. He observed the back of another, covered in multiple slashes, the skin having healed and welded itself to a piece of protruding backbone.

"Gord Jesus. It's 'im from Essex," said Magwitch under his breath. Somehow aware of the scrutiny, the man turned to face him.

"It's 'im all right, bit bigger than me, ruddy 'n fair, more hair, and that scar 'e got when they chased 'im in Chatham docks." Magwitch's mind flashed back, recalling the disposal of the swag from Compeyson's burglaries. He wanted to turn and run. Put as much distance between them as possible, but it was too late. Reluctantly, he walked over to the other men.

"Well, well, well, what have we here?" taunted Hath, eager to recruit Magwitch into his rotten little band.

"Pretend I'm not 'ere," replied Magwitch, attempting to keep himself to himself as he jumped into the creek for a long-needed wash.

"Ah, but you is 'ere, old chap."

"I'm a different person, Hath. And my new name is Provis," replied Magwitch, squatting down to wash his face in the creek water.

"We'll see about that." Hath walked over to Magwitch and pushed him backwards onto the bank of the creek.

"Wot yous do that for?" grumbled Magwitch. Attempting to ignore the situation, he turned his back and scrambled out of the creek.

"Now what the hell's going on, Hath?" shouted Frost from the top of the bank.

"Nothing, least nothing to concern you," replied Hath rudely.

"Lights out in half an hour, don't be at large after that, or you know what's coming," threatened Frost. Hath cursed, gave a deep, deliberate snark and spat tobacco-saturated sputum into the crystal-clear creek water. Magwitch quickly excused himself and scurried back to the barn. Safely inside, he held his breath whilst watching Hath through the vertical planking until he had finished talking with Frost. He breathed a sigh of relief as Hath arrived back at the convict quarters with the rest of his gang and disappeared into one of the smaller huts. "Thank gord for small mercies. Don't want to get tangled with 'im again."

Magwitch was awake long before the first bell. Eyes and ears conscious of his new surroundings as other convicts snored and tossed in their sleep. He screwed around in the hammock to observe the faint glow in the east; almost immediately, he heard the five rings from the homestead bell heralding one hour till work. He didn't have any. At least, he had yet to be assigned to his new duty. Over a year up in the high pastures, with only a few trips down to the farm had left Magwitch ignorant of the aggressive build-up of attitudes of the convict community and the developing political intrigue. Anyway, he wasn't interested in their petty squabbles; the whispered conversation between the other convicts in the barn after lights out having given him the low-down. He swung his legs over the side of the hammock, grabbed his washing things, and made his way in the dawning light to Mudies Creek. He was the first there. Kneeling, he scrubbed his face and hands and armpits, then with cupped hands, threw water over his back and chest, toweling down with an old piece of hessian saved especially for ablutions.

Eleven of them emerged from Hath's hut, their sullen faces setting the wind-up Magwitch, forcing him to change direction and skirt around the back of the barn. Mangles, the overseer, was already doing the count as he entered the barn.

"Ah, there you are. Clean bugger, eh?" scoffed Mangles, applying a mark to the side of Magwitch's name. The other convicts began to disperse to the creek and the latrines. "Be quick and get to your work. 20 minutes," shouted Mangles after them. "Now, Magwitch, you are to report to Mr. Larnach at the house straight after the bell to commence the day's work. A bell will also sound at nine o'clock, and you will be back for breakfast. Is that clear?"

"That be right, boss. Do you know what Mr. Larnach wants me to do?"

"Just report after the bell, that's all I know, and no more questions. Questions get trouble. Just say yes and be humble, or it'll be the lash for you." Magwitch's eyes crossed to the heavy, wooden, three-sided, pyramidal triangle; iron rings on all three legs from which hung stout, leather strops to secure the convict whilst the scourge was administered. Mangles noticed the anxiety in Magwitch's eyes.

"That's Larnach's instrument of discipline. After lashing, he'll have salt chucked on and then leave you to bake in the afternoon sun. No water, of course." Magwitch shuddered. He had received the birch in England, but nothing approaching this sadistic punishment. He had heard the rumours of men receiving 300 lashes before passing out and, again, the sight of the man's back at the creek yesterday and that one piece of his white backbone sticking through as if he had been born like it.

No-legs-Lennie, the nickname he gained after having had both legs amputated to save his life, slid across the deck on his leather skid-tray and placed his hand on the bell-cord while Magwitch waited at a discrete distance from Larnach's office.

Located some 100 yards from the homestead, the office was basic consisting of vertical planking, barn door, and a gable roof. In the corner was an open fireplace built in stone, with a stone chimney exiting through the rear of the hut, and two casement side-windows through which Larnach could observe the fenced compound and convict quarters. The ground was worn through foot traffic and dust during the long hot summers. He had strategically located guards to monitor the 50 odd convicts who occupied the buildings. The rest of the convicts were accommodated further afield in temporary quarters nearer their places of work. The bell struck just as the orange sun cleared the horizon in the east. In fear and trepidation, Magwitch walked brusquely to the office, stepped up the two wooden steps, crossed the heavy planking of the deck, and knocked gently on the closed door.

"Yes."

"Tis Provis, guv'nor," replied Magwitch sheepishly.

"You mean Magwitch. Enter," growled the guttural Scottish accent from within.

"Er, sorry, sir. Magwitch, sir. Asked to report this morning, sir." Magwitch stood to attention in front of the desk, behind which sat Larnach prodding indiscriminately, with his sheath knife at the ridged grain in the top of the desk.

"What do you know about cattle?" demanded Larnach.

"Didn't know much about sheep 'til you trusted me in the pastures," replied Magwitch with a quizzical expression.

"Aye, that may be so, but this is different."

"Beggin' yourn pardon, sir?"

"Aye, man, but you lost not a sheep and worked alone without complaint, so the Major and I have decided to put you in charge of a small herd of experimental cattle." Larnach raised his knifed hand and drove the blade vertically into the top of the desk, the ivory handle wobbled as he removed his fist. He stood and walked to the sidewall of the hut. Picking up his silver-tipped Black-Watch cane, he pointed to the map on the wall and the boundaries of Castle Forbes.

"You have spent the last year in this area here, but on the other side of the hill is a new pasture, specially fenced. This blue line is a small spring that feeds into Mudies Creek." Magwitch nodded, recognising the area in which he had attended his flock. "Good, so you can read maps too."

"Well, sir, not exactly, sir, but I can recognise the hills and the rivers and the buildings," replied Magwitch, becoming more relaxed.

"What do you know about coolies?"

"Beggin' yourn pardon, sir, but is that a prison, sir, wot we call the slammer, sir?" Larnach burst out laughing and returned to his seat. Grabbing the handle of the knife, he wrenched the blade from the desktop and looked harshly back at Magwitch.

"So you dunna ken, man. It's an Indian worker, fool!"

"Oh, er, sorry, sir. I didn't know, sir."

"Well, you know now, and next month, you and two other convicts, Eads, and our head stockman, will travel with Major Mudie to the steamship port of Morpeth to take delivery of the experimental-horned cattle shipped from Calcutta. Four coolies who are travelling with the herd and have worked with the breed in Calcutta will help you drive the herd back to Castle Forbes. Do you have any questions?"

"No, sir, and thank you, sir."

"Aye, you surprise me, Magwitch. No questions, aye," said Larnach sarcastically.

"Er, well, sir, er, I do 'ave one, sir. When would I meet Mr. Eads, sir, and the 'ead stockman, sir?"

"That's better, man. Start thinking and you may just keep out of trouble. Now, go and report to overseer Frost."

A further three weeks passed during which time Magwitch was exposed to cattle management at Castle Forbes. The plan was made including a practice drive to the collection point at the Morpeth wharf and a meeting with the Sikh, the Indian trader responsible for concluding the financial exchange. Packing his small case with a change of clothing, shaving tackle, and the money to be exchanged for the cattle on the morning of departure, Mudie was disturbed by a heavy knock on the front door of the homestead.

"Magwitch wishes to speak with you urgently, sir," announced the maid, Mary Stewart, having responded and opened the front door.

"I'll be there when I'm ready, Mary. Tell him to wait on the deck," snapped Mudie, irritated that a convict should have the audacity to approach the homestead.

"What the hell is it, Magwitch?" said Mudie, storming out to the front deck.

"It's Eads, sir; 'es gorn, sir."

"What?"

"Er, 'es gorn; disappeared, sir, went last night with two others, sir, their hammocks were empty when I woke, sir."

"Why the hell didn't you say so earlier?" he challenged.

"Mary." Mudie shouted over his shoulder.

"Go and fetch Mangles and tell him to sound the alarm." Mary ran from the kitchen; her bare feet padded across the deck and descended the steps onto the dusty ground.

"Er, didn't know earlier, sir, thought they were down washing in the creek, sir."

"Aye, all right, all right, stop whining; it's not your fault," replied Mudie. "Now, go and tell Mangles to allocate another cattleman. Better still, tell Mangles to get up here right away. We must leave within the hour, and he's to be the replacement."

"Yes, sir, certainly, sir." Magwitch turned and ran back to get his horse, mounted, and galloped off to find overseer, Mangles. Over an hour late, Mudie's party left for Morpeth and made haste to catch up the time.

Breathless and steaming after nearly an hour's ride from the farm, the horses began flagging. They slowed as they entered the narrow track of road, heavily flanked by the trees and undergrowth just before Greta village. Rounding the bend at a trot, there, sprawled on the left side of the road, his head hidden by a clump of long grass, lay a man dressed in slop clothing. The rig's driver reined in the horses; the wheels stopping a few feet past the man's booted feet.

"What in heaven's name has happened to him? Is he dead?" said Mudie, leaning over the left side of the rig. "Magwitch, get down and see if he's alive."

"God almighty, it's a trap," shouted Mangles, hearing the undergrowth snapping on the other side of the road. Mudie swung round to be confronted by a scruffy convict on horseback, his face concealed by a red and white scarf. Mudie stared down the twin barrels of two flintlock pistols. "What the hell do you think you're up to?" Mudie challenged. "Highway robbery is a hanging offence!"

"Only if you get caught," scoffed the convict who had been lying on the edge of the road. He stood up, brushing himself off as he approached the side of the rig.

"It's Eads, sir," called Magwitch from the back of the rig, recognising the voice behind the scarf. Surprised at the identification, Mudie looked back at Magwitch for confirmation.

"That's enough talking. Now get out of the rig," instructed Eads, reaching for the harness of the lead horse, preventing the team from galloping off. In an attempt to conceal it, Mudie slid his small case under the bench seat. Mangles and the driver climbed down and stood to the side of the rig.

"What's that?" challenged Eads.

"What's what?" growled Mudie, furious at the bushrangers. Eads waved the barrel of his pistol at the rig.

"That case."

"What case?" replied Mudie obstinately, still seated in the rig. Eads stood in his stirrups to see the case hidden beneath the seat. He let go of the rig harness and spurred his mount forwards to get a closer look. "Get that case."

The other bushranger pushed Magwitch backwards and grabbed the side of the rig, stepped on the footplate and mounted. Shoving Mudie in the chest, he grabbed the handle of the case. The skittish horses fidgeted. Eads backed up to regain the harness. Magwitch moved surreptitiously to the front of the rig. Seeing his chance, he ducked in front of the horses and flew at Eads, grabbing him by the leg. Eads cursed, his horse bucking at the action, disturbing the rider. Magwitch yanked harder, dragging Eads from the saddle. Off balance, Eads pointed his cocked pistol at Magwitch's neck and fired at point blank range. In the commotion, Mangles leapt across the tray of the rig, grabbing the throat of the other bushranger, his right fist punching him on the temple. The convict released the case as he fell backwards, dropping to the ground instantly. The bullet creased Magwitch's face as he pulled Eads to the ground. Blood gushing from his torn cheek, Magwitch struggled to his feet, punching Eads in the throat, knocking him to the ground again before he could regain his feet. Mudie grappled for the reins and struggled to hold the team of horses from bolting. The second bushranger was dead, his temple crushed from the blow inflicted by Mangles. Minutes later, Mudie was back in control, the knuckles of his right hand bleeding.

"Good work, Magwitch."

"Tis me job, Major," said Magwitch, pleased to receive the compliment.

"Driver, you and Mangles tie that Eads up and get him loaded on the rig," instructed Mudie. "And get back up here. Leave the other one to the vultures. We have some sacred Hindu cattle to bring home."

Chapter 46

The Sikh was a tall, slender man, supporting a tightly wrapped turban. Jewelled at the centre with a single large ruby set in gold filigree, his turban rose to a frontal peak, beneath which shone bright intelligent eyes and distinguished facial features. His English was near perfect, save his accented West-Bengalian tongue, indicating a British education and an understanding of that eloquent Anglo-Indian culture of the *'Venice of the East,'* Calcutta.

The 12 cows and one bull had already been disembarked from the steam-assisted sailing vessel, from the centre of which protruded a vertical funnel still discharging wisps of smoke from the coal-fired boilers buried in the depths of the ship's hull. Grazing lazily on the vacant piece of land opposite the J. Campbell and Co. stores in Morpeth, the cows seemed healthy and lively, considering their five-week sea voyage. The most striking feature was their skinny, almost-emaciated bodies, emphasising the span of the grand U-shaped horns thrusting away from their heads. Healthy wet noses beneath hazel-brown eyes snuffled amongst the dew-damp grass while teeth chomped and plucked at the tender green shoots. An exaggerated hump appeared above the bony shoulder blades and there was a distinct sag to the backbone, beneath which hung an ample underbelly and udders capable of sustaining volumes of rich, creamy milk. Musky-brown in colour and distinguished by a white pencil-wide trim, their fine-haired coats added an air of majesty to the sacred beasts. The bull was different, highly spirited, and inquisitive. He had been penned separately; his head rising every time he bellowed for his ladies. He snuffled and trumpeted in frustration.

"They're called *'Singhai'* in Hindi," said the Sikh. Mudie smiled.

"Horned cattle is far more simple." They shook hands as the Sikh gave a gentle bow, his eyes dropped to focus on the floor in respect for the buyer.

Chapter 47

Infested with rats beneath the rough-sawn floor planking, the hut that housed Hath and his gang was located at the side and towards the rear of the group of convict's quarters at Castle Forbes. For the past year, debris from stolen food and empty bottles of illicit alcohol, mostly rum and gin, had been disposed of under the floor through the removal of half-a-dozen, short floor planks at the end of the solitary room. Beneath another set of short, loose planks, to the side of the stone foundation built to support the cylindrical, cast-iron, wood-burning stove, they had secreted their stash of full bottles. Each time there was a trip to Maitland, one convict would be nominated to replenish stocks from any one of the three sly-grogshops along the heavily rutted road.

Rats had bred in profusion and when trapped and gutted, would be roasted in their furry jackets on a makeshift iron spit pushed through the front-loading door of the stove. The furthest end of the spit would be supported on a metal hook suspended from one of the rear bolts of the cylinder, whilst the front end of the spit rested on the cast-iron aperture. Turning constantly, the rat took less than 12 minutes to cook through. When ready, the spit was removed from the heat, the charred, furry skin was peeled back revealing well-done flesh, augmenting their meagre protein supply. Tonight, they grilled three at a time, and, exhausted after each day's work in the fields, the 11 convicts lay on their wretched beds, complaining to each other. They brewed discontent and treachery as they spoke in lowered tones for fear of being overheard by the roving night watchman, a convict specially selected and bribed by the overseer for informing on his mates.

Sleep evaded them this night, clear starlit yet ink-black sky heralded a cold night, but winter would soon give way to spring. In its second quadrant, the silvery light of the clear spring moon threw shadows from the group of huts across the rough grass. Shrubs and bushes had been mostly cleared to a distance of a hundred yards from the camp. Over an hour had passed since the familiar call of 'lights-out,' but most failed to drift into their usual fatigued sleep.

Unconcerned, David Jones watched the shadow of a rat, the size of a jam jar, scurry across the top of the horizontal transom of the thick roof truss and reach the corner; its feet spanned the corner planking as it descended head first down to the floor and squeezed through the enlarged knot-hole in the floor. Ryan, the current rum gofer, lay on his belly, yesterday's flogging making it impossible to get a night's sleep. He lay groaning, the crusting salt applied to his back, aggravating the wounds. He struggled to turn on his makeshift scratcher, the straw and horse-hair mattress seemed to move with the infestation of fleas and bugs. He propped himself up on his left elbow and looked out through the cracks in the buckled vertical planking. Only 17, Ryan thought back to the stupidity of events that had taken place in Britain leading to his capture and transportation over two years ago.

"You awake?" whispered Hath.

"Yeah," groaned Ryan.

"So am I," muttered Jones from the other end of the hut.

"Shhhhh. Get to sleep," muttered another voice. The wood-burning stove had all but died whilst the sound of boots crunching on the dry ground outside floated into ears within. The door flew open, followed by a fist, below which swung an oil lantern, thrusting light into the gloom.

"Wanting another flogging in the morning, is it, then?" threatened the overseer. "Now get some sleep, you're going to need it." The overseer scoffed as he exited and slammed the door behind him. All awake, they listened to the diminishing sound of gravel crunching as the raised steel nails on the leather-soled boots ground their way over to the far side of the compound.

"That'll be right," growled Hath from his dark corner at the back of the hut.

"Up yours," cursed James Reilly and John Perry, now also wide awake.

"I'm getting out of here. Next chance I get," announced David Jones.

Hath sat up and listened to the banter; the complaints continued, becoming more aggressive. He swung his legs from his bed and crawled to the loose boards, carefully removed two, and placed them to the side. Lying on his stomach, he dropped his shoulder, pushing his arm beneath. He groped in the darkness beneath the boards until his gnarled fingers brushed the bottle. Clutching it by the neck, he retrieved the rum, rolled on his side and took a healthy swig and passed it on. Watching the silhouette of the bottle progress around the hut, he knelt down, dropped his hand into the dark hole again, and grabbed a second bottle. The cork squeaked as he twisted it out with his teeth and spat it across the room. After taking another swig, he dragged the back of his hand across his stubbled face.

"What's wrong with tonight?" growled Hath.

"Be Jesus," blasphemed Perry. "They'll hang us for sure."

"No worse than what's happening to us now if we stay."

"I'm game," groaned Ryan. "Just look at me."

"So are we," came three more voices, their owners sitting up, excited at the prospect of absconding *en masse*. Hath grinned to himself in the darkness and then peered out through a knot in the vertical planking.

"Give it another hour. One hour after midnight. The quarter moon will have moved away and it will be darker. The guard'll probably be asleep."

"What do we do for horses?" whispered Perry.

"Leave the compound to the north, circle around to the paddock on the far side of the homestead," replied Hath, taking another heavy swig of rum and passing the bottle to Ryan, the scabbing slashes to his back cracking with the movement. Thin trickles of blood and puss began to ooze from the wounds on his exposed back.

"Halters and saddles?" muttered Jones.

"Who the hell needs saddles? And there's rope hanging up on the fence at the back," argued Hath. "Reilly, over here. Use my spare knife and go cut 40 yards of the stuff. Bring it back here."

"Gord, Hath, why me?"

"'Cause you're nearest, mate! Now, go before that night-watch returns." Reilly took a final swig of rum then tiptoed to the door. He placed his hand on the latch and pressed down, muffling the clank with his other hand. The door squeaked as Reilly slunk out and made his way across to the barbed-wire fencing. The distance was further than he remembered, but the darkness obscured his passage.

He ducked between the scattered huts and pausing, looked over his shoulder at the homestead up on the hill, Rosemont, the home of Emily and John Larnach, Major Mudie's eldest daughter and husband. His eyes scanned the vast property and then back to his pathetic refuge. He advanced further, stopping to catch his breath under the solitary bush 20 yards from the fence. His heart thumped in his ears and mouth, obliterating the imaginary night-watch boots that would surely raise the alarm. Four coils of hemp rope hung tantalisingly from the fence post.

"Bugger. No cover from here to the fence," muttered Reilly. He sat down to get his energy back; the rum having taken its toll. He looked up the hill again and focused on the homestead; a faint light came from one of the rooms.

"That Emily'll be feeding her brat. What's its name?" cursed Reilly. "William James Mudie Larnach. Christ, that little Scottish bigot sucking up to his father-in-law. Makes me wanna vomit." Hath reached into the stash and pulled a third bottle.

"What's keeping the fool?" growled Hath, eager to make the break. All 11 convicts made ready, packing their meagre possessions into individual cloth bundles knotted at the top. Hath removed the remaining bottles of gin and rum and handed them out. The rats continued gnawing, oblivious to the urgency above.

"Shhhhh," whispered Jones. "Watch is coming back." The boots were heard approaching the hut. They stopped outside. Breathlessly, they waited.

"Bloody fool don't come back now," mused Hath, his knife at the ready as he slid behind the door, ready to jump the night-watch. They waited and listened. So did the night-watch, his left ear poised within three inches of the door, curious that there was no snoring or the garbled nonsense of nightmares from within. He continued his rounds.

Crouching, Reilly made his decision. "Two coils should be enough, and cut them back in the hut." He looked around and then stealthily crawled to the fence line. He stood up, unhooked the two coils and crouched back down, steadying himself on the fence post.

"So far so good. Now, to get back." Reilly knew he shouldn't be talking to himself, especially out loud. "God, I could do with another swig of that rum," he muttered, as he turned and, dragging the coiled rope behind, crawled back to the cover of the bush. It took another half an hour to cut the rope and prepare the halters. All-consumed by his hatred of Castle Forbes, Hath took the lead. "Mudie and Larnach would pay." Bitterness blinded him to caution.

"Get caught as a bushranger, yous a box of dead meat, but so what? What future was there in this God forsaken place?" muttered Hath.

"What's the matter with you? Not coming, eh?"

"No, it's not that, Hath, but I don't want to die," replied David Jones, suddenly getting cold feet. "At least I don't want my sentence to be increased with another transportation to Norfolk Island. I've only got two years to go, then I get my Conditional-Pardon."

"In your dreams, laddie, in your dreams," goaded Hath. "And you can't stay behind, 'cause you know too much." The 11 bitter members of Hath's gang slid out of the hut and skirted the compound, slowly making their way over to the paddock.

"Must be 20 or more in there," whispered Perry to Hath, estimating the number of heads outlined above the paddock rail.

"Go in over the fence and secure your mounts," instructed Hath in a low, grating voice. The horses shuffled around at the sight of the men. A couple of horses neighed.

"Hush, my beauty," whispered Reilly, as he gently slid the rope halter on and swung himself up onto the back of the animal. Skittish hooves scuffled, creating a fine veil of dust to drift up into the night sky. They slowly mounted, presenting rounded-back silhouettes topped with salt-dry sweat hats and were ready for the signal.

"Open the gate," instructed Hath, his grating voice louder than before, disturbing the Newfoundland dogs dozing around the homestead. The barking became infectious. Lights turned on at the homestead.

"Drive all the horses out, including the spares. They'll panic and follow anyway. We have a long ride in front of us." Heels dug heavily into ribs, spurring the horses; the commotion delivering an escalation of barking. Seconds later, they galloped to freedom, chased by nine, black, Newfoundland dogs.

Chapter 48

Eads lay trussed up like a chicken on the back tray of the rig.

"Outspan the cattle at Molly Morgan's and the second night at Greta village," instructed Mudie from the front bench seat. "I'll deal with this character at court in the morning." Mudie looked angrily back at Eads.

"Yes, sir," acknowledged Magwitch, stroking one of the cows.

"Don't drive them hard either."

"No, sir."

"You're to stop for watering along the river at midday as well. Take the whole week to get back if necessary. I want the herd to be in prime condition when you reach Castle Forbes." The sepoys nodded and looked towards Magwitch.

"Yous can rely on me, sir," replied Magwitch, eager to prove his worth with his new charge. "I swears on my trusty book to yous, them cows'll have the best care from me. Gord strike me dead if I don't." Magwitch clutched his little, black, pocketbook. Mudie nodded in approval. They left for Castle Forbes at first light reaching Molly Morgan's early in the afternoon.

"Well, bless my soul," said Molly Morgan, as Magwitch appeared at the doorway of the inn.

"In charge, is it? The Major must be losing his mind." Magwitch strode up to the bar, delighted at the recognition. A confident smile appearing across his proud face; the gunshot wound in his cheek hidden beneath a week's stubble and his neck scarf.

"The Major knows a good man when he sees one."

"Didn't think he thought any convict could be good," chuckled Molly Morgan. "Now, what'll be your pleasure, hey?"

"Name's Provis, and I'll just have some coffee."

"It gets worse," scoffed Molly Morgan. "Turned over a new leaf, is it?"

"Let's just say that I's important, and I don't want to lose me sel' just yet." Still muttering, Molly Morgan turned to the rear shelf and put the dented kettle onto the hot stove.

"And what for those skinny Indians?"

"They'll have the same as me," replied Magwitch quickly, looking over his shoulder at the two sepoys who had come into the inn behind him. The kettle began to wobble, indicating the presence of boiling water, as steam burst from beneath the lid and the spout spat lumps of brown coffee-laden water, hissing the instant it hit the cast-iron stove beneath.

"Must be nearly three years," volunteered Molly Morgan whilst adding milk to the mugs of steaming coffee.

"It'll be three years later this year. See, I did more than a year in the high pasture," confirmed Magwitch, settling himself at the nearest table.

"You look well on it. The Major must be looking after you. Been flogged yet?" asked Molly Morgan as an afterthought, a frown appearing on her troubled brow.

"Seems everybody thinks we all get the flogging at Castle Forbes, but truth is the lazy ones get bad, then Larnach takes it out on them all the time. O' course the Major and his daughters can't forget that assault neiver. I dunno wot happened, so I dunno. Never did find the convict wot dunnit. The Major reckons he must 'ave came from Singleton's place. Before my time though, so I dunno nuffing." Magwitch indicated to the sepoys they should sit on the table over on the other side of the room.

"Can yous give a good man a minute?" Magwitch winked, inviting her to join him at the table.

"So you want another reading?" quizzed Molly Morgan, returning the wink as she moved from behind the bar to sit with Magwitch.

"Yous got it right last time, luv."

"All right, Provis, you know the rules. Cross my palm with silver, not copper, and I'll see what I can do." Molly Morgan reached under her apron and produced the well-worn Tarot cards. Magwitch dug deep into his baggy trouser pocket. He selected a silver three-penny piece and placed it on the outstretched palm.

"That's better, Provis," grinned Molly Morgan, remembering the old penny Magwitch had given her when they had first met. "You know the ropes, Provis."

"How many cards this time?" asked Magwitch innocently.

"12. Four cards a penny," replied Molly Morgan, smiling.

"Gor blimy. I get's treated proper this time."

"You're a special customer," jested Molly, handing over the deck. Before shuffling, Magwitch lent back on the stool, slipped his right hand inside his jacket, and withdrew his clay pipe. His left hand dug out his penknife and plug of tobacco from his lower jacket pocket. Deliberately, he scraped the clay bowl and then shaved two fresh slices of tobacco from the plug, rubbed them between his palms and re-loaded. Left elbow resting on the table, he leant forward and lit up. He shuffled, placed the deck in the center of the table, cut the deck with his left hand, and spread the cards sideways into a fan. He selected 12 cards, handing each one carefully across the table to Molly Morgan, who laid them face down in rows of four.

"This time," said Molly Morgan, pausing for thought, "we will look at your past, present, and future." Magwitch shuddered and took a deep drag on his pipe, inhaled, sucking in every last wisp of smoke, and then exhaled across the table.

"That stuff'll kill you," she said, criticising. Coughing a couple of times, she waved her hand to dispel the pollution.

"These first four show your past. Maybe a girlfriend or wife?" Molly Morgan pointed to Ace of Cups. "But you did a bad thing." Her finger moved to the Reversed Fool.

"The trouble on Hounslow Heath," mused Magwitch, his cheeks flushing. "Not as bad as wot she did to Madonna and little Estella."

"I see a woman here. She often wonders what happened to you." Molly Morgan continued with the interpretation of the cards, almost speaking as if she were Magwitch's mother.

"No chance of her finding that out," mused Magwitch, aware of the special interest Molly Morgan was taking.

"This card," she paused and pointed to the card. "The Emperor says she is working for a big Whig. Who could that be? Justice! See this. It's to do with justice. What's she to you, Provis?"

"Don't wanna say," said Magwitch, taking another panicky suck at his pipe.

"But you know 'im. This Whig, you know 'im," said Molly Morgan, excitedly tapping the card with her index finger and looking suspiciously back at Magwitch's questioning expression.

"Does I now?" replied Magwitch with a wry smile.

"Certainly do, luvy. And given where it sits in the spread, he's going to become involved again in your future, or something to do with your future." Magwitch took another heavy suck on his pipe; the tobacco glowing as oxygenated air forced its way through the leafy drug. His eyes watered at the thought of his little Estella and the image she conjured up in his mind.

"She would be about eight years old by now," mused Magwitch. From nowhere, he was again back on the marshes. Suddenly, he was drinking that fiery brandy in the freezing cold with his young saviour, Pip. He could taste the pork pie and that burning sensation as the brandy hit his empty stomach.

"A penny for your thoughts, Provis?"

"Just thinking. Just thinking," sighed Magwitch.

"And now, to your future, Provis. Yes, you are going to travel, but before you do, you have important work. It'll make you a rich man. Any ideas about that?" she inquired, a more inquisitive expression appearing across her ageing and wrinkled face.

"Only I must look after these special cows," said Magwitch.

"The Indians have the answer you need. Listen to them." Molly Morgan scanned the cards again. "Then there is a strange man who enters your life, and he brings change and security to you for the coming years. Lots of bright light and, yes, here it is, the Charioteer, that's him." Molly Morgan reached and turned the next card. "The Wheel of Fortune, excellent, that's what the Charioteer will bring to you, so be ready. But then it fades; you're at a crossroad." Molly Morgan began to frown as she turned the next card.

"The Broken Tower," she gasped. "But it's further into the future, a big change, a land you have known before, yet I see darkness, maybe death, so be careful. There will be trouble, but someone you knew in the past will see you again. Or you will see them again. A child, but he or she will be grown up by then."

"How far away?" asked Magwitch nervously.

"Maybe ten years," replied Molly Morgan with a serious expression and sadness to her voice. She gathered the cards up and re-stacked the deck and silently looked from the cards into Magwitch's questioning eyes.

"I'll be nearly 60," chuckled Magwitch, attempting to lighten the meeting. "May not even live that long," he sighed.

Chapter 49

The breathless horses stood tethered at the side of the dilapidated wooden building. They had ridden throughout the night, skirting other settlers' homesteads and eventually, billeting themselves in an old, disused, wool shed, three hours ride to the north of Hunters River.

Poole drew his knife and slunk into the shadows at the sound of the approaching riders. He had absconded from Singleton's farm close to Castle Forbes a week earlier and hidden in the disused shed. Hath was the first to dismount and enter.

"Well, looky here," smirked Hath at the sight of Poole cowering in the corner.

"Should announce yourself properly," sneered Poole, blinking through his one good eye, his left socket covered with a tatty, black, leather patch. "A man could get his throat cut out here."

"Agh, shut up, Poole, but not by the likes of you. Christ, what happened to your eye?" asked Hath in surprise.

"That bitch I screwed at the Major's place. Stuck her thumbnail in and buggered it up proper, she did," growled Poole.

"Old score to settle then?" grinned Hath. "Best join us 'cause we're going back to settle a few scores."

"Dinner?" jested Hath, pointing at the two stolen lambs bleating behind Poole.

Poole turned and drew his knife across each lamb's throat; the bleating turned to a gargle as the slain animals dropped to the floor. Lifting the twitching animals by the back legs, Poole led Hath out through the backdoor to find Ryan lighting the campfire. The wounds on his back from repeated flogging had opened during the ride and were bleeding profusely, but the excitement dulled the pain. John Perry prepared the coffee pot. Hath settled himself on a discarded rum barrel, bit down on the cork of his next bottle of rum and, aggressively twisting it out, threw his stubbled head back, snarked, and spat into the fire. He took two hearty swigs and handed the greenish bottle to Ryan.

"This'll help," said Hath. Ryan nodded. Taking the bottle from Hath, he stuck the neck in his mouth and upended it, swallowing two gulps of the fiery liquor.

"Yep, now this is what I calls freedom," smirked Hath as he loaded his clay pipe with tobacco. "But we're not finished here yet." Confused at Hath's last statement, Reilly looked up from the fire.

"Not by a long shot neither."

Both lambs slowly bled to death and minutes later, Poole had beheaded, skinned, and gutted the young animals. Next, he cut two stout pieces of bamboo from the overgrown bamboo growing behind the shed and made a single spit and two bamboo supports. A pair of rusty spurs acted as fulcrums to cradle the spit. He sharpened the bamboo spit with his dagger and drove it down the neck of the lamb, exiting below the rib cage, finally wiring it to the pelvic girdle with a rusted piece of barbed wire. He repeated the operation with the second animal, then loaded the spit onto the inverted stirrups and began to turn.

"As I see it, we have a score to settle with that Larnach. Mudie's away in Maitland, so it's as good a time as any," said Hath.

"What do you mean? Go back again?" asked Reilly, steadily turning the spit, fatty droplets of lamb dripped into the lengthened fire, causing bursts of flame.

"That's right," said Hath. "Pillage Castle Forbes first and get firearms from Mudie's homestead, and then attack Larnach's place. Kill him I reckon," continued Hath. "Whilst that old bugger, Major Mudie, is in Maitland on the Bench, convicting and demanding floggings for nothing. We can settle a few old scores. Torch the place too." Ryan listened intently, the pain in his back dissipating through rum. Nonchalantly, he pointed to the coffee pot steaming at the edge of the fire.

"Later," said Poole, preferring to quaff the rum. David Jones stayed on sentry duty, oblivious to the developing attack plan, but his nostrils savoured the wafts of roasting lamb. He salivated at the thought of a breakfast of succulent lamb, his first taste of freedom for years.

Chapter 50

Hungry for his next feed, baby William James Mudie Larnach kicked frantically at his swaddling clothes. Delicately woven by crochet fingers during Emily's confinement, the soft-wool blanket had all but been kicked off the makeshift cradle. Mildred, the nanny, bent forwards and rescued the little infant. Lifting him from his cot, she handed him gently to Emily, Mudie's eldest daughter. Strewn with baby toys either jettisoned from the cot or suspended overhead, the veranda to Larnach's Rosemont homestead had become the daytime nursery. Combined with natural elevation overlooking the Castle Forbes farm, the eight-foot wide deck with a pole railing and three steps down to the ground, provided its occupants with tranquility from the hustle and bustle of farming activity. Oscillating quietly in her creaking rocking chair, Emily began feeding whilst observing the activity down at Mudies Creek where a dozen or so convicts busied themselves washing the great volumes of wool sheared from the spring shearing.

Magwitch knocked on the backdoor and patiently waited. Receiving no answer, he quietly proceeded around the side of the house to the veranda.

"Excuse me, Miss Emily," said Magwitch as he rounded the kitchen corner of the homestead. Emily rapidly covered herself and little William.

"What are you doing here?" snapped Emily at the gross intrusion.

"Beggin' yourn pardon, ma'am, but I need to speak with Mr. Larnach," said Magwitch, his head appearing just above the pole handrail.

"Well, he's not here," replied Emily curtly. Mildred had already stood up to usher Magwitch away.

"What a bootiful son you have, Miss Emily," said Magwitch, swiftly removing his leathery old hat to reveal his balding, white pate; his sun-burnt, hooked nose adding character to his weather-beaten face. Emily relaxed at the compliment but discretely pulled her cover up further.

"I once had a little girl in England named Estella."

"So you know about little children then?" questioned Emily, not inquiring further for fear of receiving too much information into Magwitch's past.

"That I does," said Magwitch proudly, but thought better and added, "Well, I did." His glistening eyes distracted by a bluebottle fly landing on the underside of the rafter above Emily's head. Quickly, he changed the subject.

"Got a little poem for 'im if he'd like to hear it, ma'am." Slowly relaxing, Emily nodded back to Magwitch. "Goes like this, ma'am:

Little fly upon the ceiling,
Lummy, ain't yous cold?
Ain't yous got no shirts nor trousers?
Ain't yous got no skirts nor blouses?
Lummy, ain't yous cold?"

Magwitch gave a gentle smile as he recited his little poem and watched the delighted expressions appear on both Emily and Mildred's faces.

"Thank you, Magwitch, that's very good, but Mr. Larnach is down at the creek with the wool washers," announced Emily, suddenly aware of William fidgeting beneath the blanket.

"Certainly, ma'am," acknowledged Magwitch with a slight bow, his hat crumpled under his nervously clenched fingers.

"In case I miss 'im, ma'am, would you kindly let him know that I have returned with the 'erd, and they's all safe up in the new paddock. And, oh, I have left the sepoys to guard 'em, ma'am." Emily nodded again and waved her hand in final dismissal. Magwitch made his way down the hill towards Mudies Creek.

Chapter 51

They ate and they drank and they plotted, ultimately falling into an inebriated sleep, waking where they had dropped the night before. The fire had diminished to a smouldering heap of ashes. It was still dark as they ate the remains of the lamb and then mounted. Quietly, and in three separate groups, Hath's gang made its way back to Castle Forbes. More bushrangers had joined the gang during the previous few days and, as expected, Mudie's homestead was deserted save the three servants from the female factory and No-Legs-Lennie. The dogs were tied up on chains. Teeth bared, they barked incessantly, snapping at the chains to free themselves.

The women screamed as five selected bushrangers kicked in the front door. The sixth bushranger bashed the back of No-Legs-Lennie's head with an iron bar before he could skid across to the alarm bell. Hath dismounted, tethered his mount to the rail, and climbed the front steps behind the others. He strode in to witness the three women convicts being knocked to the floor. Hath went to the first, grabbed her by the hair, and dragged her screaming backwards, striking her across the face in an attempt to induce silence. Poole was busy ripping the clothes off another, intent on forcing himself on her before moving on.

"Leave her," bellowed Hath. "We're here for the guns, not friggin' women."

Ignoring the command, Poole stuck his gnarled hand up her skirt and feeling her soft knickerless buttocks, buried his fingers deep in her qwim. Writhing and kicking and punching, she attempted to protect herself, but Poole pinned her to the floor and held on like a limpet, his body weight too much to escape and with his other arm around the woman's neck, began choking her, as she lay prostrate on the bare boards of the floor.

"Leave her I said," bellowed Hath, striding over and punching Poole on the back of the neck. "Where are the weapons?" Hath shouted at the terrified woman.

"In the dining room," she whimpered breathlessly as Poole rolled over to the side, half unconscious from Hath's blow, his black patch dislodged to reveal a gaping eye-socket beneath.

"Get up, you fool," ordered Hath as an afterthought, then walked briskly to the dining room. The other two convicts had beaten him to it and were rifling the gun cabinet. The heavy poker ripped from its stand by the fire, serving as a suitable hammer and jemmy to break the glass and force open the lock. They ripped out a double-barrel and single-barrel shotgun and two muskets from their rests. Hath reached in and grabbed the two flintlock pistols from their green velvet case, while Perry grabbed the tomahawk and bone-handled hunting knife. Reaching up, Hath grabbed the two powder horns and the spare shot. Dazed, Poole got to his feet and sniffed his fingers.

"Here, catch this," said Hath, chucking one of the flintlock rifles to Poole. Next came clothes and food. Clothes were Reilly's job, while Perry and another would grab all the food and grog. They emptied the wardrobe and larder, hurling everything of use out of the double-hung window onto the deck for the other bushrangers to load onto the horses.

"We'll change into Mudie's clothes for disguise later," shouted Hath. Men were everywhere. Seven bushrangers hung around outside, whilst the rest tried on the clothes and ate what they could. Hath pocketed the bottle of cognac. David Jones drank the rum as he found it.

"Right, that's enough," ordered Hath, stuffing the butt of his flintlock through the glass-panelled door of the second display cabinet. Splintered glass dropped to the floor. Ryan moved slowly in an attempt to lessen the aggravation to his back; he searched the bedrooms, delighted to find the cash box. Secretly, he pocketed the 63 pounds, ten shillings, and three pence and slid quietly back outside.

"Where've you been," challenged Hath, already mounted and busily lighting an oil lamp.

"Just checking the bedrooms," replied Ryan sheepishly.

"Get mounted," ordered Hath, failing to notice Ryan's happy countenance as he hurled the lighted lamp in through the open doorway; the glass mantle shattered instantly, splashing the burning oil across the wooden planking. Hath turned his mount and, beckoning the others to follow, galloped off in the direction of Larnach's Rosemont homestead. Riding Point, Hath raised his hand to bring the 20 or more bushrangers to a halt before reaching the top of the hill. Hidden from view behind a clump of bushes at the crest, they prepared for the attack on Larnach.

"Load up," instructed Hath, pouring powder into the barrel and tamping down the muslin-wrapped ball. He also loaded his two pistols, jammed one into his belt, and handed the other to Poole.

"Reilly, and you others, leave them women alone; we only want that bastard Larnach. After I've dealt with him, we make a break for it. Poole, Reilly, Jones, Perry, and Ryan, you come with me. We head for Lamb's Creek to the north of Greta village, spend a couple of nights, and then head farther north into the bush. You others make for the high ground out to the west. Skirt around Singleton's place, then split up so the federal authorities get confused with tracking. Half of you head down to Wiseman's ferry and on to Sydney; you others make for the high plains. Give it a couple of months, then we all head for Sydney and jump a ship for Feejee or Calcutta. May be safer to just to get lost in Sydney. Twenty thousand people there now, so they won't notice the likes of us."

"Get eaten in Feejee!" shouted Poole, the black patch over his left eye socket making him an unlikely cannibal's meal. Hath grinned at the thought, but was confident.

Chapter 52

It was just past noon with blue skies and not a cloud in sight as the temperature rose into the hundreds on the Fahrenheit scale. Humidity was low, and rain had failed to fall for nearly three months, leaving the ground hard and dusty.

Having finished feeding, Emily felt the sun on her neck as she carefully bedded baby William back in his cradle. She sat back on her rocking chair and watched Magwitch disappear in the distance, picking his way between the various outcrops of rock as he made his way down to join the men at Mudies Creek over half a mile away. From behind, she heard the sound of galloping hooves. It sounded like a whole battalion. She beckoned to Mildred to go to the end of the veranda and see what was happening. Seconds later, Mildred returned, distress written across her face.

"Riders, ma'am," announced Mildred in a fluster. "Lots of them, riding fast, and they are coming towards us from the hill behind." Emily stood and walked back into the homestead to see from the kitchen window what the commotion was all about. Instantly, she recognised the lead horseman.

"Hath," she whispered under her breath. "Heavens, no, and John is down at the creek!" she exclaimed.

"Shall I run and fetch the master, ma'am?"

"No, stay here," ordered Emily, "just get the pistols out from the cabinet and load them for me."

"Never loaded a pistol, ma'am."

"For heaven's sake, Mildred," gasped Emily, running through to the gun case and retrieving both pistols. She reached up for the powder horn and quickly loaded, completing just as the horses arrived. Minutes later, out of the corner of her eye, Emily noticed one of the convict's hats beneath the window as he skirted round to the back. "Mildred, bring little William in from the veranda."

Emily was near to panic as she emerged on the front deck to confront Hath. Mildred rushed through the house to the back, just in time to see the weather-beaten convict bent over baby William's cradle. He lifted the infant out. Mildred screamed, lunging with her full body weight and clawing at his eyes. With little William tucked under his left arm, the convict punched Mildred in the face, breaking her nose and dropping her instantly to the floor.

"What is it, Hath?" challenged Emily, her head turning, distracted by Mildred's scream from the rear deck, both loaded pistols still pointing menacingly at Hath. The sound of shattering glass within brought further urgency to the panic-stricken women.

"Where's Larnach?" growled Hath, ignoring her pistol threat. The other bushrangers fidgeted on their breathless mounts, eager to be given the signal to trash the homestead. Emily turned further to see what was happening to Mildred and baby William.

"You evil sodding devils," she cursed, turning her pistols away from Hath and running back into the house. Blood streaming from her broken nose, Mildred struggled from the deck as Emily came through. The convict looked up and, instantly seeing what was happening, tried to lunge to the side to escape. With lightning speed, Emily shot him through the temple, her accuracy easily missing the child. He fell backwards over the railing, breaking baby William's fall, narrowly missing the top of William's forming soft skull as he landed on his back in the long grass. Mildred rushed forwards and grabbed the baby, her nose bleeding profusely over her mouth. Emily raised the second pistol in her right hand, preparing to kill again. Emily quickly turned back to confront Hath. Mildred cowered behind, carrying baby William. He cried in confusion and struggled in her arms, disturbing Emily further.

"Where's Larnach?" shouted Hath again.

"Not bloody well here!" shouted Emily, her face red in furious rage at the attempted kidnap of her little William.

"Don't believe you," argued Hath.

"Poole and Reilly search the bloody place. I only want Larnach," bellowed Hath, as the two convicts disappeared into the house, emerging a few minutes later, their pockets full of silver ornaments and jewellery.

"No one inside," growled Reilly.

"Damn you, woman, where is he?" cursed Hath, getting agitated that his plan was already failing. Emily stood silently, still pointing the pistol, aware that she had only one shot left. Mildred stood behind, comforting William in her arms, blood still trickling from her nose.

"One more time; where the bloody hell is he?" raged Hath; Emily remained silent. Her pistol clicked as she cocked the frizzen threateningly.

"He's down at the creek with the wool washers," wailed Mildred with a wave of her hand in the direction of Mudies Creek.

"Shut up," snapped Emily back at Mildred.

"Thank you, Mildred," sneered Hath, wheeling his horse round and signaling to the others to follow. They galloped off down the hill, leaving Emily and the servants powerless to help but to watch the attack at the creek.

"Tell the stable lad to harness the rig," ordered Emily, having raced out to the veranda as the riders disappeared in the distance. Mildred handed over little William and ran down the steps. She raced across to the barn and shouted to the convict idly cleaning harnesses. She arrived at the great barn door and gave instructions.

"Harness the rig for Miss Emily. There's bad business down at the creek."

The young convict sprang to his feet and reached for the nearest leather and bronze harness set. He briskly walked to the end stable, secured the harness, and led the horse out of the pen. A light rig stood opposite, and, within five minutes, he drove the rig up to the homestead with Mildred at his side. Emily rushed to the gun cabinet, but it had been forced open and stood empty. She swiftly strode along the corridor to the bedroom and retrieved the two flintlock rifles secretly hidden beneath her large double bed. Adept at shooting, she efficiently loaded both weapons and the pistol and refilled the powder horn. Holding the rifles under her right arm and pistols, powder horn, and pouch of spare shot in her left, she walked out to meet the rig.

"Mildred, get down from there, you will stay with little William," instructed Emily as she placed one flintlock with the spare pouch of shot under the seat in the front. Still clutching the second weapon with the powder horn slung around her neck, she rushed back for two wool blankets and the medical kit. Mildred helped load the blankets onto the rig as Emily climbed up and sat on the wooden bench seat next to the convict driver. The sight of the puff of white smoke made Emily gasp.

"Drive like the wind," instructed Emily. "They're already firing at them in the creek."

The convict driver made the familiar clicking sound with his tongue and sent waves rippling along the leather reins, slapping the back of the horse. Instantly, the rig jolted forwards and accelerated to an extended trot; the ground too rough to canter, let alone gallop.

Chapter 53

The motley bunch of convicts stood knee-deep in Mudies Creek, washing the recently sheared lamb's wool. Larnach, his bullwhip clenched in his right hand, shouted instructions.

Magwitch reached the top of the bank and looked down. He heard the horses in the distance behind and swung round. Half a mile away, they were coming at a gallop, leaving a trail of dust behind. Through the distant orange cloud of dust, he could barely see the homestead. He focused on the lead rider.

"Christ Jesus, it's Hath and his gang," shouted Magwitch. Larnach glanced up.

"Come down here," he shouted threateningly with his bullwhip.

"Yes, sir, certainly, sir." Obediently, Magwitch scurried down the steep bank. "There's horses comin', sir," he announced breathlessly; anguish written across his face.

"Who is it?" grumbled Larnach. The other convicts stopped work and stood, watching the commotion between the pair. "Hitchcock, sir, and a gang of riders, sir."

"Bastards," cursed Larnach. "The murdering bastards are back for revenge." Larnach slung his bullwhip over to the bank of the creek and stumbled through the water to get his loaded flintlock lying on the far side.

Still hidden from view by the high bank, the horses had covered the distance from the homestead in minutes and could now be clearly heard as they galloped up to the creek. Three, weather-beaten faces, one with a black patch over his left eye, appeared at the top of the bank. Pointing menacingly down at the men in the creek were two rifles and a pistol, their hammers already cocked. Hath, Poole, and Reilly gloated at the sitting ducks. Hath waved his pistol to the other bushrangers to spread out along the top of the bank.

"Got the drop on us," muttered Larnach, forced to freeze before reaching his weapon on the far side of the creek.

"Get out of the water every bloody one of you, or we'll blow your bloody brains out," shouted Hath from the top of the bank. "It's no use thinking to make an escape 'cause I'm going to take good care you never take another man to court for flogging." Larnach moved in behind Magwitch.

"Get out of the way, Magwitch. Yous and me goes back a long way," sneered Hath, enjoying the sport.

"Stay where you are. All of you," ordered Larnach, using the convicts as shields against the mounted bushrangers. Larnach backed away behind the other convicts. He made it to the far bank of the creek and reached for his gun. Hath raised his piece and took aim, losing a shot at Larnach's back. The ball winged him at the base of the shoulder blade, shattering the bone and lodging itself deep in his ribcage. Pieces of bone punctured his right lung. Magwitch ducked and swung round. Coughing blood, Larnach cursed and fell back into the creek. A cloud of burnt cordite and smoke obscured Hath and his weapon. Quickly, he reached for the powder horn and ball to reload.

"Fool," shouted Hath, waving his pistol at Magwitch. "Why didn't you get out of my way? I'd have killed the bastard." Slowly, the light breeze pushed the smoke away. Heavily wheezing, Larnach grovelled at the water's edge and, still struggling, crawled out of the creek and up the bank; his left hand reached across to support his limp arm hanging from his shoulder. Blood oozed from the corner of his mouth.

"Shoot the bugger," shouted Poole, following Hath's lead.

"Fire again. I'll make sure you'll never get another man flogged." Poole fired the second shot. The ball struck Larnach in the left calf muscle, tearing away a chunk of flesh, instantly dropping him to the ground.

"Fire again. Let's settle him. He's almost finished." Reilly blasted off the third shot, creasing the side of Larnach's skull, ripping off the lobe of his left ear. Blood ran down Larnach's cheek and dripped from his chin as he continued crawling up the opposite bank. Then Ryan called out.

"Fire again. Let's follow him." Larnach disappeared into the scrub at the top of the bank.

"No, take care of your powder and ball. It's almost finished," argued Perry.

"Settle him with a knife," shouted Hath in frustration. Reloaded, Hath spurred his horse down the bank. Poole and Reilly followed. "He's mine," growled Hath in a thick gravel voice. His horse entered the water and began crossing the creek. Poole and Reilly waited. Magwitch slipped behind two convicts and reached for Larnach's flintlock. It gave a heavy click as he pulled the frizzen back. He swung round and pointed the muzzle at Hath's back.

"Yous done enough bad business 'ere," growled Magwitch. "The Federals'll be hunting yous down like rabid dogs."

"Curse you, Magwitch. Reckon you're a big man, is it?" challenged Hath, turning in his saddle; his horse bucking and tramping water.

"Don't look at me like that, Hitchcock. Done yous a favour, that's wot I done," shouted Magwitch, waving the loaded rifle. Hath grabbed a moment to look down at his pistol; his skittish horse making it difficult to aim. Magwitch took aim with the flintlock.

"You win this round, Magwitch, but watch your back 'cause I'll get you later."

"Gord listen to 'im. Federals ain't arter me, mate. Best put distance to save yourn neck. Now get." Magwitch waved the muzzle menacingly. Cursing, Hath spat in the creek, then signalled to his men.

Magwitch stood his ground as the last of the gang spurred their horses and galloped off to Lamb's Creek. Magwitch splashed across the creek and up the bank to rescue Larnach lying like a wounded animal in the thicket. Blood dripped from his chin and poured from his calf muscle down his leg onto his wet boots. His arm hung limp from his shattered shoulder-blade and blood trickled from the corner of his mouth. "Well done, Magwitch," wheezed Larnach, his breath coming in short, agonising gasps.

"Tis me job, sir," said Magwitch, tending to Larnach's shoulder.

Emily arrived at the top of the far bank and jumped down. She ran around to the back of the rig, grabbed the medical kit and one blanket. She had seen the smoke from the gunshots and then the bushrangers gallop off when she was still a hundred yards or so away. The sight of Magwitch scrambling up the opposite bank was enough for her to know that someone had been shot. Walking sideways, bending forwards to steady herself, she made her way down the bank and waded across the creek. Magwitch and two other convicts helped Larnach from the thicket and laid him out on his back. Breathless from the climb, Emily spread a blanket over Larnach.

"Oh God, John, what have they done to you?" She cut his trouser leg to inspect the wound. The ball had lodged against the bone and required surgery for removal. Giving the bandage to Magwitch to tie as a tourniquet around his thigh in an attempt to stem the bleeding, she cut the back of John's shirt. There was only a thin trickle of blood where the bullet had entered. Again she dabbed the wound and decided they should carry him back to the rig. Congealing blood clung stubbornly to the lower part of his ear, left cheek, and chin. Cradling his head in her lap before moving him, she attempted to wipe away what she could before giving the order to carry him down the bank across the creek and up to the waiting rig.

"Magwitch choose three of your best men and send one for Peter Cunningham, the surgeon, another for the constable at Singleton's, and the third for the federal authorities in Maitland. Newcastle should also send help. The authorities should report to James Mudie at the magistrate's court first.

He'll know what to do," ordered Emily, climbing up onto the back of the rig to comfort her husband, his eyes slowly closing through loss of blood and shock. Magwitch turned and issued instructions to the riders to go for the surgeon and the constable.

"Ma'am, I'll go myself for the Major and the authorities," volunteered Magwitch.

"Thank you, Magwitch," replied Emily, busily tending John.

"Drive to Rosemont quickly," instructed Emily, as the rig driver took up the reins. Quickly mounting, Magwitch grabbed the reins and two spare horses and cantered off towards Hunters River, following the tracks in the long grass as he made his way to Maitland. Aboriginal trackers sat roasting a large, blue-tongued lizard on a thick stick at the water's edge when Magwitch arrived. "Seen any riders?" questioned Magwitch. The two Aboriginals acknowledged.

"One of yous must come with me and the other must follow them tracks," said Magwitch urgently.

"Come where?" said the fattest Aboriginal.

"Maitland. One pound each, when you find them," said Magwitch, anticipating the next question. The Aboriginals stood up and reached for the reins. They rode together, changing horses at Greta and continued on to Maitland. Just east of Greta village, the tracks veered off north.

"The copse at Lamb's Creek I reckon," suggested the fat Aboriginal tracker. He had dismounted to study the hoof prints. "Six or seven of them," volunteered the tracker, still squatting; his fingers tracing the broken stems of grass and imprints in the dry ground.

"Find 'em, but don't be seen," ordered Magwitch. "We'll be back with the federals and the Major in a couple a days." The tracker acknowledged in his native tongue.

Chapter 54

"All rise," said the sergeant. He stood, issuing the instruction, as James Mudie completed his seventh case that morning and retired to his private room at the back of the Maitland courthouse. Magwitch had been let in by the backdoor and sat patiently, holding his sweaty leather hat between his trembling knees. He jumped to his feet as Mudie swept in.

Having arranged with the Colonial Secretary, Alex McLeay, Mudie posted a 70-pounds reward both in Sydney and Maitland. Riders went about, nailing the reward notice to trees and circulated the notice through the mail service to every farmer in the area. Mudie sought information on the ringleaders. Reports said the gang was nearly 20 strong and that they had split up. But Mudie wanted the seven men who had attempted to kidnap his newest and only grandson, William James Mudie Larnach, and who had rifled and torched his private home and who had attempted to murder his family. Seven convicts in all, for which he would pay ten pounds each, a year's wages for an ordinary assigned convict for information leading to the arrests and conviction of the bushrangers.

Armed to the teeth, the posse consisted of 13 men. Two local constables and the rest, Free Settlers and farmers. They rode with hatred and anger, tired of the escalation of bushranger activity along Hunters River. Almost every week, there was another atrocity committed. Murder, larceny, arson, rape, highway robbery. There were even reports of cannibalism of Chinese amongst the Aboriginal communities. The list was endless.

These crimes were too serious to be dealt with at local magistrate level. Supreme Court trials by military jury were held in Sydney, much to the delight of Major Mudie, sickened by the favouritism meted out by the time served and conditionally-pardoned convict jurors of local courts.

The 140 miles from Sydney left Free Settlers vulnerable, as the federal authorities had insufficient manpower to provide adequate policing, and half of those dispatched consisted of convicts who had served their time now classified as emancipated. A developing situation that did not rest well with Major Mudie and many of the other Free Settlers in Hunters River district. The swell of convict sympathies threatened mutiny on the large farms, the most notorious being at Castle Forbes, converted from densely wooded fertile land over the past ten years, through the blood, sweat, and irons of convicts to become a highly successful farm yielding a multitude of arable crops, sheep, and cattle. Mudie vowed to bring the matter to a head with Governor Bourke. The posse rode past Lochinvar farm and continued northwest along Hunters River, anticipating interception of tracks by the second day's ride.

"Too lenient," Mudie muttered to himself, his mind flashing back to Macquarie's words in the early days which still rang in his ears. "Hang them all. Wasters the lot of them. Once a convict, always a convict. *'A leopard never changes its spots.'*"

Changing horses, they spent the night at Greta village and continued at first light. Magwitch rode ahead with the Aboriginal tracker and slowed the pace as they approached the river crossing. He pointed to the yellow cloth he had tied to the tree at the point where the tracks had entered the water.

"They crossed here, Major," said Magwitch, turning in his saddle to inform Mudie. Spurring the horses into the water, the posse crossed the wide section of river; the three-month drought making the crossing possible without boats. Cautiously, they made their way to Lamb's Creek, following the tracks on the west side. Magwitch raised his hand, pointing towards thin wisps of smoke rising from the far side of the derelict wool shed.

"Something going on over there, sir," whispered Magwitch.

"Frost take one man and scout the camp; I want to know how many there are. Report back as quick as you can. We need to be in position by nightfall and attempt the arrest at first light," instructed Mudie. Frost wheeled his horse and disappeared into the trees and bush. Mudie and the rest of the riders dismounted behind the copse. Tethering his horse to the nearest branch, Mudie took command of the other men. "When Frost gets back, we spread out. Henry, you will take one man and circle out to the east and work your way back, concealing yourselves in the brush. Walter, you will take John and another two men and work around the west side of the small range, then split up, leaving John and his man to come in from the west whilst you two head farther north and make your approach from the north. For heaven's sake, don't get spotted."

It was late afternoon, and the decision was taken to move into position preferably before nightfall and, on Mudie's signal, they would close in and make the arrest. If they failed to make the arrest, they would drive the bushrangers south and trap them at the narrow and deepest part of the river.

"Seven bushrangers, sir," said Frost breathlessly as he dismounted.

"Good, that makes odds of two to one. What were they doing?"

"Couldn't make out much, not really close enough, but it looked as if they were just sitting by the fire and drinking, sir."

"Good," said Mudie. "They should all have thumping, great hangovers by the morning. Walter, you'll be the last in position. Remember, no fires tonight, and we strike on my signal at first light. I will be the first into the camp from the south, and the signal will be two shots in quick succession into the air. The six of you will gallop down into the camp and back us up. I will have six men with me, so it will be one-on-one 'til you arrive, so don't be sleeping. Doubt they will have time to get up off the ground. I want them alive to stand trial." Mudie was adamant.

Henry, Walter, John, and the other three men mounted and rode quietly off through the trees.

Chapter 55

"Why the hell did you punch me on the neck?" slurred Poole, scraping the underside of his blackened nail with his nine-inch dagger.

"You stupid fool. You can do the women any time. We wanted the loot, and guns, and grog, and take Larnach out for good," replied Hath angrily.

John Perry was busy helping James Ryan rubbing ointment into the wounds on his back from the recent flogging.

"Wish I hadn't absconded," groaned Perry.

"Same here," agreed David Jones; the thought of being hanged suddenly too much to bear.

"Shut up the lot of you," growled Hath. "We got what we went for, including money and guns and food, didn't we? Enough for a couple of weeks at least, and that Larnach got what was coming to him. Reckon he's as good as dead anyway."

"I'm heading for the coast tomorrow and grabbing a boat for Sydney, then do a crewing job to get to Feejee," said James Reilly, kicking the fire and throwing another log on.

"When do we eat, Hath?"

"As soon as it gets dusk. Better hack up that sheep now. Small chunks; takes too long to spit roast. Each grills his own meat," instructed Hath, taking another swig of whisky.

Poole handed the dagger to Robert Mason and rubbed the bruise on the back of his neck. He twisted his head from side to side, stretching his bruised muscles in his neck.

"Best put more wood on to stop the fire smoking," said Reilly, conscious of being followed.

"For Christ's sake, it looks like we're sending Indian smoke signals!" cursed Jones; he felt his neck as if he had a rope burn. "Pass that whisky."

The sun set behind the range and, slowly, the light faded. They stoked up the fire, now less concerned about smoke. The lamb charred against the flames; impatience and nerves forcing arguments as to what to do in the morning. They ate charred lamb, mostly raw in the middle, care and attention lost to the alcohol.

"Stay here until after the weekend," said Hath finally deciding what their next move should be. They argued into the night, eventually falling into a drunken, stupified sleep as the fire burnt down and smouldered.

Chapter 56

Magwitch and the Aboriginal crawled next to Mudie, with the other men spread out either side. Mudie had two pistols whilst the men and Magwitch had rifles. First light was nearly an hour before sun-up. They approached the camp from the south, catching sight of John to the west and Walter to the north. There was no sign of Henry to the east.

"Magwitch, I'll fire first and you fire immediately afterwards," whispered Mudie. "And fire in the air in case Henry is coming in from the east through the undergrowth." Magwitch and the Aboriginal nodded. Mudie signalled to John and Walter, then slowly stood. Five of the bushrangers lay sleeping by the smouldering fire. Mudie fired, followed instantly by Magwitch. Both Walter and John and their men immediately mounted and galloped down from their vantage points, entering the camp within minutes.

"You bastards," cursed Hath, his gun lying just out of reach as Mudie held his pistol at pointblank range. The other men, rifles loaded and cocked, covered Hitchcock, Poole, Reilly, Ryan, and Mason, their physical condition leaving them in no condition to fight back.

"Where are the others?" challenged Mudie.

"How the blazes should I know?" cursed Hath.

"They were here yesterday," growled Mudie, waving his pistol menacingly.

"Is that a fact?" Hath made a move for his gun. Mudie fired, hitting Hath in the leg. Moments later, Henry rode slowly into camp. David Jones and John Perry, their wrists tied and a noose knotted round their necks, walked behind Henry's horse.

"Found this pair making a bid for freedom," said Henry. "They reckon they had nothing to do with the bushwhack." Henry dismounted and having tethered his horse, tied Jones and Perry to a tree.

Chapter 57

"All rise, Supreme Court is in session, Sir Francis Forbes presiding," announced the sergeant under his handlebar moustache. Crown prosecution and two, uniformed, police constables stood, as did Barrister Roger Therry for the defence. The public gallery, mostly dressed in scruffy clothing, some of whom were erstwhile convicts who had already received their Conditional Pardons and some still on Tickets-of-Leave, all shuffled to their feet in anticipation. Isabella and Maria, Major Mudie's other two daughters, were dressed in flowing crinoline frocks formally topped off with lace bonnets. They had been positioned in the centre front of the public gallery and held hands. Earlier, Mudie had agreed with the police to drop the lesser charges, provided the death sentence was given for a conviction on the remaining ones, negating the need to introduce the charge of attempted kidnap and the production of the attempted-rape victim as a witness to the burglary and arson at Castle Forbes. Justice Forbes entered from his private chambers to the rear of the court and settled himself in his great leather chair behind the carved wooden bench.

"Be seated," announced the sergeant. Hubbub ensued from the public gallery in anticipation of the trial.

"Silence in court," shouted the sergeant, as Sir Francis Forbes crashed his gavel down repeatedly onto the lumpy wooden anvil to retain order.

In the centre of the court stood a heavily barred cage containing six wooden stools, ready to receive the prisoners. The prime witnesses, John Larnach, Emily, and Mildred, along with two convict witnesses, John Sawyer and Samuel Marsden, both of whom were with Larnach that day, were held in the witness room at the side of the court, awaiting summons to give evidence. Silence fell in the courtroom as the military jury was summoned.

Led by James Mudie as jury foreman, the retired officers filed into the jury box in military precision. All formerly dressed in dapper suits or military uniform bearing their rank, the retired lieutenants, sergeants, magistrates, and colonels stood to attention before seating themselves on the twin benches. A sound of disapproval and muffled boos rose from the gallery, which angered Sir Francis, inducing him to reach for his gavel again to order silence. Finally, amid tumultuous uproar from the public gallery, the six accused were led into court. Chains clanking, they shuffled into court in single file, wrists manacled and both feet chained together, the four-inch diameter, cast-iron ball held up in front as they processed across the polished wooden floor and only released on entering the claustrophobic iron cage.

"Silence in court," shouted the sergeant again, accompanied by rapid strikes of the gavel from a now highly irritated chief justice.

"If I have to call for order again, the gallery will be emptied and the trial will be held in private. And that includes the press," growled Sir Francis Forbes, scowling across at journalists from the Sydney Gazette, his face reddening with fury.

Isabella froze at the sight of Poole, his ugly patch confirming the damage she had inflicted during the rape in the barn nearly six years ago.

"That's him," whispered Isabella to Maria; a sick feeling developing in her stomach.

"You sure?" Maria looked back at Isabella.

"I remember poking the bastard's eye out with my thumb nail," whispered Isabella, a hint of a smile grew on her thin lips and her eyes glinted.

"Soon, he won't be able to look out of his good eye either," smirked Maria, developing a bigger hate for the convict. They stopped whispering as the sergeant began reading out the prisoners' names.

"The prisoners at the bar, Anthony Hitchcock alias Hath, John Poole, James Reilly, David Jones, John Perry, and James Ryan, transported for heinous crimes against His Majesty in the Mother Country, stand accused of the further crimes in this country of attempted murder and stealing, and putting residents in fear." The Crown had decided not to dredge up the earlier rape, attempted kidnap, attempted rape, and arson charges, as they were more than confident that the first three charges, each of which carried the death penalty, would be proven and, given that a man could only be hanged once, Mudie's decision to save the court's time and drop the latter charges was made.

Crown prosecution rose to lay before the court the prime offence. Anthony Hitchcock, alias Hath, and John Poole were indicted for maliciously shooting at Mr. John Larnach of Castle Forbes in the district of Patrick Plains, on the fifth of November last, with the intent to kill, and James Reilly, John Perry, David Jones, and James Ryan for counselling, aiding, and abetting the said two first-named prisoners in the commission of the said felony. A second count charged the offence with having been committed with the intent to do the said John Larnach some grievous bodily harm. John Larnach was summoned and duly sworn in the witness box.

"On the morning of the fifth of November, 1833, I went to the river to superintend sheep washing, and it all started between 12 noon and one o'clock." John Larnach continued to relate events as they had unfolded on that fateful day.

Barrister Roger Therry rose and conducted cross-examination, and the trial proceeded, with all witnesses summoned and sworn and bringing to the court's attention evidence of excessive brutality at Castle Forbes and misuse of corporal punishment, more particularly the use of the scourge and miserly distribution of food rations and clothing that had contributed to the convicts seeking revenge. Finally, both Crown prosecution, and Roger Therry acting as counsel for the defence, had completed their summing up.

"Prisoners at the bar, you have heard the case put before the court. Have you anything further to add before I instruct the jury to retire to consider their verdict?" said Sir Francis. Hath raised his manacled hand.

"May it please, your Lordship, the court may see proof if we can remove our shirts and show you our backs with the scars and wounds inflicted at Castle Forbes," said Hath, immediately pulling his shirt from his belt and undoing his front buttons. Laughter enveloped the public gallery to be met with castigation from the Chief Justice's gavel.

"That will not be necessary," came the retort. "Jurors, you will now retire to consider your verdict." In the privacy of the jury room, Mudie took charge.

"Hands up those who agree with me that we should return a verdict of guilty." Mudie was keen to get on with the business. Less than an hour later, the jury filed back into the court. Mudie remained standing.

"Have you reached a unanimous verdict?" asked Sir Francis.

"Yes, your Lordship, we have," replied Mudie gruffly.

"How do you find the accused?"

"We find the accused guilty on all three counts, with the exception of David Jones." Sir Francis sat back to consider the response, ultimately passing the death sentence on five, with David Jones being transported for further punishment to Norfolk Island. Next came the mercy pleadings. Mr. Therry hoped that there was another tribunal before which the plea of mercy might be raised and the extenuating circumstances of the prisoners' case met with due attention by the court. Sir Francis replied.

"Undoubtedly, there is another tribunal where the plea of mercy might be raised and it is also competent for that tribunal to grant the remedy for which the learned counsel applies. However, it is not in the province of this court to interfere, and I can make no order to the application just made." Sir Francis concluded with a single tap of his gavel, introducing the Solicitor General who would now perform the painful part of his duty in praying the judgment of the court on the prisoners at the bar. Proclamation having been made, the Chief Justice, Sir Francis Forbes, placed a black cloth on top of his fading white wig and addressed the prisoners.

"You have all, with the exception of David Jones, been convicted of two capital felonies and, during the course of your trial, have further pleaded guilty to a third capital indictment. Independent of this, your crimes have involved open rebellion against your master. I, therefore, have the painful duty to pass on to you, namely Anthony Hitchcock alias Hath, John Poole, James Ryan, John Perry, and James Reilly, the lawful sentence of directing that you be executed at such a time and, at such place, as His Excellency, the Governor, shall be pleased to appoint. Further, I am at liberty to direct that, for prisoners James Ryan, John Perry, and James Reilly, your time and place of execution shall be at Sydney, on the 21st of December, being 11 days hence. As regards prisoners Anthony Hitchcock, alias Hath, and John Poole, I direct that by way of example to other would be bushrangers in the Hunters River district, that your time and place of execution shall be at Castle Forbes on Hunters River, on the 21st of December, also being 11 days hence." The gavel crashed as the public gallery erupted. A smile of satisfaction spread across Mudie's face, but the relief may have come too late for Mudie and his future plans.

Chapter 58

Mudie kept Hath and Poole under lock and key in his solitary hut known as the black hole and had hastened up to the new cattle pasture to check on the condition of the herd since their arrival at Castle Forbes. Magwitch had seen the dust trail in the distance and quickly extinguished his pipe by tapping out the glowing tobacco and slipped it back into his jacket pocket. Minutes later, Mudie dismounted in the upper pasture and thanked Magwitch for his contribution to the capture. He took pleasure in handing over 50 pounds, Magwitch's reward for aiding in the hunt for the felons. Half an hour later, he had briefed his now-trusted cattle overseer, explaining that his presence, along with every convict and Free Settler in Hunters district was expected to bear witness to the hanging of the felonious murdering traitors, Hath and Poole.

"When's the 'anging, sir?"

"This Saturday," said Mudie, "and I have decided the great tree at New Freugh should serve us adequately for the gibbet." Magwitch scratched his chin.

"Them felonrys has been convicted to 'ang 'ere?" quizzed Magwitch. "And I must come to watch? Beggin yourn pardon, sir, but why, sir?"

"Yes, Magwitch, and all will witness what happens to bushrangers."

"I's sorry for to see that, sir, and them criminals will get wots owed them." Mudie sighed; his respect for Magwitch over the past few years had grown, given the number of occasions that he had helped the family with the growing problems with the convicts.

"The problem is, Magwitch, that the way the convicts are beginning to take over in New South Wales is becoming a big problem. The new Governor General doesn't help much either."

"Can't speak about that, sir."

"I know, I know. Any problems with the herd?" Mudie decided to change the subject.

"No, sir, they's been as good as gold, sir. 'Appy to be 'ere, I reckons." Holding onto the distinctive horn, Magwitch began stroking one of the cows on the neck.

Chapter 59

"Keep their wrists manacled and one leg-iron with the ball attached. The extra weight will make sure of it," instructed Mudie, popping his last forkful of eggs and bacon into his mouth.

Larnach left the table, painfully mounted his horse, and rode across to the black hole to prepare the prisoners. Polished for the occasion, the best four-in-hand carriage drew up outside the homestead. Mudie assisted Isabella into the carriage and tapped the driver to head off for New Freugh. They approached to witness hundreds of men swarming around the great tree.

Federal guards had been dispatched from Newcastle and Maitland, maintaining a clear passage which the felons would be paraded along before execution. Two, thick, hemp ropes hung ominously from the stout branch. Isabella counted seven rings of rope, forming the slipknot on each rope beneath which hung the empty nooses. Larnach was the last to arrive on his 16-hand, black stallion. He walked to the two horses pulling the prisoner's rig.

Resigned to their fate, Hath and Poole sat heavily chained in the back. Slowly, he brought the pair of horses forwards, guiding the rig under the branch. He handed the reins to Mangles who had been appointed to steady the horses. An eerie silence descended, broken only by the scuffle of horses' hooves. Even the morning bird song had gone, as had the wind, increasing the claustrophobic humidity. Grinning, Larnach jumped up onto the back of the rig and dragged Poole to his feet. He leant across and placed the noose over his head and jerked the knot down. The noose tightened. Accidentally, Larnach's elbow knocked the black eyepatch down over Poole's nose, revealing the ugly gaping socket.

"Woopsy," jested Larnach. "Don't want to spoil your good looks." Poole gave a guttural growl in disgust, snarked, and spat at Larnach; the dollop of yellow sputum hitting Larnach in the eye. Enraged, Larnach punched Poole in his good eye, nearly knocking him off the back of the rig; the near fall inducing premature hanging.

"Stop that," bellowed Mudie from his carriage. "Don't spoil the moment." Larnach cursed as he wiped his eye on his cotton cuff. He reached up and finished tightening the noose and then proceeded to Hath and did likewise. Hath smiled in contempt as he spouted the Lord's Prayer. The noose tightened on his neck, with the knot strategically tucked behind his ear as he uttered his last words.

"Yeah, as I walk through the valley of death, I fear no evil from you savages. You know what you do," Hath's gruff voice trembled with each word. Eventually, he stopped ranting.

"Have you anything to say before I give the order to carry out your sentence?" shouted Mudie. Both men remained silent. Mudie lent across to Isabella.

"My dear, would you like to use my stick on the rump of the lead horse?" Mudie made the offer as revenge for the rape Isabella had suffered all those years ago. Poole had remained hidden at Singleton's place until now. His void eye socket bearing testament to the desperate struggle in the barn.

"I'd rather not, Father, especially in front of all these men," replied Isabella, staring at the ground beneath the tree.

"I think it's best to let John finish the job." Mudie looked up and nodded to Larnach, who, in turn, pulled his pistol from his belt, nudged his black stallion to the back of the two horses harnessed to the rig, and just behind the nearest horse's withers, fired in the air, spooking both horses straight into a gallop. The leaves on the end of the live gibbet shook as the branch jerked under the load of two pairs of booted bodies. The bodies twitched in spasm. Their necks broken and windpipes strangulated. Clamped to each ankle, the chained cast-iron balls dangled beneath and swung silently to and fro; a mere six inches from the dusty ground.

"How long 'til I cut 'em down?" shouted Larnach.

"Hell no, John, leave them hanging as a warning to the others," retorted Mudie, tapping the driver to indicate that the show was over and they should return to the homestead.

Chapter 60

The collapse of the economy in New South Wales, combined with the ongoing drought, was forcing Mudie's hand to sell up. His daughters were all now satisfactorily married off and had land of their own. The final insult had been his dismissal as magistrate in Maitland. Admittedly, 32 other names had been left off the list of acting magistrates, but that did little to stop Mudie taking the decision personally. He had acquired the allotment at Morpeth about 18 months earlier and with the exception of acting as an outspan area for horses and cattle, for which it had been fenced, no other improvements had been added. In all, it consisted of five acres, with a long, deep, river frontage on the outside of an ancient oxbow bend.

"One penny per annum," said Mudie, with a twinkle in his eye. "And a lease for 99 years." Magwitch was expressionless, never having been given anything in his life before, that hadn't come back and bitten him. He scratched his stubbled chin, dug out his clay pipe and began his ritual of preparing a smoke. The two men leaned against the post and rail fence to the allotment. "Is it a deal, Magwitch?" asked Mudie, confused as to why Magwitch wasn't talking.

"Well, sir, I never got nothink 'afore, guv," stuttered Magwitch, taking a panicky suck on his pipe.

"Aye, but then you have probably never done so much for anybody before," replied Mudie; an appreciative smile spreading across his rugged face. "And there's more I have for you, so you had better get used to being a receiver of fortune."

Mudie's growing conflict with Governor, Major General Sir Richard Bourke, had escalated and precipitated his decision to sell Castle Forbes and return to England to carry his personal fight about the performance of the Governor and the virtual mutiny of the emancipated convicts in New South Wales to the Houses of Parliament in Westminster.

"Thank you, sir. I only does me job, sir." Magwitch had no idea where the conversation was leading.

"Saving my life during the highway robbery and then saving the life of my partner and son-in-law is a lot more than just doing your job. And on top of that, you have also done well with the sheep and the cattle." Mudie recalled the list of extra achievements that Magwitch had accomplished during his first five years.

"Also, never complaining or faking sickness. No, Magwitch, you have done well. And, of course, there are the horned cattle. You are to have one for yourself. Keep her here if you want. It makes no difference to me, as I am selling the main farm, Castle Forbes, so you won't be able to keep her there after I'm gone. You must get some help and move your hut down here so you have somewhere to stay." Mudie continued handing over the gifts until he got to Magwitch's status. Magwitch sat down on the lower rail of the fence to ponder the generosity. He dug deep into his jacket and produced his tatty black notebook. The gold edge had become frayed over the years, but it still had its presence.

"'Scuse me, sir, but could I ask yous for to kindly write in my little black book, sir? Words wot I can see so I knows I'm not havin' a vision like."

"I shall be pleased to do that for you. Better to write everything down," agreed Mudie, taking the black book from Magwitch. Mudie walked across to the rig for writing materials. Placing the book on the flat tray of the rig, Mudie carefully wrote an abbreviated list, including other legal matters still to discuss. Magwitch peered over his shoulder, and whilst recognising some of the words, struggled to understand their meaning. Beneath the list, Mudie wrote:

These gifts, I gratefully bestow upon Abel Magwitch, alias Provis, a man who has proven himself to be honest and trustworthy, and a man who exhibits integrity and strength during times of adversity, particularly whilst in my employ, and before God.

James Mudie
22nd February, 1836.

"Don't forget to swear on it, guv. Swear it to the Lord, sir, so he can look over both of us, sir." Mudie smiled, clutched the book, and closed his eyes; his lips moved in silent prayer.

"Amen," said Mudie, respectfully handing the book back to Magwitch.

"Amen," said Magwitch, nodding, glancing at the new writing. He tucked it carefully back into his jacket pocket. Magwitch looked up at Mudie and with a fake cough, quickly cleared his throat.

"Er, 'scuse me, sir, but are yous going to England, sir?"

"That I am, Magwitch, sailing in a few weeks' time."

"Er well, sir, I wonders, sir, if I could ask yous to find someone, sir?"

"Who?" quizzed Mudie, surprised at the request.

"That Jaggers I told yous about could maybe help, sir."

"That's fine, Magwitch. I know where to find Mr. Jaggers, and I've already written to him, but who's the other person?"

"Well, guv, er, sir, he's a boy, 'bout seven; no, not seven now, 'cause that's when I left, sir. He's 'bout 12 or 13 now. 'E lives near Rochester, sir. Name's Pip, sir, and his father drinks at the Three Jolly Bargemen, four mile out of Rochester. Yous could ask 'em there. His father, no, not really father, but 'e looks after Pip. 'E's a blacksmith wot works near Cooling Church, sir."

"And if I do find him, what then?"

"I humbly asks that yous write me when yous found him, sir."

"Aye, man, I'll see what I can do. I shall write if I have news."

"Thankee, sir. Gord speed yourn ship, sir."

The two men shook hands. Mudie climbed onto the rig and shook the reins, sending ripples along the horses' backs. Magwitch watched until the rig disappeared in the distance, that familiar lonely feeling began creeping back into his soul.

Chapter 61

The first available ship sailing for England raised anchor at high-tide Sydney Cove at the end of March. Mudie settled himself in his private cabin, having only just completed documentation for the sale of Castle Forbes. Finally, he had packed up his personal effects and prepared for the voyage. The largest part of his luggage, packed in wooden packing cases, being his personal notes, the beginnings of his memoirs, copy documents, newspaper cuttings, hastily acquired reference letters, and copies of letters to and from Government House at Parramatta.

There were letters from London and Edinburgh, and notes of the responses, copies of court records, and previously circulated printed material and pamphlets. Mudie had used the efficient steam service from Morpeth to Sydney and spent a number of nights in the Royal Hotel, giving time for the completion and registration of the sale of Castle Forbes to a certain James Baxter at the bargain basement price of seven thousand pounds. There was the issue of registering the Magwitch Lease and the application to regularise Abel Magwitch's emancipated status within the colony. However, greed had overtaken the government clerks and their respective administration departments, leaving Mudie to provide Magwitch with additional funds with which to personally oil the wheels to facilitate the extraction of the necessary certification; the only matter being properly concluded before sailing, being the sale of Castle Forbes.

"Walls do not a prison make, nor iron bars a cage," mused Mudie as he glanced around the cramped cabin aboard his ship bound for the Port of London. Sailing on the 31st of March, 1836, gave him 14 years of material. The last few years would be the best, and he would assemble the facts in the form of a non-fiction novel.

Sailing out from Sydney Cove, he ran over the events of the past few years, deciding to name names, exposing those enemies who were conspiring to defraud the colony. He would publish in London. "That'll send them running for cover. Bunch of perjuring rotten traitors, the lot of them," he chuckled to himself, imagining the outcome as he poured himself another large whisky.

Mudie unpacked his papers and carefully spread them around the cabin. He settled down to write his literary masterpiece, *The Felonry of New South Wales*.

The voyage went in a flash and before knowing it, he was sailing up the Thames. They had entered the Thames estuary at low tide as the sun rose astern and, having packed his papers the previous night, excitement had driven sleep from him. He stood on deck, brimming with emotion, drinking in the sights and the hustle and bustle on the river and at the piers, and, suddenly, rounding Blackwall Reach, he could see the familiar sight of Greenwich.

"God, it's been a long time, and what an experience," he mused as he thought about the task before him. "Magna Carta – June 15, 1215. The Barons had been right, forcing King John to sign at Rummymede, agreeing to civil rights and political liberties for the English. But what of those disenfranchised convicts? Stripped if you like, and non-persons under the rule of law." Mudie frowned.

"This one's for the politicians al'right."

His suit smelt musty, even his old tie, but London air would soon deal with stuffy odours. Mudie was ready and, with most of the writing completed, he was looking forward to discussing his work with the publisher. His eyes searched the waiting faces of people from the description John Plaistowe, Mudie's commercial lawyer in Maitland, had given him.

"He's a big burly man of exceedingly dark complexion, with a huge head, almost too big for his body, and a bulbous nose. He is very distinguished with bushy, black eyebrows. He'll probably be wearing a dark city suit and have a massive, silk, spotted handkerchief protruding from his top pocket and, if he's not there, go straight to the restaurant; any driver will take you." Plaistowe had studied law under him in London before he had travelled to Maitland in New South Wales.

It was sunny and hot when the ship finally docked, and the sun was almost directly overhead, indicating midday. A few welcoming figures paraded along the dockside, but mostly those in attendance wore flat hats or cheese-cutters and consisted of dockside workers scurrying about their business. There were massive working cranes and derricks and gantries and horses and carts. He noted the Clydesdale and Suffolk-Punch horses selected for strength to haul great loads both to and from the quayside. The ship moved closer, sailors rushed about throwing ropes and turning capstans. Slowly, they winched the steam-assisted, square-rigged ship onto the bollards.

"Fountain Tavern, Strand," instructed Mudie, placing his foot on the black, cast-iron step and climbing into the Hackney carriage.

"Simpson's Grand Divan Tavern, guv?" corrected the driver. "Changed its name didn't it?"

The horse-drawn carriage bumped its way past the end of Smithfield market and made its way west towards the Strand. The first sight was the familiar figure of the monument, then the Mansion House, then Sir Christopher Wren's Saint Paul's Cathedral, consecrated in 1710. After passing the cathedral, the carriage, drawn by matching twin geldings, trotted down Ludgate Hill, across the circus, up Fleet Street, past the law courts on the right, and into the Strand.

The carriage pulled up outside Samuel Reiss's Tavern and, since joining with John Simpson, it had become known as Simpson's Grand Divan and Tavern and had become the meeting place for London's epicureans, delighting in chess, fine wines, cigars, and coffee. Mudie alighted and paid the three-penny three-farthing fare. He stepped up to the entrance and paid the tuppence ha'penny entrance fee to the tailed doorman who instantly doffed his top hat in appreciation. Mudie stepped through the heavy, mahogany and bevelled glass door and, admiring his plush new surroundings, walked sedately through to the Grand Divan.

Mudie chose a booth to the side, slipped in, and waited to be served. He looked around the panelled room, marvelling at the high ceilings suspended from which hung magnificent, whale-oil burning, crystal chandeliers. It had been 14 gruelling years since he had been in London and, although well into his 50s, he felt the power and thrill of the city.

"Good day, sir," said the waiter.

"Aye, it certainly is and a delight to be back in London," said Mudie.

"Been away, sir?"

"Aye, lad, you could say that. Australia," said Mudie, chuckling.

"Then you will be thirsty, sir."

"Indeed, I am, and whilst I am waiting for my colleague, I think a bottle of red burgundy wine and two glasses would serve my purposes." The waiter disappeared and minutes later, returned, opened the bottle, and poured. Mudie sat back and savoured the wine and his surroundings.

Part 3

Chapter 62
England – 1836

The grotesque weapon lay on the ground beside Mrs. Gargery, and there was a huge gash in the back of her skull, extending down to the top of her spine. She was unconscious and only just breathing. Death appeared not far away. Aghast, Pip knew immediately that the weapon was his convict's old leg-iron. Near to tears, his stepfather, Joe Gargery, bent down and picked up the offending rusty ball and chain. Examining it with his smithy's eye, he declared it to have been removed years ago with a blacksmith's file.

Instantly, Pip's mind raced back to that freezing cold and dank Christmas Eve in the graveyard and the next day out on those misty marshes. Pip thought back, shocked that his old secret had come back to haunt him. The dreadful secret that had almost consumed his whole being nearly six years ago, and that it should have dared to rear its ugly head again. He looked at the gaping wound on the back of his sister's head and spine. She had been brutally struck from behind; the rusted leg-iron having been thrown down beside the prostrate body. As if history was repeating itself, he had heard the sound of the escape warning cannon the night before as it rolled lazily through the deadening mist outside. There had been two more convicts escape from the hulks last night. Within hours, one convict had already been recaptured, but his leg-iron was still on. This leg-iron had certainly come from a convict on the hulks, but it had been discarded years ago.

The Peelers were about Joe Gargery's house for weeks, interviewing everybody who had come and gone recently; the prime suspect being her husband, Joe Gargery, the blacksmith. But Joe had been at the Three Jolly Bargemen, smoking his pipe from a quarter after eight to a quarter before ten. While he was there, his wife, Mrs. Gargery, had been seen standing at the kitchen door, exchanging good nights with a farm labourer going home. Joe had discovered her body when he had gone home at five minutes to ten. His innocent mind had no idea that the Peelers suspected him. They hung about the

Three Jolly Bargemen, questioning this one and that one, making everybody feel guilty. But at the end of it, they never did find the culprit.

Standing in the little stone cottage beside the forge, Pip's mind flashed back to the very beginning; he revisited that fateful day again when he himself had become a thief to help his convict on the marshes. Then, had come that strange invitation to attend Miss Havisham. In his mind's eye, he saw the window to Satis House raise and heard that girl's voice.

"What name?" she had called out.

"Pumblechook," Pip's uncle had replied.

"Quite right." And the window had shut again. She had come across the courtyard, with keys in her hand to let them in.

"This," Pip's uncle had said, "is Pip."

"This is Pip, is it? Come in, Pip." Uncle Pumblechook had attempted to follow, but she had rudely stopped him.

"Oh!" she had said. "Did you wish to see Miss Havisham?"

"If Miss Havisham wishes to see me," Pip's uncle had replied.

"Ah!" the girl had said, "but, you see, she don't." The girl had locked the gate and turned her back on him, leaving Pip to follow. Long ago, the yard had been paved and was clean, with tufts of grass growing from every crevice. Cold wind had seemed to whistle through the disused brewery buildings like the noise of wind in the rigging of a ship at sea.

"You could drink without hurt all the strong beer that's brewed there now, boy," she had said as they crossed the yard.

"I should think I could, miss," Pip had replied in his shy way.

"Better not try to brew beer there now, or it would turn out sour, boy. Don't you think so?"

"It looks like it, miss," Pip reminisced. He had assessed her to be about the same age as himself.

"Don't loiter, boy." Her final words still echoed in his ears.

Inside Satis House, it had been dark and dismal, and they had climbed the back staircase by candlelight. There, Pip had found himself alone. He had knocked on the door at the top of the stairs and been instructed to enter. As he thought back, he could still vividly see it all; the experience as a young lad still shocked him.

He had entered cautiously, finding candles lighting the room, for all the windows had been closed and the curtains drawn. Most prominent had been the great dining table draped in a delicate lace tablecloth and laden with dishes of rotted food; the most striking feature being a five-tiered wedding cake. He had first seen it in the reflection of a gilded looking glass. In an armchair, with her left elbow resting on the table and her head leaning on her hand, sat the strangest lady he had ever seen, or shall ever see. She was dressed in rich materials. Satins and lace and silks. All of white. Her shoes were white. And she had a long, white veil pinned to her hair, and she had bridal flowers, but her hair was white. Some bright jewels sparkled on her neck and on her hands, and some other jewels lay sparkling on the table. Dresses, less splendid than the dress she wore, and half-packed trunks were scattered about. She had not quite finished dressing, for she had but one shoe on. The other was on the table near her right hand. Her veil was but half arranged, her watch and chain were not put on, and some lace for her bosom lay with the trinkets and with her handkerchief and gloves and some flowers and a prayer book, all confusedly heaped about the looking glass. The powerful memory shattered him like some ghastly waxworks where time had stood still.

"Look at me," she had said. "You are not afraid of a woman who has never seen the light of day since you were born?"

"No," Pip had replied.

"Do you know what I touch here?" she had said, laying her hands, one upon the other, on her left side.

"Yes, ma'am."

"What do I touch?"

"Your heart," Pip had replied.

"Broken."

He hadn't said anything further, and she had continued talking out her strange fantasies. Suddenly, she had called for Estella, who had quickly arrived.

"Play. I want to see you play."

"With this boy? Why, he is a common labouring boy," Estella had complained.

"Well, you can break his heart," Miss Havisham had said. She had picked up a deck of playing cards and they had started to play. Then, he remembered the embarrassment he had felt at calling knaves, Jacks.

His mind began filling in more details since that first strange day, after which he had been instructed to visit regularly. He particularly remembered the second visit when he had bumped into that burly man coming down the stairs as he, Pip, was groping his way up the dark staircase. The man had grabbed his chin in his large, scented hand as they passed.

"Boys!" he had said, shaking his head, instinctively mistrusting Pip's purpose.

Each time he visited, his feelings had grown more and more for Estella. Then, finally, on his 14th birthday, when he had discovered he was to become a blacksmith's apprentice to Joe at the forge, he vividly recalled the morning when he had to bid farewell to Estella and Miss Havisham. That painful moment when Joe had accompanied him to Satis House, and the interview, exposing him to the shame he had felt for his stepfather.

"Well," Miss Havisham had said. "And you have reared this boy with the intention of taking him for your apprentice. Is that so, Mr. Gargery?" Joe had confirmed, but he had directed his comments to Pip, never looking at Miss Havisham.

"Has the boy," Miss Havisham had continued, "ever made any objection? Does he like the trade?"#

How could I have told Joe that I now hated the thought of being a labouring boy and wanted to be a gentleman instead? Pip thought back to yet another embarrassing moment; the shame growing again. *Miss Havisham had graciously given over 25 guineas as a premium for me. Then had come the indentures for Philip Pirrip, alias Pip, for me to be sworn down at the Town Hall in front of all the justices.*

Oh, God, the wretched excuse I had made to go and visit Miss Havisham to thank her for everything after the first year as an apprentice, but, in reality, a hopeless excuse to see Estella again. What tragedy to have the gate opened by that Sarah Pocket, her walnut-shell countenance, explaining to me that Estella had been sent away to a finishing school in France to become a lady, and there I was, being a common boy in a forge. I hated it, Pip mused, his mind racing ahead as he interrogated his memory, searching into his past for the potential murderer of Mrs. Joe Gargery.

Momentarily breaking his thoughts, Pip looked up, as the Peelers helped Mrs. Gargery to the bed and the gentle yet plain Biddy, Pip's erstwhile teacher, began dressing the wounds.

Pip's mind drifted back to his earlier apprenticeship life and his decision to revisit Miss Havisham on his next birthday. For his effort, Miss Havisham had given him a golden guinea and told him to come again the same time next year. Each and every birthday after that, he had visited, each time receiving a golden guinea and each time enquiring after Estella. But he had always received the usual, harsh rebuke from Miss Havisham. Each time, Sarah Pocket had been on gate duty at Satis House, and Pip had begun to wonder when, if ever, Estella would return. Biddy had grown closer and, after the attack on his sister, had moved into Joe's house to help look after her and, between them, his sister was never left alone, providing the opportunity for Pip and Biddy to become even closer friends.

It was summertime and on this particular Sunday, the weather was lovely, affording the opportunity for Pip and Biddy to walk together in the beautiful English countryside. They quietly walked through the village to the church, across the churchyard, and eventually found themselves out on the marshes. They spoke little, as they studied the ships sailing on the Medway estuary. Pip began to combine Miss Havisham and Estella in his imagination with the possibility of future prospects.

Across the marshes, they came to the quiet riverside and sat down on the bank. Rippling at their feet, the water flowing in the brook made it all the more tranquil than it would have been without the sound of running water and, as they settled themselves on the grass, Pip resolved that now was as good a time and place as ever to make his secret admission and to take Biddy into his inner confidence.

"Biddy, can I speak to you in confidence?" asked Pip gently.

"Why, of course, Pip. Haven't you known me long enough to be able to answer that yourself?" replied Biddy calmly. Pip smiled warmly back.

"Biddy, I want to be a gentleman."

"Oh, I wouldn't, if I was you," she replied cautiously. "I don't think it would provide the answer you are looking for."

"Biddy," responded Pip, a sternness appearing in the tone of his voice. "I have a particular reason for wanting to be a gentleman."

"You know best, Pip. But why? Don't you think you are happy as you are?"

"Biddy!" exclaimed Pip impatiently. "What an absurd thing to say. I am not at all happy as I am. I am disgusted with my calling and with my life. I have never taken to either since I was bound to being an apprentice at the forge."

"Was I absurd?" said Biddy, quietly raising her eyebrows at Pip's outburst. "I am sorry for that. I didn't mean to be. I only want you to do well and to be comfortable."

"Well, then, understand once and for all that I can never be comfortable, or anything else but miserable, Biddy, unless I can lead a very different sort of life from the life I have now."

"That's a pity," said Biddy, shaking her head with a sorrowful air.

"If I could have settled down," said Pip, plucking up the short grass within reach.

"If I could have settled down and been but half as fond of the forge as I was when I was little, I know it would have been much better for me. You, and I, and Joe would have wanted for nothing then, and Joe and I would have become partners when I was out of my time, and I might even have grown up to keep company with you, and we might have sat on this very bank, on a fine Sunday, being quite different people. I would have been good enough for you, shouldn't I, Biddy?"

"Yes. I'm not over particular," sighed Biddy, gazing out at the tall ships sailing by.

"Instead of that," said Pip, raising his eyebrows at Biddy's last unflattering remark and plucking up more grass and chewing on the stems.

"Instead of that, see how I am going on. Dissatisfied and uncomfortable, and what would it signify to me being coarse and common if nobody had told me so?"

"That's neither a very true, nor a polite thing to say," said Biddy, frowning, suddenly turning to face Pip. "Who said it?"

"The beautiful young lady at Miss Havisham's, and she's more beautiful than anybody ever was, and I admire her dreadfully, and I want to be a gentleman on her account," announced Pip, agitatedly tearing more grass and throwing tufts into the trickling brook.

"Do you want to be a gentleman to spite her, or to gain her over?" asked Biddy sensitively.

"I don't know," replied Pip moodily.

"Because, if you want to spite her," Biddy pursued, "I should think, but you know best; she is not worth your anger."

"That may be quite true," replied Pip. "But I admire her dreadfully," he said, his rough hands angrily tugging at his own hair before burying his face in the grass. Biddy reached out and tenderly stroked the back of Pip's head; her hand reaching across to stop him from uprooting any more of his hair. Slowly, his misery and anger subsided.

"I am glad of one thing," said Biddy, eventually breaking the silence, "which is that you feel you can confide in me, Pip. And I am glad of another thing which is that, of course, you know you may depend upon my keeping it a secret between us." Biddy sighed as she stood up from the bank and dusted down her frock.

"Shall we walk a little farther, or go home?" Biddy gently suggested with a fresh and pleasant change to her voice.

"Biddy," cried Pip, also getting up and putting his arm round her neck and giving her a kiss. "I shall always tell you everything."

"Till you're a gentleman," said Biddy, raising her eyebrow.

"You know I never shall be, so that's always. Not that I have any occasion to tell you anything else, for you know everything already."

"Ah," said Biddy, her voice in a whisper. "Shall we walk a little farther, or go home?" Pip took Biddy's hand in his and, deep in thought, they walked along the riverside together. He began to question whether he was more comfortable with Biddy in these circumstances, or when he was playing beggar-my-neighbour by candlelight in the room with all the stopped clocks and being despised by Estella.

I wish I could get her out of my head. All those fancies gone, leaving me to get on with a real life and doing work that I could enjoy and making the best of the time I have, mused Pip as they walked home hand-in-hand.

If Estella were beside me now instead of Biddy, would she make me miserable? Pip questioned his thoughts.

"I just don't know for certain. Pip, what a fool you are," he said moodily to himself.

"Biddy," said Pip suddenly. "I wish you could make me right."

"I wish I could too," whispered Biddy, squeezing Pip's hand.

"If I could only get myself to fall in love with you, Biddy. I hope you don't mind me saying so?"

"Oh dear, not at all," said Biddy. "Don't mind me."

"If I could only get myself to fall in love with you, that would be the thing for me."

"But, you see, Pip, you never will," said Biddy, finality in her voice.

Chapter 63

"Heavens, no, James, I propose you select a hotel anywhere from Soho to Covent Garden and have your luggage delivered to your suite straight from the docks. Be a good base to start with. You can deal with your business from there," suggested Jaggers, sipping on the red burgundy. Jaggers had arrived 15 minutes after Mudie and, meeting in the exclusive haunt of gentlemen chess players, Simpson's Grand Divan tavern proved the perfect venue.

"Excellent," said Mudie, having no idea where anything was in London.

"May I suggest the Ox and Hound?" Jaggers pulled his spotted handkerchief for effect, tucking it swiftly back in its home. Mudie nodded.

"Waiter?" Clicking his two fingers, Jaggers raised his voice across the room for service.

"Yes, sir; can I be of service, sir?"

"Be a good fellow and bring the porter." Jaggers slipped the boy a penny for his effort.

"There is one other matter, if I may trouble you, Mr. Jaggers?" said Mudie.

"Certainly, and what matter is that?" said Jaggers, reaching for his wine.

"A certain convict by the name of Magwitch asks for your help in locating a lad by the name of Pip." Jaggers nearly choked on his red wine, his eyebrows raised as he recollected the names.

"Indeed," he said, after regaining his composure.

"Aye, Magwitch works…or, should I say, worked for me at Castle Forbes. Did me an invaluable service for which I hope I have justly rewarded him," said Mudie, looking at the expression on Jaggers's face.

"I see those names are familiar to you," said Mudie.

"Put the case that I am aware that the first person you mentioned was a client of mine a number of years ago, and that further evidence existed at that time which concerned the second name you have mentioned, then I may be able to be of some assistance, depending upon the nature of your enquiry."

"Aye, actually, quite a simple question; Magwitch asks to know the whereabouts of the lad known as Pip." Interrupting Jaggers's reply, the concierge arrived at the private booth to be given instructions to transfer Mudie's luggage from the ship to the Ox and Hound in Meards Street, Soho.

"Present the bill to my office clerk in Little Britain," said Jaggers, squeezing his business card and half a crown into the concierge's hand and turned back to Mudie. "Shall we order?" suggested Jaggers, biting the side of his large index finger as the waiter came over, his pad at the ready.

"Why did you choose the Ox and Hound?" quizzed Mudie, after ordering roast beef.

"One of the oldest timber-framed inns left after the great fire," replied Jaggers, pouring the red burgundy. "Anyway, it's near to your publisher and, if it takes your fancy, there's plenty of nightlife. Get a meal any time of night or day if you want." Mudie and Jaggers sat, enjoying a three-hour luncheon together. Beef carved at the table, followed by cheese and port. Jaggers savoured his Montecristo cigar whilst Mudie declined the smoke, preferring to have a second helping of rhubarb crumble and custard.

Simpson's Grand Divan and Tavern in the Strand stood the culinary test.

Chapter 64
New South Wales – 1836

The horned cow was the first gift Magwitch could remember ever receiving in his entire life, and the riverside allotment in Morpeth, which he had leased for a penny an acre a year from James Mudie, had become home. He had built his little cottage with the aid of his recently acquired Aboriginal friend, Moola, the eldest son of a tribal chief.

Before his departure for England, Mudie had allocated one of the larger accommodation units at Castle Forbes before the sale, and Magwitch had relocated the building to his Morpeth lot. He had built a huge stone fireplace at one end, big enough to cook on. In the centre of the hut, he had erected a central barrier with a door between to form a separate room at the other end, which he now used as his bedroom. The lavatory was outside and consisted of a large limed pit above which he had slung a horizontal plank and handrail. He had rebuilt the cottage on the highest part of the land for fear of flooding. The jugerum of land along the waterfront conformed strangely to the ancient Roman measurements, in all, two-thirds of an acre of the best, rich, dark, alluvial soils. Lying dormant beneath the grasses at the water's edge, the humid, well-drained, sandy loam waited patiently to be sown. Skillfully, Magwitch had erected fencing from old, discarded wire and posts, allowing the cow, which he had named Buttercup, and the clutch of hens, freedom to graze and range at will.

The drought had broken with the spring rains, and it had been raining constantly for the past three days, in consequence, Hunters River had risen substantially. Magwitch sat on the top step of his little cottage looking across the 20 yards to the river, now running higher than he had seen before. He looked up at the sky and noticed a change in the cloud formation.

"That's the last of the rain for this year," volunteered Moola.

"Hope yourn right," commented Magwitch, concerned at the level of the river.

"Be gone tomorrow." Moola looked around for natural signs. He had been with Magwitch since the breakup of Castle Forbes and had assumed duties at the little cottage. Magwitch kept himself to himself, preferring Aboriginal companionship to that of rogue convicts. He had planted maize and potatoes which, combined with milk and butter from Buttercup and the odd bird and kangaroo, provided ample food. Slowly, the sky was clearing, and the sun began to force its way through.

"Moola, I need a lady to help us here. Yous agree. Working at milking and cleaning and cooking. Working just like the other farmers wot has maids so that we can go about men's business." Moola looked across at Magwitch and smiled.

"An Aboriginal wife?"

"No, a London lady."

"Where from? I mean, where will you find a lady like that?"

"The Female Factory," replied Magwitch, chuckling at the thought that armed with his Conditional-Pardon; he could have a lady assigned to him for domestic duties.

Magwitch jumped up and disappeared inside the cottage. Behind the stone fireplace, he had hidden his secret stash of money that he had converted to guineas, and the papers he had kept for the past six years since transportation, the last of the proceeds of the burglaries with Compeyson. He carefully removed the logs to the left side of the open fire and leant over the great stone slab at the side of the fireplace. At the back was a half-inch thick iron plate under which he had created his safe. Using a small jemmy, he eased the plate from its frame and slid it to the side, exposing an oblong, stone-lined chamber which extended under the heavy stone slab above.

The 18-inch deep chamber was bone-dry as a result of the heat from the adjacent fire. Magwitch reached in feeling under the heavy stone slab. He chuckled as his hand found the swag intact. Still having no idea what they were, he pushed the deeds to the Calcutta property to one side; his hand continued to grope in the gloom, searching for the two remaining gold coins and his little black book. Under a layer of dust, he retrieved the coins and his book. Carefully replacing the iron plate, he returned to the front step and sat back down. To Magwitch's relief, Moola had disappeared to attend to milking Buttercup, leaving him alone with his private thoughts. He fingered the two gold coins, both golden guineas minted in 1811.

Wonder if there's gold in this Land of Promise, he thought, biting down on each coin whilst considering his next plan.

Horse and trap first, food and water, and I'll take the road inland, down through Wiseman's Ferry to the Female Factory in Parramatta. He made his plans, opened his little black book, and studied the writing, tracing the smudged ink with his ragged index finger, stopping at his preferred name, Provis. He smiled at the thought of starting a new family, but then frowned.

"No, Provis, that's wrong," he said to himself. "Yous a married man still. Got to see the gypsy Elder, Sylvester, before you can do another family." Vividly, he remembered the tragedy on Hounslow Heath. *Assign a lady convict, not a wife. Too dangerous,* he mused, as the trap bounced along the new inland road.

But I'll 'ave 'er call me by my new name, Provis.

The matron lined the women up on the forecourt of the Female Factory in Parramatta. There were more than 20 of them, different shapes and sizes, with ages ranging from between 18 to 39, he reckoned. He studied their facial features and hair and the bagginess of their hand-woven slop-clothing. He noted the coarse material fell bulkily down to the ground. His eyes scanned the line of expectant female faces.

"Medical checks are down to you, Mr. Provis," said the portly matron.

"Wot? Don't yous do that? I'm no doctor."

"We do, but best check; there are so many women here and they try to hide their problems, especially if there's a chance of getting out. But take a tip, have a good look, maybe she's already pregnant. And feel for fatty or swollen lumps on glands for yourself," suggested the unconcerned matron as she looked down the list of selected names. "And don't forget to drop your handkerchief," she said as an afterthought. Magwitch stepped forwards and starting at the beginning of the line, walked steadily past each of the first 16 women. Smiling expressions of anticipation written across their faces, their heads turning to the right as he moved forward, expressions changing to sadness as he passed.

"Wot's yourn name?" asked Magwitch, stopping at the 17th woman.

"Polly, sir." Magwitch chuckled, enjoying his new title. He estimated her to be mid-30s, six to nine inches shorter than he; her brown hair neatly tied in a bun. Her pale skin appeared clear, and she had a straight back with broad shoulders and ample bosom. Magwitch reached for her hands to inspect her fingernails. He stopped mid-inspection, his attention drawn to the arrival of another horse and trap, as it noisily entered the courtyard. In the back of the trap sat a woman with a red ribbon tied to a single, fat plait at the back of her head. She was tied to the back of the front bench-seat of the rig with hemp rope that had also been tied in a noose around her neck. Having untied the rope from the bench seat, the driver climbed down and tugged at the woman.

"Get out, you old bag," he growled at her, yanking aggressively on the frayed rope. Led by the rope, the coarse man dragged the grumbling woman into the courtyard and tied the loose end of the rope to the tethering post.

"This one's barren and argumentative, luv," shouted the driver to the matron.

"Wife returns are processed by the superintendent," the matron shouted back, pointing to the end of the huge stone building. "Over there," the matron shouted again, pointing out the office with an untidy gesture and turned back to the business at hand, nodding to Magwitch to continue. Prudishly, Magwitch pushed Polly back behind the line-up, out of sight of the other women.

"How old is yous, my dear?" asked Magwitch.

"29, sir," replied Polly with a slight curtsy.

"Open yourn mouth, Polly," he instructed, reaching forwards and cupping her jaw whilst peering in at her teeth, scrutinising both top and bottom sets. He noted one of the molars had been removed.

"Ah, wot happened here?"

"Bit on a cherry stone and broke the side of it, sir. Rest of my teeth is strong though," Polly replied with a Cornish accent laden with irritation, as if she had been insulted, having compared her mouth to Magwitch's gapped and tobacco-stained teeth.

"Thank yous, Polly, now just stand still." Magwitch slipped his right hand into the top of her blouse and round under her armpit. Polly giggled; his fingers probing for swollen underarm glands, the action tickling Polly. Magwitch grinned, repeating the inspection of the other armpit; their eyes studying each other as he withdrew his hand.

"Oh, sir, you're so gentle," said Polly, returning a cheeky smile.

"Sorry, luv." Magwitch bent down and lifted her ample frock, plunging his coarse, unskilled hand in between her legs, probing for points of entry. Polly lent forwards and whispered.

"You can look, sir, when we get home, sir, if you like."

"Matron said to feel first," said Magwitch, feeling embarrassed.

"Men love to feel, don't they, sir?" He pretended to tut at the insinuation, quickly removing his hand.

"What do you feel for, sir?" whispered Polly into his left ear.

"Lumps, Polly, matron said for to do it." Magwitch chuckled whilst finishing his physical examination and then rummaged in his trouser pocket for his tatty handkerchief.

"Polly to get back in line," he said, turning to the matron and deliberately dropping his handkerchief, signalling that he had made his choice.

Having completed formalities in the superintendent's office, they prepared to leave for Maitland again via the inland road.

"I have another question," said Polly.

"And what may that be?" responded the snobbish superintendent.

"What is to happen to my daughter, Alice?"

"She'll be cared for at the orphanage until you have served your time."

"But, sir, she's only six. Can't she come home with us? Promise she'll be no trouble, sir," Polly quickly turned her request and addressed it to Magwitch.

"Wot? I'm to be an orphanage, is it?" said Magwitch, suddenly regretting his outburst and feeling sympathy for Polly. Polly threw a pleading glance back at Magwitch.

"She can work for you too, milk cows and grow vegetables and clean, sir." Magwitch pictured the little girl on a three-legged stool, milking Buttercup. His mind filled with thoughts of little Estella.

"Gord bless me soul if I's not going soft or something." Polly sat in the front of the trap with Magwitch and little Alice squeezed in the middle between them.

"Instant family without the nightmare of marriage," chuckled Magwitch, as they bumped along the rutted road on their 140-mile journey home.

"Mr. Provis," said Alice. "Thank you for saving Mummy and me, and I promise I'll be a very good girl when we get home." Magwitch suddenly felt he could make up for all those lost years he had missed with Gypsy Molly and Estella. By the time they reached home, they had become more than master and servant.

"Polly, put the kettle on," chuckled Magwitch, as he added the finishing touches before planting the vegetable patch on the jugerum of sandy-loam alluvial soil.

Moola had spent the past three weeks preparing the soils. The heat and drought had intensified, if that was possible, but there was still plenty of water in Hunters River, and they had skillfully created an irrigation system. Domestic food was ample, but other forms of income were failing. Most farmers who did not have a river or creek frontage had suffered successive losses of crops through the ongoing drought, and those who had survived were being robbed almost daily by roaming bushrangers.

"Polly, put the kettle on," was Magwitch's cry for attention and his regular instruction at the end of the day as he completed washing in the river. "We'll all have tea." It was approaching dusk when Moola and Magwitch arrived back at the cottage for tea. The weather had presented blue skies since they could remember, and the table had been set up permanently on the deck. Pestered by aggressive flies, they sat down. "Alice, go and see wot yourn mum's up to," said Magwitch, lazily swatting a bloated bluebottle. Little Alice, now dressed in her night dress and ready for bed, ran quickly into the cottage. Magwitch sat brooding on the deck, becoming angry at the delay.

"I'm coming, I'm coming," the words floated on the air. "Be patient."

"Be patient, she says. All we want is something to drink," grumbled Magwitch, his nerves becoming tense with the frustrations of lack of work in the district.

"Must find another way to make some money." Polly arrived with the tea and some bread and butter.

"Master, now what's all the noise about?" said Polly, hurrying back into the kitchen to bring the newly baked biscuits and the last of the cream.

"We need to be making more money. I can't keep supporting yous lot without a job." Moola sat quietly on the steps and listened.

"There's more trouble than that," replied Polly.

"Wot do you mean?"

"It's Buttercup."

"Wot's wrong with her?"

"She's stopped giving milk, and I think you should take her to the market and sell her."

"Polly, Polly, Polly," said Magwitch. "Stop clucking around. Have yous upset my Buttercup or something?"

"No, master, it's just that she's getting old, and I think you should sell her and get some money." Polly quickly poured the tea.

"But she's sacred to me. If we were in India, we would never dream of selling her. We would let her roam forever."

"This isn't India," argued Polly, "but 'cause of the drought, there's no grazing and no food for her. That's probably why there's no milk," replied Polly thoughtfully, concerned for their need of money.

"Gord's truth, Polly, I can't sell her."

"You must. First thing in the morning," said Polly, clearing away the table. Magwitch slumped back into his chair; his eyes looked towards Moola for inspiration.

"'S truth, mate," said Magwitch almost jumping from his chair and blurting out his favorite blasphemous expression, "Wot's that?" Sitting on the deck, Moola fiddled quietly with two stone-like nuggets. Nuggets the size of fat, king marbles sat glinting in the palm of his left hand.

"For good luck," replied Moola, looking back at Magwitch.

"Where in gord's name did yous find 'em?"

"A hard day's ride west of my home at Myall Creek," replied Moola. The night was hot and humid, with mosquitoes and flies and moths conspiring to defeat any possibility of a decent sleep for Magwitch's troubled mind. After breakfast, the temperature quickly moved into the high 90s as Magwitch walked towards Maitland Market, Buttercup in tow, her soft doleful eyes set in her smooth, brown-haired face hung sadly between her magnificent horns, adding a further air to the misery of the pair as they trudged to their destiny.

Chapter 65

The sun refracting through the ruby caught Magwitch's eye. He stopped, embarrassed that a Sikh, of all people, should bear witness to his almost sacrilegious deed of selling Buttercup.

The Sikh stepped out from the dappled shade into full view, his white turban highlighting the richness of the central ruby, his purple and gold tunic and shimmering satin of his ample, silken trousers adding crispness to his presence. He brought his hands up and gently pressed his palms together in prayer, with his head bowed in reverence. Magwitch and Buttercup stood together on the dusty road, observing the elegant stranger. The Sikh approached, repeating his salutation.

"Where do you travel?" asked the Sikh respectfully.

"Maitland cattle market," replied Magwitch, looking sheepishly down at Buttercup's forlorn expression.

"We know each other?" suggested the Sikh.

Magwitch pretended not to remember the first time when the new herd had arrived. That had been years ago.

"For money? And what then? Mere money, to be spent in the blink of an eye," continued the strange Sikh, digging his hand into the small, gold-braided pocket of his purple jacket. Magwitch took a shallow breath to respond as the Sikh withdrew his hand and revealed three ripe beans sitting proudly on his palm. Magwitch watched, mesmerised by the man's actions.

"Wot's them?" asked Magwitch innocently.

"Magical beans to make your fortune."

"Nah, money's wot I needs."

"If you follow my lead, you can become a rich man," insisted the Sikh.

"Wot's that? If, if, if. If my auntie had balls, she'd be my uncle," grumbled Magwitch; his instincts warning him of being conned. A gentle smile appeared on the Sikh's distinguished face. Quietly, he placed his thumb to secure the beans and brought the palms of his hands together and, again, raised them to beneath his lean chin in the form of prayer. He nodded respectfully and then delivered his message:

Good flax and good jute, for to have of your own,
In spring, a good housewife will see it be sown.
And afterward, trim it, to serve at a need,
The fimble to spin, and the carle for your seed.

"Where do them beans come from?" asked Magwitch, his interest alerted at the Sikh's theatrical display.

"From the banks of the Hoogly, a tributary of the great holy River Ganges in Calcutta," replied the Sikh, dragging a heavy sack full of jute seeds from behind a massive, red, cedar tree. The mention of Calcutta triggered Magwitch's memory of the strange papers he still kept in the little hidey-hole at the cottage. His mind flashed back to the robbery in Marylebone, his first with Compeyson; rightly or wrongly, Magwitch smelt money, the mental connection urging him to trade.

"S'pose its better than selling Buttercup, I'd rather she got a good 'ome," mumbled Magwitch, reaching out to receive the beans. He studied the seeds and then opened the top of the sack to check that they were the same.

"How can these make me a fortune?" said Magwitch, warming to the idea.

"Ah, when grown and harvested and properly treated, you will make more delicate and beautiful garments for the people of New South Wales. Better and stronger than the finest flax. Clothes as delicate as the spider's most attenuated web. For the variety of clothing you can produce will be more numerous than can be made with flax or even cotton. And from the coarser material, you will make rope and sacking and webbing. Indeed, the ladies of the Parramatta factory weave and sew from materials imported into your home country and shipped here by your own government. And then there are the oils that come from crushing the seed, oil for oil-cakes for fattening oxen and hogs and poultry and all domestic livestock."

It was late afternoon by the time Magwitch set out to walk the few miles back along the dusty road towards home. But he walked sprightly, although the weight of the sack on his shoulders caused him to stoop. He chuckled at the thought of the encounter with the same Sikh who had delivered the *'Singhai'* cattle years earlier and now, here he was, introducing yet another idea. But, this time, an idea which could potentially deliver riches.

He had been right the last time, why not this time as well. *The cards have foretold.* Singing with euphoria, he swung open the gate to his allotment, almost breaking into a run as he approached the cottage. "Polly, put the kettle on," he sang out as loud as he could. "Polly, put the kettle on." His left fist clutched the three magic jute beans while his right steadied the sack on his shoulders. He climbed the few steps to the deck and dropped the sack on the floor planking. Still clutching the three beans, he burst in through the old wooden door. "Polly, put the kettle on, we'll all have tea," he sang out, laughing, desperate to tell his story.

Polly and Alice and Moola listened intently as Magwitch related the encounter verbatim and finally reaching the end, he carefully laid a handful of beans in the centre of the table.

"Goodness gracious, master, have you gone quite mad!?" exclaimed Polly, shocked and near to disgust. Magwitch said nothing in reply. Distraught, Polly jumped up from the table, grabbed the beans, and hurled them out of the open window. They reached the rich, dark, alluvial soils of the riverside vegetable patch, disappearing from view in the furrows of the recently hand-tilled earth. Magwitch gasped in horror. "And you can forget tea," she shouted, having forgotten her position in the household. Moola slunk out of the room, leaving Alice confused at the reason for the row between her mother and the master. "That's right, and you can forget dinner," continued Polly, taking the kettle off the stove.

"Polly, take it off again," sniggered Alice from the deck. Avoiding the brewing domestic argument, Magwitch slipped away, leaving Polly ranting and raving.

Chapter 66

The Angel Inn had changed since Molly Morgan had retired, but her memory lived on. Half a dozen assigned convicts sat drinking opposite in the dining room as Magwitch scoffed his breakfast opposite. Their absentee masters working away down in Sydney had given them full reign to come and go as they pleased. Magwitch noticed they carried muskets. They spoke in lowered tones, dredging up hatred and grumbling about the Aboriginals.

But Major Mudie liked the Aboriginals and said they was helpful people and should be respected? mused Magwitch, scratching his stubbly chin as he considered their conversation. He had found the same with Moola. *Major Mudie said they were honest people compared to the likes of us.* Magwitch considered himself to be emancipated and better than those still serving their time. He listened again.

"They live up around Myall Creek," said the curly-haired convict with the blotchy-red shirt. The names of their employers floated on the air.

"Work for Henry Dangar," and another settler's name mentioned, "Glennie."

That's near Castle Forbes, thought Magwitch, wondering what they were discussing. He overheard one of the convict's names, 'John Russell.'

He's the one wot got the blotchy-red shirt. Nasty bit of goods, observed Magwitch as he left his table and slipped unnoticed out of the backdoor. Disturbed by the conspiracy, he hung on, listening at the door as the conversation became heated.

"Or my name's not 'Charles Kilmaister.'"

"Gord, there's another name, loud-mouthed and boasting through the effects of rum," whispered Magwitch to himself. He closed the door quietly and walked slowly back to Morpeth. Adding to his misery during the two weeks he had been away from home, the weather had been overcast and drizzly. But it had cleared his mind; the sight of new green shoots in the fields and jacarandas beginning to blossom lifted his heart. He felt his skin soften in the gentle mist and drew comfort from dust free roads. "Wot in gord's name is them?" he said to himself, rounding the corner to his little allotment, his eyes focusing on the vegetable patch. Great green bunches of stalks thrust up into the heavens.

"Weeds. Your weeds," accused Polly.

"Now don't start that again," said Magwitch angrily, remembering the man who had dragged his wife back to the female factory at the end of a rope.

"Them weeds is jute!" exclaimed Magwitch, strangely confident that the Sikh knew something he didn't.

"What's jute?"

"Indian word for hemp, you foolish woman," Magwitch's voice began to rise.

"God save us," replied Polly. "Spent all my time in the factory where you found me weaving and spinning that blessed stuff."

"But that came from England. This, we've grow'd here." Magwitch stomped out of the little cottage and walked across to the thicket of jute. He ran his finger up the thickening stems. "Where to from 'ere?" he muttered to himself. "Where to from 'ere?"

A scruffy, Ticket-of-Leave, convict clerk managed the information section of the government office in Sydney. He was approachable, and he knew his subject. Magwitch had slipped him a tarnished shilling for the information.

"Uses? You want to know the uses of hemp?" he replied, flicking the grubby coin two feet into the air with his thumb nail, smartly catching it during its descent.

"If yous can," replied Magwitch, settling himself into the ragged chair in the corner of the tiny office. The clerk, quickly tucking the coin in his waistcoat pocket, turned and pulled a buff file from the lower shelf behind. He removed the fading ribbon to reveal a bundle of papers. Silently, Magwitch waited, watching the clerk progress through the papers.

"Says here that botanist, Sir Joseph Banks, sent seeds out with the First Fleet in 1788, wanted to make New South Wales a hemp colony," muttered the clerk. "But nothing much else."

"Does they grow the stuff 'ere now?" asked Magwitch. The clerk sat down on his wooden armchair and began to leaf through the wad of paper.

"A few references, but nothing important." Magwitch kept quiet as the clerk continued reading, "Big market though, says that England imports 40,000 tons a year from Russia. They spend over a million pounds on it." Magwitch's ears pricked up. The clerk raised his eyebrows in surprise as he studied the next paper; a picture of a fully rigged man o' war took up most of the page and underneath, appeared the words: "*180 thousand pounds' weight of hemp are required to completely rig a first-rate ship of war,*" he read aloud. The clerk wrote the figure on a piece of paper and divided it by 2240. "That's nearly 80 tons of hemp for one ship!" He stopped and looked across at Magwitch.

"Anything else?" asked Magwitch innocently.

"We import the woven material in bundles and have it sewn together for slop-clothing and other uses by the women in the Female Factory in Parramatta."

"Government contract then?" suggested Magwitch. The clerk nodded.

"Ah, also says the women weave flax," scratching his chin as he thought. The clerk closed the file, retied the ribbon, and put it back on the shelf. "Got to have money for a government contract," added the clerk, a wry smile slowly spreading across his face.

A simple bribe to secure the contract, thought Magwitch, winking back without comment.

Chapter 67

They loaded the trap with fossicking equipment, pans, buckets and the single small tent before dawn and, whilst still dark, gobbled breakfast consisting of thick omelettes and crusty bread rinsed down with copious amounts of tea. They were on their way before sunrise. The sun broke the horizon behind them as they passed through Wallalong and, by midday, stopped for a break and lunch at the Aboriginal camp at Wallaringa. Magwitch looked at the ominous Wallarobba Range, deciding to follow the track to Dungog where they would pitch camp. Tomorrow, they would head northeast to intercept the Myall track, then turn westwards to cross the Malumla Range of mountains, aiming to establish their prospecting base at Woolooma, close to where Moola remembered finding the two gold nuggets. Moola talked incessantly whilst they erected the tent and lit the campfire. He talked of his childhood and fishing in Myall Creek and how life had changed for his Aboriginal people since the arrival of the white man.

"Does that include me?" quizzed Magwitch, wiping the watery gravy from his tin plate with a chunk of stale, crusty bread. Moola was about to answer when Magwitch cut him short.

"Let's see them nuggets," grunted Magwitch, having lit up his clay pipe. Moola fished deep in his baggy shorts, retrieved his two, irregularly shaped, yellowish worry toys and handed them to Magwitch. "Gord bless my soul." The weight of them was more than Magwitch remembered. He put one between his teeth and bit down. "Gor blimy, best not tell a livin' soul." Moola looked on in disbelief that a couple of speckled, little, yellow stones should be kept secret. Magwitch read his mind. "Different values, mate. Different values."

Chapter 68

Close to the end of summer, the jute programme had escalated. Taking seeds from the first plants had produced a far bigger crop, taking up most of the area allocated for vegetables. Polly had become resigned to Magwitch's activity. She watched as the jute plants grew three times as tall as a man in as many weeks and slowly warmed to his objective of making cloth from the strands. The first stalks were strong, but to manufacture and weave and produce was the next problem. And to produce finished goods to a quality befitting the government contract seemed a long way off. It would take time, more land, and money. Prospecting for precious stones seemed the short-term solution, but as to gold, there had been no reports other than small amounts of alluvial deposits. Magwitch rattled the two nuggets in his right hand and then handed them back to Moola.

"We dig and pan for three months and take back whatever we have at the end of winter, and be back home in time for the spring planting," said Magwitch, lying down on his bedroll and gazing up into the starlight sky.

At Moola's insistence, the following day, they made a detour further north and arrived at the Aboriginal camp by nightfall. Big Daddy, the Aboriginal closely related to Moola and Davey, Moola's brother received them, proudly introducing them to the family. The camp, located on the edge of Henry Dangar's cattle station, contained a number of families. A dozen or so piccaninnies played, kicking an old rusty tin about the yard as the women prepared the evening meal. Wisps of smoke from clay pipes floated up into the still air as the more-senior men sat round the campfire, discussing business and telling stories since Moola had last been home. Magwitch broached the subject of alluvial gold, receiving nods of interest and information that there were similar deposits of the yellow stones and particles on the beds of other creeks and rivers sourced in the Malumla Range.

Magwitch added the information to his little map, noting two points: the first they had already passed was north of Dungog, halfway to the base of the mountain range and, secondly, Moonan Flats, to the west of the range. He grinned at the thought.

How simple is this, keep in with the Aboriginals; Major Mudie was right, they've been here for thousands of years and know where the stuff is. O'course it's no use to them, thought Magwitch, squeezing his little black book into his pocket. He looked up as the little piccaninny approached with a wooden plate laden with squirming grubs. He shivered at the thought, but reached out and took one. Throwing his head back, he dropped the wriggling thing into his mouth and chewing quickly to stop the wriggle, swallowed hard. His frown slowly turned to a smile. The sweet taste struck his taste buds as it slid down his throat, prompting him to reach for another to the satisfaction of the expectant Aboriginal eyes.

"Wot's yourn name?" said Magwitch, preparing his pipe.

"Charley," grinned the little boy, his light, olive-coloured skin setting him apart from the other Aboriginal children.

"Yourn mother's been eating too much white bread?" jested Magwitch, looking at little Charley, a cheeky grin spreading from ear to ear.

"She eats your bread, mister, and likes it," said Charley, offering Magwitch another witchetty grub.

Chapter 69

Running his own cattle station on Liverpool Plains, emancipated convict, John Russell, freed by servitude a year or so ago, had sent a message to all the bitter convicts running the neighbouring cattle stations in the district on behalf of their absent landowners. The convicts had been conspiring for weeks, bearing grudges against their masters, but more so, against the Aboriginals living peacefully in the area. Apart from the occasional drunkenness and tomfoolery with the convicts sleeping with their Aboriginal women, the Aboriginals posed no threat to the cattle, preferring to live separately, follow their culture and traditions. But that wasn't enough to bigoted and mean convicts who saw them as nothing better than animals to be hunted as wild game.

"There's a big Aboriginal camp up by Myall Creek," said Russell, swallowing another cup of colonial gin. Edward Foley, assigned to Flemming's cattle station, slid his rusted sword from its scabbard and harpooned an apple from the bowl of fruit on the dresser. Bending his wrist, he brought the fruit stuck on the end of his sword within reach of his left hand without leaving his seat. Pulling it off, he bit a chunk from the side. Juice ran down his chin.

"Leave a couple of hours before the sun gets up," said Foley, his mouth full of masticated apple. "Go from station to station and collect a few more men and jump the camp at dawn." Busily oiling and polishing his musket, Russell started his infectious laughter, spurring the others to drink more. "End up at Henry Dangar's hut, reckon Hobbs, the overseer, is down in Maitland, but Anderson and Kilmaister should be there." As planned, half an hour before sun-up, they mounted and rode between stations, building their numbers for the live human hunt.

Chapter 70

Magwitch and Moola bid farewell to Big Daddy, Davey, and the rest of Moola's friends and family and, leaving before sun-up, rode in their trap westwards towards Moonan Flats and Woolooma. There had been small rains during the night, laying the dust and leaving silty-mud and isolated puddles on the track.

"Be there by nightfall," volunteered Moola. Magwitch nodded, preferring to keep sucking on his clay pipe. An hour out of the camp, they saw the riders. Magwitch pushed his old hat back and peered into the distance; the half-moon forming a ghostly image of the distant riders.

"More than ten," he mused. "Wonder where they's going?"

"Bushrangers, master," replied Moola; his voice quivered as the terror filled his body. Magwitch yanked the left rein, steering the horses into the bush to the south of the track. They parked behind a thicket and waited for the riders to pass.

"9 – 10 – 11 – 12. Looks like 12 of the evil buggers," muttered Magwitch as they approached.

"Don't think they saw us, master."

"Gord save us if they did! They look awful mean." The sound of galloping hooves, slapping leather, and rattling metal buckles of livery shook the air. They crouched down in the back of the trap and watched. Moola nudged Magwitch.

"Look, master, they're armed with muskets and swords and pistols."

"I sees that," acknowledged Magwitch, holding his hand over his mouth as if silencing himself. The horses and riders were on top of them in minutes.

"Christ Jesus, now yous know wot Major Mudie was on about," breathed Magwitch through his trembling hand. As quickly as they had come, they passed, disappearing into the east, the silhouette of their bobbing heads beneath weathered-leather hats, more distinct from the aurora of the yet hidden sun beneath the horizon.

"Thank the good Lord for that," said Magwitch, slapping the reins and moving the creaking trap from the cover of the tree and sneaking out from behind the bush to get back on to the track. Magwitch looked down at the mob's hoofed tracks in the silty mud. "Gord, let's get out of here before they come back."

Led by John Russell, the gang of horsemen galloped into the Aboriginal camp, sending men and women and children running for cover. Big Daddy and some others made it to Dangar's hut, leaving Davey, two women, and two piccaninnies out of sight behind the hut.

"Quick, down to the brook," said Davey, grabbing the two, little, black children and running for the banks of the creek. Shrieking in panic, the two Aboriginal women scrambled down to the creek.

Anderson, Dangar's hutkeeper, stood in the doorway of the hut as Russell dismounted, turned to his saddlebag and unbuckled a long rope. He strode into the hut and, assisted by the other convicts, tied nooses around the necks of the Aboriginals, spurred the horse and dragged them off to the creek. Big Daddy had been tied by the ankles and feet first, was dragged in the dirt by another horse behind the others.

"Hobbs not here then?" challenged Kilmaister.

Anderson shook his head, fear etched in his face. The other convicts marauded around and were itching for blood by the time they reached the creek a quarter of a mile away. They had rounded up over 30 Aboriginals who now lay trussed together on the banks of the creek. Big Daddy struggled and, unnoticed, had managed to untie his wrists. He bent forward and hurriedly attempted to untie his ankles. Blood dripped from his knees, feet, and elbows; a six-inch gash lay gaping in his cheek, all caused by stones as he was dragged by the horse. Kilmaister saw, pulled his pistol and, at pointblank range, shot him in the chest and head. Foley jumped forwards and thrust his sword into another, its tip snapping as it struck the inside of the man's shoulder blade after passing through the lung. At the same time, Hawkins, Foley's sidekick, drew his sword and took a swipe at little Charley, taking his head off in one cut, leaving it to fall to the ground and roll towards the women. The women screamed at the bloody sight. The initial shots panicked the other convicts, as they too opened fire. They kept firing until nothing moved.

"Get the firesticks from the hut," ordered Russell, dragging dried branches into a heap creating a funeral pyre. Davey, the two women, and children, watched in horror from their hide on the far side of the creek. Trembling, they stayed hidden. Foley slung his broken sword into the creek and raced back to the hut. He returned with the firesticks and handed them out to the murderous mob. They loaded the wretched bodies onto the bonfire. It was ablaze in minutes.

"Human fat burns well," commented James Oats in between gulping great swigs of rum. Sick grins and satanic laughter filled the air as they drank and relived the human hunt. The pyre took all day, but as the sun dipped in the west, all that remained were charred bones. Aboriginal bones left to bleach in the cruel sun. Children's skulls predominated. The mob dispersed into the bush and back to their respective cattle stations, unconcerned at leaving evidence and tracks behind.

Chapter 71

"Gord, look at this, will ya? I's got some," shouted Magwitch, swirling the water around in his pan. He carefully tipped the water out and lifted each grain of gold from the wet alluvial sample and placed them in his little muslin pouch. His heart pounded with excitement at his first ever find. For weeks, he and Moola kept panning, collecting several ounces of clean gold. They worked their way back up towards the range. They learnt that the gold nuggets seemed to drop in certain parts of the river, particularly on the inside of meanders and places where the river ran more slowly.

"The mother lode must be in the Malumla Range," concluded Magwitch, looking up at the range behind them. He opened his little black book and added a note to his map, marking the position of each find. He noted that the further they went up the river, the finds were bigger. He began to develop his hypothesis as to the location of the mother lode. "Next year, we come back and start on the southeast, north of Dungog," said Magwitch, as they finally loaded the trap and began the slow trek home.

Aghast, Magwitch and Moola listened to the dreadful news in the Angel Inn in Maitland. The murderous attack on the Aboriginal village was talked about as the Myall Creek massacre of which they knew nothing until they had reached home. During his absence, Governor Gipps, who had replaced Governor Bourke, had sent a party of mounted police to hunt down the murderers and, once caught, would be tried at the Supreme Court in Sydney. Moola had breathed a sigh of relief to hear that Davey had escaped and volunteered to be a material witness in the trial later in the year, but had broken down in tears when he had heard of the murder of Big Daddy and the rest of his family. Local gossip had embellished the attack, but the details of the butchering of little four-year-old Charley were impossible to stomach. Hardened by such atrocities, Magwitch had sat quietly, horrified at the news and had chosen to suck away on his pipe and focus on his success with the jute and the gold.

Come the spring, he would act.

Chapter 72

The tiny crucible designed for re-smelting lead ball for muskets would be perfect. Having scrubbed the rusty bowl, he held the crucible over the fire and waited for it to glow red, while the gold particles sat patiently in the bottom of a small glass before smelting. Removing the glowing iron cup from the fire, Magwitch carefully introduced the particles of gold and watched as they melted, forming a thin, crusty skin on the surface. Five minutes later, he tapped the newly smelted nugget from its mould. The glittering fat bullet was heavy, had a rounded top and flat bottom, and was slightly knurled on the barrel from the rusted sides of the crucible. But nevertheless, the bullet-shaped ingot was shiny and attractive. He inscribed the letters 'AMP' on the flat bottom and stood it in front of him on an inverted, rusty, bean tin.

"My first bullet. My good luck charm." Magwitch felt pleased with himself and prepared to smelt the second. He estimated there to be enough alluvial gold to smelt a further two bullets. Little by little, he dropped grains of gold into the red-hot crucible. He was able to produce two more bullets, one bigger than the first and the last, smaller than the first. He chuckled to himself as he mounted his horse and rode south.

Straight-faced, Magwitch placed the smallest gold bullet on the desk in front of the government clerk. A cantankerous smile slid around the clerk's crooked mouth as he lent forward and picked up the gratuity.

"Bullion?" was the first word to be uttered whilst weighing the precious metal in his cupped hand. He raised the bullet to his mouth and bit down. His smile grew while he reached down to his lower desk drawer and, opening it, rummaged around and finally pulled out a sheaf of paper tied together in the top left-hand corner with a thin green ribbon.

"This year's hemp supply contract," said the clerk. The contract had gone to some London company. Surreptitiously, the clerk slid the copy contract across to Magwitch, the bullet still held tightly in his greedy little hand. "And next year, the contract will be double the amount from what I hear."

"Can I get a lend 'e it?" asked Magwitch politely.

"I'll need it back by the end of the month," replied the clerk. Magwitch tucked the document into his tatty jacket and was gone.

Chapter 73

"Are you here for Buttercup?" asked the Sikh, surprised to see Magwitch after such a long time.

"Gord alone knows wot I'd give to take 'er home along-a-me. But no," said Magwitch, having travelled back from his meeting with the purchases clerk in Sydney.

"I needs a supply of proper jute 'til I gets mine growed enough."

"How much jute and for what purpose?" Magwitch smiled and handed over the copy contract.

"Double that!" exclaimed Magwitch, unable to read the document. The Sikh quickly glanced through the first three pages, fixing his eyes on the quantity summaries at the end. "And how would you propose to pay?"

"With these?" The Sikh found it difficult to hide his pleasure at the sight of Magwitch's largest gold bullet and the aging deeds to the salubrious property that Magwitch had kept with him since the Riverside Terrace robbery for nearly seven years. To the Sikh, the sight of the deeds was incomprehensible and, potentially, vastly more valuable.

"I know this property," said the Sikh in surprise as he studied the Calcutta property deeds. "It's currently occupied by part of the East India Company specialising in imports and exports," he continued, leafing through the document. "Where did you get them?"

"London. Found 'em before I got shipped 'ere," replied Magwitch with a wry smile, unable to understand what the documents were.

"Found where?" the Sikh probed.

"Chiswick, a business acquaintance, goes by the name of Compeyson." Magwitch pointed the finger of blame and quickly changed the subject.

"And wot does they trade in?"

"I'm thinking jute and cotton and silks. Some spices," commented the Sikh. "Do you know the people?"

"No."

"And you want me to be your import agent to meet this contract until you can grow enough jute?" Magwitch nodded, wondering where this would lead.

"Samples first?" quizzed the Sikh, rolling the bullet between his fingers.

"Enough for to get a start," replied Magwitch, looking at the shiny gold bullet in the Sikh's hand.

After securing the beginnings of a source of supply of jute from Calcutta, Magwitch made his way back to his little cottage in Morpeth.

Polly helped bring in the last jute harvest of the year before winter. Slashing at the sinewy stalks, she laid the 12 to 16-foot strips out in the sun to dry. Two weeks later, she prepared the strips, peeling off the coarse outer cover to reveal the internal stringy material. There was enough to fill their small cart; the length of the strands making it necessary to fold the stems halfway along to fit on the cart without dragging on the ground during the overland trip down to Parramatta and the Female Factory west of Sydney.

Chapter 74

The first trial of those connected with the massacre at Myall Creek turned into a farce. The worst of the treachery was the caliber of the jurymen, having been formed of mostly time-served, emancipated convicts, who, after their short deliberation, had emerged from the jury room, sniggering and laughing, as the foreman blatantly returned a unanimous verdict of not guilty.

Immediately, the Chief Justice was forced to order a mistrial and a few days later, a second trial was held, this time chaired by Justice Burton, supported by a military jury. They quickly returned a unanimous verdict of guilty. During the trial, a series of objections had been raised, not least of which was that 19-year-old Davey, an Aboriginal who had come forward as a material witness, would need to be instructed by a competent person before his evidence could be considered acceptable in a court of law.

After the trial, Judge Burton looked shocked and tired, disturbed at the depths to which these men had sunk. Somberly, he placed the triangular black cloth on the top of his wig. "It is my solemn duty that I now award the sentence due for your crime." He paused to collect himself. "I direct that each and every one of you be taken from this place to the place from whence you came, and from there, be taken to a place of public execution where you will be hanged by the neck until you are dead, and may God have mercy on your souls."

The murderers, still in the belief that they had done nothing wrong, were taken away to the military barracks in The Rocks. Days later, they were all simultaneously hanged in front of hundreds of spectators.

Chapter 75

First opened in 1817, the Bank of New South Wales was located in George Street, Sydney, and the manager, Mr. Worthington, considered the bank to be his own and acted accordingly.

Magwitch was ushered into the backroom; his presentation of seven golden bullets, the proceeds from his second prospecting trip to Dungog, had done the trick. No questions asked at the front desk, but inside the confines of the well-appointed office, the questions came thick and fast.

"My name is Worthington," said the manager, his right hand extended.

"Thank'ye, Mr. Worthington." They briefly shook hands. Mr. Worthington indicated a seat where Magwitch quickly settled himself.

"Where?" quizzed Worthington.

"Begin yourn pardon, sir, but all I can remember is north of 'ere, sir," replied Magwitch, not wishing to spill the beans. Nervously, he slipped his hand into his pocket for his clay pipe, the other hand clutching his penknife and plug of dark tobacco. Carefully, he shaved off two slivers, rubbed them together, and rammed the loose tobacco into his pipe; he sat back and lit up while the manager fingered and inspected each bullet carefully.

"By fossicking or panning?" Worthington continued probing.

"Well, sir, seems I done both, sir," said Magwitch, calmly sucking on his pipe, the resultant smoke thickening in the room. Accidentally, his frayed straw hat fell from his lap onto the floor, beads of perspiration formed on his brow through exertion as he bent down and reached under the desk.

"Took a long time, sir," commented Magwitch breathlessly as an afterthought, hiding the fact that he and Moola had made the find within weeks. Worthington smiled benevolently and opened a thick-covered, hard-backed accounts ledger, bound with a burgundy leather spine, the words, 'Asset Ledger,' embossed in gold on the front. Dipping his quill pen into the crystal inkwell, he carefully made an entry. A double knock on the door broke the silence and in walked an elegant, red-haired, female assistant. Her eyes glittered at the sight of the seven golden bullets lined up on the manager's oak desk. In her left hand, she carried a set of brass scales supported on a polished mahogany base. Both men looked up. Magwitch took another suck on his pipe.

"Ah, thank you, my dear." Worthington indicated with the feather end of his quill that she should place the scales in front of Magwitch. Magwitch shuffled his chair to the side to give her room; her tight-fitting frock brushing against his elbow. He looked up and smiled politely; his stomach screwing up with excitement, treatment like this was a new experience. Carefully, Worthington placed the seven bullets on the left pan, neatly clustering six bullets in a circle with one in the centre, their flat bases allowing the rounded bullet-noses to point up at the central pivot of three delicate chains where they hooked on the end of the balance beam. The pan sat heavily on the mahogany base.

From the skillfully crafted weight box, Worthington carefully removed one weight at a time with a slim pair of tweezers steadily increasing the weights on the right pan. Ultimately, the gold pan lifted gently from its rest, whilst the downward pointer of the pendulum swung slowly from the right to the centre until both pans sat level. Worthington smiled, retrieved his quill from the stand, replenished the ink, and completed the entry in the ledger.

"This is more than enough to cover your Calcutta shipment. Indeed, all the jute shipments to fulfill the government contract for this year, Mr. Magwitch."

"Yous can call me Provis, sir," said Magwitch with a serious expression. Picking up his quill pen again, Worthington added the additional name to the entry.

"And Provis, may I enquire as to who you would nominate as your next of kin?"

"Next a kin?"

"Yes, Mr. Magwitch, er Provis," he repeated himself, pausing for the next entry.

"Why does yous need that, sir?"

"Only a precaution, Provis, in case something were to happen to you." Magwitch frowned, pausing to scrape out the bowl of his pipe into the crystal ashtray. Worthington sat back and waited for his client to speak. Magwitch produced his tobacco, patiently sliced another two slivers, rubbed them together, and, with his stained thumb, rammed the ball of tobacco into the bowl and relit his pipe, inhaling deeply.

"I was married once. Had a beautiful daughter an' all." Magwitch's delayed delivery bemused the manager. "Likely, still is? Lady's name was Gypsy Molly. Before me, her family name was an Ingram. Daughter's name's Estella." He puffed again and then thoughtfully turned his head to gaze out of the double-hung window, his mind vividly recalling his affair on Hounslow Heath.

"Do you want me to enter those names?" asked Worthington.

"Maybe I's not married no more," suggested Magwitch. "And maybe Estella's dead." Worthington raised his eyebrows.

"But I need to make a record, Provis. It's the bank's procedure and family would be the best." Magwitch sucked harder, the new tobacco glowing red in the top of the bowl. Tamping down the burning, loose ends of tobacco, he felt nothing through the thickened skin at the end of his thumb. He carefully considered his reply.

"Well, em, there is one other name, but not family yous understand. Name only. 'E'd be 'bout seven'een."

"A young lad then," inquired the manager.

"Yes, 'e helped me see, as a boy like, and 'e's to become my gentleman."

"And his name is?" urged the manager.

Magwitch paused, looking carefully at Worthington poised to write.

"Pip."

Chapter 76

There were more prospecting trips. A few made to Woolooma, Dungog, and the last, to Moonan Flat. Magwitch's asset holdings in the Bank of New South Wales began to swell. He had also opened his cash account with which he traded the jute. The cash balance increasing substantially with each shipment and delivery to the Female Factory.

During the winter months of the next few years, Magwitch and Moola had worked the creeks, getting higher and higher into other alluvial deposits, but the mother lode had escaped detection. During the hot summer months from late September through to May, Magwitch pursued jute. Income increased dramatically and, using other emancipated convicts to help in production along the banks of Hunters River, combined with assigned female convict workers from the Female Factory weaving and sewing to produce finished garments, government money began to dwarf gains from his meagre gold finds. Magwitch made further graphic entries in his little black book, eliminating locations where he was sure there was no more alluvial gold. He carefully noted one area to the side of the Malumla Range where he had found the source of one creek, as it cascaded from its subterranean spring and potential origin of the mother lode.

"One day," he muttered, marking the point with a small cross on the tatty page and then slipping the little book back into his jacket pocket. He turned his attention to packing up for the return trip home, preferring to focus on jute. It was cash money, government money.

"Better than gold," he muttered to himself as he arrived back at his little cottage in Morpeth, ready for the next planting season. Magwitch took the overnight steamship from Morpeth to Sydney Cove. Having eaten a hearty breakfast on board before docking, he proudly disembarked in the bustling cove and took a carriage for the short trip up George Street to the Bank of New South Wales. He arrived just after the heavy mahogany doors opened and was ushered into the carpeted inner sanctum. He busily loaded his new pipe whilst Worthington visited the lavatory to wash his hands; a habit of ritual cleansing between meetings with wealthy clients formed in his early banking years.

"Good morning, Mr. Provis, it is fortuitous that you should be here, as I am in possession of a letter from London for you. By all accounts, it is from a certain Mr. Jaggers of Little Britain."

"Would yous open and read aloud?" The letter contained the whereabouts of Pip in that he was still working at the blacksmith's. It commented that Pip was nearing the end of his apprenticeship and would soon be 18 years of age. Worthington completed the reading and placed the letter back down on the desk before him. Inquisitively, he looked up at Magwitch.

"Pip is to be made a gentleman," announced Magwitch, his sunburnt hand rubbing the top of his furrowed pate, disturbing his long iron-grey hair at the sides.

"Quite so, quite so," replied the manager.

"Yous are to give 'im 500 pounds fur to start. For clothes and proper lodgings in London and for to be educated to learn in readin' and for to write," instructed Magwitch, reclining in the thick, comfortable chair opposite the manager. He sucked fatherly on his newly lit pipe.

"And where can we find Gentleman Pip?"

"No, not a gentleman yet; this money is fur to make 'im a gentleman, see," said Magwitch, inspiration flooding into his mind. "Yous'll 'ave to ask Mr. Jaggers that."

"And pray tell, who is this Mr. Jaggers?" quizzed Worthington, replacing the pen back on its stand and sitting back in his leather chair to listen further.

"London. He's a big lawyer near Newgate prison, see, office be in Little Britain if I remembers right." Worthington withdrew a small buff file from his desk drawer and commenced making notes. "And best to write to 'im wot I want for me gentleman," concluded Magwitch as an afterthought.

"I understand, Mr. Provis."

"Oh, er, an' another thing. If anything takes me to 'im above, Gentleman Pip is to get the lot. Says so 'ere in the little black book." Magwitch waved his book at the manager.

"Will you sign the letter?"

"Be me pleasure; I got fur dreaming these past years," said Magwitch, chuckling through copious clouds of rich, blue-brown tobacco smoke. The memory of the penny he had paid the giant tramp for teaching him how to sign his name on the way down to Epsom Downs came flashing back into his mind.

"Are there any special instructions for Mr. Jaggers?" enquired Worthington, continuing to make notes.

"Good Gord," grunted Magwitch, his mind racing. "Pip must always be Pip, but 'e's not to know I's the one wot sends the dough. I'll tell 'im mysel' later." Nodding, Worthington made further notes in the file, raised his head from writing and again looked respectfully towards Magwitch.

"It would be a good idea to ask Mr. Jaggers to be young Pip's helper. Perhaps it would also be easier to send the money via him and to know what is happening. You could engage Mr. Jaggers for that purpose and appoint him as Pip's guardian if you wish. Even ask him to send you a regular report on progress," Worthington suggested. Magwitch took another thoughtful suck on his pipe.

"Oh, an' tell Mr. Jaggers fur to give Pip wot he wants 'til he's of age. But pay 'im 500 pounds each year, reglar like. No questions, yous understand?" The manager dropped his eyes to the ledger and added the final instruction to his notes.

Magwitch felt he was walking on air as he left the impressive stone building housing his bankers. For the rest of the day, he entertained himself around Sydney and late afternoon, decided to make his way to the Rocks. As dusk approached, he entered the red-light district. In need of a celebration, he justified his decision to treat himself to a few nights in different company. It had become a ritual every time he did his banking, but he had to reason with himself that he had earned the right to pleasure and to tour the pubs and brothels. He knew the girls and they knew him. He had his favourites, one in particular, Sheilagh, who had lived in Chiswick before being transported and was familiar with the London area and his stories of housebreaking with Compeyson. Unwittingly, he would confide in her, having no idea that she also knew his arch enemy and, afterwards, when he had satisfied his soul, he would make his way home.

Chapter 77
England – 1841

A wintry Saturday night saw the three men, Pip Pirrip, Joe Gargery, and Mr. Wopsle, the clerk of the church, gathered together around the fire in the Three Jolly Bargemen. They had been in a heated discussion debating a highly popular murder and led by Mr. Wopsle, had cosily created a state of mind in all interested parties who had gathered to listen to the loose-tongued pub talk. They had arrived at the conclusion that the verdict should be that of wilful murder. Pip had enjoyed the debate, but towards the end, he had become aware of a strange, but familiar gentleman, leaning over the back of the settle opposite the group, who was looking on.

Suddenly, the stranger had stood and challenged Mr. Wopsle. With his head on one side and himself on the other, and in a bullying interrogative manner, he threw his large forefinger, pointing at Mr. Wopsle as if it were to mark him out.

Aggressively, the stranger challenged those who had participated in the discussion. His words, "Innocent until proven guilty," deliberately targeted at Mr. Wopsle, forced him to back down in embarrassment. With an air of authority and a manner suggesting he knew something secret about each and every one of the group, the strange gentleman left the back of the settle and came into the space between the two settles in front of the fire. He remained standing, his left hand in his pocket. He aggressively bit the side of the large forefinger of his right hand.

"From the information I have received," he said, changing the subject and looking round, "I have reason to believe there is a blacksmith among you. He is the blacksmith who goes by the name, Joseph, or Joe Gargery. Which is the man?"

"Here is the man," said Joe. The strange gentleman beckoned Joe out of his place.

"You have an apprentice," he pursued, "commonly known as Pip. Is he here?"

"I am here," cried Pip, nearing the end of his fourth year of apprenticeship. He looked cautiously at the stranger, confident that the man had not recognised him, but certain that he was the same burly man he had met on the stairs the second time he had visited Miss Havisham.

Definitely him, thought Pip. *Although it was a few years ago. I'll never forget his large head and bulbous nose, his dark complexion, those deep-set eyes and bushy black eyebrows, and strong black dots of beard and whiskers. Probably have that distinctive smell of scented soap on his great hands too.*

"I wish to have a private conference with you two," the man announced, having had time to survey Pip. "It will take a little time. Perhaps we had better go to your place of residence. I prefer not to anticipate my communication here. You will impart as much or as little of it as you please to your friends afterwards. I have nothing to do with that," concluded the stranger.

They took a carriage and after the short ride, reached the forge and the little stone cottage. Courteously, Joe stepped in front and opened the door. The three entered the parlour lit by a solitary candle. After seating themselves at the table, the strange gentleman drew the candle nearer and looked over some entries in his pocketbook, ultimately setting the candle aside. He peered round the side of the candle into the darkness at Joe and Pip.

"My name," he said, "is Jaggers, and I am a lawyer in London. I am pretty well-known. I have unusual business to transact with you, and I commence by explaining that it is not of my originating. If my advice had been asked, I should not have been here. It was not asked, and you see me here. What I have to do, as the confidential agent of another, I do, no less, no more." Finding that he could not see the faces very well from where he sat, Jaggers got up, threw one leg over the back of a chair and leant on it, leaving one foot on the seat of the chair and the other on the ground.

"Now, Joseph Gargery, I am the bearer of an offer to relieve you of this young fellow, your apprentice. You would not object to cancelling his indentures, at his request, and for his good. You would want nothing for so doing?" began Jaggers.

"Lord forbid that I should want anything for not standing in Pip's way," said Joe, staring back at Jaggers.

"Lord forbidding is pious and not to the purpose," returned Jaggers. "The question is, would you want anything? Do you want anything?"

"The answer is," returned Joe, sternly. "No."

"Very well," said Jaggers. "Recollect the admission you have made and don't try to change it later."

"Who's going to t...try?" stuttered Joe.

"I don't say anybody is. But you'd do well to keep your mouth shut at what I'm about to reveal. Bear that in mind. Will you?" repeated Jaggers, shutting his eyes and nodding his head at Joe as if he were forgiving him something.

"Now, I return to this young fellow. And the communication I have got to make is that his life is about to change." Joe gasped and looked from Jaggers to Pip.

"I am instructed to communicate to him," said Jaggers, throwing his large forefinger sideways at Pip, "that he will come into handsome property. Further, that it is the desire of the present possessor of that property that he be immediately removed from his present sphere of life and from this place, and be brought up as a gentleman. Simply stated, Pip is a fellow of *Great Expectations*." Pip's dream was out. His wild fancy was surpassed by sober reality.

Miss Havisham is going to make my fortune on a grand scale, thought Pip, his heart pounding.

"Now, Mr. Pip," pursued the lawyer. "I address the rest of what I have to say to you. You are to understand first that it is the request of the person from whom I take my instructions that you always bear the name Pip. You will have no objection, I dare say, to your *Great Expectations* being encumbered with that easy condition. But if you have any objection, this is the time to mention it."

"I, er, have no objection," stammered Pip, his heart beating so fast, making his ears sing, obliterating any further thought on the matter.

"I should think not! Now, you are to understand secondly, Mr. Pip, that the name of the person who is your liberal benefactor remains a profound secret until that person chooses to reveal it. I am empowered to mention that it is the intention of that person to reveal it at firsthand by word of mouth. When or where that intention may be carried out, I cannot say. No one can say. It may be years hence.

"Now, you are distinctly to understand that you are most positively prohibited from making any enquiry on this head, or any allusion or reference, however distant, to any individual whomsoever, in all communications you may have with me. If you have a suspicion in your own breast, it is not the least to the purpose what the reasons of this prohibition are. They may be the strongest and gravest reasons, or they may be mere whim. This is not for you to enquire into. The condition is laid down. Your acceptance of it and your observance of it, as binding, is the only remaining condition that I am charged with, by the person from whom I take my instructions and for whom I am not otherwise responsible. That person is the person from whom you derive your expectations and that I solely hold by that person and this secret. Again, not a very difficult condition with which to encumber such a rise in fortune, but if you have any objection to it, this is the time to mention it. Speak out."

"I, er, have no objection," stammered Pip, again almost fainting with excitement.

"I should think not! Now, Mr. Pip, I have done with stipulations." Jaggers paused before proceeding. "We come next to mere details of arrangements. You must know that, although I have used the term, expectations, more than once, you are not endowed with expectations only. There is already lodged in my hands a sum of money amply sufficient for your suitable education and maintenance. You will please consider me your guardian." Pip took a breath to speak, but Jaggers had already read his mind. "I tell you at once, I am paid for my services, or I shouldn't render them. It is considered that you must be better-educated in accordance with your altered position and that you will be alive to the importance and necessity of at once entering on that advantage."

"I said I had always longed for it," said Pip quickly.

"Never mind what you have always longed for, Mr. Pip." Jaggers retorted. "Keep to the record. If you long for it now, that's enough. Am I answered that you are ready to be placed at once, under some proper tutor? Is that it?"

"Yes, sir," replied Pip, his voice deepening with respect.

"Good. Now, your inclinations are to be consulted. I don't think that wise, mind, but it's my trust. Have you ever heard of any tutor whom you would prefer to another?"

"No, Mr. Jaggers," replied Pip, declining to mention Biddy and uncle Pumblechook's stuffy old great-aunt.

"There is a certain tutor of whom I have some knowledge, who, I think, might suit the purpose," said Jaggers. "I don't recommend him, observe, because I never recommend anybody. The gentleman I speak of, is one Mr. Mathew Pocket." Pip's face lit up at the name.

Another connection to Miss Havisham, assumed Pip, developing further circumstantial evidence as to the identity of his undisclosed benefactor.

"I see you know the name," said Jaggers, looking shrewdly at Pip and then shutting his eyes while he waited for an answer.

"Yes, sir," replied Pip. "I would be much obliged to try him, sir."

"Good. You had better try him in his own house then. The way shall be prepared for you and you can see his son, Herbert Pocket, who is also in London. When will you come to London?" asked Jaggers abruptly, glancing at Joe for a reaction.

"I suppose I should come directly," replied Pip, a quizzical expression suddenly appearing across his brow.

"First," said Jaggers. "You should have some new clothes to come in, and they should not be working clothes. Say, this week. You'll want some money. Shall I leave 20 guineas?" Jaggers produced a long purse and, with the greatest of coolness, counted the golden guineas out on the table, stacking them in four stacks of five guineas each and pushed each stack over to Pip.

"Well, Joseph Gargery, you look dumbfounded?"

"I am!" exclaimed Joe, in a decided manner.

"Well, Mr. Pip, I think the sooner you leave here as you are to be a gentleman, the better. Let it stand for this week, and you shall receive my printed address in the meantime. You can take a hackney coach at the stagecoach office in London and come straight to me. Understand, I express no opinion, one way or the other, on the trust I undertake. I am paid for undertaking it, and I do so. Now, understand that, finally. Understand that!" Jaggers rose and repaired to his waiting coach outside the forge to return to the Three Jolly Bargemen. Pip ran after him.

"Begging your pardon, Mr. Jaggers."

"Halloa!" replied Jaggers, swinging round on his heel. "What's the matter?"

"I wish to be quite right, Mr. Jaggers, and to keep to your directions. So I thought I had better ask. Would there be any objection to my taking leave of anyone I know about here before I go away?"

"No," replied Jaggers.

"I don't mean in the village only, but uptown?"

"No," said Jaggers again. "No objection."

Clad in his new suit, shoes, tie, shirt, leather gloves, top hat, and cane, courtesy of Mr. Trabb, the tailor, Pip made his way discretely through the back roads to Satis House and, on arrival at the wrought-iron gates, struggled to ring the bell on account of his stiff new gloves. Sarah Pocket came to the gate and positively reeled back at the sight of Pip in his new clothes. Her walnut-shell countenance slowly turned from brown to green and then to yellow.

"You?" she said. "You, good gracious! What do you want?"

"I am going to London, Miss Pocket," replied Pip. "And I want to say goodbye to Miss Havisham."

The room was lit as before, and they found her taking exercise by walking around the long spread table. She stopped just abreast of the rotted bride cake and leant on her crutch stick. She turned as Sarah and Pip entered.

"Don't go, Sarah," said Miss Havisham, noticing Sarah on the point of withdrawing. "Well, Pip?"

"I start for London, Miss Havisham, tomorrow."

"This is a gay figure, Pip," she said, making her crutch stick play round Pip, as if she were the fairy godmother who had changed Pip and was enjoying bestowing the finished gift.

"I have come into such good fortune since I saw you last, Miss Havisham," said Pip respectfully. "And I am so grateful for it, Miss Havisham."

"Ay, ay," replied Miss Havisham, looking at the discomforted and envious Sarah with delight. "I have seen Mr. Jaggers and have heard about it, Pip. So you go tomorrow?"

"Yes, Miss Havisham."

"And you are adopted by a rich person?"

"Yes, Miss Havisham."

"Not named?"

"No, Miss Havisham."

"And Mr. Jaggers is made your guardian?"

"Yes, Miss Havisham."

"Well. You have a promising career before you. Be good, deserve it, and abide by Mr. Jaggers's instructions," she said, looking at Pip and then to Sarah. A cruel smile appeared on Miss Havisham's watchful face at the sight of Sarah's jealous countenance.

"Goodbye, Pip. You will always keep the name of Pip, you know."

"Yes, Miss Havisham," said Pip, his back straight and head bowed in acknowledgement.

"Goodbye, Pip!"

Chapter 78
New South Wales

The underground spring emerged from a swollen orifice on the side of the escarpment. Inaccessible from the bottom of the cliff, it was clearly visible, some 40 feet down from the top of the scarp face. Over the past few months, Magwitch had designed and built basic equipment with which he could access the aperture from the top. For this winter trip, Magwitch had loaded the rig with rope woven from his homegrown jute.

On the back of the rig, he loaded his fabricated man-hoist. Forged metal spikes had been purchased from the government stores that would provide the anchorage for the second-hand pulley system. He had built the man-hoist, a bamboo basket which comprised four, light, bamboo frames woven together and secured with jute to form the sides, and a thicker frame for the floor. Around the top, woven into the side frames was a thicker piece of bamboo, providing four lifting points on each corner. Four, handwoven jute ropes, woven and tied into each corner, two each side, came together in a triangle about six feet above the basket and, from there, forming into two single ropes, one each side, to raise and lower the basket through a system of pulleys. It was only big enough for one man at a time.

Magwitch would descend first. The basket jerked and bounced like taught elastic as the Aboriginals paid out the fraying rope. The pulleys squeaked in opposition. Magwitch cursed for forgetting either beef or pork fat, concerned that the pulley system may lock up through lack of lubrication, causing the basket to stick, putting additional strain on the jute ropes. He fended himself off the rocky face as the team lowered the basket. Moola acted banksman, his left hand holding onto a separate rope wrapped around his waist secured behind to a spike driven into a fissure in the rock. He leaned out over the rocky edge, able to see the basket descend whilst giving hand signals to the four Aboriginals lowering the basket.

He wound his finger in a circle pointing downwards. The pulleys creaked and the basket descended jerkily, bouncing as the ropes paid out. Magwitch looked down. Light scrub vegetation looked up at him some 300 feet below. He loved the chase, determined to find the mother lode before the end of winter. The basket stopped with a jolt, caught by a scraggy twig protruding from a weathered fissure. He waved above to stop lowering. Moola clenched his fist, relaying the message to the others. The basket stopped, its floor already tilting, forcing Magwitch to slip to the side. Moola opened and closed his fist, the signal to gently raise the left side of the basket inch by inch. But the twig had burst through the gaps in the bamboo and held the basket fast. Magwitch signaled to hold fast. Moola clenched his fist again. Beads of perspiration appeared on his forehead and deep furrows acted as channels discharging to the sides of his eyebrows. Grabbing his small fossicking pick in his belt, Magwitch reached over the side and hacked away at the twig until the basket freed itself and swung precariously away from the rock face.

"Only five feet more," Magwitch assessed, giving the signal to lower away.

The continuing drought had affected the flow of water, and the subterranean creek had virtually dried up. The basket reached the critical point, presenting an elliptical hole to Magwitch's chest. No bigger than three feet from top to bottom, but the hole was big enough for a boy to crawl through. Magwitch noted that the base of the orifice was worn away through the passage of water. His heart thumping, he peered in. He ran his hand around the mouth of the outfall; the trickle of water cold and refreshing to his skin. He scratched the mould on the bottom; his fingernails filling with the soft slimy substance. He turned to the sun and with his tobacco-stained penknife, scraped the residue from beneath his nails. The tip of the knife glinted. Fine gold particles lay embedded in the mould, evidence that the river must touch the gold seam of the mother lode. Silently, he reached inside his jacket for his pocketbook and, on the last page, made a six-sided star, recording the position of the find.

Chapter 79

It had been over 15 years since Magwitch had been deported. Of those years, he had worked about one-third of the time for James Mudie and achieved his Conditional-Pardon when Mudie had left. The drought and lack of money had made him trade Buttercup for the jute beans, and, following Moola's lead, he had also prospected successfully for gold. England seemed a lifetime away.

"Now, I can see me gentleman," announced Magwitch, as he sat in front of Mr. Worthington at the Bank of New South Wales.

"Are you sure you should go back? You know what they say about going back. Besides, you're a free man here, but over there, even with Governor Gipps's reference and the application for a full pardon, it's a different matter. Mr. Jaggers's last letter said so, and he should know." Magwitch considered carefully, enjoying his importance as a client.

"I can send a letter inviting Gentleman Pip to come here," suggested Worthington.

"Face to face is wot's right." Magwitch had made his decision. "Whilst I's gorn, invest the money from the jute in Sydney buildings," instructed Magwitch, beginning his pipe-lighting ritual. "Without me, there would be no more prospecting. And no more gold fur to invest."

"And yous got to register my interest for to graze sheep in this area on the Malumla Range." Magwitch sketched the location on the blank paper on the desk. "Better still, buy the land with all the rights."

"Any particular reason, Mr. Provis?" Magwitch was about to blurt out about his belief in the location of the mother lode but suddenly stopped, preferring to note it in his little black book.

"Only Aboriginals live there, and my man, Moola, will look after it for me whilst I'm gorn." Magwitch sucked greedily on his pipe, filling the banker's ornate office with his customary blue-brown smoke. Worthington smiled, suffering the pollution, not wishing to offend his wealthy client.

"So be it, Mr. Provis. So be it. Should I write to Mr. Jaggers and advise him that you are returning to England?" suggested Worthington courteously.

"Struth mate, no!" gasped Magwitch. "Just tell 'im I'll be enquiring fur to look arter my gentleman. And best put everything 'ere in Mr. Pip's name, but don't tell a livin' soul. Them'll knows soon enough that I've arrived home."

Chapter 80
London – 1846

The despotic monster of a four-poster bedstead was jammed into the tiny room. One of its huge wooden legs was stuck in the fireplace and another partially blocked the doorway. In what little space there was left, stood a chest of drawers and washing stand on which rested a basin and water jug, both were empty except for a few dried-up flies. The room provided little comfort, but at such short notice, it was the only accommodation they had left at Hummums, a hotel built on the site of an old Turkish bathhouse on the corner of Russell Square, Covent Garden.

The night watchman had brought in a good, old, constitutional rush-light, appearing as the ghost of a walking cane that would instantly break its back if it were touched and from which nothing could ever be lighted. For protection, it stood in solitary confinement at the bottom of a high-sided tin, perforated with round holes, such that it threw wide-awake sunflower patterns on the walls. Pip got into bed, exhausted from the past few days and the final devastating revelation discovered during his visit to Miss Havisham and Estella in Rochester. He lay in the four-poster bed, footsore, weary, and wretched. Unable to sleep. In the gloom and dead of the night, stimulated by the ghostly patterns on the walls, he saw again the sinister words of the desperate message written in Wemmick's hand on the outside of the envelope that had been handed to him by the night watchman at the gate to his London apartment.

'PLEASE READ THIS, HERE.'

And inside the envelope, the brutal message had read.

'DON'T GO HOME.'

"How could they have found out that I was harbouring a returned convict?" muttered Pip, as he lay on his back, staring at the ceiling, imagining sleepy insects silently losing their grip above his head as he slept, ending up in the back of his throat should he open his mouth in an unconscious yawn or snore.

'DON'T GO HOME.'

It hit him again with all the viciousness and fear that the unknown could induce in his 23-year-old mind in the small hours of the night. Only a few days ago, he was oblivious, but, suddenly, now he knew the truth.

All your chickens come home to roost, he mused, ruminating why. "Why me?" he whispered aloud. *That frightful graveyard on Christmas Eve, and me becoming a thief on Christmas day.* Pip's thoughts flew back 16 years.

Then they trapped me into attending that cruel and bitter woman, Miss Havisham, driven to insanity by treachery.

Pip blushed in the dark at the thought of playing cards with Estella and that he hadn't known the name was knaves when he had ignorantly called them jacks. He smiled at the thought of fighting that pale-faced boy and knocking him down in front of Estella, prompting her to allow him to kiss her for the very first time.

God, how could I have been so low as to reject Joe in the belief that these people were better. He felt sick as he thought about the forge and his years as an apprentice, and that Sunday with Biddy when he had suggested that one day, he might fall in love with her.

How wise Biddy had been, and I should have listened, but I didn't because I wanted to be a gentleman. And, God, that feeling of euphoria when Mr. Jaggers had announced that all my dreams were to come true and that I had Great Expectations. How stupid to think that my secret benefactor could have ever been that miserable and senile Miss Havisham. But what of Estella? Had she a hand in it? No, I think not. Estella was like she was because of Miss Havisham. Thank heavens that the pale-faced boy turned out to be my dearest friend and confidant and roommate at Garden Court Temple Bar, dear Herbert Pocket.

Pip went over and over the past 16 years in his mind and until a few days ago, he had known nothing, unwittingly accepting everything on face value, blind to the fact that there may be other forces at work. He rolled over onto his other side, hoping his eyes would close. They didn't. He peered through the slightly open door into the dark corridor beyond. His mind focused again.

And that wretched weather when the news had broken. It was stormy and wet, muddy streets and winds raging, day after day, driving rain in from the East.

From the top floor of Pip's chambers, the building had shaken with each gust of wind. Lead had been stripped from roofs and, in the country, trees had been torn up and the sails of windmills carried away. He remembered that he had been quietly reading and planning to retire at 11 o'clock, with his pocket watch strategically placed on the table before him. Occasionally, he had looked out of the window at the tempest as it raged. Pip had noted that the lamps in the courtyard below had blown out. His clock had indicated 11 and, just as he had closed his watch, Saint Paul's, and all the many church clocks in the city, some leading, some accompanying, some following, had struck the 11 o'clock hour.

For the briefest of moments, Pip had heard a strange noise. He had listened again and heard the footsteps stumble in and continue on. He remembered the staircase lights had also blown out so had grabbed his reading lamp and gone to the stairhead. Whoever it had been down below had stopped.

"There is someone down there, isn't there?" Pip had called out, nerves tightening in his stomach.

"Yes," a voice had replied from the darkness beneath.

"What floor do you want?"

"The top, Mr. Pip."

Pip groaned and rolled over again as he recalled the details of that fateful night and the first few days that had followed. But the intruder had explained everything, not least of which was the attention given to his little, black pocketbook, thickened and bursting with loose papers, holding years of innocuous secrets and wealth.

"There's something worth spending in that there book, dear boy. It's yourn. All I've got ain't mine. It's yourn. Don't you be afeerd on it. There's more where that came from. I've come back to the old country fur to see my gentleman spend his money like a gentleman. That'll be my pleasure. My pleasure 'ull be fur to see 'im do it. And blast you all." The dishevelled man had wound up, looking around the room and snapping his fingers once with a loud snap.

"Blast you everyone, from judge in his wig to the colonist a stirring up the dust, I'll show a better gentleman than the whole kit on you put together."

Pip visualised his determined weather-beaten face as he uttered the words. The whole episode had left Pip in a psychological mess. Eventually, putting his convict to bed in Herbert's room, Pip had fallen asleep in his armchair to be awoken as the clocks of the eastward churches were striking five, the candles were wasted out, the fire was dead, and the wind and rain had intensified the thick, black darkness. Turning again, he lay on his back, staring at the rush-light pattern of dots running up the wall onto the ceiling, analysing in his mind the weeks that had followed.

"My feelings of revulsion for him when he came to breakfast that first morning," Pip conjured up the conversation.

"I do not know by what name to call you," he had said in an ashamedly low voice.

"But I have said that you are my uncle."

"That's it, dear boy. Call me uncle."

"You assumed some name, I suppose, on board ship?"

"Yes, dear boy. I took the name of Provis."

"Do you mean to keep that name?"

"Why, yes, dear boy, it's as good as another. Unless you'd like another."

"What is your real name?" Pip had asked in a whisper.

"Magwitch," he had answered and, in the same tone, "chrisen'd Abel."

"What were you brought up to be?"

"A warmint, dear boy."

Pip sat up on the sagging, horsehair mattress of the four-poster, scratching the bites from the bedbugs. He considered the realisation and double shock that all the time, Magwitch had been in touch with Jaggers, paying him and appointing him his guardian, and Wemmick for giving out his address when he had illegally returned to England via Portsmouth. In the darkness, Pip lay back down and went over and over the events.

Confirmation from Jaggers in his usual, non-committal and arm's length manner, that Magwitch was, indeed, his secret benefactor and not Miss Havisham. And with help from Herbert Pocket, more revelations had emerged, not least of which were the events leading up to Estella's adoption by Miss Havisham and that, by deduction, Magwitch must, therefore, be Estella's father. Pip's dreams and success had become a nightmare. Lying on his back, staring at the ceiling, he decided his next move must be to have it out with Miss Havisham.

He sat up again, the bugs gnawing into his skin as he thought of that dreadful chance meeting with Bentley Drummle, Estella's suitor, in the Blue Boar Inn, before attending Satis House. And, finally, the heart-shattering moment when Estella, quietly knitting with her long distinctive fingers, sat at Miss Havisham's feet whilst she had cut him dead, deriving pleasure that Estella was now betrothed to Bentley Drummle, Pip's last vestige of hope in gaining his loved one dashed for eternity.

Sleep discovered Pip an hour before it grew light, relaxed by the open bedroom door and the cheery light where the night watchman sat, dozing. He drifted off, but the night fancies had done little to ward off the terrors of the message:

'DON'T GO HOME.'

"Why was I not to go home and what had happened at home? One thing was obvious, the message had been written by Wemmick, Jaggers's clerk," Pip whispered.

Suddenly, Pip knew his next step.

As instructed, the chamberlain knocked on the bedroom door at seven o'clock. Pip needed no second call. He washed and dressed quickly and made his way to the country.

The walls of the private residence arose from the mist, and it was a little past eight o'clock in the morning. He entered the home to find Wemmick making tea. They exchanged pleasantries. Half an hour later, the warning came. Pip's apartment was being watched and a man named Compeyson was involved. Wemmick advised that Magwitch had already been moved to a safe location; the choice being a furnished upper-floor set of cabin rooms in a house between Limehouse and Greenwich at Mill Pond Bank, Chink's Basin, recognisable by the large bow-window on the Thames riverside. From there, plans could be made to get Magwitch out of the country onboard a foreign packet-boat. Hamburg, Rotterdam, Antwerp, the foreign destination port would be incidental, simply get Magwitch out of England.

Leaving at eight o'clock the following morning, Pip and Herbert took a small boat down river. Their nostrils filled with the pleasant scent from different wood materials floating in the air as they passed by the chips and shavings of the long-shore boat builders and the mast and oar and block makers of upper and lower Pool below Bridge.

Eventually, they found the spot called Mill Pond Bank, Chink's Basin. The best guide had been the Old Green Copper Rope-Walk. Observing the large, bow-shaped window Wemmick had described, they moored and, once ashore, studied the brass plate bearing the name, Mrs. Whimple, the owner. Momentarily pausing, they knocked on the door, announcing their arrival. She was an elderly woman of pleasant and thriving appearance who opened the door and led them into the parlour. There was a corner cupboard with glass and china. Shells stood neatly on the chimneypiece, and coloured engravings hung on the wall representing the death of Captain Cook. There was a picture of a ship-launch and His Majesty King George the Third in a stage-coachman's wig, leather breeches, and top boots on the terrace at Windsor.

"Perfect," said Pip. Herbert nodded. Curiously, there was a heavy thump on the floor above. Pip looked up.

"Oh, don't mind him, that's old Bill Barley," said Herbert. Pip smiled. "I am afraid he is an old rascal, drinks rum as well, but I have never seen him."

"To have Provis here for an upper lodger is quite a godsend to Mrs. Whimple, because most people won't stand that noise."

"A strange place isn't it?" agreed Pip. They went upstairs. Magwitch sat comfortably settled beside the fire, looking out of the window across the river. He looked up but expressed no alarm as Pip and Herbert entered.

"Ay, ay, dear boy," said Magwitch with a pleasant nod. "Jaggers knows."

"Good, I have also talked with Wemmick," said Pip, "and have come to tell you what caution he gave me and what advice." Pip explained their actions and why he would be much safer here than in London. Pip prepared to leave to attend to the arrangements.

"Dear boy," said Magwitch, reaching out and clasping Pip's hands. "I don't know when we will meet again, and I don't like for to say goodbye. I says goodnight."

For fear of being followed, Pip visited irregularly. Each time, he carried with him Magwitch's little black book. Grudgingly, he had taken Wemmick's advice regarding the security of moveable property and taken possession of Magwitch's precious book.

"Ay, Mr. Pip, there's more money in that their book o' yourn than you can spend in a lifetime. And in case, just in case, it's also written in yourn name at the bank," confirmed Magwitch each time they met. Pip took no notice.

Weeks later, the plan was in place. They would target the two steamers sailing later in the week, one for Hamburg, the other for Rotterdam. Monday evening, instead of going home to dinner, Herbert would go straight to Mill Pond Bank and alert Magwitch.

Pip would wait in Temple until the appointed time on Wednesday, then, with Herbert, take their small boat and make their way down river. The tide would begin to run at nine and be with them until it turned around three. After it turned, they would creep on, rowing by the bank against the tide until dark. By then, they planned to be well into the long reaches below Gravesend, between Kent and Essex, where the river is broad and solitary, where the waterside inhabitants are very few, and where lone public houses are scattered here and there, one of which they would choose for a resting place. There, they planned to lie low all night.

Both steamers started from the Pool of London at about nine on Thursday morning, and they knew at what time to expect them according to where they were and would hail the first vessel as she steamed past. If, by any accident, they were not taken aboard the first, they would have a second chance.

"Wednesday is the time to go, Provis," said Herbert in the cabin apartments at Mrs. Whimple's.

"Ay, lad, I's as ready as I'll ever be," replied Magwitch, pointing to his boat-cloak and black canvas bag packed neatly on the wooden chair in the corner. Herbert had borrowed an old telescope and surveyed the water before handing it to Magwitch.

"Remember, come down the stairs hard by the house on Wednesday late morning, but only when you see us," said Herbert. "And today is Monday."

Last night's moon had been nearly full, and it was one of those March days when the sun shines hot and the wind blows cold. Pip and Herbert donned their pea-coats, the thick wool providing warmth on the wintry morning whilst the short length avoided getting soaked by trailing in the water. They descended the Temple stairs and boarded, Herbert in the bow and Pip steering. It was around eight-thirty, half an hour or so before the tide turned. Soon, they passed under Old London Bridge and by old Billingsgate market. Next came the Tower and Traitor's Gate. Full of craft all around, the *Leith*, and *Aberdeen*, and Glasgow steamers dwarfed them as they loaded and unloaded along the wharfs. Suddenly, there they were. Tomorrow's foreign steamers, *Hamburg* and *Rotterdam*. Around the next bend, heart's beat at the sight of Mill Pond Bank and Mill Pond Stairs.

"Is he there?" said Herbert, peering around the obstruction.

"Not yet."

"Patience. He was not to come down until he saw us. Can you see his signal?"

"Not well from here, but I think I see it. Now. I see him now. Pull both!" The oarsmen pulled heavily towards the stairs. Minutes later, they reached the submerged bottom of the stairs at Mill Pond Bank.

"Easy, Herbert, easy. Oars!" The boat scuffed the stairs gently, and Magwitch, looking like a river pilot in his boat cloak, jumped in, his muscular build distinguishing his entry.

"Dear boy," he said, putting his arm around Pip as he took his seat. "Faithful dear boy, well done. Thank'ye, thank'ye." Pip gave a nervous smile and looked around, comfortable that nobody had seen, and they were not being followed. The oarsmen pulled off. Pip looked back at Magwitch seemingly untroubled at the presence of danger. Almost as if he had read Pip's mind. Magwitch acknowledged.

"If yous knowed, dear boy, what it is to sit here with my dear boy and have my smoke, baccy an' all, arter having been day by day imprisoned betwixed four walls, you'd envy me. But yous don't know wot it is."

"I think I know the delights of freedom," replied Pip respectfully.

"Ah," replied Magwitch, shaking his head gravely and taking a heavy suck on his black pipe. "But yous don't know it equal to me. Yous must have been under lock and key, dear boy, to know it equal to me."

The oarsmen rowed strenuously against the incoming tide. The dusk arrived, and the sun turned red, lowering towards the horizon, eventually disappearing into the night. They kept rowing, every ripple and unusual sound delivered fear, inducing prickly skin at the thought that they were being followed. The sign outside the riverside pub had a picture of a square-rigged ship, underneath, in gold letters on black, 'The Ship.'

It was lonely and deserted and provided perfect cover for the night. Next morning, watching the river from a double-hung window, Pip froze, as a small dingy drew alongside their boat for a routine custom's inspection. Observing discretely from the pub window, he breathed a sigh of relief as the men departed without comment. Having breakfasted late on eggs and bacon, they waited patiently for the sign of steamer smoke. It was half past one in the afternoon by the time the first steamer was sighted. Running with the tide, the steamer puffed away not far off and minutes later, came the other, directly behind, pumping out its familiar trail of sooty, yet wispy smoke.

"Here she is," said Pip, his stomach rebelling against the eggs and bacon. "Hurry, they're steaming at full speed."

They chucked the bags in and shook hands whilst boarding. Pip's eyes filled and Herbert copied involuntarily. The oarsmen pulled. From nowhere, the secreted four-oared galley with Thames River Peelers shot from under the bank, rowing powerfully in the same direction. Pip swung round, nearly vomiting at the sight.

"Keep before the tide!" shouted Pip. "She might see us lying before her." The steamer was coming head on.

"Provis, keep quite still and cover your face," urged Pip, terror mounting in his heart.

"Trust to me, dear boy," replied Magwitch cheerily, clutching his smoldering pipe.

The skillfully handled police galley cut through the water heading between them and the steamer. They slowed and came alongside, leaving just enough room for their oars, yet drifting parallel as if tied by an invisible rope.

"Two sitters," muttered Pip. He watched their actions, one busy with the rudder, the other, eyes peering above a blanket, had the rest of his face hidden. He leaned to the other and whispered something. For minutes, nobody spoke.

"It's *Hamburg*," whispered one of the oarsmen. The steamer bore down on both boats, her paddles thrashing at the water, turbulating anything that dared to stand in her way.

"You have a returned transport there," shouted the man on the rudder.

"That's the man, wrapped in the cloak. His name is Abel Magwitch, otherwise Provis. I apprehend that man and call upon him to surrender and you to assist."

Instantly, his oarsmen pulled twice and returned their oars inboard as he suddenly swung the rudder and ran athwart, the men grabbed the gunwale before Pip knew what had happened. The heavy vessel was on top of them in seconds; confusion broke out on the deck of *Hamburg* as the order was given to reverse engines. The paddlewheels stopped and reversed. Picking up power, they skidded and scooped at the frothy water. The steersman of the police galley grabbed Magwitch as the force of the tide swung the boats round. Magwitch leaned across the steersman and aggressively wrenched the coat from the other sitter.

"Compeyson," cursed Magwitch, recognising the scars and white terror in his bitter evil face. With Olympian force, Magwitch leapt across at his old enemy, grabbing him by the scruff of his coat.

"Who telt yous I were here?" growled Magwitch, his face inches from Compeyson's jaw.

"Our mutual girlfriend."

"Gor lummy, who?"

"Sheilagh!" sneered Compeyson. "The Sheilagh who work down in the Sydney Rocks. She writes to me for old time's sake." The final comment inflaming Magwitch's temper to boiling point.

"Yous a bastard, make no mistake," growled Magwitch, clenching his right fist and driving it into Compeyson's jaw, the force propelling them both over the gunwale as the steamer struck. The galley corrected, but Pip's boat was crushed under the steamer and disappeared beneath the reversing paddlewheel along with Magwitch and Compeyson. Minutes later, Magwitch surfaced, blood spread from a huge gash to his head. He wheezed, having sustained serious damage to his chest where he had gone under the reversing paddlewheel of the steamer. There was no sight of Compeyson. The police hauled them all into the galley and returned to 'The Ship Inn.'

"Officer, may I have permission to change the prisoner's wet clothing?" asked Pip respectfully.

"Indeed, you may, but whilst I remember, you are to hand over all his personal belongings," replied the officer. Inside the inn, Pip purchased certain articles of clothing from the publican, then, in an attempt to lighten Magwitch's sentence, handed over his personal effects, including the little black book. Magwitch sat in the corner, his wrists and ankles now manacled. He raised his hands at the sight of Pip's honesty, beckoning him over.

"Dear, dear, dear Pip. Yous have just give away yourn fortune."

"But what's so important about a little black book?" said Pip, more concerned that he had upset Magwitch than for his memoirs.

"Has me life's work, dear boy. A fortune, I tell yous," said Magwitch. "But then yous won't miss wot yous never 'ad, now does yous?"

"No," Pip replied sheepishly.

"Get me my smoke, dear Pip, I've a big thought to share," said Magwitch with a wry smile.

Pip dug into the pockets of the wet clothes and prepared a fresh pipe. When ready, he pushed the chewed stem between Magwitch's stained teeth and helped him light up. Two hearty sucks, antagonising his chest further made him cough, inducing his eyes to water. Slowly, he settled.

"Now, my boy, here's wot yous must do," he whispered secretly. "Yous tell Jaggers I give you that book and its yourn, not mine, and he's fur to get it back from those Peelers. Is that clear?"

"But why bother?" argued Pip disinterestedly.

"Did yous look at it, Pip? Did yous ever look at it?" challenged Magwitch, his chest hurting.

"No, not exactly."

"I telt yous to, 'cause it has signatures, and maps, and names. Names yous will need for to find for when yous go on the treasure hunt on Australia," replied Magwitch, a grin appearing across his weather-beaten old face. "And another fing, yous lot don't know here is 'cause of me jute, I got given a special appeal from the Gov'nor. Guv Gipps is his name. Says so in the book, and there's papers to prove." Magwitch sat back and quietly puffed.

"See, dear Pip, I'm right famous down under, but hated up top."

"No, Provis, not hated here, only by one man, and he's gone now. It's all over for him."

"Gorn, but not forgot. Not never forgot by the like's o' me."

The Peeler signalled the turn of the tide and they all left the inn, boarded the galley and headed for London. On arrival in London, Pip took a Hackney carriage and went straight to Jaggers's private residence in Gerrard Street, Soho. Jaggers listened intently, the confiscation of his personal effects by the police irritating him the most.

"I shall deal with that first thing in the morning," retorted Jaggers.

"Molly, bring the whisky."

Moments later, Molly scurried in with the decanter and two crystal glasses. Jaggers moved to stand in front of the fire, his hands behind his back. He rocked backwards and forwards on the balls of his feet, intermittently chewing on his great forefinger.

"Pour Molly, pour," instructed Jaggers, waving his huge bitten finger. Molly did, two inches deep into the Royal Stuart glasses, handing the first to Jaggers and the second to Pip.

"The Macallan single malt," announced Jaggers, raising his glass to Pip in a mock toast. Pip copied, transfixed at the uncharacteristic change in the man.

"Thank you, Molly," said Pip, concentrating on her fine physical features; he had seen delicate hands like those before.

Just like Estella's hands. But older. 20 years older? thought Pip. *She could be Estella's mother.* His eyes watched her fingers clutching the neck of the decanter, memories of Estella sitting, knitting on the floor beside Miss Havisham flooded back. He silently winced at the thought that Estella would now be married to that Bentley Drummle.

"Yes, of course I will represent him, but I hold little hope of success less, per chance, there is some shred of evidence buried in Australia exonerating him from his actions. Indeed, I see no redemption in the eyes of the law, and upon their production of a witness as to his identity, I fear the trial will be over in minutes," said Jaggers. Molly moved towards the door.

"Wait, Molly!" Jaggers hurled the instruction. Molly froze and turned. "Continue, Pip."

"Yes, sir," said Pip. "Should we lose, then I would like the loss of his wealth to the Crown be kept from him, if that be possible, Mr. Jaggers." Jaggers frowned and began his typical theatrically presented hypothesis.

"Put the case, Pip, that certain hearsay information came to my ears concerning a particular client who was unaware of a single, living, blood relative and, that the hypothetical relationship I am suggesting were that of Father and Daughter, both parties being unaware of the other's existence." Jaggers paused to allow his words to sink in. "And in consequence, through the fluxion of time, both had developed the belief that the other party, were, in fact, deceased, Pip, then there would be two matters to resolve before the courts."

Jaggers took another healthy mouthful of whisky and before swallowing, appeared to wash the liquid around his teeth and gums behind closed lips. He swallowed, marginally opening his lips and gently inhaled, drawing in cool air over his tongue and gums.

"Pip, inheritance can be a dirty business," Jaggers began again. "Put the case that there are other living relatives and that there may be notes in existence, directing the deceased's wishes, what then? For all deceased estates, where the deceased has made no clear provision, then the rules of intestacy are applied by the deployment of the press to advertise to other interested parties. A veritable Pandora's Box. Howsoever, for simplicities' sake, let us assume that there exist no other hidden parties that may wish to lay claim to the estate, then the two matters to be resolved before the courts would be firstly, that the daughter were, indeed, the true blood relative, and that the child were born in wedlock. And, secondly, that the child had come of age and, indeed, had the assistance of a man through whom would rest the binding contract of legitimate inheritance. And, further, there is still the overwhelming criminal act of his return to these shores as a convicted felon, exposing all assets to the crown."

"Yes, sir," said Pip. Becoming irritated at the lawyer's evasive manner, Pip stood up in frustration and began pacing round the large room.

"I see you find the prospect of a case such as I have put somewhat daunting, Pip."

"Yes, and surely you are not surprised, sir," muttered Pip, raising his glass and sipping the whisky.

"You will now understand the advice you received from Wemmick, in that all efforts should have been made at the appropriate time to secure all moveable property before the event."

"I had hoped that my actions in handing over his personal effects, indeed cooperating with the Peelers, would go a long way to helping the case."

"Then it was you who has let it slip through your fingers. Was it not, Pip?" Jaggers waved his forefinger threateningly. Pip opened his mouth to explain, but Jaggers held up his hand, halting his words before they could flow.

"And," Jaggers continued, having withdrawn his large handkerchief. "For the future, we must memorialise by and by and try all events for some of it. Indeed, Pip, there are many cases where the Crown does not succeed with forfeiture. This case, in the final analysis, however, may prove a lost cause." Molly stood, silently watching.

"Ah, Molly, bring another glass," instructed Jaggers. Molly scurried off and, in seconds, had returned, clutching a matching crystal glass.

"Pour, Molly, pour." Jaggers held his glass out for Molly to top up, then directed her to Pip. Molly began topping up Pip's glass.

"And pour for yourself." Molly stopped amid pour.

"Go on, Molly. Pour a large one for yourself. You may need it!" Silently, Molly poured.

"And now, a special toast, shall we? A toast to Australia, the Land of Promise." Jaggers raised his glass and Pip followed. Molly flushed, and turning slightly away, secretly sipping at the amber liquid too soon. Nobody noticed.

"Australia."

Attempting to weigh his thoughts, Pip studied Jaggers over the top of his sparkling crystal glass.

"Magwitch said that there was a fortune written in his little black book. And, oh, at his bank too," said Pip in passing.

Molly pricked up her ears at the mention of the name, Magwitch, immediately taking another huge quaff of whisky. Her shamanistic eyes darkened and flashed towards Jaggers and then back to Pip.

"Pip," said Jaggers, "you have neither evidence, nor are you related, which makes it an even more hopeless task."

"But," said Pip.

"No buts."

Well, then, I know two people who are related, and one of them is standing in this room, and the other I am in love with, mused Pip, his eyes flashing at Jaggers, but deciding it were better if he just shut up rather than pursue the misery of attempting to establish a legitimate connection.

At the magistrate's court the following day, Magwitch's committal for trial was postponed, pending physical confirmation that the arrested man was, indeed, Magwitch, a transport, who had dared to return to Great Britain. Churned in the tides, the primary witness for the Crown, Compeyson, had been found massively mutilated, and horribly disfigured, the only clue to his identity being the contents of his pockets and folded, yet still legible notes, contained in the case he was carrying at the time of the collision.

Either way, he was dead. Three days later, during which Crown prosecution had stood over, awaiting the production of an old witness hastily brought up to the Old Bailey from the prison hulk from which Magwitch had escaped all those years ago. Magwitch was finally committed to stand trial at the next sessions scheduled for early April.

Jaggers immediately set about with delay tactics and caused an application for postponement, pending the healthy recovery of the prisoner.

It was denied. The trial was short and very clear. The jury's verdict given for a returned transport was swiftly delivered – guilty! To give weight and deterrent to other would be murderers and returnees, sentencing was set down for the following week. Jaggers had made no comment.

Glittering in the warm spring sun, the April raindrops joined together and ran down the outside of the courtroom windows. Pip stood to the side of the dock, whilst Magwitch, along with 32 men and women, some defiant, some stricken with terror, some sobbing and weeping, some covering their faces, some staring gloomily about, awaited sentence in the dock. There had been shrieks from among the women convicts, but they had been stilled, and a hush had succeeded as they stood before the judge to receive sentence. The public gallery was crammed to bursting point as the judge arrived and seated himself, ready to address the prisoners. Speaking generally at first, he then focused on one prisoner in particular.

"Almost from infancy, this prisoner has been an offender and, after repeated imprisonment and punishments, this prisoner had been at length sentenced to exile for the term of his natural life. That miserable man would seem, for a time, to have become convinced of the errors of his ways, and, when far removed from the scenes of his old offences, had lived a peaceable and honest life. But in a fatal moment, yielding to those propensities and passions, he quitted his haven of rest and repentance and came back to the country where he was proscribed. Being denounced, he took flight and in resisting arrest, caused the death of his denouncer, either by accident or by intent. Howsoever, notwithstanding this act, for which he is not on trial, the appointed punishment for his return to the land that had cast him out being death, he must prepare to die."

Angrily, the gavel crashed.

Jaggers immediately registered an appeal, requesting a stay of execution pending the discovery of further evidence from afar. Separately and unbeknown to Jaggers, Pip set about writing to the Home Secretary of State, setting forth his knowledge and the reason for Magwitch's temporary return. He wrote to the Crown for clemency, and that here was a man who was, and still is, an asset to Her Majesty's colonies. Further letters were sent to others in high places, and every day, the number of Pip's appeals grew. But, as each day passed, Magwitch grew weaker from his injuries. He had been moved from the raw gaol to the prison infirmary, allowing Pip greater flexibility with visiting. The number of days since sentencing had risen to ten. Magwitch's eyes lit up as Pip entered.

"Dear boy," he said, "I thought yous was late. But I knowed yous couldn't be that."

"It is just the time," said Pip. "I waited for it at the gate."

"Yous always waits at the gate, don't yous, dear boy?"

"Yes. Not to lose a moment of time."

"Thank'ye, dear boy, thank'ye. God bless yous. Yous've never deserted me, dear boy." Pip pressed his hand in silence.

"And what's best of all is yous've been more comfortable along with me since I was under a dark cloud than when the sun shone. That's the best of all."

Magwitch lay propped up but, on his back, breathing with great difficulty. Pip watched as the light faded in his expression and a calm, placid film came over his face as he looked at the ceiling above.

"Are you in much pain today?"

"I don't complain of none, dear boy." He fell silent.

"You never do complain," commented Pip in a whisper.

Magwitch briefly opened his eyes and looked affectionately at Pip.

"Dear Magwitch, I must tell you, now at last." Magwitch slowly closed his eyes.

"You understand what I say?" whispered Pip. Magwitch gave a gentle squeeze on Pip's hand.

"You had a child once, whom you loved and lost." Magwitch squeezed Pip's hand more strongly.

"She lived and found powerful friends. She is living now. She is a lady and very beautiful. And Magwitch... I love her."

With a last faint effort, Magwitch raised Pip's hand gently to his lips, momentarily held a kiss to the back and gently let it sink back upon his breast, with his own hand lying on it. The calm, placid look on his face returned, and as he passed peacefully away, his head dropped quietly on his breast.

"O Lord, be merciful to him, a sinner," whispered Pip, his closed eyes unable to stop the flow of tears.

Chapter 81

The horse-drawn hearse arrived at Cooling Church. There were no mourners, and there was no procession. The Minister had already been paid, as had the gravediggers and the flower lady. Two, elegant, slim ladies, both veiled in black, one short, the other tall, waited in the vestibule at the side of the church as Magwitch's casket was brought in through the wide, Norman arched door at the front. Top hat in hand, Pip walked behind and alone. The service was short.

"Ashes to ashes, dust to dust," said the Minister, as the casket with a solitary red rose on top was lowered into the grave behind the group of parallel children's graves. Pip dabbed his eyes and, turning round for the first time, noticed the two ladies. He acknowledged their presence, failing to recognise the faces beneath their thick black veils. He also failed to question as to who they were and why they were attending the funeral. Alone and emotional, he proceeded to his carriage and was gone.

Chapter 82

Jaggers's office in Little Britain became a hive of activity. Two runners and an additional researcher were hired specifically to focus on the case. Jaggers had risen to the bait. The researcher had been installed at the Old Bailey, his function, to trawl through decades of court records relating to past cases dealing with intestacy and the treatment of the property of convicted criminals. He was to research all cases, particularly those since 1788, of criminals who had been transported and died in the colonies. In all, he was to research a period of half a century, during which time the numbers of transports approached 80,000 souls. His brief was to find a precedent.

"Wemmick!" shouted Jaggers. In the outer reception, Wemmick hastily concluded his discussions with the junior and quickly proceeded to conference with Jaggers. He entered the brooding atmosphere of the office, took but a few nervous paces forwards; his mind riddled with questions.

"Wemmick, go to Scotland Yard and politely point out the error of the confiscation of private and personal property. Personal property of Mr. Magwitch cannot be considered a ward of state, the Old Bill have no right to make such demands. All papers and loose items handed over on the day of the arrest should be returned to his lawyer immediately." Wemmick nodded, sensing the hunt. "And Wemmick, have this letter copied by the junior. No, on second thoughts, copy it yourself, then walk all the way to Whitehall Place and concentrate on your words to extract that little black book." Wemmick raised his eyebrows.

"And Wemmick, ride back at my expense, but only if you have the book. If you fail, which you won't, walk!"

"I won't fail, wild horses –"

"Yes, yes, yes, Wemmick, I have heard all of that before, just keep to your purpose," grumbled Jaggers, waving his bitten forefinger in dismissal.

Rapidly departing, Wemmick walked briskly down the hill past Saint Paul's Cathedral and along Fleet Street into the Strand. He stopped briefly at Simpson's for a cigar and coffee, and half an hour later, continued on via

Charing Cross and Whitehall, reaching Scotland Yard just before luncheon. He summoned the Chief Inspector and handed over the letter.

"Ah, what have we here?" asked the Inspector with a slight frown as he read the stern letter.

"It's all explained in the letter," said Wemmick, choosing to be economical with his words.

"And to what purpose is this?"

"Mr. Jaggers just wishes to close his file on the matter, Chief Inspector."

"Such a strong letter, if that is all this is about. Still, we would probably be disposing of his things anyway," said the inspector, turning to the four-drawer, wooden, filing cabinet at the back of the stark office. Tucked into the ornate brass frame, the index card on the front of the third drawer down read M-R. Opening it, his grubby hands retrieved the fat buff file. He returned to the counter. There were two envelopes, one contained the little black book, brim full of differing sizes of scruffy paper, the other, Magwitch's tobacco-stained pipe, the stem almost completely chewed away, and a half-smoked plug of dark dry tobacco. The inspector poured the contents of the envelopes out before Wemmick.

Wemmick's eyes lit up.

"That's the most important item," said Wemmick, pointing to the pipe.

"Gord bless him," grinned the inspector. "What on earth would Mr. Jaggers want with that?" A damp grey mould had grown around the bowl and it stank.

"Frankly, I have no idea, my good man. Now, where do I sign?"

"Ah, quite right." The inspector reached for the standard form, dipped the quill into the inkwell. The swan feather was mostly crumpled and bent to the side. He dated and headed the document, writing a simple list of the items beneath and marked a cross for Wemmick to sign. Looking at Wemmick, he turned the paper and handed him the quill. Wemmick started to sign.

"Wait a minute." Wemmick completed his signature, resisting the temptation to grab the book and run.

"What is it?"

"There's something else besides," said the inspector. Wemmick kept silent in fear of what was coming next.

"Mr. Jaggers's letter is not specific except it says nothing is to be accidentally forgotten."

"I know."

"Do you want his jacket and boat cloak? I think there's also a cap."

"Oh, Mr. Jaggers said he would like these to be donated to the retired police, if you wish, but asked me to look at them first. He doesn't have room back at the office," said Wemmick, relieved.

Minutes later, the inspector returned with the clothing. Wemmick checked through the pockets, noting tears in the lining of the jacket pockets. He made his decision quickly.

"I'll take the jacket and the cap," said Wemmick, handing the boat cloak back.

"How thoughtful," said the Inspector.

"Tell Mr. Jaggers we thank him for the donation, it's gratefully received, every little helps, you know."

Wemmick smiled, stuffed the little black book bulging with loose paper into one pocket and the pipe and tobacco into the other, hailed a Hackney carriage, and rode in style back to Little Britain.

Chapter 83

With his best friend, Herbert, having left for Cairo to open a new branch office of the family business, Pip had an increased feeling of desolation. Within days of the funeral, he fell ill and lay partially unconscious and delirious for months. His creditors had foreclosed since his source of income had been stopped immediately following the death of Magwitch. Recovering slowly, later in the year, he felt ashamed to find that Joe Gargery, his stepfather, had secretly settled his creditors and that he was a free man. But with a broken heart and nothing to do in either London or Rochester, he decided to take up the offer of a position with his dear friend, Herbert, in the new branch office in Cairo and sailed for Egypt towards the end of the summer of that tragic year.

Chapter 84

For nights on end, Jaggers studied the illiterate hieroglyphics and sketches and random pieces of paper held in Magwitch's little black book. The gold clasp hung sadly, nearly torn from the worn binding through use over the years. All entries were undated except for relatively recent entries at the end of the book. He noted that the different entries made in New South Wales were literate entries, but being irrelevant to his cause to establish earlier family connections, he decided to pursue these later. Jaggers focused on the early years. Years during which Magwitch had worked and socialised before he was exiled to Australia.

The first major breakthrough came when he recognised the name, Moses, under a terrible sketch of a horse. It had taken him weeks to make the connection that this could refer to the winning horse, Moses, in the Epsom Derby.

"If that be the case, the start date of the first entries in the book indicates the summer of the year 1822," said Jaggers, holding the book in his right hand as he paced the floor of his office.

He sat back down behind his desk and again flipped through the pages. The volumes of information contained expanded, and Jaggers decided to allocate the little unused room to the side of his office for a display of the material. He erected four easels on the front of which he fixed vertical battens made from soft balsa wood, soft enough to pin his interpretation of each page of the book as he deciphered the contents. The first two pages in the book contained sketches he believed to be of Tarot cards. There were six sketches and what appeared to be a glass ball with a sun and a pound's, shilling's, and pence's sign. From this, he determined Magwitch pursued and believed in, the occult and supernatural. As was his habit with unusual clients, Jaggers had driven three square nails into the huge, oak, timber post in the centre of the wall at the end of the room, one below the other, on which he hung Magwitch's personal possessions.

On the top nail, he hung Magwitch's tatty old cap. On the next nail, he hung the stinking old pipe, hooking the chewed tooth hole in the stem over the nail and then rubbing the remaining tobacco into a cone, he squeezed it into the bowl; the fat part of the cone of Negro-Head tobacco sat proud of the bowl by nearly half an inch. Before hanging the jacket up on the third nail, he searched the pockets. As with Wemmick, he noted holes in the lining of the pockets. But investigating more effectively than Wemmick, he felt around at the bottom of the jacket between the lining and the woollen, outer material. His fingers identified a hard lump, the size of the tip of a man's little finger. He slipped his thick wrist through the hole in the lining of the inside pocked and reached down, his other hand holding the lump through the material. Feeling for the object with his bitten forefinger and thumb, he closed on the lump and pulled it out. Jaggers couldn't believe his eyes.

"A single gold bullet," he said, breathing the words aloud.

His eyes focused on the base of the shiny object, the distinctive initials, A.M.P., hit him. Hurriedly draping the jacket over the back of a wooden chair, he retreated to his massive black chair in the main office and sat down, placing his find on the desk before him. He poured a huge whisky and golloped two swigs of the amber liquid, the motivation and challenge to unravel this man's discoveries charging him with renewed energy. A third of a bottle of whisky later, he returned to his display and, using a wooden coat hanger, reverently hung Magwitch's jacket on the third nail. He walked around his office, rolling the golden bullet in between his thumb and bitten forefinger, stopping in front of the row of death masks. The top one, a particularly grizzly face, suited his purpose, having a protruding bottom lip that formed a perfect platform underneath a hooked nose. Smiling, he reached up and placed the bullet on the lip. He stepped back to admire the display, conscious that the gold bullet appeared as an overly large gold tooth.

"Motivation indeed," chuckled Jaggers to himself, delighted at the enormity of the legal challenge before him.

Printed in thick bold letters on the top of a new sheet of paper to be pinned to the first easel, he listed the order in which he would develop the case and the evidence he would need to substantiate his client's claims.

Under the heading:

'Evidence,' he wrote:

1. Proof of wedlock for Molly and Magwitch.
2. Proof of wedlock before conception, negating claims of illegitimacy.
3. Proof of wedlock at the time Estella was born.
4. Proof that Magwitch was, indeed, Estella's father.
5. Proof that Molly was Estella's mother.
6. Proof of the identity of Estella.

7. Proof of the marital status at the time of Magwitch's death.
8. Proof that Magwitch had nominated Pip heir to 'The Magwitch Fortunes.'

Under the heading, 'Statutory Research,' he wrote:

1. Laws relating to the wedding ceremony.
2. Laws relating to probate.
3. Laws relating to the Statute of Limitations.

Under the heading, 'Prime Witness,' he wrote:

1. Molly.
2. Pip.
3. Estella.

Under the heading, 'Jurisdiction,' he wrote:

1. England.
2. Australia.

On the second sheet of paper, he prepared a tabular life programme, entering the years and events he already knew from his client files, deciding to fill in the gaps as the relevant information came to light.

Programme of Life

Year	Magwitch	Molly	Estella	Pip
1786	Born			
1805		Born		
1822	Epsom Derby			
1822	*Wedding?*	*Wedding?*		
1823			Born	Born
1826		Madonna Murder	Havisham	
1829	Larceny Trial			
1830	Transportation			Havisham
1837				Apprentice
1841				Gentleman
1846	*Age 60 (Died)*	*Age 41*	*Age 23*	*Age 23*

On the second easel, he decided to schedule his initial outgoing correspondence, being conscious that communication with Australia would, at best, require a turnaround time approaching eight months. He would employ the services of his corresponding lawyer, John Plaistowe, resident in Maitland.

Under the heading, 'Correspondence – Plaistowe, Australia,' he wrote:

1. Governor New South Wales
2. Manager Bank of New South Wales
3. Status Ticket-of-Leave
4. Conditional-Pardon
5. Full-Pardon

Under the heading, 'Correspondence – England,' he wrote:

1. Employer – James Mudie
2. Register of Births, Marriages, and Deaths. (Church records)
3. Home Secretary – Sir Robert Peel
4. Her Majesty Queen Victoria

On the third easel, using fresh paper, he prepared to copy the contents of each page of the little black book up until Magwitch had been transported and, on the fourth easel, copied the entries made during Magwitch's time in

Australia. He copied each and every loose page, leaving blanks where he was unable to decipher meanings. He would start this work later in the week, but in the meantime, he planned to interview Molly and extract everything she could recall in the early years. Estella, at this time, would have little to add, in consequence, he decided to refrain from communication and likewise with Pip, as in any event, he was out of the country, working in Egypt. It was three o'clock in the morning and having consumed over half a bottle of whisky, Jaggers was exhausted. Satisfied with his night's work, he donned his heavy, black cloak and top hat and took a carriage back to his home in Gerrard Street.

By Easter the following year, Jaggers had completed his analysis of the little black book and loose papers. He had achieved another windfall by securing Compeyson's briefcase. A few golden guineas in the right direction at Scotland Yard had delivered the case and its contents. Original documents and letters providing a clear trail to unearth further information in New South Wales. A personal letter from a woman called Sheilagh in Sydney caught his attention. Compeyson's deceit and cunning sickened Jaggers, but added further grist to the mill. He now had a framework in place and all that remained was to fill in the gaps. He was yet to receive a first reply to his enquiries sent through his correspondent, John Plaistow, in Maitland. His optimism grew, but it was taking time, more time that he believed possible at the beginning of the quest.

Jaggers ordered Dover sole for dinner, enough for two, and requested Molly lay the table for himself in his usual seat at the head of the table, with another place setting to his right, four feet away from the top for his guest. From across the other side of the dining table, the guest would be looking directly at an original oil of the Old Bailey, in the foreground to the left, the artist had featured the last burning of a hanged woman and to the right, the five men known as the Cato Street conspirators, hanged and then beheaded as traitors for conspiring to kill the cabinet.

A smaller oil painting to the right depicted the carnival of a medieval procession to Tyburn, with mobs of spectators following the prisoners' cart from Newgate to the gallows. Further along the wall was a portrait of himself, Queen Victoria, and Windsor Castle. Fresh flowers stood generously in the centre of the table on top of an oblong piece of white lace. The wine would be white Burgundy which would be lightly chilled outside before dining commenced. In front of the central, brass, candlestick holder, he deliberately placed the little black book, covering it with a ladies lace handkerchief. Molly had instructions to serve as the grandfather clock struck eight o'clock, whether the guest had arrived or not. On the last stroke of eight, she appeared with the

Burgundy and plated vegetables on a tray and returned to the kitchen for the Dover sole.

"Dinner is served, sir," announced Molly.

"Thank you, Molly. And, Molly, tonight, you are to be my guest; shed your apron and please join me, we have matters to discuss." Molly's face went white. She had worked for him for nearly 20 years but had never been invited to dine.

Taking the lead, Jaggers sat first, indicating that she should sit next to him. He poured the wine delicately and offered a toast, thanking her for all her years' service, commenting that she had assisted him far more than she could possibly imagine. Great silences rained. During each pregnant silence, Jaggers poured more wine. Eventually, Molly relaxed.

"You are an excellent cook, Molly," said Jaggers, complimenting her again.

She blushed. Jaggers believed it to be the wine. Molly enjoyed the compliment. She started to talk. The main course finished and with a smile on her face, Molly removed the plates and crumbed down. For pudding, always her domain, she had chosen raspberry pie and custard.

"How interesting is this, Molly?" said Jaggers, unable to believe the coincidence, remembering the evidence of bramble scratches at her trial.

Molly stood whilst dishing up. The raspberry pie had a golden crust, and the custard had thickened with a light skin developing on the top.

"Why do you say that sir?" Molly's ebony eyes smiled as she watched him salivate and lick his lips before his first taste. He greedily shovelled the first couple of mouthfuls before replying.

"Delicious, Molly, absolutely delicious," he said, his mouth still containing custard, raspberries, and crust. She quickly sat down and followed, revelling in the compliment. "Reminds me of something that happened which brought us together." Jaggers dabbed the corners of his mouth with his napkin; this time, his mouth had emptied when he spoke. Molly continued eating, almost choking on his last words.

"Yes, Molly, Epsom Downs and Hounslow Heath." Molly dropped her spoon in the plate and stared back, wondering what he would say next. "Later, Molly, later, we finish dinner first. As Confucius said, *'May you live in interesting times!'*"

Jaggers finished his raspberry pie and custard, and sat silently as Molly finished hers. He leant forward and lifted the lace handkerchief covering the little black book. Molly gasped, abruptly stood up, collected the pudding plates, and scurried to the kitchen. Jaggers sat back and lit a cigar and waited. After five minutes, she returned. Jaggers rose from the table as she entered.

"Come, my dear, let us sit together in the lounge." Strangely, Molly went first, Jaggers picked up the little black book and followed.

Uncharacteristically, he seated Molly in a comfortable chair in his lounge. She had recognised the book immediately and watched as Jaggers placed it on the occasional table between them. She remembered the occasion when she had sold it to Magwitch on Epsom Downs.

"Now, Molly," said Jaggers. "Would you like to join me with whisky?" Molly nodded and watched as Jaggers poured whilst briefly explaining his mission. He invited her to relay everything she knew. Molly confirmed her shock discovery when she had witnessed the meeting with Pip and the connection with Magwitch. She knew nothing of the years since the murder of Gypsy Madonna. Prompted by the first few pages of the little book, she confirmed their first meeting to have been on Epsom Downs, and that she was an Ingram, a pure Gypsy before marrying the Georgio, Magwitch. Jaggers cut her short when she started talking about the Punch and Judy show, saying it was irrelevant to the case. He did not tell her why he wanted the information.

"Molly, I am interested in what kind of wedding service you had, and where?"

Molly explained it to be a Romany Gypsy service on Epsom Downs, confirming it was in June, actually midsummer's day and the Summer Solstice, longest day of the year, in 1822. Jaggers made copious notes as she spoke.

"Were there any witnesses?"

"All the Ingrams and all the Woods were present. The Elder, Sylvester, who tied the knot, will confirm that," she said. She went on to explain the service and finally, jumping over the broomstick. She explained that immediately after the wedding, they had left for Hounslow Heath where they had lived in her Bow-Top wagon. She confirmed that she had fallen pregnant with Estella almost immediately after they had been married. She laughed, saying that she had read the cards for Magwitch and that he had drawn the Empress, Goddess of fertility, which must have been correct. Jaggers made continuous notes on his pad, mostly single words and one-liners.

"Will you confirm that Magwitch was, indeed, Estella's father?" Molly's ebony eyes flashed at the insinuation, angry that Jaggers should suggest otherwise. He apologised.

"So what happened next?"

"The Gypsy tradition of *'marimē'* forbade relations during pregnancy, which was when Magwitch started to pursue that other woman. I found out after. It must have been going on for years, even went on after Estella was born, and you know the rest, sir," she said, getting aggravated at the memory.

Jaggers nodded, pouring Molly another whisky, relaxing her further. Jaggers thought back to her trial, then a flash of inspiration burst into his mind. The evidence produced by the Bow Street Runners at the trial of the Crown vs. Molly Magwitch had challenged Molly to advertise the whereabouts of her husband and, at that time, he was definitely in the country and working with Compeyson.

If that evidence was acceptable to the Crown, then the same would apply today, proving their marital relationship, thought Jaggers, quaffing more whisky. "When was Estella born?" probed Jaggers, pacing up and down excitedly.

"I remember it well, second of April, 1823. A few years earlier, Magwitch had also started getting involved with that evil man. I think it may have been around the time when we first met, because every so often, he had to go to Brentford. I never went there," said Molly, thinking back.

"Did you ever get divorced?" asked Jaggers.

"The Elder has to do that because he keeps the bloodied cord."

"Did you?"

"No!" exclaimed Molly.

"Does he still have the cord then?"

"Most likely."

"Right, Molly, tomorrow you will go and find this Sylvester man and bring him to me with any evidence he may have of your wedding, particularly the bloodied cord."

Sylvester also brought Ursula for Jaggers to interview. She confirmed that she was Molly's twin sister and had officiated at the wedding. Both Sylvester and Ursula confirmed everything that Molly had said and signed the statements prepared by Jaggers. As evidence, Jaggers retained the ageing broomstick that Molly had made and the bloodied knot. He drafted a statement in relation to symbolising the marriage as per ancient custom originating in India, a ceremony older than that of the Christian church and that, according to the Elder, although separated for many years, under Romany law, the couple were still married at the time of Magwitch's death.

Having dismissed the witnesses, Jaggers returned to his office in Little Britain and ticked off items one to seven on his list of evidence. The articled clerk assigned to research had also achieved the desired result in that probate would be passed on the basis of evidence of the blood relatives being the wife, Molly, and the daughter, Estella. Jaggers had also established that there existed a precedent through the appeals process to achieve Full-Pardon, but never posthumously. Jaggers's objective was to ensure Magwitch's wish that Pip was to be his heir and, for this to happen, he would need to look deeper into his activities in New South Wales. Regarding the acceptability under English Law of the Romany ceremony of marriage, he would challenge this through the courts.

Finally came the matter of time and his need to establish a timeframe of 15 years for the Statute of Limitations, basing his claim on recent powers given to the Inland Revenue Department by the Chancellor of the Exchequer.

Then came the official adoption papers for Estella, signed by Miss Havisham, but the introduction of this served only to complicate Pip's right as nominated beneficiary and could potentially stall probate.

In the fifth year, Jaggers summarised his achievements. He had gathered all the necessary statements and succeeded through the courts to establish relationships. It was 1851 when he received official confirmation of the timeframe being extended for cases of inheritance requiring international probate from seven to 15 years, projecting his deadline for proving Pip as sole beneficiary to 1861.

He now set about reviewing Magwitch's social and business status in the years following his transportation up until his return to England in 1846. He believed that the possibility existed that he may, indeed, have been qualified to return, but that Compeyson had deliberately misled the authorities who would have been unaware of the huge success Magwitch had achieved in his last few years in New South Wales. Jaggers wrote to James Mudie, his last known address being in Tottenham. The reply had been returned, saying that he was now resident in Paddington, but the invitation had been accepted.

Since their last meeting surrounding the publishing of *The Felonry of New South Wales* and the political furour it had created, Mudie had aged. He had just turned 70, was exceptionally bald, and had grown bitter with his memories of betrayal. The letter from Jaggers, inviting him for luncheon at Simpson's in the Strand, had come out of the blue and, for the first time in years, Mudie felt the excitement of a legal challenge.

"Roast beef and Yorkshire pudding of course," smiled Mudie, placing a silver sixpence on the mobile beef stand as the chef carved.

"Medium rare, with a little burnt piece," continued Mudie, pointing to the charred piece of beef on the side of the joint.

"Thank you, sir," said the chef, discretely slipping the coin into the pocket beneath his dark blue and white-striped apron. He placed three delicately carved pieces of pink beef onto the plate and proceeded to carve the crusty burnt piece.

"Horse radish, sir?" Mudie acknowledged. "One roast potato, and a little mustard and gravy as well," said Mudie, as the chef completed his serve.

Jaggers poured the red wine, also ordering roast beef. They exchanged light conversation until the Stilton and port had been finished and coffee, cigars, and cognac had been served. Jaggers sucked hard on his Montecristo, retrieved the little black book and opened it at the page where Mudie had signed the entry on 22nd February, 1836, before returning to England and his foray into the world of publishing.

"Good heavens!" exclaimed Mudie, his eyes nearly popping out of his head. "Where on earth did you find this?" Jaggers smiled.

"That's for me to know and for you to find out," he said with a wry smile.

"James, what can you tell me about this man?"

"Good fellow saved my life more than once, and loyal, very loyal. One of the rare ones, one in a million I suspect. Had a bad start though, by all accounts." Mudie explained all he knew.

"James, you returned to New South Wales in 1840. Was he doing well then?"

"I believe so, but I was only there for a few months. Had my own problems," replied Mudie with a sadness to his face. Jaggers turned towards the end of the book.

"What does this government stamp represent?" Mudie sipped at his balloon glass, then reached forward and spun the book round.

"It's evidence of the application of his appeal for a Full-Pardon. Amazing! I first gave him a Ticket-of-Leave and, before I left the first time, converted it to a Conditional-Pardon for everything he had done for me. In truth, he still had about eight or so years to serve. To get this," Mudie explained, "he must have been brought to the attention of Governor Gipps. Only the governor can recommend a Full-Pardon. He must have done enormously well."

"What was his main work after you left the first time?"

"Jute, I think; he was pioneering jute in the colony, and getting other emancipated convicts to help grow the stuff, and the women convicts in the Female Factory to weave and produce all manner of products from clothing to webbing and string. That's all I really know."

It had gone dark by the time they finished their meeting. Jaggers sat and studiously prepared a statement setting out the facts pertaining to Magwitch whilst assigned to Mudie at Castle Forbes. Mudie signed for the years 1829 to 1836, adding his comments to the facts he knew for the years 1836 to 1840, commenting on the government stamp in the little black book, indicating the application for appeal seeking a Full-Pardon dated 1844.

Jaggers entered his final appeal to overturn the conviction Magwitch had sustained on his return and capture. There, now, came the final leg of the case, to prove that Magwitch had nominated Pip as his heir. Jaggers had until 1861 before the time ran out.

Chapter 85

December, the 21st, the shortest day of the year, and darkness fell around four o'clock in the afternoon as Pip laid his hand softly on the latch of the old kitchen door of the cottage at the forge where he had spent his childhood.

Thank God I was here when Joe and Biddy got married, thought Pip.

Since then, Pip had been away in Egypt for nearly ten years. Nobody heard him enter and, for a moment, he looked in, unseen. Sitting opposite was old Joe. A little greyer, but as strong as ever, and fenced in by his leg, his foot resting on the fireguard, was a little, seven-year-old boy.

In my likeness, thought Pip without further comment.

"We giv' him the name, Pip, for your sake, dear old chap," said Joe, grinning from ear to ear at the sight of Pip in the doorway. "And we hoped he might grow a little bit like you, and we think he do."

"I think so too," said Pip, walking in and resisting the temptation to ruffle young Pip's hair.

The following morning, Pip took Little Pip for a morning walk. Talking continuously, they made their way down to the churchyard where Pip lifted Little Pip on top of the tombstone, the same tombstone he had been sat on by Magwitch on that fateful Christmas Eve and which held the sacred memory of his parents, their weathered names etched into the face of the stone still read, 'Philip Pirrip, late of this Parish, and also Georgina, wife of the above.'

"Biddy, one of these days you must give Little Pip to me, or lend him at least," said Pip after dinner that night.

"No, no," said Biddy, gently. "You must marry."

"So Herbert and Clara say, but I don't think I shall ever get married, Biddy. I have settled down in Cairo and it's not likely that I shall meet anyone suitable. I'm already quite an old bachelor."

"Dear Pip," said Biddy, "you're sure you don't fret after her?"

"Oh no, I don't think so, Biddy."

"Tell me as an old friend, have you quite forgotten her?"

"Dearest Biddy, I have forgotten nothing of importance in my life. But as to my selfish dreams, well, that's all gone, Biddy. All gone now," said Pip, hiding from the truth that he intended to revisit Satis House sometime in the hopes of rekindling his memory of Estella.

"Do you hear anything of Estella, Pip?" probed Biddy, her female intuition sensing Pip's emotions.

"I had heard that she was leading a most unhappy life. But now, I understand she is separated from her husband, Bentley Drummle. Apparently, he used to beat and bash her regularly. He was renowned for his brutality and meanness. But he got his comeuppance, I heard. Trampled to death by a horse he kept ill-treating. After that, I heard that she married her doctor. He had witnessed some of the outrageous beatings she had received. Apparently, the doctor was poor, so since then, they have been using some of her money to live on," replied Pip, with sadness in his voice.

Joe listened and nodded.

Chapter 86

Jaggers's main legal work had been and still was, the defence of criminals where the cases involved serious felony, the punishment for which would be death, leaving him relatively inexperienced in the field of wills and probate. He decided to employ the services of specialist counsel.

With all the evidence analysed, counsel advised that it was unlikely that the illegible notes made by Magwitch in his little book would direct the inheritance towards Pip, but rather, it would go firstly to Molly, his wife. This, however, could be challenged, given the marital relationship at the time of the breakup, since Molly was on record as threatening to murder her husband, Magwitch. It followed that next in line was, therefore, Estella. But here too, the water had been slightly muddied through her adoption by Miss Havisham, but since Estella had now come of age, she would be free to exercise her rights as an independent citizen.

In summary, counsel believed that given there was no other blood relative, the courts would look favourably upon Estella as the sole beneficiary. Finally, counsel pointed out that under English law, the ownership of fixed property in England and Wales required the assistance of a man, but given that the property was located in Australia, different rules may apply.

After the lengthy consultation with counsel in Lincoln's Inn, Jaggers returned to his office and updated his programme.

Programme of Life

Year	Magwitch	Molly	Estella	Pip
1786	Born			
1805		Born		
1822	Epsom Derby			
1822	*Wedding?*	*Wedding?*		
1823			Born	Born
1826		Murder trial	Havisham	
1829	Larceny Trial			
1830	Transportation			Havisham
1837				Apprentice
1841				Gentleman
1844	1st Appeal			
1846	*Age 60 (Died)*	*Age 41*	*Age 23*	*Age 23*
1847			Weds Drummie	Travels to Cairo
1856				Return from Cairo
1857	11 years later	*Age 52*	*Age 34*	*Age 34*
1861	Statute of Limits		*Australia? 38*	*Australia? 38*

London was sunny and warm, horse-drawn carriages conveyed gentlemen in top hats and ladies in crinoline frocks; their gentle hands supporting parasols to protect their fair skins from the sun. Walking hand-in-hand with Little Pip on his first outing to London, Pip and Little Pip watched as the horses pulling elegant carriages went trotting past. Biddy had reluctantly given permission for Little Pip to be taken to the big smoke.

Having had an early picnic on the grass in Hyde Park and after feeding the swans on the Serpentine with the leftover sandwiches, it was still before midday when they began sauntering along the road to Piccadilly Circus, where they would take the afternoon stagecoach back to Rochester. They were still looking in the shop windows at the magical displays when a servant came running up to them.

"Excuse me, sir, there's a lady back there who wants to speak with you, sir," said the woman with a curtsey. Pip took Little Pip's hand and turning, walked towards the pony and carriage the woman had pointed out. Pip's eyes focused on the face of the slim, elegant lady driving the pony, the reins still in her delicate hands. She leant forwards; her floral bonnet and face catching the midday sunshine.

"Estella," gasped Pip, noting her gentle expression. Pip read her mind, but before he could say anything…

"I am greatly changed too, I know," said Estella. Standing by the front tyre of her carriage, Pip looked down at Little Pip.

"Would you like to shake hands with Estella, Little Pip" He was stuck for words, consumed by her classical face and mannerisms, even more beautiful than ever.

"Lift up that handsome little child and let me kiss him," said Estella, believing he was Pip's little boy and charmed at the sight of the smartly dressed lad.

The chance meeting was strange for both, and Pip noticed that her face spoke volumes and his ears told him also from her voice, and the feel of her touch confirmed to him that she had suffered more in life than during any of the cruel teachings she had received from Miss Havisham. He suddenly recognised that in her brutal life with Drummle, she had found her heart and now, she could understand how his heart had felt all those years ago.

Pip handed up Little Pip and climbed up onto the carriage, squeezing Little Pip between them.

"I have been summoned to Mr. Jaggers's office tomorrow morning," said Estella with a bland expression. "It's something to do with my father. If you know anything about it, you should come too."

"I will," replied Pip. "But first, I need to take Little Pip home."

"Oh," said Estella. "Where's home?"

"With Joe and Biddy, down at the forge, you remember, near Satis House." Estella blinked in surprise.

"You're not Little Pip's father then?"

"No, Estella, I'm still an old bachelor, living and working in Cairo. Little Pip belongs to Biddy and Joe. They called him Pip for my sake," explained Pip.

"Shall I ride down with you? We could visit Satis House together. Catch up on a few things," suggested Estella.

"I'd like that, Estella." Pip's heart beat faster, a feeling he had forgotten since their last parting.

Joe and Biddy invited them to stay for dinner, which was always early; meat and veggies either boiling or roasting for hours, the aroma wafting around the kitchen and making everyone hungry before they should have been. After dinner, with plenty of daylight left, Pip and Estella excused themselves and went for an evening walk. Joe winked at Biddy as the latch on the kitchen door clanked shut.

"How lovely to see them together at last," said Biddy.

Silently, they picked their way through the lanes and backstreets. Estella, a little taller than Pip, her blond-red hair tied neatly in a ponytail and Pip's dark hair and swarthy complexion made them a striking couple; their minds perplexed at what to say or ask next. They arrived at Satis House. The entire place had been knocked down and all that remained was the wall of the old garden and weeds growing through the cracked paving slabs.

"I still own the land," volunteered Estella, conscious that Pip was shocked at the demolition of the old mansion.

Pip remained silent, his mind flashing back to the sight of the fire licking up the curtains of the second-floor window after his last visit well over a decade ago. That painful memory had remained with him when he had rushed back into the mansion and up the back staircase, bursting into Miss Havisham's room. In her pathetic attempt to extinguish the flames, the fire had caught her cotton and silk wedding dress. He still carried the scars of the burns he had suffered, attempting to save her life. His ears filled with her screams as she had collapsed, her body, face, and hair consumed by the flames.

"After the fire, they had to demolish the building," continued Estella, as they arrived at the rusting wrought-iron gate; the lock, long since corroded away. It squeaked as Pip gently pushed it open. A silvery mist was descending as dusk approached. They walked in without speaking and made their way over to the one remaining wrought-iron garden bench and sat down together.

"After so many years, it's strange that we should meet like this, Estella, especially here where we first walked together. Don't you remember telling Uncle Pumblechook that Miss Havisham didn't want to see him?" said Pip with a lump in his throat. Estella didn't answer. Pip continued, "Do you often come back?"

"I have never been here since."

"Nor I."

The full moon began to rise, yellowish in colour, magnifying the shadowy shapes on the surface. Pip's mind imagined it to be Magwitch's face when he had stared placidly up at the ceiling in his prison cell in those last few moments before he died.

"I have often hoped and intended to come back, but have been prevented by many circumstances," said Estella sadly, tears forming in her eyes. "Poor, poor old place."

The silvery mist touched by those first rays of the moon became ethereal as shadows grew across the now-vacant spot.

"As we walked along, were you wondering how it came to be left in this condition?" asked Estella, struggling to keep her emotions under control.

Pip had seen the single tear run down her cheek; his emotions too were bursting.

"Yes, Estella, I would love to know what has happened."

"The ground belongs to me. It's the only possession I have left. Everything else has gone."

"Is it to be built on?"

"At last, it is," said Estella with a long sigh. "That's why I wanted to come down to Rochester with you. It's strange to think that we will be saying goodbye to the place together."

Tears began to form in her eyes again as she quickly changed the subject. "Do you still work abroad?"

"Still," said Pip, his voice sad.

"And you do well, I am sure."

"I work pretty hard for a sufficient living, and I suppose, yes, I do well."

"I have often thought of you, Pip."

"Have you?"

"Of late, I think of you very often. I have found a place in my heart."

"You have always had a place in my heart," said Pip. They fell silent.

"I never thought," said Estella, "that I should be saying goodbye to you at the same time as saying goodbye to this place. But I am very glad to do so."

"Glad to part again, Estella? To me, parting is a painful thing. To me, the memory of our last parting still remains both mournful and painful."

"But when we parted then, you said to me," said Estella earnestly, "God bless you; God forgive you." She paused for thought, and Pip held the silence.

"If you could say that then, you would say it now, especially as I have been bent and broken in life. But I hope I am a better person through that horrible experience. Pip, be as considerate and good to me as you were before and tell me we are friends." Estella felt desolate.

"We are friends," confirmed Pip, rising and bending over her as she rose from the bench.

"And we will continue friends apart," agreed Estella.

Pip gently took her hand in his and they went out of the ruined place together, and as the morning mists had risen long ago when Pip had first left the forge, so the evening mists were rising now, and in all the broad expanse of tranquil light, silently, Pip and Estella realised that there was no shadow of another parting.

Chapter 87

"What a pleasant surprise?" said Jaggers, as Wemmick ushered Estella into his office in Little Britain. "How good of you to come."

"Your message said it was about my father?" said Estella, remaining aloof.

Jaggers confirmed the purpose of the meeting being to do with Magwitch's affairs and, placing his large hands on his desk, he prepared to rise, when excited voices were heard from the reception. Wemmick knocked the door and entered.

"Sir, there is a gentleman here to meet you, just returned from Cairo!" exclaimed Wemmick, pleasure oozing from every facial muscle. Estella smiled at Jaggers's surprised expression as Pip strode in, his arm outstretched.

"Well, bless my soul, young Pip."

They shook hands and Jaggers offered Pip a seat. Jaggers moved back behind his desk and settled himself in his great, black, coffin-like chair.

"Good morning, Estella." Pip bent down and gave her a light peck on the cheek before settling himself.

"Your timing is impeccable, Mr. Pip, and, indeed, opportune."

"Thank you, Mr. Jaggers," replied Pip. "I arrived a few days ago." They exchanged pleasantries for a few minutes, and Jaggers invited Wemmick to join the conference.

"It has been a long, hard road for us all," began Jaggers, "not least of which has been the unravelling of your father's estate, Estella."

"I didn't know he had one," replied Estella with a sound of astonishment to her voice. Pip took a sharp intake of breath at the mention of Magwitch's affairs after more than a decade.

"Indeed, he has, but the matter before me has been firstly, to secure it from the rights to confiscation by the Crown, following Magwitch's potentially illegal return, and, that up until recently, it was difficult to prove the existence of an heir."

Pip pricked up his ears.

"Wemmick, be kind enough to arrange some tea." Wemmick nodded and departed.

"May I respectfully enquire into your relationship?" quizzed Jaggers, looking from Estella to Pip.

"We're friends," said Estella quickly.

"Close and old friends," added Pip.

"You are presumably still married to Mr. Bentley Drummle, Estella?" Estella winced at the sound of Drummle's name.

"No, Mr. Jaggers," replied Estella, going on to explain the circumstances of his death and that she had remarried her personal physician. Pip sat silently, grieving internally.

"But it seems that I am doomed never to find a happy married life with children, as he too recently passed away in consequence of a tropical disease. Nobody knew what it was and they believe he had caught it while treating a patient who had returned from central Africa with the illness." Estella went into detail at the lingering death and how she had nursed him for many months.

"Ah, maybe the answer to a maiden's prayer," interjected Jaggers, holding up his hand, indicating he had heard enough of the grizzly medical details and the sadness she had endured.

"Put the case, that between husband and wife, the matter of a questionable will and blood relative making it difficult, if not impossible, for the Crown to interpret the wishes of the estate when the deceased had failed to make proper provision and, therefore, the rules of intestacy were to be applied. Put the case, that only a few years remained before reaching the fluxion of the Statute of Limitations, then it would appear the solution would lay through wedlock."

Jaggers stood, removed his great spotted handkerchief, and walked over to his side office, beckoning Estella and Pip to follow.

The papers pinned to the easels had turned yellow with age, and volumes of paper lay strewn across the temporary trestle table erected along the end wall of the little room. He picked up his ivory-handled cane and began to explain his discoveries. He started by pointing to the few remaining artifacts pinned to the heavy timber post. Pip choked at the sight of Magwitch's cap, pipe, and jacket.

"In summary," concluded Jaggers, "the final success may lie with you as a couple, jointly delivering the final challenge to inherit the fortunes of your father, Estella, also your secret benefactor, Pip, who was known in Australia as Provis."

Pip nearly dropped his teacup as Jaggers reached the end of his dissertation. He steadied it with his left hand and placed it on the trestle table. Both Estella and Pip were speechless.

"I see that my proposal requires consideration and time. Since you both have a justifiable claim, yet Magwitch directs that Pip is his heir, you must, therefore, answer the question in your minds as to what directions he may have made, should he have possessed the knowledge that his one and only beloved daughter, was, in fact, alive and well."

Pip and Estella watched as he delivered his summation.

"For the purpose of resolving this matter, may I suggest you take one week, at the end of which, you return here and deliver your final instructions." This time, he blew his nose loudly, returning the handkerchief to its regular place.

"I can only speak for myself," said Pip, the first to speak. "And I will simplify the matter, as I have already made my decision and it will be Estella's answer you must rely upon."

Pip dropped to his right knee in front of Estella, his head bowed slightly. He took her slender arm by the wrist, slipping down to her hand and halfway along her slim fingers, gently holding the back of her hand to his lips. He looked up into her soft, blue-green eyes.

"My dearest, sweetest, Estella, would you do me the infinite pleasure of accepting my hand in marriage?" His eyes watered as the words emerged.

"Oh yes, Pip," she said without a pause, her other hand tenderly stroking the hair on the side of his head.

"Oh yes, Pip, oh yes, my love," she spoke in a whisper, tears flooding down her cheeks.

"Wemmick. Bring the champagne!" shouted Jaggers, moving back and settling himself in his chair.

Pip stood and held Estella close to him and hand-in-hand, they returned to their seats in front of Jaggers. Wemmick poured the champagne.

"To the *Magwitch Fortunes*," announced Jaggers. The crystal glasses clinked and they drank the first toast.

"To my bride and our wedding day," said Pip, raising his glass to Estella.

"To our children," whispered Estella, her slim hand trembling with years of pent-up feelings.

"And where would you like the ceremony" said Jaggers, getting down to business immediately.

"Cooling Church, of course," replied Pip, bursting with pride.

"Not a gypsy wedding, Estella?"

"I don't think so, Mr. Jaggers, and Mr. Jaggers, would you be kind enough to give me away?" asked Estella, nearly bursting into tears again; the happiness surging into her every limb.

"And I'll have Herbert Pocket as my best man."

"Guests?" quizzed Jaggers.

"Molly, of course," said Estella, smiling, their mother and daughter relationship having blossomed since they had been reunited just before Magwitch's funeral.

"And I will have Joe and Biddy and Little Pip," interjected Pip.

"And I had better ask Uncle Pumblechook too. Mr. Wopsle will be there anyway, but I suppose he should get an official invitation."

"Don't forget Wemmick," whispered Estella into Pip's ear.

"And the guest list would not be complete without dear Mr. Wemmick," said Pip quickly.

Wemmick flushed at Pip's invitation.

"Would you like Molly and I to handle the arrangements?" volunteered Jaggers.

Pip and Estella agreed instantly, comfortable that they were in capable hands.

"Now, before we finish today, I must warn you that to complete matters of the estate, you should consider travelling out to Australia immediately after the wedding." Jaggers paused for reaction.

"What a wonderful honeymoon," they both replied as if they had prepared earlier. Jaggers laughed nervously, a strange and unusual show of emotion never witnessed before by Wemmick in all his 35 years with Jaggers. Estella suddenly stood up and looked accusingly back at Pip.

"And don't you dare do to me what that swindler Compeyson did to Miss Havisham!" Both Jaggers and Wemmick exploded into fits of laughter.

Molly suggested the date should be the same as her wedding day, the 21st of June, midsummer's day and the Summer Solstice and, the longest day of the year, but Estella disagreed, insisting on May Day, the first of May, and the spring celebration with dancing around the maypole and the crowning of a May Queen to add to the merriment at the reception.

Chapter 88

On the ends of the oak pews down either side of the aisle, Molly had arranged white lilies surrounded with lush, deep-green leaves. At the sides of the altar, she arranged voluminous bunches of flowers, and the same both sides of the podium where the sermon would be read. At the base of the diamond-leaded windows to the sides of the church, she had arranged scented herbs and grasses on the sloping stone windowsills. Outside of the main entrance, she had arranged, against a lush-green background of ferns, copious bunches of red and white roses together with bunches of lilac, their fragrance and mauve flowers adding a touch of passion. And, finally, she had wedged the front gates open and tied bunches of yellow flowering gorse. A general invitation was made to the residents and traders along Rochester High Street and the neighbors of the ground where Satis House once stood. The reception was to be held at the Blue Boar Inn.

Herbert sat next to Pip and fiddled with the ring, talking quietly in an attempt to calm Pip's nerves, although Herbert was probably much worse. They sat in the front pew on the right-hand side of the aisle and occasionally glanced across at Molly who was seated with Clara, Herbert's wife, on the left-hand side. The Minister waited patiently as the hour approached. The church was crammed full. Mostly dressed in their finery, with some seated at the back still in their working clothes. They all wore a little sprig of white heather received from Little Pip, dispensed from his wicker basket as the guests arrived. The wind-organ pumped at the sound of the hooves of a team of horses approaching.

The open, four-in-hand carriage, driven by two gentlemen dressed in red jackets and shiny, black top hats slowed to a halt at the front gates. Wearing top hat and tails, Jaggers stepped out first, carrying his ivory-handled cane. He offered his hand as Estella emerged from the carriage. Gracefully, her slender figure clad in an antique, ivory-lace dress, stepped from the carriage onto the dry gravel. The sun shone above the few trees inducing dappled shade along the short walk to the church entrance. Estella linked her arm through Jaggers's stout arm. Glancing through her delicate veil, Estella thanked him with her eyes. He winked back; a smile broadening underneath his huge, bulbous nose.

"Everything will be just fine," he whispered, giving her reassurance. "And then you sail for New South Wales."

She smiled back.

"How can I ever thank you enough, Mr. Jaggers?" she whispered.

"Pay my bill when you can from Australia." He winked again.

"Of course," she said.

"It's a big one; 12 years is a long time," he laughed. "But I wouldn't have missed it for anything."

They stepped into the shadow of the Norman archway and entered the church. Estella squeezed his arm. Chuckling, he squeezed back. The organ played and they walked slowly down the aisle. Pip turned to look back; the sight almost too much to bear, his eyes filled.

"Ladies and gentlemen, we are gathered together in the sight of God…" the Minister began, finally he reached the vows.

"I do," said Pip, his voice strong and proud.

"I do," said Estella, almost in a whisper, hardly audible past the front pews, but Molly heard, instantly bursting into tears. She clutched at her own broomstick brought in specially to bless Estella.

"You may now kiss the bride."

A round of applause went up from the guests, almost as if it had brought to an end a lifetime of misery since the death of the town's brewer, Brewer Havisham, all those years ago.

The Blue Boar Inn was jammed to bursting point. Food was a simple affair, and the toasts and speeches were completed with the exception of Jaggers, who, vehemently considering himself to be the official family friend, wanted to say a few words.

He spoke for 15 minutes, touching on the fascinating story of Estella, leaving out the sadness and highlighting the best. He spoke of the couple's destiny together and as he drew to the end, he reached behind to a small, polished, mahogany box he had commissioned to be made.

"Now, Pip, this is for you, and its contents will assist in what I would cautiously term your treasure hunt." Pip stepped forwards to receive the box.

"Open it," said Jaggers. Pip did and gasped at the sight of the contents. Magwitch's little, black book stuffed full of numerous pieces of paper snuggled into the padded, burgundy, silk lining.

"I had no idea you had recovered it," said Pip, fingering the tatty leather binding.

"You will find information and sketches and maps. I have provided a separate analysis of my findings over the years which may also be helpful." Pip shook Jaggers's hand and returned to Estella's side.

"And for Estella," he said, rummaging in his small waistcoat pocket. He retrieved Magwitch's golden bullet to which he had had a gold chain added so that she could wear it as a necklace.

"This is the first gold bullet your father smelted in New South Wales. Your task is to find its origin." Estella stepped forward, her eyes focusing on the unique and exquisite piece of jewellery.

"Thank you, Mr. Jaggers," she said, lowering her head, allowing Jaggers to slip the necklace on. Stunned and speechless, she stood with Pip, their shoulders touching and holding hands, mesmerised by Jaggers as he stood before the gathering.

"And now, ladies and gentlemen, it remains for me as the old friend of the family, to propose the toast to the bride and groom. And it gives me the greatest of pleasure, ladies and gentlemen, in wishing nothing but the best for Pip and Estella, and we wish them every success with their future in the Land of Promise, Australia."

He paused, raised his glass, and said with a wry smile, "And this time, ladies and gentlemen, they clearly do have *Great Expectations*."

Part 4
New South Wales – 1857

Chapter 89

The clipper, *Dunbar,* had already achieved the near record time of 81 days for a passenger ship sailing from Plymouth to Sydney. In total, 121 persons, of which 63 were passengers and 58 were crew. Their departure had been delayed for 23 hours, pending the arrival of late passengers, forcing them to wait for the next daylight tide, frustrating both Captain Green and passengers. Built by James Laing and Sons at Sunderland from British oak and boasting East India teak decks, she weighed nearly 1200 tons. Her crew tended to her every need, almost more so than for the passengers.

First-class cabins were luxurious, with vast sums of money having been lavished in the fitting out of the ornate quarters. Ticket costs were up to 30 per cent more than for other vessels, but then the clipper's speed would slice nearly a month from the normal sailing time. Onboard entertainment was provided, not least of which would be the snobbish waving at passengers on other slower vessels as they overtook, singing a boisterous chorus of Rule Britannia. Passengers and crew had all participated during the two-and-a-half-month confinement, providing daily-organised activities, filling the voyage to the Land of Promise. Sailing at the end of May, Plymouth had buzzed with the excitement of the continuing gold fever in Australia, the gold rush having now entered its fourth year, increasing the need for luxury passenger ships, mostly travelling between Great Britain and Australia.

The passengers were a mixed bunch from returning colonists and business tycoons and families deciding to throw in the towel in England to seek their fortunes Down Under. There were many single men heading for the gold fields, even a young couple straight from their marriage ceremony, their few worldly goods packed in a single trunk.

Having made the journey a number of times before, Captain Green was no novice. The sun had shone as they sailed in pleasant conditions from Plymouth, passing Lizard Point into the North Atlantic. Flocks of gulls had squawked overhead and followed the *Dunbar* well past the Azores as they headed south, and deeper into the Atlantic; a few gulls staying with the ship until the Cape Verde Islands. Partially becalmed in the Doldrums before crossing the Equator, west of Ascension Island, where they had all participated in the usual equatorial drenching ceremony, they eventually gathered speed as they tacked south through the southeast trade winds off the west coast of Africa and down to re-victual in Cape Town. After less than 48 hours in Cape Town, they had sailed down into the Roaring Forties, almost flying as the clipper came into her own. The weather had darkened as they reentered the southeast trade winds heading north up the east coast of Australia. August, the depth of winter in the southern hemisphere, and it was cold, freezing cold. *Dunbar* was still over 1200 miles south of the Tropic of Capricorn as they approached Port Jackson. Darkness came early, but with their imminent arrival, excitement grew amongst the passengers, yet hardly tempered by the onslaught of the tempestuous storm. Whipped up by near cyclonic winds, the seas became mountainous.

Heading on a starboard tack, Botany Bay was estimated to be just off the port bow. It was hugely dark, no moon and, the setting sun in the west had long gone, if it was ever visible at dusk in weather like this. The crew knew it was hopeless to anticipate the silhouette of the North and South Heads cliffs and the entrance of the mouth to Port Jackson and safety. Peering into the horizontal blinding rain, Captain Green screwed up his eyes for the faintest clue to his location.

"Bo'sun, double-reef fore and main topsails," he instructed, shouting through the megaphone, hardly audible above the winds; the seas too strong to maintain any degree of canvas.

"Aye, aye, sir. Double-reef fore and main topsails."

It was a dirty, dark, and satanic night. The seaman's terror.

"Where the hell am I?" agonised Green, the first feeling of doubt entering his mind. He thought of his instruction to passengers some three hours earlier that they would be in the lee of Port Jackson by the early hours.

"Best get below and turn in for the night, far too dangerous to be out on deck," he had said, the fear of being swept overboard in the growing tempest mounting. He planned to enter the protection of the port before midnight and hove to before heading for Sydney Cove. God willing, they would be docking by breakfast. He wiped the driving, ice-cold rain from his gas.

"First Mate fo'ard," ordered Green. "Look out for the North Head." They waited for the light to guide them through the entrance between the cliffs.

"Second Mate, fo'c'sle," ordered Green. "Look out for South Head."

"Lighthouse ahoy," shouted the First Mate an hour later. Green wiped the driving rain from his face and shielded his eyes.

Thank the good Lord for small mercies. Reckon that must be North Head, pondered Green.

"That sets us between the Heads."

Green was wrong. The lighthouse signalled The Gap. That jagged break in the rock face just south of South Head. He gave the instruction to change course westerly as he stared at the intermittent flashing light breaking the cloak of treacherous darkness. The *Dunbar* slowly turned, sliding down the mountainous waves and disappearing into the trough, then back up the other side, breaking sight of the navigation light. Two men struggled to hold the ship's wheel, the force of the aggressive seas smashing against the hull and rudder as the rear of the vessel emerged from the waves.

"Square away," ordered Green, confident that he was entering the mouth of the port.

"Aye, aye, Captain," shouted the two seamen hauling the ship's wheel in an anticlockwise direction, one seaman instantly knocked off his feet by another mountainous breaking wave.

"Keep the luff," shouted Green through his megaphone as the clipper headed broadside into the wind. He felt weary as he looked up into the close-reefed fore and main topsails. He ordered the foresail to be clued up, adrenalin alone keeping him awake, having had no rest for the past two days.

"Breakers ahead!" screamed able-seaman, Johnson.

"Hard to starboard," shouted Green; he looked desperately up at the sail-less rigging. The wind having forced him to strip most of the canvas and with no small sail hoisted, the clipper failed to respond. In the ink-black heinous night, they drifted towards the rugged cliffs. Trapped broadside to the wind and parallel to the mountainous waves, *Dunbar's* hull became a sail.

The next massive wave lifted *Dunbar* onto the jagged rocks at the base of the cliffs, smashing her as the wave subsided, breaking her back. Panicking and screaming passengers in nightdresses and pyjamas scurried on deck only to be washed over the side and smashed on the vicious, unforgiving rocks below; their bodies pummelled mercilessly like rag dolls, lifted and smashed again and again.

Able-seaman Johnson, the last man to be washed from the crushed and dying vessel and hurled high into the cliff face, was left hanging to the side of the rocks, as he managed to climb higher and clear of the worst of the waves.

In the dawn, the sight was of bodies torn to shreds, dead women and children in nightdresses, their arms and heads and legs severed from the thorax and pelvis, and couples locked together in a desperate embrace, together in their final moments and together for eternity.

With the dawn, the wind had dropped, but cruel seas still tore at the ragged rocks at the entrance to Port Jackson. Slowly, daylight arrived to expose split and broken driftwood littering the rocks. Driftwood and shattered pieces of

Dunbar rose and fell on the swell around South Head. The scene was one of dreadful carnage. The alarm went up as evidence of the wreck was discovered onshore. The port master, Captain Pockley, reported 12 bodies ashore in Middle Harbour, one of which was an officer. Then, a mailbag marked, *Dunbar*, Plymouth, May 29. Next, a cask of tripe marked, *Dunbar*. A large portion of the wreck supporting handrails with the carving of a lion was also washed into Middle Harbour. Another two beer casks with Tooth's brand and the bodies of a respectably dressed man and woman with a ring on her finger floated silently beside a solitary grand piano, on the top of which was a slim young woman, partially clad in her delicate cotton nightdress as she clung spread-eagled to the lid. The cruel sea had claimed her.

Chapter 90

Since Magwitch had departed, never to return, Mr. Worthington, the manager of the Bank of New South Wales, had continued to act as requested, by siphoning off surplus funds from the jute trade and investing heavily in Sydney property. The success and size of the property portfolio now required independent management and, following advice from Jaggers in London, he looked forward to the arrival of the heirs to the Magwitch estate, relieving him of further responsibility. The Sikh had coordinated the Jute trade and shipping, whilst the Chinese trading house in George Street, Tin War and Yee Tick, had acted as agents from the fancy goods shop of Sam Choy and S. Dockson. Sydney had changed dramatically, in particular, the amount of new construction and property development and prices were escalating as a result of the gold rush. Great numbers of Chinese with the gold fever had arrived. There was also a near doubling of European migration, many of whom had come down from the gold fields of California, all seeking their fortunes in the burgeoning gold fields of Australia.

"But what do we do with the jute business? That is the question." Mr. Worthington and the Sikh had been going over the books of the trading company for the past half hour, discussing the prospects for the next trading year.

"If you don't mind me saying, sir," said the Sikh. "Has not the time arrived to sell?"

"Dispose of my little business? You may be right, especially with the trouble brewing in West Bengal."

"The sacred cow," corrected the Sikh. "Would you like me to make discrete enquiries in the Indian community, sir? I believe I know an Indian businessman who would be interested, providing the price is acceptable," volunteered the Sikh.

Worthington stood from behind his desk and began pacing. Deep in thought, he walked to the twin, double-hung, mahogany window and absently gazed out onto George Street. He watched the myriad of horse-drawn carriages going about their business. There were ladies carrying parasols and dressed in gay frocks, and crisply dressed gentlemen in top hats. Gone were the earlier days of convicts in irons clanking their way up the untidy streets and, in their place, had arrived the rush and tumble of free human spirit. Sydney had become a city accommodating every form of life and business imaginable. It had become a truly cosmopolitan society supporting Asians and Europeans, all in the pursuit of wealth.

"Yes," replied Worthington after a moment's silence. "Tell him that I will consider any reasonable cash offer. No delays. A clean contract with one payment at settlement. And his offer will be accepted or declined within 24 hours. Payment will only be accepted in gold or British currency."

Chapter 91

Midnight, 20th August, Thursday, the *Dunbar* crushed, splintered, and disintegrated on South Head. Abel-seaman James Johnson climbed higher and finding a thin ledge, clung on until first light. Below, the sight sickened him. Above, he saw a group of people, spectators who had gathered, stunned at the enormity of the tragedy, but they failed to see him. He slept as Friday came and went. The skies opened again, aggravating any hope of early rescue. The conditions were freezing. Saturday, Johnson was seen waving a sodden, white handkerchief. Miraculously, a rope ladder dropped to his ledge from above, providing his escape. The first reports of the shipwreck hit Sydney, bringing a surge of spectators, all with a connection to someone who had sailed on the *Dunbar*, be they friend or family or business associate, no one in Sydney was unconnected. It was the worst maritime disaster ever in Port Jackson.

Under the North Head, a group of rescuers found themselves suddenly attacked by a shark as they attempted to drag the remains of bodies from the turbulent seas. Rescue teams, lowered from The Gap, spent half of Saturday picking up mutilated body parts wedged between crevices in the fractured rocks and ledges. Caught between two boulders, the trunk of a mature female from the waist upwards. Farther along, the legs and pelvis of a male to his navel. Then, part of a shoulder, neck, and head of a female supporting a bleached arm and extended hand, with the wash of the receding water, almost as if it were in life, beckoning for help. Then, a leg, and a thigh, and a human head hurled along by the remorseless sea, tearing furiously in a concerted effort to devour its prey. Many bodies were identified, but equally as many were not, and the funeral procession to the mass grave at Camperdown Cemetery provided the final resting place for them all. Only later would the copy manifest from London confirm the names of those who had perished.

Chapter 92

Overtaken by the newer, sleeker, and faster clipper *Dunbar*, three weeks out of Plymouth, the *Maid Marion* finally entered Bass Straits nearly a month behind the clipper. Passing Cape Howe at the extreme southeastern point of Australia, late September, with spring in the air, they sailed sedately up the eastern coastline. The sights of the distant mountain range interspersed with low hills covered with thick bush and dwarfish olive-coloured trees led down to sandy beaches. Tranquil and sunny weather brought passengers onto the top decks of the *Maid Marion,* where they could witness the full beauty of the Great Dividing Range and Illawarra country and the lofty Mount Keera pushing up into the heavens. For the first time since leaving England, passengers delighted at the delicious sight of waving wheat fields and the bright grass of clover-meadows lying between the belt of mountains that encircled the rich valley of Illawarra and the shore. From the aromatic leaves of trees and shrubs along the margin of the Illawarra beach, a perfumed breeze wafted across the decks of the *Maid Marion*.

"Darling, how wonderful is this?" said Estella, squeezing Pip's hand. "It reminds me of Southern Italy."

"I wouldn't really know," replied Pip, having previously only sailed past Gibraltar, holding well to the south of the Mediterranean and hugging the North African coast each time he had travelled back and forth to Cairo.

"It's like the Bay of Naples and Capri," continued Estella.

"We're both lucky to have been abroad before," said Pip. "A lot of the other passengers have never been out of the country."

During the voyage, Pip and Estella had got to know most of the other passengers whilst exercising and dining on deck during the balmy weather between the tropics. The winter months off the Skeleton Coast and down into the Roaring Forties being spent below decks, analysing the information Jaggers had given them before their departure. Estella had sifted through the little black book, redrawing the maps and diagrams and various references Magwitch had made during his 16 years in New South Wales before returning to England. She had decided that the book was becoming so fragile that they should interpret as much as they could before arriving and keep the book protected in its mahogany box.

They had a short list of names both from the book and from Jaggers's notes that had come down to an Aboriginal village well north of Maitland, and an Aboriginal man named Moola, the bank manager at the bank of New South Wales, the name given by Jaggers as Mr. Worthington. There were references to an Indian Sikh, but there didn't seem to be a name. A lawyer named Plaistowe in Maitland, and Polly, Magwitch's housekeeper in Morpeth, and her daughter, Alice, who must now be in her 20s.

They had a copy of the map of Sydney that James Mudie had included with his book, *The Felonry of New South Wales*, and a topographical map of New South Wales. The rest, they hoped to find in Sydney. The most interesting page of the little black book contained the map Magwitch had sketched when he had been out planning to graze sheep on the Malumla Range, but the map itself made no comment as to its purpose. Estella noted Magwitch had modified it on numerous occasions, marking what appeared as an important point in charcoal with a striking six-pointed star.

"The captain says we should be docking in Darling Harbour tomorrow," said Pip, his mind turning to thoughts of their disembarkation.

"Just can't wait to start exploring," said Estella, the long voyage becoming tedious.

"Shall we send our trunk to the Royal Hotel first and walk around town for a while?" suggested Pip.

"Let's see what time of day it is first," said Estella. "We don't want to be out after dark. I've heard terrible stories of the Rocks area, and we will not be far from there."

"I reckon we will find everything we need to know at night in the Rocks," commented Pip.

"Let's wait and see first. Maybe get some advice from this Mr. Worthington," suggested Estella. As dusk approached, they went below to their small cabin, and Estella retrieved her copy of the map of Sydney.

"See here," said Estella excitedly, "find Market Street and walk along it, cross Sussex Street, Kent Street, Clarence Street, and York Street, and then turn left into George Street. The Bank of New South Wales should be just about here." Estella's slim index finger traced the route.

"We should really take a carriage."

"But why, darling?" challenged Estella, becoming dominant and preferring to walk to see the town.

"Just thinking about our safety," replied Pip indignantly.

"We've got this far, haven't we?" retorted Estella, unconcerned. "Just depends on the time of day and the weather." Pip capitulated.

They had been married for four-and-a-half months; the confinement below decks bringing them closer together. Making love had been a total failure initially when in England, but at sea, their inhibitions had dissolved, leading them to discover each other's fantasies, daily exploring each other's passions, fired with a fine blend of port wine and whisky. They were never separated and having excitedly planned their arrival, decided to dine below decks that evening and turn in early.

The sight of the North and South Heads was awe-inspiring. With two rocky precipices like guardian giants about three quarters of a mile apart, rising abruptly from the swell of the sea to a height of about 200 feet, appearing on sentry duty whilst guarding the entrance, stunningly stark, as they were bathed in the morning sunshine.

It was the calmest of mornings, but still the *Maid Marion* rose and fell in the heavy swell as she passed from the Pacific Ocean into the protection of Port Jackson. From the f'o'csle, Pip and Estella gazed at the small islands and little harbours, all part of Port Jackson. Middle Harbour, Sydney Cove, Darling Harbour, Rose Bay, and in the distance, the Parramatta River disappearing into the hinterland. On a slope at the eastern side of a very snug sunny bay lay an English lawn, meadow-like verdure in front, providing added splendour to the handsome stone mansion. Every space now occupied by one type of mansion or villa and down at the water's edge, small private jetties sported private sale boats. There were cheerful gardens and bright shrubberies with varied hues of trees and plants of European, and tropical climates danced in the wind. Tranquil blue waters with light sailboats skimming the waters like an inland lake and numerous small beaches glittering with siliceous sands, suitable for the production of the finest glassware. Myriads of oysters clinging to metamorphic rocks, occasional people harvesting, scraping the oyster from its wrinkled home and eating it there and then, rinsed down with watered rum or colonial gin. Pip took Estella in his arms and sighed.

"What a wondrous sight, darling," he whispered, burying his face into her long blond hair and kissing her lightly on her ear and long neck.

"Perfect to raise our family," replied Estella with a twinkle in her eyes.

Pip held her hand and looked deeply into her eyes.

"Is there something I should know?" Estella nodded.

"Are you?" Estella nodded again, her eyes smiling.

"When?"

"Easter next year, I think," said Estella. Pip exploded with laughter.

"Miss Havisham taught you about the birds and the bees as well then?"

"Not exactly, we never ever spoke of such things."

They both fell silent, their attention returning to the sights of Sydney and the glorious little coves and harbours.

"When do you think it happened?" asked Pip innocently.

"Stellenbosch. The two weeks we stopped for repairs and to re-victual in Cape Town. You know, when we stayed at that magnificent vineyard," said Estella, remembering the splendour of Cape Town and the sight of Table Mountain before they had docked and then that carriage ride to the winery. Her mind darkened as her thoughts suddenly flashed back to her failed marriages.

"Bentley Drummle didn't do much either," volunteered Estella. Pip winced.

"I mean, he was better at being cruel, and he couldn't make love properly. He was a big man and all that, but small where it mattered, if you know what I mean." Estella tried to explain that he had failed her as a lover. Pip made no comment. The thought of that evil man interfering with his Estella was unbearable. "We hardly ever made love," Estella kept on. "Only when he got drunk!"

"I don't want to know, Estella," replied Pip irritably, deep down, rejecting the thought from his mind.

"You are much better, my darling," said Estella, nuzzling Pip in the ear. Pip ignored the comment; his head retreated momentarily from Estella's whispered warm breath.

"When do we start thinking of names?" said Pip, changing the subject. Estella stroked her stomach and then turned her head and kissed Pip on the cheek. He slid his arm around her waist.

"Now, if you like."

"Can't think of any names right now," sighed Pip, distracted by the sudden flurry of activity in the rigging as the captain made preparations for the *Maid Marion* to enter Darling Harbour.

Chapter 93

Having arrived from Morpeth earlier in the day, Alice was waiting in the reception area of the Bank of New South Wales as Mr. Worthington emerged from his plush offices.

"Good afternoon, Alice, thank you for coming." After exchanging brief pleasantries, they exited the bank building and mounted a Hackney carriage for Sydney Cove. There, they boarded a private steam launch to Blackburn Cove and Woollahra. Set towards the rear of green lawns with manicured beds of spring flowers and shrubs and roses, Worthington's stone mansion sat separately and distinguished by its baronial architecture. They dined early on oysters and shellfish and green salads. Alice, now nearly 27 years of age, declined the wine, preferring not to mix drinks, sticking to her whisky and ginger. Worthington had briefed his wife about the successful sale of the jute business, advising her to talk about different subjects over dinner. But he did touch on the success he had achieved with Mr. Jaggers's information request, an investigation that Alice was delighted to hear that she had been of service.

"Dreadful tragedy here three weeks ago," interjected Mrs. Worthington. Alice raised her eyebrows.

"Worst shipwreck ever in Port Jackson," she continued. "121 souls lost. There was only one survivor."

"That's awful," agreed Alice, remembering how Polly, her mother, had died on the steam ship disaster in Morpeth four years earlier.

"The worst is that we aren't sure of the passenger list yet. Many of the bodies were unrecognisable, all were buried in the mass grave at Camperdown cemetery along with the mutilated remains of those without identification," said Mrs. Worthington.

"When will you know?" asked Alice absently.

"Next mail ship," interjected Mr. Worthington, pondering whether his client's heirs were already in the cemetery.

"What's on your mind, Mr. Worthington?" said Alice, aware that he was holding something back.

"I didn't want to say anything until later, but you will find out anyway, so it's best you hear it from the horse's mouth," replied Worthington, finishing his whisky.

"In heaven's name, hear what!?" exclaimed Alice, wondering what was coming next.

"It's about Mr. Jaggers's clients, the ones connected with the information request that you and John Plaistowe helped to unravel."

"What of them?"

"Sadly, they may have been on the *Dunbar;* I've never met them, so it was no use my going in to identify any of the bodies, even if my stomach could take it." Worthington excused himself from the table to retrieve the whisky decanter and returning, topped up Alice's glass and poured another for himself; Mrs. Worthington preferring to remain virtually teetotal, sipped quietly at her homemade ginger beer.

"When were they meant to arrive?" Alice probed, becoming interested in the intrigue.

"They were married in May, so they could have easily sailed on the *Dunbar* at the end of May," said Mrs. Worthington, having developed a keen interest in the wedding and honeymoon arrangements.

"Maybe they sailed earlier?"

"If that were the case, they should have been here already," replied Worthington.

"I wouldn't worry until you know for sure; they'll probably walk into your office just like I did," said Alice, smiling, as she warmed to the idea that they were on a different ship.

"And when they do, Mr. Worthington, would it be possible for me to meet them?"

"Of course, and that would be my pleasure." Worthington beamed at the thought. "I think it is highly important that you should know them, especially as Estella is Mr. Magwitch's, oh, er, sorry, Mr. Provis's only daughter."

"But he treated me as if I was his daughter, you know."

"Quite so, quite so, Alice," agreed Worthington, not wishing to pursue the legal relationship until later. "And, definitely, you will be meeting them."

"I would like that very much," Alice replied, swallowing another oyster.

"Em, Mr. Worthington, how old is Estella?" Worthington laughed.

"As far as I know, both she and her husband, Pip, will be in their early to mid-30s. Not sure exactly. You can ask her yourself."

"Yes, I'll do that, and should I call them aunty and uncle?" Alice chuckled.

"What an excellent idea," said Mrs. Worthington.

"Actually, you should consider Estella as your stepsister, and Pip, your brother-in-law. Anyway, you will have ample time to get to know them, as initially, I would like you all to stay here. We have masses of room in my home, as you can see."

"Thank you, ma'am," said Alice. "You are very kind. That will be lovely."

Chapter 94

By the time the *Maid Marion* docked and the official formalities with customs and the authorities were completed, it was already mid-afternoon. The weather was still fine and warm, and Pip and Estella decided to walk to their hotel, postponing their visit to the bank. Their plan was simple, find out everything they could from the bank manager and establish the relationship Magwitch had had with Governor Gipps before he had returned to England. Later, they could spend a couple of days enjoying themselves in Sydney, including exploring the nightlife in the Rocks and then, by steamer, head north to Morpeth and Maitland.

The following day, they swallowed an early breakfast of eggs and bacon and, as it was still early, decided to walk the city, agreeing that it would be folly to spend money buying until they had met with the bank manager.

Straight after their wedding in England, they had arranged a shipment of funds to Sydney through Jaggers which should have already arrived at the bank; in the meantime, they had a little over 200 pounds between them, which was more than enough to cover the hotel and food and clothing for a while until they got their affairs sorted out. After breakfast, they walked briskly down to the Rocks. Fascinated at the variety of goods on sale in the shops, they walked at a more leisurely pace, gazing in on windows displaying spices and jewellery and tinned foods, all items they had never seen before. There were oriental shops with fine fabrics and huge haberdasheries.

"We should get stocked up before we head north," suggested Estella. "We will need lots of these sorts of things for the baby."

"We need to deal with the banking before we spend a penny," replied Pip, the bitter memory of his debts in England that Joe had settled for him when he was ill, still lingered. They stopped under the three balls of the pawnbroker.

"I'm coming back to buy those gypsy's things," said Estella, pointing to a display in the window.

"Whatever for?" challenged Pip.

"They are exactly like my mother's, even the clothes and headscarf and beads." Estella pointed her slim finger, the tip bending against the thick glass window. "Oh, and look, there's also a set of Tarot cards!" she exclaimed, her breath quickening.

"But what on earth do you want that stuff for? Do you really believe in all that gypsy mumbo jumbo?" grumbled Pip, totally against the practice.

"You shouldn't scoff at things you don't understand, Pip," Estella retorted; her nose now pressed against the window as she examined the collection. Totally disinterested, Pip walked off, stopping at a little Chinese shop displaying an array of oriental china and furniture.

"Now this is more like it," said Pip, turning back to see Estella disappearing into the pawnbrokers. "Silly woman, wasting money on that stuff," he whispered under his breath. He continued on to the next shop.

"Who owned them before?" asked Estella, browsing through the collection.

"I'm not sure, luvy," said the scruffy old woman sitting behind the counter. "They came from somewhere up north, Greta village, I think. I heard they belonged to Molly Morgan. Dead now, o'course." The name similarity spurred Estella. She counted the Tarot cards, satisfying herself that they were complete. Resting on a thick piece of purple velvet, the crystal ball glistened, tempting her further. She scratched around to discover a little book with Tarot pictures and explanations and then another different set of cards, slightly curling at the edges.

"How much?" said Estella; her fingers caressing the crystal ball.

"15 pounds the lot," replied the woman in a coarse voice. She sniffed, scratched her unkempt hair, releasing fine scurf to float down onto the shoulders of her dark, knitted cardigan.

"That's an awful lot of money," sighed Estella.

"Luvy, that's for everything, including the two oak chairs and the table and the candlestick holders. Cheap if you asks me." Estella rummaged in her bag, retrieving her purse.

"Can you deliver them to the Royal Hotel?" The woman stood up, sensing a sale.

"At lunch time, luvy, when I close," she replied, walking over to join Estella as she searched through the various articles of clothing draped over the back of the two chairs and table.

"Ten pounds," said Estella.

"Gord, luvy, you're a hard'n, but seeing as how you seem to know what you're doing, it's a deal," said the woman, still happy at receiving ten pounds. Estella withdrew two, crisp, five-pound notes and handed them to the woman.

"Could I have a docket?" asked Estella, excitedly fingering the Tarot cards.

"I'll take these and the little book with me," said Estella, tucking the cards and explanation book into her bag. She grabbed the docket, wrote her name and hotel in the woman's sales register, and rushed into the street to catch Pip.

It was 10:30 when they arrived at the steps of the bank. Pip was furious, but he too was just as guilty, having made a purchase from the impressive gun shop, treating himself to one of the new Enfield rifles and a box of cartridges, spending half an hour with the gunsmith, learning how to *'bite the bullet.'* They had laughed at the dilemma the new cartridges posed to Indians being lubricated with either pork or beef fat.

"We're as bad as each other," laughed Estella, looking at the Enfield. By the time they entered the bank, they had forgotten about their purchases and, hand-in-hand, walked up the three, wide, stone steps.

"Mr. Worthington, please," said Pip to the dapperly dressed teller behind the iron grill.

"Certainly, sir. And whom shall I say is calling?"

"Pip and Estella Pirrip." The fresh-faced young gentleman disappeared from his perch on the stool, leaving Pip and Estella talking pleasantries as they waited. Moments later, dressed in winter tweeds, Worthington arrived in the front.

"Mr. and Mrs. Pirrip, I can't say what a pleasure it is to see you here," he said with a slight bow of his greying head. He clicked his heels and extended his right hand. Estella flushed, surprised at such formality.

"A pleasure to be here," replied Pip, shaking the manager's hand.

"Come," said Worthington, turning and walking back to his office.

Pip winked at Estella as they followed. They settled on the sofa; Worthington seated himself in the single armchair.

"You were surprised to see us?"

"Ah, Mr. Pirrip; naturally Mr. Jaggers had informed me of your sailing and estimated time of arrival, however, he omitted to notify me of the ship," said Worthington, going on to explain his concern regarding the wreck of the *Dunbar* last month.

"We sailed on the *Maid Marion*. Left a week or so before the *Dunbar*, in fact, she overtook us as we were leaving the Doldrums. Upset us a little when we saw her race past us. Our ship was much slower, you see."

"Very lucky for you, *n'est pas*," said Worthington, showing off with a little French. "Now, let me show you Mr. Magwitch's records, or should I say, Mr. Provis's." Worthington went to the small annex at the back of his office, returning with the hard-backed accounts ledger bound with a burgundy leather spine, the words 'Asset Ledger' embossed in gold on the front. He settled himself, rang the little silver bell and ordered tea and coffee.

"An amazing man," commented Worthington. Pip and Estella nodded, wondering what the ledger contained.

"May I enquire as to how you met him?" asked Worthington seriously, before opening the ledger. Pip spoke first.

"It was in a church graveyard at the edge of Romney marshes. Actually, it was a Christmas Eve over 25 years ago." Worthington sat back in his chair, his face full of questions. Pip smiled at the reaction.

"But correct me if I am wrong, Mr. Pirrip, are you not the lad Mr. Magwitch wished to be his gentleman as he would refer to every time, he made his deposits."

"That's quite correct, but I didn't know it was him then," explained Pip.

"Ah, of course," muttered Worthington. "And yourself, Mrs. Pirrip?"

"He was my father," explained Estella. "But I hardly remember him, you see, I was only three when he and my mother separated."

"Curiouser and curiouser," said Worthington. "But none of that matters now. You see, it all began just after I had taken over from my predecessor at the bank. I had only been in the position for a few weeks and we had only a few regulations in place to record such situations as that which Mr. Magwitch, I mean, Mr. Provis presented to us. Howsoever, the first entry in the leger was a deposit of seven gold bullets." Worthington opened the ledger and turned it around for Pip and Estella to read. Estella undid the top two buttons to her cotton blouse, her gold bullet glistened against her soft white flesh, barely above her cleavage.

"Like this one?" said Estella, holding the gold chain in her fingers, the bullet swinging beneath.

"Well, bless my soul," said Worthington with surprise.

"May I?" said Worthington, reaching forward, his thumb and index finger closed on the swinging bullet. Smiling, Estella nodded.

"Exactly like that one, and look here." He turned the bullet, revealing the engraving, A.M.P., on its base.

"Abel Magwitch Provis," he announced reverently, allowing the bullet to swing back onto Estella's fair skin.

Worthington stood and went to the glass cabinet on the sidewall next to the stout mahogany door and pointed through the beveled glass window. "You see, it's the same as this, your one must have been in with the very first he smelted. Very kindly, he allowed me to keep one on display. Mr. Magwitch, I mean Mr. Provis, used to say that there was a lot more where that came from, but he never said where." Estella stood up from the sofa and walked gracefully over to the cabinet to compare the bullets.

"It's the same," she agreed, nodding to Worthington as they both compared the bullets. "Cast in the same mould."

"Magwitch was finding gold long before the gold rush started here in 1853, four years ago. With the gold as his first deposit with us, we were able to provide a guarantee for the shipments of jute from Calcutta whilst he was growing and processing his own. I have had the good fortune to watch the jute business grow. Then, he began receiving regular government payments for his jute cloth. Although small in comparison, there were also many more small gold deposits. When I took instructions from him just before he left for England, his assets had risen enormously, but other than funding Mr. Jaggers for his gentleman, he had no use for the money himself, preferring to stay with his own way of life."

Estella and Worthington sat back down. Worthington reached for his coffee and took a few sips as Pip and Estella continued to study the numerous entries. Pip nudged Estella when he came to the entry bearing his name and the addition of Magwitch's chosen name of Provis.

"Yes," acknowledged Worthington, aware that Pip's finger had stopped at his name, nominating him as next of kin and heir.

"But at that time, he would not have known about you, Mrs. Pirrip, so you shouldn't feel left out. From what I hear from Mr. Jaggers, had he known that Mr. Magwitch was your father, he would certainly have made a handsome provision for you as well."

"Where did the rest of the money go to?" asked Estella. Worthington turned to the center of the ledger. The heading, *'Jute,'* opened up, showing entries for the jute business, with large transfers out occurring about every six months and one final entry of ten thousand pounds sterling, having been received only seven weeks ago.

"Well spotted," complimented Worthington.

"Magwitch's final instructions were that, in his absence, we should invest the surplus cash; by the way, he called the jute business, his sacred cow." Worthington smiled at the analogy before continuing, "His instructions were that we should invest the surplus cash into Sydney property." Worthington stood and walked back to the annex and returned with a pile of official papers neatly tied together with a red ribbon.

"These are the deeds to the properties we purchased," said Worthington proudly. "Of course, the purchases have been made over the past 11 years. Since then, it has grown into a sizeable portfolio. We established a property company, the shares held in trust through a nominee, the ultimate beneficial owner being your good self, Mr. Pirrip."

"Heavens above, I had no idea. Now I understand why Magwitch was so insistent about my looking after his little black book."

"Indeed, Mr. Pirrip."

"Please call me Pip, Mr. Worthington." Worthington nodded.

"I took the liberty of appointing a private property management company, and I shall arrange for you to meet the chairman in the next day or so. I am sure you will be comfortable with the arrangements."

"And that last entry of ten thousand pounds?" quizzed Estella.

"Ah, yes, another sound decision on the bank's part," replied Worthington. "I decided the time had come to sell the jute business and that was the amount of the settlement."

"But why sell if the business was going so well?" interjected Pip.

"Good point, Pip; however, we hear that there has been a mutiny and open rebellion in West Bengal, which could affect jute supplies from Calcutta, but take it from me that the timing was perfect," said Worthington, ringing his tiny silver bell. The secretary appeared in the doorway.

"Ah, Miss Frobisher, can you attend the Royal and see if Alice is available to join us for luncheon?"

"Certainly, sir; can I tell her where to meet you, sir?"

"Oh, please, if you would," said Worthington, withdrawing his gold Hunter pocket-watch and glancing at the time. He looked up.

"One o'clock at the Banker's Club in Pitt Street. My usual table. I will leave word at the front desk for Alice to join us." Miss Frobisher curtsied and was gone.

"Who's Alice, Mr. Worthington?" asked Estella.

"She came with her mother, Polly, as domestic servants for Mr. Magwitch when he was in Morpeth, Estella. Tragically, Polly drowned in a ferry accident a few years ago. Since then, Alice has been looking after the property in Morpeth. You'll like her, I'm sure," said Worthington.

"Which reminds me, before we leave, there are just two other points I must mention. Firstly, Mr. Magwitch had a land lease in Morpeth at one penny per year, but only during his lifetime, and secondly, he asked us to secure grazing rights in this area, preferably purchase the land with all its rights." Worthington tabled the rough map drawn by Magwitch, outlining the area he wanted in the Malumla Range. Worthington thumbed through the bundle of papers and withdrew the relevant deed.

"This is the extent of the property, and his man, Moola, I believe, is still there, acting as shepherd." Worthington removed the rest of the deeds from the table and returned them to the annex.

"Come, you must have seen enough for one day, shall we repair to the restaurant for luncheon?"

Under the warm midday sun, Worthington escorted Pip and Estella on foot; the various buildings providing a modicum of shade as they walked to the club. They arrived early, going straight to the banker's usual table. Worthington sat with his back to the wall, affording him full view of guests as they entered and with the ability to summon the waiters as and when necessary without turning in his chair. He seated Estella on his right and Pip next to her, leaving the fourth seat for Alice next to him. He instructed the hovering waiter to bring a bottle of Bordeaux and indicated to the headwaiter to proceed with the wine, delaying their order until Alice arrived.

"I have another question," said Pip, taking a large sip of wine.

"Fire away," replied Worthington, enjoying the refreshing company.

"Do you hold any records of Mr. Magwitch's appeal?"

"Hmm, now that's an interesting one," said Worthington, frowning. "Why would you need proof of that? Anyway, it would have been over 15 years ago now, and even the Governor may not have retained records; indeed, they would have already been transferred to London."

"Mr. Jaggers says he may need it to complete probate," explained Pip.

"But why would the Crown require that? I have a record here that you, Pip, are his rightful heir," argued Worthington; his attention suddenly attracted at the arrival of his third guest at the reception. "Ah, here she is." Worthington excused himself and walked briskly over to receive Alice.

Small and buxom, she stood to the side of the reception, clad in a brown and green frock made from fine jute. Her sunburnt face slightly flushed through the midday sun, was radiant. Worthington greeted Alice and escorted her over to the table. The headwaiter removed the chair, allowing Alice to slide in, tucking it back in behind her calf muscles. Alice lent forwards, her ample bosom resting on the table as she lent to the side and slid her jute handbag under her chair. She sat back up, ruffled her locks of hair whilst acknowledging Pip and Estella.

"Allow me to introduce you," said Worthington. Pip had immediately stood as she approached and instantly likened her to the flower girls of Covent Garden, yet her cockney accent was replaced with Strine.

"Miss Alice, please meet Mrs. Estella Pirrip and her husband, Philip." Estella smiled, her old cold and aloof manner, ingrained by Miss Havisham, suddenly returning.

"Alice," said Estella.

"Lovely to meet you, Alice," said Pip, shaking her pudgy hand, sincerity lacking in his tone.

Stilted conversation threatened to derail Worthington's chairmanship until the wine took hold. The luncheon lasted all afternoon with Alice's humour entertaining the Londoners, as she explained her years with Magwitch in Morpeth and all the work she and her mother had been doing to maintain the allotment since Magwitch had left. As the wine took hold, both Pip and Estella revealed some of their secrets in Rochester, and Alice responded with stories of Hunters River.

Delighted that the three were finally getting along, Worthington discretely sent word home to Mrs. Worthington that he would be bringing the three guests home that night and to have their rooms prepared. It was late afternoon by the time they departed. Estella and Alice talked continuously, whilst Pip and Mr. Worthington surveyed the surrounding town and people going about their business. Estella stood ten inches or more over Alice, and they made a strange sight; the mixture of London tailoring and Australian, homemade, jute clothing seemed incongruous as they boarded the four-in-hand carriage and trotted off across town to Woollahra. Alice had her same room, and Pip and Estella had the guestroom in the east wing.

"My darlings, you will see a wonderful sunrise from here," said Mrs. Worthington, as she departed to make the dining arrangements.

Chapter 95

Jaggers's correspondent, John Plaistowe, occupied an office in Morpeth that turned out to be two shabby rooms above a new bakery house owned by David and William Arnott. Only later did Pip and Estella discover that Plaistowe's main office was in West Maitland. Strangely, it gave them comfort, given its similarity to the scruffiness of Jaggers's office in Little Britain, but without the death masks and coffin-like chair. He seemed to be of the same ilk as Jaggers, with caricatures of convicts depicted, suffering various stages of punishment, hung on the walls, and one particularly macabre painting of two convict bushrangers being hanged from a tree off the back of a rig. The title given was, *The Hanging at New Freugh – 1833*.

John Plaistowe had been fully informed by Jaggers about the Magwitch Estate and agreed with Worthington's assessment that the need for evidence of Magwitch's status was irrelevant, but he warned that it would be London who would finally complete probate on the estate. Until probate was passed, none of the assets could be touched, leaving Pip and Estella reliant on their own funds for the time being. Deciding to base themselves where Magwitch had spent most of his time, Pip and Estella rented cheap rooms in Morpeth whilst they made new plans to pursue Magwitch's other interests.

Chapter 96

Estella and Pip had remained cooped up in their Morpeth apartment, watching the rain lash down day after day. It had poured incessantly in the whole area for more than a week, and Hunters River through Maitland approached flood conditions. Fields of wheat and barley had been flattened, and travel in the area was out of the question.

"We must try and find Alice," said Estella, as she pondered over the strange sketches Magwitch had produced in his little book and on the scruffy sheet of paper Worthington had given them. Jaggers's notes helped to crystalise the history, but failed to satisfy questions about topography and location.

"She must have moved away," suggested Pip. "I wonder why Alice didn't say when we were with Mr. Worthington."

"Moved where?" replied Estella, trying to find a comfortable spot on their second-hand sofa; her pregnancy, now towards the end of the fourth month, beginning to restrict her normal, lithe movements. She stood up and walked to the window looking down to the river.

"When there is a break in the weather, I'm going over to Maitland to ask a few questions."

"Just be careful, Estella," said Pip, conscious that Hunters River and parts of Maitland were liable to flooding. Pip sat, considering his options.

"I think," said Pip cautiously, "that we should split up for a couple of weeks." Estella swung around and looked intently at Pip. He sat back on the sofa and expanded on his plan.

"Whilst you are searching for Alice, I will head north and find this Moola chap."

Estella frowned, holding onto her swelling stomach.

"And leave me here?"

"You won't exactly be alone," pleaded Pip. "You know the Arnotts, and John Plaistowe is here at least half of the time. And, of course, there is also Dr. Charles Towers-Long if you need medical help. We also know the other women over at the tavern and at Campbell's store." Pip stood and walked to the window overlooking the street.

"See, there are lots of people around."

"But why can't I come too?"

"Darling, it's a rough road, and there are no doctors in case anything should happen to you with all the bouncing around in the rig. Anyway, the weather is just too bad."

Pip had been gone for a week when Estella decided to chance a trip to Maitland. The morning had started with hot sunshine and Estella felt confident. David Arnott had become the family friend delivering bread daily, and this morning, he had offered to take her into town on his bread delivery.

"Wagon's loaded, Miss Estella," he shouted up from the street below. Estella opened the double-hung window and stuck her head through the opening.

"Be down in five minutes," she replied, adding the final touches to her hair and frock. She emerged into the street which was still muddy from the night's rain; steam rising as the sun cooked the brown-rutted clays. Estella climbed up onto the rig next to David.

"What a lovely smell of yeast and crusty bread." David smiled at the compliment, the back of the rig laden with loaves and rolls of every description. For a while, they rode in silence, Estella mulling over where Alice had gone.

"David, do you have any idea where Alice went?"

"Not exactly, but the bakery was built on part of the land that she used to occupy."

"So their bank should know?" commented Estella.

"I'm sure they would; banks always know about land. Anyway, business is going well," said David Arnott, as he emitted a clicking sound from the back of his throat.

They set off, crossing by Hunters River over the new bridge. Beneath the bridge, the river was badly swollen, but as yet, had not burst its banks and flooded into Maitland. They both looked down at the ominous river.

"Government surveyor, George Boyle White, records that the river could flood any time," said David.

"Have you seen it flood?" asked Estella, feeling dizzy at the sight of the swirling waters below.

"Actually, no, the last recorded flood was over 25 years ago. Nobody can really remember it, and since then, there have been lots of changes and new buildings constructed."

The rig lurched as the front and rear artillery wheels left the planking of the bridge and struck the muddy track.

Chapter 97

Pip had secured the assistance of two Aboriginal guides on the outskirts of Morpeth and by the end of the first week, had made contact with Moola. He had noted small references in Magwitch's book that the Aboriginal guides would serve well and remained loyal rather than use emancipated convicts who would steal and register claims behind your back. Hardly any rain had fallen on the Range, or on Liverpool Plains, and before heading off to locate the areas where Magwitch had been prospecting, Moola had insisted that Pip stay at the village for a couple of nights. While they rested and prepared for the trip up onto the Malumla Range and across to Moonan Flat, Moola filled in some of the gaps on Magwitch's map. A few days later, they arrived at Moonan Flat to find a mob of Chinese had set up camp and were busily panning for gold.

"Did you know about this?" asked Pip. Moola laughed.

"Lots of them now," he replied.

"Do they have a licence?" said Pip, angrily watching them working illegally on his land.

"They don't care about that, too far away from Sydney to worry. Funny looking people," said Moola. "Ate some of them once, before we knew what they were." Moola chuckled. Pip shuddered as he looked on at the activity below, their wide-brimmed, peaked hats and buckets slung on the end of ropes hanging from a crooked pole stretched across their shoulders, bouncing as they took the selected ore up to the sluice trough for washing.

"Come, let's get out of here, I've seen enough," said Pip, irritated that the area was overrun with Chinese.

"Magwitch believes that's the important place," said Moola, pointing up the scarp face of the escarpment on the range behind. Pip pulled out his map and studied the range.

"That's it," he said, recognising the similarity of the terrain against features identified on the drawing.

"But I've been away from Morpeth long enough, and we should head back to see how Mrs. Pirrip is faring," said Pip, feeling a nervous premonition.

Chapter 98

It came like a tsunami, sweeping everything away in its path; rigs overturned and caught in between the shafts, horses drowned, unable to swim to safety, their harnesses anchoring them as the floodwaters rose.

Estella had no sooner left John Plaistowe's office that a two-foot wall of water came swirling around the corner of the end building and roared down the High Street, instantly knocking her slender frame off her feet. She clawed at the stony ground beneath the turbulent water attempting to stop herself from being swept away. The water rushed over her back as she lay face down, all vestiges of female grace shattered; she fought to survive against the torrent. David Arnott shouted from the doorway as he watched helplessly then jumped in, struggling against the raging water. He reached Estella and, grabbing her flailing arms, pulled her out of the murky swirling waters and dragged her back into the doorway and safety. The water rose further, now almost halfway up the doorframe. They retreated inside, Estella shivering and coughing in the dank cold of the flooded building. David sat her on the stairs and wiped the muddy water from her terrified face. The first spasm struck, forcing her to bend forward, clutching her swollen stomach.

"Oh no," she gasped. "Not now."

"What's the matter?" said David, his arm around her shoulder trying to keep her warm; while her light cotton frock offered little protection.

"It's my baby," said Estella, looking pathetically at David. She winced again, the stabbing pain catching her breath.

"I'll try and get you to the immigrant's home; they turned it into a hospital," explained David. "Wait here, I'll try and get a small boat."

Estella sat alone, shivering, the spasms coming more quickly now. She knew she couldn't last much longer. With the warm sensation between her legs, she knew and started to cry. Terrified, the noise of the raging water added to her pain. David was back in a minute with a small boat and two other men to help. He carried Estella down the stairs and settled her in the small rowboat. It took nearly an hour as they struggled to reach the hospital, but there too was pandemonium. He carried her in, tears streaming down her pale and weakening face. She felt it begin as Dr. Charles Towers-Long entered emergency. She lay bunched up on the bed as the doctor carried out his examination.

"I fear it may be too late," he muttered quietly. "Here, take this." He handed Estella a glass full of a dark liquid. She drank it quickly, but said nothing. Her eyes receded deep into their sockets, emphasised by heavy, dark shadows beneath.

She cried out in agony and sadness as the final spasm forced her to abort.

Chapter 99

Christmas came and went, their future dreams shattered. Pip blamed himself for leaving at such a critical time and vowed never to leave his Estella alone again. Eventually, the floodwaters subsided, leaving the scars and damage behind. Nobody had escaped except those outside Maitland on high ground, but even they had lost crops or animals or property. In the New Year, Pip and Estella wrote to Jaggers, explaining their position and asking his advice. If they were conservative, they calculated that their money would last for the best part of the year, but after that, they would need more. By the middle of the year, Jaggers had replied, advising that the remaining funds in trust in England had been dispatched, providing enough for maybe another year, with enough spare to fund their prospecting sorties. Suddenly, it became imperative to locate the source of the Magwitch gold, more especially, the mother lode.

Estella, proud to be a gypsy's daughter, threw herself into her mysticism, setting herself up as a fortuneteller and medium from which she managed to make a small income. It was the spring of the following year when their circumstances changed. Firstly, there was the discovery, contained in a letter from Jaggers, that Molly, Estella's mother, was a pure gypsy. The subject had never been discussed in England before their departure, and the revelation assisted in interpreting early entries in Magwitch's little black book. Estella worked on the information for weeks, remembering the broomstick Molly had brought to Cooling Church on their wedding day. Estella studied and practiced, becoming adept with her clients in comforting their innermost feelings, whilst Pip laboriously pursued their fruitless prospecting. He was sickened and jealous of the growing numbers of Chinese who lived on nothing, and had no women to distract them from their work as they sucked every deposit of alluvial gold out of the rivers and creeks.

Chapter 100

Jaggers sat brooding in his office in Little Britain; the weather outside was darkened by the November fog. Dense fog made even heavier by the hundreds of thousands of little coal fires burning away in the private fireplaces of London, injecting sulphurous fumes into the atmosphere. More and more steam trains belched clumps of smoke and ash, adding to the lung-choking yellowish cloud swirling around the streets. Visibility outside was down to four yards as the dank wintry dusk fell, forcing carriages to slow.

The footman elected to walk in front to guide the horses; the sound of their hooves muffled by the thickening smog. Pedestrians, hand-in-hand, groped, feeling their way along grimy walls, their spare hand holding a handkerchief over their mouths and nostrils filtering grimy particles from each intake of breath as they cautiously crossed roads in order to read street signs. Sooty rivulets ran down the stone and brick walls of buildings, the acidity of the mix staining the sandstone and granite structures. Jaggers looked up at his blackened skylight above his desk and could only imagine the fresh, blue-blazing sun of Australia as the summer of the southern hemisphere arrived. He thought about Pip and Estella; it had been almost three years since they had sailed.

No further extension of time, and here we are, 1861, the last year in which to conclude probate, he mused seriously whilst waiting for Wemmick to return from the probate office, hopefully with the letter containing the final decision of the Crown.

Jaggers had provided all the necessary evidence they had called for. Items one to seven of evidence had been submitted. There were compelling statements from Molly's trial, including the evidence of the existence of a husband by the Bow Street Runner. He had used his own records for proof of the adoption of Estella by Miss Havisham. Then there were documents, ratified by the courts, naming Molly as the mother, all of which was confirmed by statements from the gypsy Elder, Sylvester, and other eyewitnesses to the wedding on Epsom Downs. He had even included the bloodied cord in evidence that Molly and Magwitch were married at the time of Estella's birth. He felt silently confident.

Jaggers had written to John Plaistowe in Maitland and Mr. Worthington at the bank of New South Wales; their replies had been positive. He had sent numerous missives to General Gipps, the Governor of New South Wales, but as yet, there had been no reply. He had written to the Home Secretary, unearthing a positive response established by Pip's earlier letters of appeal and that there had been a communication recommending the granting of a Full-Pardon from the Governor of New South Wales before Magwitch had died. He had even received a sympathetic reply from the palace, but the letter had stressed that in the final analysis, it would be a decision for the, now defunct, Select Committee for Transportation and Westminster.

Jaggers stood from behind his coffin-like chair and walked across to his annex. He had stripped the easels and put them away, leaving the room bare except for the trestle table at the end which was now laden with piles of papers and buff files. He stopped in front of Magwitch's last remaining personal effects. His cap hung limply and the plug of tobacco protruding from his pipe had crusted and grown a thick green mould with age. His jacket had drooped on its hanger; the material rotten from the Medway waters and damp atmosphere, advertising that if touched, it may disintegrate with years of exposure.

Nearly there, he mused; the tips of his large fingers gently touching Magwitch's cap. Quietly in reception, Wemmick made coffee before bringing in the day's correspondence. On top of the pile of letters lay the envelope from the probate office. Wemmick knocked on Jaggers's door.

"Enter," shouted Jaggers in a clipped voice, hurriedly returning to his desk, his long index finger flying to his teeth for a nervous chew. Wemmick entered.

"The correspondence you have been waiting for, sir," said Wemmick, placing the bundle of letters in front of him and returning to the reception for the coffee.

Jaggers reached for his spotted handkerchief and dabbed at his face; the damp atmosphere sticking to his large bulbous nose and jowls. He reached for the important letter and carefully slit the end of the envelope with his silver-bladed letter opener. Wemmick returned and quietly set a steaming mug of coffee to the side of the pile of letters and then settled himself in the chair opposite. He sipped his mug of coffee, watching. Jaggers sat back and silently read. He reached the third and final page and sighed, then went back to the beginning and read the letter again. His poker face gave no clue as to the contents, and, finishing his second read, he placed the three pages of the letter face down on his desk, reached for his coffee, and took two great sucking sips. With twinkling eyes, he sat back and returned Wemmick's gaze.

"Well, sir, may I be so bold as to ask?" said Wemmick.

"Item eight in evidence, Wemmick. Item eight is the remaining need."

"I don't quite follow, sir,'" said Wemmick, his face searching for direction.

"Put the case that a lawyer has worked for 14 years, Wemmick," replied Jaggers, ruffling his spotted handkerchief. "And consider that the remaining evidence, item eight, is subject to the jurisdiction of Australia and, accordingly, the evidence that is held within the archives of the office of the current Governor of New South Wales, Governor Gipps, Wemmick." Wemmick nodded as if understanding. Except, he didn't.

"Now, put the case that the said lawyer is approaching his three-score year and ten, indeed, retirement, Wemmick. Now, consider carefully, Wemmick, what next move should the said lawyer make, given his advancing years and given his client's needs and consumption of time?" Jaggers's chewed forefinger pointed aggressively at Wemmick, forcing a response.

"Retirement, sir?" guessed Wemmick with a quizzical frown.

"Excellent work, Wemmick, excellent. Now, what would the said lawyer require in retirement, Wemmick?" His finger wagged again and the ruffled spotted handkerchief arrested in its travel halfway to his nose.

"An income, sir?" replied Wemmick, his voice almost in a whisper in case he had answered incorrectly.

"Perfect, Wemmick. And how would the said lawyer achieve an income?"

"Draw an invoice, sir?"

"Ah, Wemmick, and now I know why you have been with me all these years."

"Yes, sir, thank you, sir," replied Wemmick, bemused at the direction the conversation was headed.

"The sum should be in excess of six, but less than seven figures, Wemmick. Please attend to the invoice," instructed Jaggers, finally trumpeting his great bulbous nose; his nostrils reverberating deep in the folds of his silk handkerchief. Wemmick stood slowly, confused as to whom and for what quantum he should prepare the invoice. Jaggers read his mind.

"Tut, tut, Wemmick," said Jaggers, enjoying his private thoughts. "For whom have we worked these past 13 or more years without raising a single invoice?"

"Magwitch, sir?"

"Correct."

"Then to whom should the invoice be dispatched?" asked Wemmick, perplexed. Jaggers chewed his finger, his eyebrows full of expectancy as he waited for Wemmick to work out whom he should invoice and where.

"Mr. and Mrs. Pirrip, sir. Australia?"

"Exactly, Wemmick; please see to it immediately, if not sooner. We have places to go and people to see," said Jaggers, with an unusual note of optimism in his voice.

Chapter 101

Pip and Estella had been nicknamed, the *Miners of Malumla,* the mountain diggers of Liverpool Plains, but having recovered only nominal amounts of gold after more than two years, the money was running out fast through the payment of wages at their prospecting dig high in the Malumla Range. They did their pitiful financial calculation, deciding to return to Maitland for Christmas in six weeks' time. They would leave Moola in charge with two Chinese miners, one old and wizened who professed to have experience, and the other, a mere boy who Pip estimated to be only 13 years old. But he remembered himself at that age, full of energy and ideas, and, most of all, he came cheap and ate little. Estella estimated they could afford to maintain the team for another six months, but if no gold was found during that time, they would be forced to abandon the workings by the middle of the following year.

The weeks before Christmas, the rain had again fallen, but this year, there was no sign of floods; the Hunters River catchment having missed the deluging storms left Maitland safe for the inhabitants.

"This is our Yule log," said Estella, covered in mud and leaves from foraging in the rain-soaked woods.

"Yule log?" replied Pip with surprise.

"For Yuletide," explained Estella, strangely unaware of her gypsy powers. "And David Arnott will be baking some special, Christmas, sour dough for us too." Pip nodded, oiling and polishing his Enfield.

"And what are you going to do with that?" she added, pointing at the Enfield rifle.

"Roasted kangaroo for Christmas lunch," replied Pip with a wry smile.

"I'll leave that to you, darling. I don't like killing furry animals," replied Estella, shuddering at the thought of shooting a bouncing kangaroo and then skinning and gutting it.

"I'll do all that and then butcher it. We can cook it on a spit, and for the vegetables, I shall make a stew in our thick iron pot. Maybe have some rum too." Pip considered his menu.

"On the first day of Christmas, my true love said to me," sang Pip, not at all concerned at being near penniless; the vivid memories of his childhood flooding back. "That time of year when my future is about to change," he jested happily.

"Change is as good as a rest," said Estella, smiling, as she added the final touches to the dry arrangement in their fireplace; the weather too hot to consider lighting the fire.

Christmas turned into a party, with the Arnott brothers providing an assortment of breads and Pip's kangaroo big enough to feed the whole street. The publican from the local bar had contributed, and the grocer had donated enough vegetables to feed an army.

"On the fifth day of Christmas, my true love said to me – five gold rings," Pip added a new line to the old song every day after Christmas day. Unexpectedly, there was a knock on the door and there stood Alice, clad in the scantiest of summer clothing, almost inappropriate for the churchgoers of Maitland.

"Four calling birds. Three French hens. Two turtle doves and a partridge in a pear tree," sang Alice, well-familiar with the Christmas song.

"And a very merry Christmas to you, Alice," said Estella, delighted to have some female company.

"Two turtle doves, that's you," said Alice, projecting her smile from the doorway.

"Come in," said Pip, standing up.

"Where in God's name have you been for the past couple of years?" asked Pip.

"Give her a chance to get through the door, Pip," scolded Estella. "Would you like a drink or something?"

"London dry gin, pink gin if you can do it, and plenty of bitters," said Alice. Pip greeted her with a light kiss on the cheek and began setting up the drinks.

"I went to Melbourne."

"Ballarat gold fever?" quizzed Pip, returning with pink gins for Alice and Estella, and a whisky for himself.

They spent the next two hours catching up, Estella explaining about her discovery that she was faye, her regular private readings supporting her sixth sense, proving an asset to those who had lost loved ones back home.

"Can you do a reading for me?" asked Alice.

"On the seventh day of Christmas, my true love said to me – seven swans a swimming." Pip chuckled and sipped at his whisky, midnight having just struck on the grandfather clock.

"24 hours to Hogmanay," said Pip, screwing his neck around to look at the clock face.

"What's Hogmanay?"

"New Year's Eve," said Pip, studying Alice's calm face; she smiled innocently as he explained the Scottish tradition.

"You knew?" quizzed Pip.

"Not exactly," said Alice.

"But I have a question also. What is your connection with Mr. Jaggers? I know he communicated with you and that you had to talk with Mr. Worthington at the bank, but there's something else, isn't there, Alice?" said Pip, adjusting the cuffs of his cotton shirt.

"I called him my uncle, and he liked that. In one letter, he said that if he ever came to Australia, I may call him Uncle Jeremy."

"Amazing. I never thought he had a soft spot," commented Pip. Estella re-entered the lounge room and indicated to Alice she was ready for the reading.

"Ready?" said Pip, slightly inebriated.

"Pip, behave," said Estella, annoyed that Pip still made fun of her work. By the time the reading was over, Pip was snoring quietly on the sofa. He woke with a start as the ladies came back into the lounge.

"Well?" said Pip.

"Sleep on it," said Estella, cutting off Pip's remark.

"Decide in the cold light of day. That's if it will ever cool down," she said, looking at Alice's glowing face, conscious that her cheeks would also be glowing with the heat.

Alice stayed for the next few days, chewing over her future, deciding she would travel back to Melbourne to tidy up loose ends and consolidate her affairs.

Chapter 102

It was late in the evening on the 12th night, and Estella had just finished a reading for a client when Moola arrived with the old Chinaman. They had been drinking watered rum and were totally relaxed.

"On the 12th day of Christmas, my true love said to me – 12 Lords a leaping," Pip sang his last line going through the entire song, taking the opportunity to show off to his prospecting team. He beckoned them in as he sang, before Estella could refuse. With fresh drinks poured, they were already seated in their small lounge when Estella, still wearing her glittering robes and headscarf and jewels, emerged from her meeting room with her client, a troubled woman who had just lost her entire family, home, and possessions during a freak bushfire outside Maitland. The woman excused herself and went to the washroom.

"Why have you come so late at night?" asked Estella, frowning at the intrusion.

"It's about the gold, ma'am," replied Moola. The wizened old Chinaman stood head bowed, nodding in agreement.

"Peng believes you may possess special powers," he said. "And be able to call up knowledge that would help in locating the Magwitch gold."

"I have never used my gift for my own benefit," said Estella.

"Maybe you should just try anyway," said Pip.

They changed the subject quickly as Estella's client appeared from the washroom. Estella ushered the troubled woman from the apartment and helped her down to the bottom of the stairs and into the street below. They shook hands and, to get some fresh air and clear her mind, Estella walked up the street in the opposite direction, her mind focusing on Moola's suggestion.

"Well, I suppose it isn't for me directly, but rather for Pip, especially as Magwitch nominated him to be his heir," Estella justified her position.

"Even the ledger at the bank and the little black book were enough evidence of that." Her thoughts gnawed away at her brain. Stopping in front of the Arnott's bakery and peering through the window, she watched the night workers cleaning out the ovens and sweeping the floors from the previous day's baking. The inspiration hit her at the sight of a single pork pie. The worker held it in his fat right hand, raised it to his mouth, and greedily bit into it. She turned and walked briskly back and up the flight of stairs to their rooms, her thoughts on gold.

Estella was silent as she reentered the apartment and went straight to her private meeting room. Quickly, she placed two more chairs at the reading table. The three men watched from the lounge.

"Moola, you sit on my right, and, Peng, you sit on my left." Pip watched from his armchair. "Pip, you sit opposite me."

"What's happening, Estella?" asked Pip, now serious about Estella's work.

"I'm going to hold a séance," replied Estella, her shamanistic eyes darkening. Pip frowned as he pulled the chair back as requested and seated himself. Estella moved the crystal ball into the centre of the table.

"Pip, please go and bring the little black book," instructed Estella.

Whilst Pip went to the bedroom for the book, Estella removed her gold bullet from around her neck and placed it on its side next to the crystal ball, the letters, A.M.P., pointing towards her and the dome towards Pip. Pip returned and handed her the little black book. She placed it carefully on the left side of the crystal and opened it at the page with the map and the diagram. The six-pointed, charcoal pentacle was smudged with age.

"Oh, Pip, bring the other map that Mr. Worthington gave us. It's under the ebony elephant on the mantelpiece." Pip returned quickly and unfolded the map, handing it respectfully to Estella. She unfolded it and placed it under the bullet, then rearranged the gold chain around the crystal ball.

"Peng, please shuffle the Tarot cards," said Estella quietly. "Then hand them to Moola." Peng shuffled, his small Chinese hands struggling to hold the deck. Having tapped them on the table to square the pack, he passed the cards face down over the top of the crystal ball to Moola. Moola received them and placed them on the table before him.

"Good," said Estella. "Now, cut the pack with the hand you use least." Moola acknowledged and reached for the cards with his left hand.

"Good. Now, place the bottom part of the cut on the top. That's right. Now, hand them to Pip –" Moola obeyed.

"With the same hand," interjected Estella.

"Good. Now, Pip, spread them in front of you with your left hand, and choose a card." Pip reached out with his left hand.

"Wait," interjected Estella. "We must hold hands for a while."

Her slim fingers reached out, left to Peng and right to Moola, her hands emphasising the difference with Peng's small bony hand and Moola's massive black hand. She looked around the table at the expectant group of faces, her eyes darkening further as she concentrated her spiritual energies.

"Close your eyes and think of a convicted man sitting on a rock with a cruel leg iron biting into his ankle. He is freezing cold in a windswept and bitter place. There is a church and a graveyard." Estella paused for the message to be received.

"Now, see him hungrily eating a pork pie. There is a small boy standing by him, holding a blacksmith's file."

Pip opened one eye and looked at Estella. Her eyes were half open, but she saw nothing. Pip had related the story a hundred times in the past. He closed his eye quickly and concentrated. Beads of perspiration formed on his brow, but he felt cold.

"Good. Now, hold your thoughts and images. Keep holding hands except for you, Pip. Use your left hand, Pip, and spread the cards out. Keep your thoughts," she said again, as Pip spread the cards across the purple cloth in the shape of a fan.

"Have you done that?" said Estella, her half-open yet non-seeing eyes reliant upon her ears.

"Yes."

"Good. Now choose one card and turn it over, face up, in front of the crystal ball." Pip moved his hand across the fan of cards and selected.

"Have you done that?"

"Yes."

"Tell me what it is."

"It looks like an angel blowing a horn. There are people in white robes and, underneath, there are stone crosses," replied Pip.

"Is it the right way up, Pip?"

"Yes."

"Good. It means judgement. The angel, Gabriel, is summoning men from their graves. The divine meaning is resurrection and the opportunity of another chance. You have reached the end of a chapter in your life and must look back over what has happened. Be aware that you did your very best in the past and can feel proud of yourself. Literally, it may also indicate that a legal matter will turn out well and justice will prevail. That's wonderful.

"Now, hold hands again, Pip, and keep your thoughts of those early years on the marshes and concentrate," Estella began in a whisper, emitting words in a foreign accent.

Pip's mind filled with Magwitch's face. Then, he saw his jaw chattering with cold. He heard the bottle of brandy rattle against the poor man's teeth whilst rinsing down the half-masticated pork pie. He felt the icy wind blowing from its cruel lair, cutting through prison clothing. Then, he saw himself giving Magwitch the file with which he started to file away at his leg iron. He looked away and through the freezing mist, saw the marshes and the river, Medway, and the rotting hulks. Then, there were high seas and blue, tranquil seas, and sheep, hundreds of sheep high on the hills, and a cow with U-shaped horns, and a Sikh handing the same man three beans.

Suddenly, flooding back into his conscious memory, came the sight of Magwitch's face gazing placidly at the ceiling of the prison infirmary. Sweat began pouring down Pip's face. Estella's voice grew husky. Peng shivered, his wispy trailing beard emphasising his wizened old face. He had removed his Chinaman's hat, exposing thinning hair and soft white skin, broken only by irregularly scattered dark-brown freckles across his balding head. From a single mole on his left cheek, two single wisps of black hair hung longer than his beard. Pip's mind filled with the image of a little Chinese boy crawling through an oval hole in the side of a hill. Suddenly, he was seeing through the eyes of the boy and he saw the walls of a dark tunnel, his knees were in ice-cold water as he crawled along, the tunnel getting narrower, forcing him onto his stomach, but the icy water kept running. He shivered, feeling cold and wet. The tunnel bent to the right, his body just scraped through beneath the crack in the roof and there, before him, glinting in the light of the flame of his oil lamp, was a huge crevice, worn away by the passage of water, exposing a wall of yellow gold, fractured as columnar jointing, but not as regular. Seven-feet high, the fractures and fissures glistened with moisture, and across the roof of the cave, hung a cluster of stalactites, the stalagmites below rounded at their tops from flooding storm water from the underground stream when in spate forcing itself across the glittering and fractured face of the golden wall, scouring away any vestiges of loose material.

Perspiration ran down Moola's big, manly face, made even darker next to Estella's pale features, and wrinkled beneath his crinkly greying hair. Moola's mind filled with the sight of himself looking down from the top of the escarpment as the jute basket was lowered a decade and a half ago, nearly tipping Magwitch to his death on the scarp face of the escarpment when it had hooked on the broken root. Magwitch had never spoken of what he had seen down there, and they had never been back. He took a sharp intake of breath at the memory.

Estella's eyes misted darker. An orange rim appearing between the whites and darkened iris and dilated pupils as her head fell forward to gaze into the crystal ball.

Faint at first, Magwitch looked back, smiling, with a smouldering clay pipe clenched between stained teeth. He winked, his face saddened and a small tear formed in his right eye. His cheeks hollowed as he sucked on his pipe. Estella straightened and relaxed again. Her words became gravelly, deepening to that of a man's. She spoke in guttural English like a man from the east end of London.

"Malumla Range 'scarpment," she croaked, thin wisps of blond hair slipped from beneath her brightly coloured headscarf and fell across her left cheek.

"Lower the jute basket wot Moola do afor with that little China piccaninny. The piccaninny wot can crawl in that there 'ole. It's a cave, see, 40 feet in. I seen it with me own eyes. That 'ole wot is more than a hundred-feet down from the top. Not nobody knows," croaked Estella, her lips barely moving.

The image in the crystal ball fidgeted and removed the smouldering pipe. Estella suddenly coughed like a smoker. The image put the pipe back in its mouth and looked from the crystal ball down to the little book on the table. The page on the book flipped and arched, the six-pointed star darkened, almost lifting above the page, and the bank's map fluttered under the gold bullet on the table, but there was no draft in the oppressive little room.

Beads of perspiration formed on Estella's brow. Magwitch winked again and began to fade. Estella's eyes glistened with moisture as the image disappeared. Exhaling through her ragged throat, her shoulders sagged, involuntarily, and her head slumped forward across the table. Estella was unconscious.

Chapter 103

The paddle steamer from Morpeth to Sydney was exciting. John Plaistowe had immediately arranged the tickets as soon as he had received word from Jaggers that the final decision on probate would be conveyed through the Governor of New South Wales. Plaistowe had sent an urgent message to Pip and Estella.

The timing had been perfect, and they would use the opportunity in Sydney to officially register the claim. Extraction of the mother lode would require specialist equipment and the support from a powerful, London-based, mining company. A provisional letter requesting an 'expression of interest' had already been sent to Rio Tinto of St. James Square off Pall Mall, in the West End of London. Pip and Estella had a double berth on the steamer and the excitement had brought them closer together.

Dawn broke around five in the morning, and Pip and Estella quickly washed and dressed, determined to witness the sunrise across the Pacific Ocean. Breakfast would be between seven and eight-thirty, and the captain advised that they would be arriving in Sydney around midday. John Plaistow joined the table for breakfast after which he elaborated on his plans. They were due at the bank any time that day, and Mr. Worthington had already been briefed by telegraph. Although behind Great Britain in its development, the telegraph links were popping up everywhere, and unless the information to be transmitted was secret, most communications were now going over the wires.

They mounted the Hackney carriage at the wharf and comfortably settled in for the short ride to the bank, watching the hustle and bustle of burgeoning Sydney.

"Walk on," said the driver to the two, well-groomed greys. The horses pulled off sedately, crossed Sussex Street and gently changed to a trot as they entered Market Street. Seven minutes later, they arrived at the Bank of New South Wales.

"Welcome and more welcome," said Worthington, rubbing his hands with delight at greeting his clients; the news that the estate would shortly be settled foremost in his mind. They walked through the foyer of the bank and into Worthington's salubrious office at the rear.

"Cool and relaxing in the middle of summer," noted Estella, as she settled herself in one of the new chairs. Worthington had redecorated his office since their last visit, preferring individual leather armchairs to soft-sprung horsehair sofas. John Plaistowe sat opposite, Worthington and Pip settled in the other two armchairs.

Miss Frobisher, Worthington's secretary, entered at the sound of the little silver bell.

"Some refreshments?" invited Worthington. Estella was the first to speak.

"A simple fruit juice," she said innocently. "Cold, if you can, please," she added, conscious that the makeup she had applied that morning was suffering in the heat and humidity. Miss Frobisher nodded understandingly, glancing across at Pip.

"I know it's a little early, but could I have a whisky?"

"Certainly, Mr. Pirrip. Would you like anything with it?"

"Another whisky," replied Pip, winking at Estella. She tutted, frowning in his direction.

"Perfect for a boy who used to work in a forge and called knaves jacks!" said Estella sarcastically, their little altercation lost on Miss Frobisher.

"And for you, Mr. Plaistowe?" said Worthington with a syrupy smile and moving the conversation forward.

"I'll have the same as Miss Estella."

"Thank you, sir," said Miss Frobisher, looking towards Worthington for his order.

"I'll join Mr. Pirrip with a whisky and have a black coffee as well." Miss Frobisher gave a beaming smile, her tight, black skirt stretching as she turned to exit the room. Worthington sat back in his chair, surveying the expectant faces before him.

"Given that there remains but one issue to resolve, an issue which I believe is surmountable, I would address my initial comments to Mr. Plaistowe."

No sooner had he spoken, than Miss Frobisher reentered the room and delivered the refreshments. She had also included some biscuits and some sponge cake filled with strawberry jam and cream. Estella swooped on the cake.

"Mr. Plaistowe, could I impose upon you to chair this meeting?" asked Worthington.

"My pleasure, Mr. Worthington, thank you. As you know, we are in the month of March," Plaistowe started his introduction. Estella reached up with her long index finger to catch a stray piece of jam and cream outside the range of her tongue. She gave a shy and embarrassed smile, then chuckled; the indiscretion lost on the men.

"That means we have less than nine months to get this matter resolved," Plaistowe continued. "The difficulty is that legal documents cannot be transmitted by telegraph and the turnaround time by sea for correspondence between here and Great Britain still approaches six months, even sailing by the Suez Canal. We, therefore, have but one chance to complete the legal requirements imposed by the government of Great Britain. I, therefore, propose that I present the case to the Governor personally whilst we are all together in Sydney and, indeed, in the event that he may require other information and sworn statements, we can oblige." John Plaistowe sat back and drank his juice, almost emptying the glass before continuing. Estella had hardly touched hers, preferring to have another slice of the sweet sponge cake.

Pip felt like a passenger, preferring to dream of his gold mother lode; a tangible reward for a man nearing middle age. At least, that's how he was beginning to feel. He took another swig of his whisky, as did Worthington, who sat quietly, allowing Plaistowe to set the stage.

"I have already appointed the Governor for this Friday. The time set is 11:30, which leads me to think we may, indeed, have the opportunity to have luncheon together. One can only hope," said Plaistowe, finishing his juice. Estella reached for another piece of cake.

"For heaven's sake," said Pip. "You're eating for two!" Estella frowned at the insinuation, but continued enjoying the sponge, finally washing it down with her juice.

Pip's eyes widened. He looked down at her slim waist, but he thought better than to mention his thoughts in public. Plaistowe continued.

"Now, I come to this latest letter from Mr. Jaggers. In the letter, Mr. Jaggers has levied his fee which, I think you will agree, indicates to us that settlement will be a function of possession of the estate. I do not comment on the quantum, but advise that in your current position, it should and must, remain unsettled." Worthington gave a fraudulent cough before swallowing a huge mouthful of whisky.

"Mr. and Mrs. Pirrip, if it pleases you, I would be delighted to offer the bank's support in settlement. Indeed, I am so confident of the settlement of the estate in your favour that the release of adequate funds is appropriate at this time." Both Pip and Estella sat forward. Estella spoke first.

"How much is it?"

"Given the stalwart performance of Mr. Jaggers, the quantum is irrelevant and, indeed, he is such a man that his presence here may benefit the final negotiations," said Worthington, handing Jaggers's letter across to Estella. Pip sat silently, remembering Jaggers's massive, scented hand grabbing his jaw all those years ago on the back staircase at Satis House.

"Jaggers's coming to Australia? Who would think of such a thing?" said Estella.

"Send him the money and a sailing ticket to visit," suggested Worthington.

"It occurs to me that he would consider it base if he were to be seen in pursuit of his invoice. I have, therefore, considered that the presentation of the invitation should be such that any commercial reason for his travelling be removed from the correspondence."

"How on earth would you manage that?" said Pip, frowning, as he drained his whisky glass. Worthington copied and then summoned Miss Frobisher to freshen drinks.

"A horse race," said Worthington with a wry smile.

"Halfway round the world for a horse race!?" interjected Plaistowe, surprised at Worthington's suggestion.

"Not just any horse race," replied Worthington. "The first race ever inviting international entries has been announced in Melbourne. Flemington, to be more precise, and scheduled for Thursday, November 7, this year, 1861. The race is to be known as the Melbourne Cup, with prize money of one thousand pounds."

"That's only eight months' time," commented Pip.

"Indeed, it is, but it would give Mr. Jaggers plenty of time to get here," added Plaistowe, warming to the idea.

"How do you know about the racing?" asked Estella, not at all concerned at the contents of the letter; her brilliant, greenish-blue eyes smiling at the thought of Jaggers gambling at a racetrack.

"Ah, one of our esteemed clients, Etienne de Mestre, advises me that he will be entering three horses, Archer, Exeter, and Inheritor. Archer and Exeter are, of course, Sydney horses, and Archer is quite the fancy of the Sydney talent, they reckon he is the best, old, good 'un in New South Wales," Worthington expanded on his inside knowledge.

"Etienne has already been kind enough to afford an invitation, and I am planning to have our own private booth on the day. Our position will be in the new grandstand, and we will be overlooking the finish and the enclosures, and on the other side of the track, we get a magnificent view across to the Salt Water River."

"Strange coincidence that a horse named Inheritor is running," said Pip, grinning. Estella reached for her handbag and rummaged around for a pencil and paper. Surreptitiously, she made a note of the names of the horses and slipped the paper back in her handbag.

"So, who should write the letter?" asked Estella, looking at Worthington as he quaffed another mouthful of whisky.

"I see it this way, Miss Estella," said Worthington, his heart beginning to pump harder. "It would be right and proper for both, you and Pip, to respond to the letter with a brief letter of your own. I will make arrangements for a bank draft to settle the invoice so that you can also enclose the draft, thanking Mr. Jaggers for his support over the years." Worthington stood up and began pacing up and down behind Plaistowe's armchair; the excitement of the occasion causing an increase in adrenalin.

"I also plan to provide you with additional funding for the rest of the year so that you will have no difficulty in maintaining your current activities and, indeed, be in a position to attend the Melbourne Cup." Worthington's broadening smile emphasising his long, whiskery, mutton-chop sideburns.

"I will personally arrange for the purchase of a ticket for Mr. Jaggers and arrange for an invitation from the bank for him to attend the Melbourne Cup as my personal guest."

"I like the idea," said Estella. "That way, Mr. Jaggers will not know that we're involved with the race."

"Exactly, my dear, and, from the bank's point of view, there would be no eyebrows raised, as both Mr. Jaggers and the bank would be seen to be acting in the best interests of our clients," responded Worthington, and as an afterthought, commented, "which, of course, we would be."

Plaistowe's meeting with the Governor on the Friday yielded little. He had been dismissed before luncheon, managing only to secure an undertaking that he would receive a written response by the end of April.

With the assistance of Worthington, Estella and Pip drafted their reply to Jaggers, and once the contents of the letter had been agreed with Plaistowe and Worthington, Estella copied it, slipped it into a plain envelope along with the bank draft, and addressed it in her own hand to Mr. Jaggers, Little Britain, London.

It was well into April by the time Worthington managed to inveigle further invitations from Etienne de Mestre, three for Mr. Jaggers, and one each for Estella, Pip, and John Plaistowe. It was nearly a month after Estella and Pip's letter had been dispatched by the time Worthington was able to write and personally invite Jaggers. He enclosed the extra invitations, suggesting he bring any guest of his choosing should he wish to have a traveling companion.

Chapter 104

The horse pulling the hansom carriage trotted down Little Britain and turned left, past Saint Paul's Cathedral. The weather in London was hot, and the forecast advertised that there would be sunshine and hot weather right up to Wimbledon week at the end of June. The horse began to sweat, although the load was light, consisting of driver and their distinguished passenger. Cheapside and Poultry roads were comparatively uncongested since it was around 11 in the morning, that static time between going to work and lunch. Minutes later, the carriage arrived outside the Old Lady of Threadneedle Street. Jaggers stepped down, paid the driver, and entered the Bank of England.

"Retiring?" quizzed the manager, clutching the Australian draft. Jaggers gave a knowing smile.

"After such a distinguished career too, Mr. Jaggers. Quite rightly so."

"After depositing the draft, would you also prepare a further promissory note in the sum of 20 per cent of that amount in favour of my trusty clerk, Wemmick? I fear he too will wish to make alternative plans, and I would like to respect his years of service to the firm," instructed Jaggers. Half an hour later, Jaggers had returned to his office.

"Wemmick!" called Jaggers.

"Yes, sir." Wemmick stood in the doorway of the office.

"Enter and sit." Wemmick did as he was bid and settled himself in front of Jaggers's desk.

"My dear Wemmick, I am delighted to say that it appears the Magwitch Estate has, or is about to be, settled satisfactorily, and, indeed, we have been paid handsomely for our services," Jaggers began with his announcement.

"Oh, that is, indeed, good news, sir," replied Wemmick with a hint of a smile.

"And, Wemmick, as I mentioned before, I have decided that I shall retire within a couple of months after having handed the practice over to a suitable legal firm, one who will continue with the work of criminal and statute law."

"Of course, sir," said Wemmick, nodding his head in agreement.

"Now, Wemmick, I come to the matter of your future. May I be so bold as to enquire as to what plans you would have following my departure from practice?"

"I shall retire also, Mr. Jaggers," said Wemmick, without blinking an eye.

"I thought you might say that Wemmick. Well, in that case, it gives me very great pleasure to hand to you an envelope, the contents of which, I trust, will help you on your way and, indeed, reflect your years of loyal service to this firm," said Jaggers, handing over the envelope.

"Thank you, sir, I am sure I can trust in your integrity," said Wemmick, slipping the unopened envelope into his jacket pocket.

By the end of June, Jaggers had settled the disposal of the practice and sat quietly at his desk as Wemmick brought in the diminishing day's post.

"Another missive from New South Wales," said Wemmick, pointing to the unusual envelope on the top. His greying, shaggy eyebrows rose to a peak above his eyes at the sight of the envelope. Jaggers grabbed the envelope and slit the end open with his silver-bladed letter opener. He raised his eyebrows further at the sight of three invitations, both from a certain Etienne de Mestre, to a horse race that he had never heard of in Melbourne, noting that the manager of the Bank of New South Wales had also endorsed the invitations. His surprise was further raised by the sight of two tickets to sail on the ship, *Jennifer*, embarking at the end of July. He carefully read the letter, explaining the invitation and the courtesy behind it. He placed it on the desk in front of him and studied Wemmick.

"Since we are both retiring in a few weeks, Wemmick, would you like to join me at the races in Australia?"

"Goodness gracious, sir! How kind of you to invite me, sir. But regrettably, I have pressing family affairs and, frankly, I am frightened of drowning, sir. You see, I cannot swim," said Wemmick, his hands clasped in terror at the front of his paisley waistcoat. Jaggers roared with laughter; the first time Wemmick had ever seen a display of such emotion in the office.

"Now, Wemmick, I respect your wishes, however, the need to swim is hardly likely to save your life in the middle of the great oceans infested with sharks and enormous creatures of the deep." Wemmick surreptitiously read the second invitation lying upside down on Jaggers's desk.

"Forgive me for asking, sir, but who will you take with you to Australia?"

"Ah, Wemmick, you will know in due course, but I must deliver the invitation first before publicising my thoughts."

"So you know someone, sir?"

"Not just someone, Wemmick, a very important lady." Jaggers grabbed his top hat and cane, walked briskly out to Little Britain and hailed the first available hansom carriage.

"Driver, Gerrard Street, Soho."

Chapter 105

The flames licked at the last few sticks Pip had placed on the fire and began to gorge on the tar-saturated lumps of coal. Pip sat back and warmed as the flames gobbled through their food. Wisps of smoke fell back down the chimney and entered the room; the draft of the chimney of the first lighting of the year not yet perfect; the flue still cold and damp. Estella arrived back from shopping. New, crusty bread rolls from Arnott's bakery created edible smells in the air, stimulating their digestive juices. She emptied the shopping, put everything away tidily, and then came and joined Pip on the sofa. He noticed she was eating more and decided to comment on her thickening waistline. Estella blushed.

"I didn't want to say anything until I was sure, Pip," she said, squeezing his hand.

"But you are sure, aren't you, Estella?" replied Pip, smiling back.

"When?"

"When we were on the paddle steamer to Sydney, I think." Pip counted on his fingers.

"That makes it the beginning of November." Pip looked up at the two invitations to the Melbourne Cup on the mantlepiece and then back down to the fire; the coal had caught and was beginning to glow.

"Do you think we should cancel?"

"Heavens, no, I am sure they have hospitals and doctors down there as well," replied Estella.

"Just so long as you are happy, we can cross that bridge when we get to it," agreed Pip.

"But that settles it. We will travel by steamer and take a holiday. And no heroics this time, and I will not be going away either."

"I'll be just fine, Pip, anyway, how could I not be there when Mr. Jaggers is coming?"

"I know," said Pip, burying his hand in his inner jacket pocket and retrieving the recent telegraph from Mr. Worthington. "Do you want to read it?" offered Pip, handing the paper to Estella.

Jaggers had made his decision to sail on the *Jennifer* and had communicated by telegraph, confirming his plans to Worthington, advising that he planned to disembark in Port Melbourne. He had confirmed he would be bringing a guest on the sailing and would keep the spare invitation from Etienne de Mestre, as he had another person in mind he wished to invite, who he believed, now, lived in Melbourne. The sailing times indicated his arrival date to be late October, only a week or so spare before the big race. Pip watched Estella's expression as she read the contents of the telegraph. That had been winter and the months had sped past through spring and into summer. October had been hot and the bushfires had started early in the year. In the days before traveling, Pip had studied Estella's growing tummy.

"Looks like you'll be having a big baby," said Pip, helping Estella struggle up the gangplank onto the steam ship, *City of Sydney*.

Hanging from her left wrist, her handbag bounced against the handrail as she leant forward, pulling herself up the steep incline of the gangplank onto the vessel, her crinoline frock disguising her size. She was not at the end of her pregnancy, but to knowledgeable eyes, she looked as if the baby was already due.

Before embarking, they had been fascinated at the loading of Etienne de Mestre's three horses and another entry from Sydney, a total of four horses in all. Loading had gone smoothly until the master had sounded the horn, spooking the last horse. The weather was wet and rainy, and winds had risen, whipping up white froth on the tops of the rolling swell in the harbour. Pip decided not to comment on the three-day sailing to Port Melbourne, preferring to concentrate Estella's thoughts on their arrival on Saturday. John Plaistowe had received verbal confirmation that the Governor had passed probate and that his letter confirming his approval had been sent on to London with a copy of the contents dispatched over the wires.

"It should be completed before the end of the year," the Governor had said. Worthington had also taken time to brief the Governor and had released further funds to Pip and Estella, especially now that she was with child, and he had also allocated one of the properties forming part of the estate in Sydney. Pip and Estella had moved down to Sydney from Morpeth and taken up residence in the simple cottage overlooking Darling Harbour. Their final action before leaving Morpeth was to instruct John Plaistowe to reply to the innocuous response from Rio Tinto, inviting their participation in the extraction and recovery of the mother lode in the Malumla range.

Settled in their private cabin on the *City of Sydney*, the few days' sail to Melbourne would hopefully be a pleasant experience, but the swirling, grey clouds above the harbor did not look promising. Neither was anybody prepared to anticipate the weather for the big race, preferring to discuss the capability of the horses should the track be heavy going.

Conscious of Estella's condition and, given that by the day of the race, Estella was scheduled to give birth, Worthington extended his spare invitation to Dr. Charles Towers-Long, Estella's personal physician. He was delighted to have the opportunity to offer his services and travel with them, comforting Estella and Pip and advising that the danger period was past.

"In any event, you are in perfect health," he had said. Secretly, he was an avid racegoer, studying form at the least opportunity.

Below decks, the horses had been stabled separately. Archer, Exeter, and Inheritor could see each other through the horizontal planking of the temporary partition and could also hang their heads over the stable door, snorting and whinnying when a person entered. Escorted by Etienne, Pip and Estella arrived at the little stables to witness two of the horses hanging their heads over their respective half-doors. Archer nodded as Estella approached. Exeter grunted, turned, and walked back into his box. Inheritor was attempting to stick his head through a porthole at the back.

"Odds should be quite generous," said Etienne, stroking Archer's neck lovingly.

"How do you know that?" asked Pip innocently. Etienne turned his distinguished face and addressed Pip and Estella through his full, well-manicured, grey beard.

"I trained him in secret at St. Kilda Park, South Yarra. Not many know his performance," said Etienne, his aristocratic baldhead shining in the shards of light that filtered down the access stairs.

"His sire was William Tell, who won the English St. Leger, and his dame was Maid of Oaks. She was foaled in Australia, but more importantly, is descended from Highflier, the sire of three Epsom Derby winners. An unbroken record, and not many know that either," he said with a wink.

"My mother was married on Epsom Downs," said Estella, moving closer to Archer and gently stroking him on his nose.

"I think I know who I will be backing. Heavens, you are a lovely animal," said Estella, kissing Archer lightly on the side of his head.

"What about Inheritor?" asked Pip, consumed with the name.

"Not good," challenged Estella, before Etienne could speak. "It's unlucky to expect to win two lots of inheritance." Etienne smiled.

Steaming south at the edge of the Pacific, and, reaching the halfway point, the steamer began to roll heavily, and for many of the passengers, nausea began to set in. Not many arrived for breakfast the next day, and the bad and windy weather continued, making the last days sailing uncomfortable, but eventually, they docked and disembarked, their hotel providing much-needed respite.

"From here, we have five choices of travelling to the race," said Worthington, a week before the race, a cheeky grin appearing across his face after breakfast. For the past few days, the party had always spent breakfast together, with the exception of Etienne, who was up at dawn every morning, attending to his three thoroughbreds. The waiter delivered fresh coffee as Worthington continued.

"We can take the steam ship, *Maitland,* up the Salt Water River. There is entertainment onboard, probably a minstrel band and liquor. We could, of course, walk, but that would not be good for Miss Estella, or we could travel by cart or carriage along the Flemington Road, but I would not recommend that either. Then, there is a new service introduced this year by the Essendon Railway Company," he said with a wry smile, already holding a bunch of pre-booked tickets beneath the breakfast table.

"A steam train," guessed Estella with delight, having never traveled on a steam train in Australia. Worthington chuckled at her female intuition.

"All aboard the first steam train for the first Melbourne Cup." The guard roared up the platform as the train puffed to a halt in front of the hundreds of passengers assembled on the platform at Spencer Street.

Crisply dressed gentlemen under top hats and carrying canes, and ladies elegantly attired in crinoline frocks with bonnets sporting exotically styled hair, emphasised the splendour of the occasion. Colour and pageantry was everywhere, and the excitement mounted as the ladies climbed in first, struggling to prevent their crinoline frocks from being crushed as they squeezed into the overcrowded compartments. Gentlemen doffed their hats and opened doors, preferring to stand in the presence of the ladies. The train driver had also clad himself in top hat and tails for the occasion, and his stoker was crowned with a rounded bowler hat. The engine sat stationary, emitting its intermittent chuffing noise like air blown into a hollow tubular tank.

"All aboard the first steam train for the first Melbourne Cup," the guard shouted again, preparing his whistle for the off.

It was a perfect day with warm sunshine and soft blue skies and a gentle southwest breeze. In the crush, Estella felt claustrophobic and clutched Pip's hand for comfort.

"Soon, be there, darling," he whispered discretely.

She squeezed his hand. Suddenly, little feet began kicking in her stomach again, this time so strongly that she felt it must be visible through her crinoline. The station guard gave a long screeching blow on his whistle and, seconds later, the steam train puffed gently from Spencer Street station; the shackles connecting the six carriages clanking one at a time as the slack was taken up by the tug of the engine. *"Chuff, chuff, chuff,"* and then a long celebratory blow on the hooter, and they were underway amidst cheers from the passengers.

Dr. Charles Towers-Long sat opposite and nodded understandingly. Estella suddenly clenched her teeth with the first spasm. She knew the feeling.

"I think something is happening," she whispered into Pip's ear. Dr. Charles stood up and leaning forward, placing the palm of his hand on her forehead.

"We'll be there in a couple of minutes," assured Dr. Charles. Eventually, the train arrived at the rear of the stands and, gliding to a halt, the passengers burst from the doors of the carriages. Gentlemen dusted themselves down and ladies resuscitated their crushed crinolines. Hurriedly, Worthington paid the one shilling each for his guests to enter the Hill Stand and led the party to his private booth and comfort.

Estella breathed a sigh of relief to find he had provided refreshments and an assortment of easy chairs, all of which had a magnificent view of the racetrack. Estella relaxed. It was not yet 11 o'clock in the morning as Worthington arranged for champagne. She took a simple juice, preferring to distance herself from the celebrations. She rummaged in her bag, retrieving a gold sovereign.

"Archer to win," she said to Pip sitting quietly by her side.

"Do you mind if I back Inheritor as well?" asked Pip. Estella shook her head and bent forward as another spasm struck, much stronger than the first.

"But my sovereign is for Archer," she groaned, her face filling with strain. Pip nodded, turning to hand over the money and instruct the runner.

"I think we should go straight to the hospital," said Dr. Charles calmly.

"Pip, would you be so kind as to hail a carriage for us?" Pip acknowledged and rushed from the booth.

Chapter 106

"Molly, Molly, Molly, don't fuss so," said Jaggers, straightening his top hat and ruffling his brilliant silk cravat before knocking on the apartment door with the silver knob of his cane. After their arduous sailing, Molly and Jaggers had docked in Melbourne a mere two days ago and had rested before the great day.

"I can't help it, sir," pleaded Molly, the excitement of seeing Estella again after such a long time was almost unbearable. Alice appeared in the doorway of her Melbourne apartment.

"Can I help you?" asked Alice.

"Good morning, madam," said Jaggers, bowing graciously. Alice looked confused.

"Put the case that there once was a lawyer in London who wished to thank his Australian correspondent."

"Em, yes, but…" Jaggers pulled his spotted, silk handkerchief, arresting her next words.

"And put the case that the said lawyer decided to travel to Australia in order to thank his correspondent in person." A smile began to form on Alice's plump face, the connection forming in her mind.

"Don't tell me you're Mr. Jaggers?" Jaggers replaced his handkerchief and smiled.

"Oh, Lordy, Lordy, what a wonderful surprise, Mr. Jaggers."

"May I introduce, Molly Magwitch, neé Ingram," said Jaggers, waving his hand ceremoniously towards Molly.

"Hello, Molly," said Alice, a broad smile spread across her flushing face. Initially, Molly remained silent, only smiling and giving a simple curtsey.

"Hello, Alice, we have talked a lot about you during the sailing, and you're exactly as I imagined." Molly reached forward and held Alice's hands.

"I wonder if I may ask if you are preoccupied today, ma'am?" quizzed Jaggers, continuing the charade. Then, reaching into his jacket pocket, he retrieved the spare invitation from Etienne.

"If I was, I'm certainly not now," she replied with bubbly charm.

"Put the case that there is a major horserace in town and consider that this certain retired lawyer and his special guest have been invited to attend." Molly looked up at Jaggers, well-practised at hearing his analogous case presentation, her eyes sparkling at his performance.

"Now, further put the case that the said lawyer and his special guest," Jaggers indicated Molly with his bitten finger, "would be delighted if a certain young lady would consider it in her heart to avail her presence as a witness to the event?"

"Oh, Mr. Jaggers." Alice considered her reply carefully before continuing, "Em, Mr. Jaggers, for the purposes of this case, would you kindly convey my wishes that I would be honoured to assist that certain lawyer and his special guest as a material witness to his gaming pursuits. However, my simple requirement would be that I shall require some 59 minutes in order to prepare for the event." Jaggers chewed away at his forefinger during her reply and reached for his spotted handkerchief as she finished.

"Consider the time allocation granted. And, Alice, do please call me J.J.," said Jaggers, breathing a sigh of relief that Alice was home and would accompany them.

They had much to discuss. Alice rushed back inside, beckoning Jaggers and Molly to follow, pointing out the lounge as she disappeared into her bedroom. Jaggers studied the invitation then checked the time on his gold pocket watch.

"10:30, gives us ample time to get to Worthington's booth well before the race," said Jaggers. Molly nodded.

"We could take drinks and snacks on the steamer up the Salt Water River," suggested Molly, looking at her invitation and noting the facilities available during the short river journey. Jaggers agreed.

Hopefully, the ladies will not want to dance to the Minstrel band on board, mused Jaggers, his social abilities somewhat lacking.

Chapter 107

Pip exploded back through the door of Worthington's booth.

"The carriage is down the stairs and waiting at the back of the grandstand, Doctor," said Pip urgently.

"Is it the time, Estella?" said Dr. Charles calmly. Estella nodded.

"I anticipated this and have made previous arrangements." Dr. Charles took control.

"Help Estella, Pip, and bring her things," said Dr. Charles, assisting Estella to her feet. They walked cautiously down the stairs and out to the waiting carriage; the flow of incoming spectators making it difficult for Estella to maintain a grip on the banister. Dr. Charles helped Estella up and climbed into the carriage himself. Pip put his foot on the cast-iron footplate. "Sorry, Pip, I think it best that you stay for the big race. The baby is a long way off yet maybe tonight. Come and visit us at the end of the race meeting and we should have some news for you."

Despondently, Pip climbed the stairs back up to the booth and proceeded to pace the floor, merely picking at the seafood lunch, preferring to drink the wine and champagne instead.

The excitement in the booth escalated at the sight of the bustling crowds estimated to be approaching six thousand as they milled around the racetrack.

Dr. Charles instructed the driver of the Hackney carriage to ride like the wind. Whipped to a gallop, the team of horses swerved in and out of oncoming carriages, frightening those driving sedately and destined for the main grandstand. It took half an hour to reach the hospital where Dr. Charles had taken earlier precautions to reserve a private room. The nurses escorted Estella into the ward and settled her into the bed as yet another spasm burst forth.

"Here, luvy, drink this," said the matron, offering Estella a mild sedative. Estella reached forward, beads of perspiration connecting and running from her brow. Estella took the glass and swallowed heartily. Dr. Charles sat with her and gently mopped her brow.

"Not long now, Estella, but you're in the right place, so just relax. I'll be with you all the way," said Dr. Charles sympathetically. He leant forward and mopped her brow again.

"I'm so sorry, Doctor, you are going to miss the great race."

"I think I am going to witness an even bigger event, Estella. Now, you just lie back and relax, maybe get some sleep if you can. I'll go and arrange something for us to eat."

"I'm not really hungry, Doctor, just some more water please."

"Nurse!"

Chapter 108

The butler assigned to the booth arrived with a silver tray and two more bottles of French champagne. The tray dripped with luxuriant foliage. He walked to the polished table in the centre of the booth, set the bottles down, and then addressed Worthington.

"Sir, you have three further guests," he advised, handing over the London business card.

"Ah, how wonderful," said Worthington, his eyes flashing with excitement. "Would you kindly announce them?" The butler returned to the door and with the heavy corkscrew, knocked distinctly three times on the doorframe. Worthington watched as his inquisitive guests took their eyes from the track and focused on the door; the first race of the day having begun to line up for the start.

Molly and Alice, their hair groomed to perfection under floral-trimmed bonnets and dressed in their fine crinoline frocks, stood smiling in the doorway. Behind them stood Jaggers, his eyes glittering beneath his greying shaggy eyebrows.

"Ladies and gentlemen," announced the butler. "Please welcome, Miss Molly and Mr. Jaggers from London, England, and Miss Alice from Melbourne, Australia."

"Oh, heavens, come in, please do come in," said Worthington, taking the initiative and stepping forward to greet the new arrivals.

"So pleased you could make it. When did you dock?"

"Ah," said Jaggers. "Literally two days ago. Delayed in Cape Town with a suspected case of cholera, but…"

'And they are off,' bellowed the commentator, drowning the polite conversation much to Plaistowe's approval. Having briefly acknowledged Jaggers, Plaistowe rudely turned back to view the first race; the horses had already reached the first turn.

"But where's Estella?" asked Molly, having scanned the room full of male faces. Only Plaistowe concentrated on the first race, ten pounds to win on the favourite, Gypsy Lady, was an investment to study.

"She's just gone to the hospital to have our baby," said Pip, proudly grabbing Molly's arm and giving her a big hug.

"Why aren't you with her, Pip? She needs you with her," said Molly, shocked.

"She's with Dr. Charles. He said I was to wait here."

"I'm to be a grandmother?" said Molly, disregarding Pip.

"What a time to choose," said Alice, chuckling, aware that Estella was due her baby any time.

"It looks that way," said Jaggers, equally surprised at the news.

"God, I know," said Pip, handing Alice and Molly a glass of champagne.

"Thank you, Pip," said Alice, conscious of Molly's concern.

"I must go to her," said Molly, unable to wait any longer. Horse racing and the party of little importance to her, she placed her champagne on the nearest table and made for the door. Cursing under his breath, Plaistowe crumpled his betting slip and stood up.

"Dr. Charles said we should stay here for the main race because the baby was still a long way off," pleaded Pip, trying to restrain Molly.

"I shouldn't worry. She couldn't be in a better place." Alice tried to bring comfort to Molly; Pip having already accepted the situation.

"Excuse me, Mr. Jaggers," said Worthington, offering another glass of champagne.

"Oh, please call me J.J.," said Jaggers, announcing his preferred name to everyone in the booth.

"Er, no more champagne. I would prefer some whisky if you have it."

"A man after my own heart, J.J.," said Worthington. "How about the Macallan single malt?"

"Down to 17 runners," announced Plaistowe loudly, hardly concerned by the human crisis in the booth, preferring to study form for the main race.

A two-mile handicap, the first Melbourne Cup was a sweepstake of 20 sovereigns, 10 sovereigns forfeit or five sovereigns if declared, with 200 sovereigns added, the final stake ending up at 930 Great British pounds.

Plaistowe had his list of horses, but there had been four scratchings in the last couple of days. Through his telescope, he read the bookmaker's odds, relaying the information to any interested party inside the booth.

"Down to six to one for Archer, and Morman is still running favourite at four to one." Plaistowe made another note on his slip.

"And for Inheritor?" quizzed Pip, holding Molly's hand.

"100 to 12," Plaistowe called back, then stood briefly before sitting back into his easy chair in the front of the private booth. He watched the horses jostling around; the jockeys leaning forwards in silk shirts under brightly coloured caps, patting the necks of their mounts. Slowly, they wheeled and began making their way to the start. Plaistowe stood again as they came under starters orders.

The dappled cloud interspersed with spring sunshine made it a perfect day, and the going was good for both horse and jockey, even more importantly, the weather allowed the ladies to show off their stunning fashion apparel as they paraded in their crinoline frocks and bonnets, their fair complexions protected with multi-coloured parasols.

Plaistowe picked out Archer and watched through his glass as John Cutts, Archer's jockey, clad in black colours, brought him to a canter and, for a few seconds, into his lumbering gallop before reining him in for the start. Suddenly, the door to the booth opened and the butler stepped in.

"His Excellency, the Governor of New South Wales," the butler announced with an urgent knock on the doorframe. Worthington quickly stepped forward to greet the Governor and proceeded to effect introductions. Standing before the other guests, His Excellency retrieved a cardboard tube from his inside pocket.

"My apologies for the lateness, and I hope I haven't disrupted your viewing of the great race."

"Not at all, Your Excellency," said Jaggers, stepping forward. "Indeed, I would anticipate another few minutes yet."

Plaistowe tutted, his eyes glued through the glass window overlooking the track at the assemblage of horses gathering at the start. Briefly, Plaistowe turned around and angrily frowned at the second intrusion.

"Mr. Jaggers, I believe you will be interested in these documents," said the Governor, offering the tube to Jaggers.

"Your Excellency, I most certainly am." Jaggers' eyes focused on the cardboard tube.

"But is it necessary to open this now?" The Governor shook his head, a wry smile forming at the corner of his lips.

"My learned friend, I am confident that you already know the contents therein."

"Thank you, Your Excellency," said Jaggers. "In that case, may I be so bold as to suggest that you personally hand the documents to their rightful heir." Jaggers waved his chewed index finger in the direction of Pip.

"This should really go to my wife," Pip started to explain.

"Good God, Twilight's just thrown her rider and bolted!" cursed Plaistowe, jumping from his seat at the sight of Twilight galloping the entire course before she could be recaptured. The other horses waited skittishly at the start. Minutes later, the spirited animals managed the line up again.

"And they're off," shouted the commentator from the Argus. Plaistowe and Worthington groaned as Flatcatcher got away too soon and reached more than one hundred yards before turning back.

"Jesus, they're off at last," breathed Plaistowe, the false start frustrating him. Worthington checked his watch and listened to the commentary below.

"And they're into the turn, Flatcatcher leads by half a length from Archer, followed by Mormon and Fireaway, then comes Dispatch, Medora, and Twilight. Twilight's coming up on the inside ahead of Dispatch now. And they're coming out of the turn. Oh my God! Oh my God! Twilight just hit the railing post, tripping Dispatch. Oh no!" exclaimed the commentator. "Medora's down as well."

The dreadful spectacle of all three horses somersaulting across the track, spreading the three jockeys across the turf to be crushed beneath writhing horses was sickening. The rest of the field raced on. The crowd roared at the spectacle. The horses came out of the final river turn lead by Morman, followed by Prince. From behind, Archer powered on, surging forward with his heavy lumbering gait.

"And it's Archer, he's coming from behind. Archer in the lead by a nose from Morman, then comes Prince. And just look at him go. It's Archer by four lengths," bellowed the commentator. "And at the post, it's Archer by six lengths from Morman, followed by Prince."

Pip reached into his pocket for a coin and handed it to the spare runner sitting idly at the back of the booth.

"Take a hansom carriage and go straight to the hospital. Find out if there is any news about my wife from Dr. Charles Towers-Long," instructed Pip. "Come back straight away and there'll be another coin for you."

"And Archer wins the first Melbourne Cup in glorious style, no contest. Archer, ridden by John Cutts and owned by the French aristocrat from New South Wales, Etienne de Mestre."

The deafening roar from the crowd conspired to drown the euphoric commentator as he relayed the field excitedly through his megaphone. "Three minutes and 52 seconds," commented Worthington.

The jubilation and noise from the crowd filled the grandstand, but Pip had lost interest; Inheritor was nowhere, and it had been over two hours since Estella and Dr. Charles had left for the hospital. John Plaistowe dispatched a runner to collect his winnings whilst proudly watching Archer sweating and frothy as he made his way to the winner's enclosure.

Chapter 109

"All three are doing just fine, Mr. Pirrip," the runner reported breathlessly, having just run up the stairs and returned to the booth.

"Three!" exclaimed Pip. "What the hell do you mean all three?"

"That's what I was told to say." The hubbub of conversation abruptly ceased in the booth as Pip interrogated the messenger.

"Did you speak to Dr. Charles?" demanded Pip.

"Only the nurse at reception. Seemed the others were too busy."

"What else?"

"I waited 'cause they were rushing about, then the nurse came back and said that Miss Estella could be visited late afternoon." Worthington checked his watch.

"Should see the next race first," interjected Plaistowe. Molly suddenly wished she had sneaked out and gone with the runner, her ebony eyes flashed at Pip.

"You know what I'm thinking?" said Alice. "John Plaistowe is right. Let's see the next race and then all visit the hospital."

"We shouldn't be too early," commented Worthington, taking the grandfather's role.

Plaistowe turned and smiled for the first time all afternoon.

Chapter 110

The nurse and Dr. Charles slipped an arm under either side of Estella and, together, pulled her up onto the pillows of her hospital bed. They finished combing Estella's hair and helped to adjust her clothing. Estella was ready to receive guests. Pip was the first to enter. It was getting dark.

"Who won?" asked Estella immediately, her eyes bright and clear, yet her face drained and pale with exhaustion.

"You did, my love; you did," replied Pip, leaning forward and kissing Estella on her forehead. Two nurses attended Estella and another two nurses assisted Dr. Charles. Molly and Alice entered next, followed by Jaggers and Worthington. Plaistowe and His Excellency had decided to wait behind at the racetrack.

"Who won?" asked Estella impatiently.

"Archer," said Pip.

"I know what I want to call our son," said Estella, smiling.

"We have a son?" Pip couldn't believe what she had just said.

"What name have you chosen?"

"Archie," said Estella, her eyes twinkling at Pip.

"Archie Abel, if you would like?"

"I would love that," replied Pip. "Where is he?" Molly smiled at the name, Abel. Arms outstretched, she reached across the bed and embraced Estella.

"Well done, darling, did you know that before I was married, even before you were born, actually when I first met your father, I managed to pick the Epsom Derby winner, Moses. Later, the same day, your father came back and gave me ten shillings as a tip." Molly quietly chuckled into Estella's ear; her eyes watered at the memory.

"You did what?" exclaimed Estella, looking from Pip to Jaggers for an explanation. Unannounced, Dr. Charles appeared in the doorway and gave a fraudulent cough to attract attention. Molly swung around and was speechless at the sight before her; the shock making her feel dizzy.

"Twins," gasped Pip.

"A pigeon pair," said Jaggers, at last using his spotted handkerchief properly by dabbing the corner of each eye and then trumpeting into the fine silk.

"It runs in the family, you know. Molly has a twin sister too. Her name is Ursula," said Jaggers with a theatrical wink. With one blue bundle and one pink bundle fitting snugly under each of his arms, Dr. Charles approached the bed and gently lowered the pink bundle and then the blue bundle into Estella's arms.

"Could we name our little girl, Pippa?" Near to tears, Pip could hardly get the words out.

"Perfect, what a beautiful name," said Estella. "Pippa Molly."

"Archie Abel Pirrip and Pippa Molly Pirrip."

Pip repeated the full names, then bending forward, stroked Estella's long, red-blond hair and kissed her tenderly on the cheek. Gently, he knelt down beside the bed, offering his forefinger for Archie to hold and then reached across so that Pippa could clutch a finger on his other hand.

I wonder what Miss Havisham would say if she were here today, mused Jaggers. Alice comforted Molly, her emotions overwhelming as she burst into tears.

"Coochi, coochi, coochi," whispered Pip, chuckling at the babies with their bright little faces.

"Poor old lady," said Estella, reading Jaggers's mind. "She never had much of a life, did she?"

"Are you strong enough to receive some other news?" asked Pip, his hand reaching into his jacket for the cardboard tube.

"Of course," said Estella. "But not too long though, I feel a bit tired." Pip carefully removed the plug from the end of the cardboard tube and handed it to Estella.

"We need a camera," said Worthington, oozing with pride as if he were the grandfather showing off his family. Jaggers came over and shook Pip's hand across the bed.

"J.J., how can I ever thank you for such loyalty?" said Estella.

Preciously, she slid the circular parchment from the tube and, there, written in the most perfect copperplate handwriting on the outside of the scroll was her father's name:

'𝕰state of t𝔥e 𝕷ate
𝕬bel 𝔐agwitc𝔥
alias 𝔓robis.'

CPSIA information can be obtained
at www.ICGtesting.com
Printed in the USA
BVHW010957010721
610825BV00018B/144